A YOUNG WOMAN
ALONE IN A COLD WORLD

"You have to understand, Hweilan, your world . . . your cities and walls and castles and fires that keep out the night. Your wizards waving their wands and warriors strutting with their swords on their hips . . . they think they've tamed the world. Made it serve them. And maybe in their little cities and towers they have. They've tamed it by keeping it out. By hiding."

FIGHTING TO SURVIVE
LONG ENOUGH TO
AVENGE HER DEAD

"But there are powers in the world that were ancient when the greatest grandfathers of men still huddled in caves by their fires and prayed for the gods to keep out the night. These older powers . . . they don't fear the dark or the things that stalk in it. They revel in the dark. They are the things that stalk it."

THE HUNTER HAS CHOSEN.

"You speak of good and evil. When a wolf pack takes down a doe, are they evil? When a falcon takes a young rabbit, is it evil? Or are they merely reveling in their nature?"

CHOSEN OF NENDAWEN

Book I
The Fall of Highwatch

Book II
Hand of the Hunter
December 2010

Book III
Cry of the Ghost Wolf
December 2011

ALSO BY
MARK SEHESTEDT

THE WIZARDS

Frostfell

Slavers stole her son and she would sacrifice
everything to get him back. In the uncaring,
frozen north, will it be enough?

THE CITADELS

Sentinelspire

With the powers of an archdruid at hand,
the mad master of the fortress of Sentinelspire
will bring death to more than just his
enemies—he will call down doom on all
of Faerûn.

FORGOTTEN REALMS

MARK SEHESTEDT

Chosen of Nendawen book I

THE FALL OF HIGHWATCH

Chosen of Nendawen, Book I
The Fall of Highwatch

©2009 Wizards of the Coast LLC

Published by Wizards of the Coast LLC

Cover art by Jaime Jones
Map by Robert Lazzaretti

First Printing: November 2009

9 8 7 6 5 4 3 2 1

ISBN: 978-0-7869-5143-7
620- 24048740-001-EN

U.S., CANADA,	EUROPEAN HEADQUARTERS
ASIA, PACIFIC, & LATIN AMERICA	Hasbro UK Ltd
Wizards of the Coast LLC	Caswell Way
P.O. Box 707	Newport, Gwent NP9 0YH
Renton, WA 98057-0707	GREAT BRITAIN
+1-800-324-6496	Save this address for your records.

Visit our web site at www.wizards.com

ACKNOWLEDGMENTS

Thanks to Mr. Ed Greenwood, for creating the Realms and letting the rest of us play in it.

Thanks to Erin Evans, for all her hard editorial work and creative contributions.

And special thanks to Brian Bell of Brunswick, Maine. If the world had more booksellers like Brian, there'd be no such thing as readers with no idea what to read next, and there'd be a lot fewer starving authors.

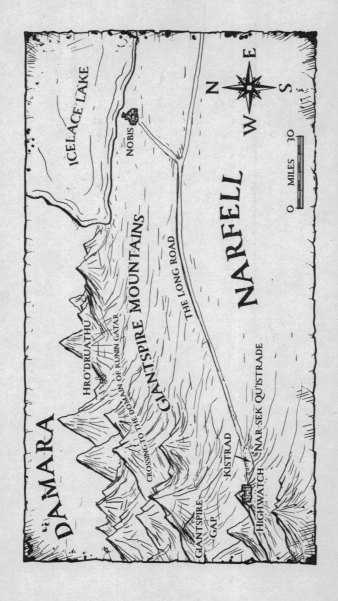

NAR-SEK QU'ISTRADE.

A spur of the Giantspire Mountains thrust into the Nar grassland. At its tip a fissure splits the mountain, only wide enough for two riders to go abreast. The Shadowed Path locals named it, for so high is the rock that even in summer the sun only shines into the path for a short time.

At the end of the path the fissure opens into a valley—a great basin of grass, surrounded by high cliffs. For generations the Nar used the valley as a winter refuge, one of the few places where rival tribes maintained an oath of peace.

In the year 1371 DR, King Gareth Dragonsbane of Damara obtained permission from Thalaman Harthgroth—the closest thing the Nar had to a supreme ruler—to mine the eastern slopes of the Giantspire Mountains. What began as a trickle of hopeful Damaran miners soon grew into a flood.

Then a warrior named Ondrahar, recently granted titles for service to his king, came to Nar-sek Qu'istrade to found a permanent settlement and a new order of knights, sworn to the service of Torm. All peoples—Damarans, Nar, Vassans—were welcome, provided that they maintained the peace.

The Nar had long been content to fill the valley with their tents for a season and then move on, but the newcomers desired a more permanent home. The shallow caves that lined the walls of the valley were a start, but their first year the settlers began expansion.

Skilled stonemasons from Damara carved the caves into halls and rooms. When rich deposits of bloodstone and iron were found in the surrounding hills, dwarves began to settle the area.

In the year 1375 DR, work on a mountain fortress began. Highwatch, the Damarans named it, for its towers perched on the peaks and looked out upon the steppe for miles. Here the Knights of Ondrahar made their home, and their lord took the title High Warden.

In the years since, the fortunes of Damara have waned, and Narfell has grown colder. But under the wisdom and fair hand of the High Warden, Highwatch has become a bastion of prosperity and safety in the Bloodstone Lands. Walled in by the mountains themselves and watched by the Knights, Highwatch has enjoyed generations of peace.

— Uluin of Merkurn, *Annals of Soravia*, 1454 DR

CHAPTER ONE

HE CROSSED THE FROZEN STREAM, KNOWING HIS pursuers would not. The knowledge of what lurked on the mount—the fear of it—would hold them back.

Still they might loose a few arrows if they caught sight of him. So he moved on. Over the ice-slick rocks of the riverbank, through the winter-bare branches of the trees that leaned over the river like eager listeners, and on into the deeper shadows of the pines.

He'd made it. He was . . . not free. But he was away from *them*.

Up the slope he ran, crouching under branches thick with snow, finding his way as much by scent as sight, for the pines blocked out the starlight. His boots kicked at old bones—and some not so old. But he kept going, up and up, to the very height of the hill. He knew the futility of trying to run or hide. His only hope was to find the horror before it found him.

Bare of trees, the summit gave him a wide view of the lands below. To the north, the peaks of the Icerim, starlit snow creased with black rock, a wall against the sky. Southward, the wooded hills fell away into the steppes of Narfell.

He had never been to this place, but he had visited others like it in other lands, had stood vigil while others sought the secrets in the holy places of the land—the Hearts. A thick tower of bare rock broke from the soil of the mount. Cracks and fissures marred it from top to bottom. Frost filled them, reflecting the starlight and giving the entire rock the appearance of being shattered by pale light.

Except near the bottom, where the largest fissure opened into blackness—the cave leading to the Heart. It waited like an open mouth, a jagged row of icicles making it seem not so much to yawn as prepare to bite. The breeze, which down in the valley had only whispered in the topmost branches, quickened to a wind and howled over the cave mouth.

A new light rained down upon the height. He looked up. The rim of the moon was climbing over the mountains. The full moon. Called by his people the Hunter's Moon. That meant—

All at once, he knew he was not alone on the mount. Eyes watched him. Hungry mouths tasted his scent on the breeze. The very air held a Presence.

He turned and looked back down the slope.

Eyes burned from the moving shadows under the trees. Dozens of them. Some large and close to the ground, their gazes mean and hungry. Wolves' eyes. Winged silhouettes watched him from the treetops, and dozens upon dozens of shadows hopped and flapped against the white background of the snow. Ravens.

Why have you come?

The voice thundered in his head, so strong that he fell, his knees breaking through the snow. He caught himself on both hands. The sharp rocks under the frost scraped the skin from his palms.

From the trees came the howl of wolves and the caw of ravens. They did not advance. Still, their meaning was clear. *You are surrounded. You are caught.*

He looked back to the cave, and something tugged his gaze upward.

The rising moonlight fell on a figure crouched on the rocks above. Larger than a man, his frame thick with muscle, his flesh patched with scars. Clothed in ragged skins, some of which still dripped and steamed in the cold air. Antlers rose like a twisted crown from the skull he wore as a mask, and from within the sockets his gaze burned with green fire. In his right hand he gripped the shaft of a long spear, its black iron head barbed. His left hand dripped blood.

Nendawen. Master of the Hunt.

Why have you come? said Nendawen.

"Salvation from my enemies," he said.

And who are you?

"Lendri," he said.

You know the covenant. To come without sacrifice means death.

Lendri felt the world shake around him, and a great roar filled his ears. He opened his eyes—he could not remember closing them—and looked up into the visage of the Hunter. Nendawen stood over him, the point of his spear on Lendri's throat.

I see no sacrifice.

"My sacrifice awaits you in the valley. A living sacrifice. Not one. I brought many."

You brought *nothing,* said Nendawen. *They pursued you. And now you come to me, begging me to save you.* He crouched, the spear never wavering, and brought his head close, the skull mask only inches from Lendri's face. The stench of death washed over Lendri, thick and close. *You have blood on your hands. The blood of a king.*

"Y-yes."

You are an exile. Cast out from your clan. Your people gone from this world. Returned home in victory. But you? Left behind in dishonor.

Lendri said nothing. He knew these things already.

But did you know that our victory was incomplete? Your people returned home, yes, but to a home despoiled by Jagun Ghen. We defeated him in the end, but he fled our vengeance. Did you know this?

"N-no."

Jagun Ghen escaped. Fled the Hunting Lands. Fled here. *To this world. And here you are, Lendri, killer of kings.*

It was not a question, but Lendri could see that Nendawen waited for a response. The point of the spear touched his throat, pressed, drawing blood.

"Wh-what do you want, holy one?"

What I ever want, said Nendawen. *Blood. I want Jagun Ghen, him and all his ilk, delivered to me.*

Lendri swallowed. He could feel the movement of his throat touching the cold iron of Nendawen's spear.

What do you want, little one?

"I . . ." He'd come here looking for no more than a night's safety. But Nendawen's question seemed to ask for more.

Salvation, you said. From your enemies.

"Yes."

I grant your request, said Nendawen.

Gratitude filled Lendri, but he said nothing.

This night, under the Hunter's Moon, I will hunt. Those sniffing your trail will not survive to see the sun. But when the Hunter's Moon sets, I may hunt no longer.

"Wh-why are you telling me this?"

Jagun Ghen cannot be allowed to roam free. In the Hunting Lands, Jagun Ghen almost conquered. Only hundreds of years of blood and sacrifice vanquished him. Here, in this corrupt world beneath its cold stars, Jagun Ghen could become a god. This cannot be allowed. You know the pact. In our holy places, within the shrines, I may enter this world, but beyond . . . only my sight may roam, except under the Hunter's Moon. Other nights, and days beneath the sun . . . another must hunt in my place. My Eye requires a Hand.

"What has this to do with me?" Lendri said, though he feared he already knew the answer.

Thunder shook the sky, and a deep rumbling filled the earth, and Lendri realized that Nendawen was laughing.

You are not to be the Hand of the Hunter. You may have ties to this world, but you are of the Hunting Lands . . . heart, soul, and blood. To hunt Jagun Ghen, I require one who is of this world.

Lendri swallowed. He could feel a trickle of blood running down his neck from where Nendawen's spear had pierced it.

You will bring me my chosen Hand, said Nendawen. *Do this, and you may return to the Hunting Lands. When next the Hunter's Moon rises, I will have my Hand, or I will have your blood, Lendri, killer of kings.*

"How will I find this . . . Hand?"

Hunt.

"And how will I know him?"

She carries death in her right hand.

CHAPTER TWO

"Hweilan?" The Lady Merah looked up, her gaze catching the young woman in the shadows. "Hweilan, is that you?"

Lady Merah was sitting on a bench near the far wall of the garden. Her long hair wafted unbound in the morning breeze, save for a braid over each ear. Scith leaned against the wall behind her, his thick arms crossed over his chest. Where she was lithe and fair to the point of paleness, he was dark and thick, giving the impression of immovable stone. Deep lines creased the corners of his eyes, and a bit of gray had begun to pepper the hair over his temples, but middle age had not softened him.

Hweilan stood in the corridor that led from the eastern towers to the garden. Clear sunlight bathed the garden. It gave little warmth. Her breath steamed in the air before her. The priests' calendar proclaimed that spring was here, but one would never know it. Both Merah and Scith wore heavy cloaks, rimmed in fur. But Hweilan wore only her "rough" clothing—suited for a day spent outside the castle walls: thick breeches, her heaviest tunic, jerkin, and boots. She had left her room in such haste that she hadn't donned a coat or cloak.

"How long have you been standing there?" said Merah. Her voice was firm, but Hweilan saw the look of guilt on her face. She was trying to hide it, but Hweilan knew her mother too well.

"I saw nothing I shouldn't, if that's what you're worried about," said Hweilan. "Is it true?"

"Is what true?" said Merah.

"That I am being sent away," said Hweilan. She walked across the courtyard. It was broad as a tourney field, surrounded by a low wall not far from the edge of a fifty-foot drop to another courtyard below. A grove of windbent pines, frosted in snow, grew in the middle of the garden, surrounded by bushes and shrubs that sprouted bright white and blue flowers in the summer. Their branches were bare and sparkled with rime. Ivy clung to the walls, forming a ring of green about the place.

The Garden of First Light. So called because it was the best place in Highwatch to watch the rise of sun and moon. Merah often came here for the latter. Though she worshiped in the temple of Torm along with the knights and the rest of the household, her heart had always tended more to Selûne. Hweilan had vague memories of other rituals dedicated to the minor gods of her mother's people. The Lady Merah was only half human. Raised among elf "barbarians" (a term Hweilan's grandmother was fond of using until her grandfather had put a stop to it) in the east, Merah had clung to her people's faith even after wedding Hweilan's father. But after her father's death, things had changed. Too many things.

Merah sighed and said, "Who told you?"

"Grandmother. I called her a liar. But it *is* true. Isn't it?"

Merah looked away, and it gave Hweilan a small flicker of hope. There was little love between her mother and her father's mother. If this was the doing of her grandmother, then her mother might—

"You will apologize to your grandmother," said Merah.

"*What?*"

"She should not have told you yet, but you will show her—"

"It *is* true!"

"You are not being 'sent away,' Hweilan. In these troubled times, alliances are important. You are going to accompany a delegation to Soravia where you will be——"

"Married off! To the highest bidder, is that it?"

"No one is forcing you."

"Really? Then I will stay here."

"You will not," said Merah. "Your family has decided——"

"Who?"

The first hint of anger entered Merah's voice. "Who what?"

"You said our family has decided." Not true. She had said *your* family. Not *our*. But Hweilan knew that sting——had felt it herself. "Was it grandfather or grandmother? I know Uncle Soran would never——"

"Hweilan, calm yourself." Merah moved over to one side of the bench——away from Scith——to make room. "Please sit. We will——"

"I don't want to sit," said Hweilan.

"Hweilan!" Merah stood to her full height. She was a formidable woman, her beauty undiminished by middle age, and she looked down on her only daughter. "You will *not* interrupt me again."

Hweilan ground her teeth, breathing heavily through her nose, and held her mother's gaze. She gave Scith a sidelong glance. He looked elsewhere.

Hweilan looked away. "I won't go," she said.

"And what will you do? Spend your days wandering the wild and hunting with Scith? You're not a little girl anymore. You will serve your people and your family."

"How? By bedding some fat lordling's son? How does that serve my people?"

"No one is forcing you into marriage, Hweilan."

"Really?"

"A delegation is going to Soravia to solidify relations

between our houses. Your Uncle Soran is going as well."

"But he isn't staying," said Hweilan.

"You will be fostered there for at least one year in hopes—"

"I know what hopes are. The duke's son—and heir, grandmother was quick to point out—is ready to marry."

"Your grandmother . . . misspoke," said Merah.

"Did she?"

Merah sighed. "Hweilan, you're seventeen. You're a member of a noble house. Did you really think you were going to spend the rest of your life wandering the wilds?"

"I can serve my people here."

"How?"

Hweilan scowled. She had no good answer for that, and it made her even angrier.

"Perhaps you will," said Merah. "But for now, you will go. As soon as the Knights deem the Gap safe for travel—"

"The Gap is never safe, no—"

Merah's voice rose to override her daughter's. "—you *will* go west, and you *will* conduct yourself in a manner worthy of your family. You will *not* shame me or this house." Her mother closed her eyes, took a deep breath, and softened her tone. "I will not lie to you, Hweilan. Your grandmother hopes that you will marry this duke's son. It would bring a strong alliance between our houses. And who knows? He might be a fine man. But your grandmother does not rule Highwatch, and she does not rule my children. You are going. If things warm between you and the duke's son . . . well and good. If not, I promise that you will not be forced into anything."

Hweilan could feel tears welling in her eyes, but she squeezed her eyes shut and took a deep breath, forcing them back.

"You will go to Soravia," said Merah. "If your fate lies elsewhere . . . so be it. But heed my words, daughter. Your childhood is over. You must find your fate, or it will find you."

Hweilan turned her back on them and walked away.

"We have her, my lord."

Guric turned to look at the man who had spoken. Argalath stood enveloped in dark robes and a deep cowl. The skin of the hands that protruded from his robes was mottled sickly white and covered with patches of blue. Argalath's entire body—every hairless inch of it—had been so scarred after encountering spellplague.

The last of the day's light was bleeding from the sky, but in the high valley night already held sway, and the men had lit torches against the dark. Even their meager light pained Argalath.

"The seals . . . ?" said Guric.

"Unbroken," said Argalath. "All went as planned."

Guric let out a great breath. "I . . ." He struggled to find the right words, then settled on, "Thank you."

Argalath bowed.

Guric pushed past Argalath and through the graveyard gates. The common folk of Highwatch and Kistrad buried their dead outside the village walls in the valley of Nar-sek Qu'istrade. The Nar burned their dead in elaborate rites in the open grassland beyond the Shadowed Path. The dwarves had carved elaborate crypts in the deep places of the mountain. But the Damarans, so far from home, still clung to their old ways. The High Warden's family had elaborate tombs farther up the mountainside, but the other Damarans of Highwatch buried their dead here, in a small valley on the mountain above the fortress, accessible only by a small path, too narrow even for horses. The hardship in getting here was part of the point. Damarans were a hard people, a proud people.

When the day's work had begun, the light had still been strong in the sky. But after the first few strikes of the workmen's picks, Guric had fled the graveyard. The sounds of iron and steel breaking through the frozen earth had been too much for him. Every blow only served to remind him of what lay below——and of what he was about to do.

The men——a few Damarans, who were loyal to Guric, overseeing the work of Nar, who were loyal to Argalath—— stood round an open grave. The Damarans held their torches high, and inky smoke wafted up into the dead air. Before them, the Nar stood over a long bundle, and one of them——one of Argalath's acolytes, Guric knew by his shaven head——was carefully using a horsetail brush to clean away the bits of frozen earth.

"My lord!" Argalath called from behind him.

Guric slowed, not because of Argalath but because of what lay before him. It looked like a large bundle of supplies, wrapped in fine linen, various symbols drawn round the knots of cord that bound it.

"Valia . . ." said Guric.

"My lord, please," said Argalath. "We must not break the seals until we have the blood."

Guric took one step forward. "I must see her."

"No." Argalath grabbed Guric's shoulder.

Guric looked down. "Unhand me, Argalath."

There was no anger in the words. No threat. Guric was not a man to threaten. People did as he told them or suffered the consequences.

Argalath released him and bowed. "My lord, I beg you. Seeing her now will only bring you pain. We are so close, so close . . ."

Guric looked down at the bundle. At his wife's corpse. He had not seen her in three years, and that last sight had haunted his dreams since.

"Those who wronged you," said Argalath, his voice pitched for all to hear, "who wronged *her,* must pay."

Guric contemplated all that lay before him. His mouth felt very dry. "There is no other way?"

"No. Kill them. Kill them all, my lord. And save the youngest for last. Her blood shall bring Valia back to you."

CHAPTER THREE

14

ONLY ONCE BEFORE HAD HWEILAN EVER FELT SUCH utter, black despair. Worse than fear was the certainty of hopelessness, and she had truly felt it only once. It wasn't the day she'd been told her father was dead. That day had been confusion. At ten years old, Hweilan had not been able to fathom the thought of a world without her father.

Until she saw his body. That had been the day. Her mother had insisted. Her child was the offspring of warriors, through both mother and father. She could weep. She would grieve. But she would not shrink from the stark reality of death.

Merah had taken Hweilan to the temple where her father's body lay, tended by priests in preparation for the last rites of the Loyal Fury. Her mother ordered everyone from the room and took Hweilan to the granite slab.

Hweilan did not resist. She was, in fact, curious in the way all children are. She had seen death before. Sheep, swiftstags, horses, even people. But never someone she knew. Never someone she loved.

Her father lay on the slab, draped in white linen up to his chest. She could not see the wound that had killed him. She'd heard the priests call death "eternal rest," but one look at her father, and there was no mistaking him for being asleep.

His eyes were closed, but the sunken cheeks and colorless pallor of his skin, gray as the stone on which he lay, and just as lifeless . . .

She reached out with one hand. Her mother didn't stop her. She touched her father's cheek. It was cold and stiff, though slightly yielding, like when the outer layer of a damp cloak froze on a winter's night. It was the most awful thing she'd ever felt.

"He's dead," Hweilan said.

"Yes," said Merah.

That was when the reality had hit her.

"Who will take care of us?"

Her father had been there the day Hweilan took her first steps. He had heard her first words, begun her lessons in fighting with blade and spear, had stayed up with her through the long nights of winter, telling stories by the fire. It had never entered into her darkest fears that he would no longer be there.

"We must care for each other now," Merah said. She turned Hweilan from her father and knelt before her. "I have something for you," she said, and reached into the folds of her robes. She withdrew a small sheepskin bundle, bound with a leather cord, and handed it to Hweilan.

"What is it?"

"Look."

Holding the bundle in one hand, Hweilan worked at the knot with the other. She could feel something hard within. She peeled back the soft folds of the bundle. Nestled within was a sort of spike, slightly curved and yellowish brown like horn. Slightly longer than her ten-year-old hand. She touched her finger to the point. It was sharp. The other end broadened into a sort of handle, and little notches had been cut into it.

"My people have given these to their children for generations," said Merah.

"What is it?"

"A *kishkoman*."

"*Kishkoman*," Hweilan said in a whisper of awe. "*Kish . . .*" She searched her memory. Her mother had taught her little of her native tongue, but this word she knew. "Knife."

"Very good, Hweilan." Merah smiled, though tears were thick in her eyes. "*Kishkoman* means whistle-knife."

"Whistle-knife?"

Her mother took the horn knife, put one of the grooves to her lips, and blew.

A sound pierced Hweilan's ears, high and so sharp that it seemed to cut right into the center of her head.

Her mother lowered the *kishkoman* and smiled. "You heard it?"

"Yes. It hurt."

"I was afraid you might not. But the blood of my people runs strong in you."

Hweilan said nothing. Simply stared at her gift. For her last birthday, her family had given her dresses, gowns, cloaks, jewelry, and a doll of silk. Gifts fit for the granddaughter of the High Warden. But gifts for a little girl. Soft gifts. This was far better.

"It is made from the antler of a young swiftstag buck," her mother said. "Among my people, mothers give them to their children when they are old enough to go off on their own at times. The whistle is beyond the hearing of most folk. But our people, Hweilan, we are . . . not like others. If you find yourself in danger, if you need help, blow this, and we will hear."

"But what if you are too far to hear?"

Merah's smile did not lessen, and in her eyes, behind the tears, a new light shone. Not pleasure. Not even pride.

Ferocity.

"Then you use it like this."

Her mother brought the sharp horn around in a punch so swift that Hweilan heard it cutting the air. Merah's fist stopped with the point of the *kishkoman* touching the soft flesh behind Hweilan's chin.

Eyes wide, breath caught in her throat, Hweilan looked up at her mother and saw not the widow of the High Warden's only son, not a grieving wife, but a barbarian queen, proud and fierce.

"Your father is dead, Hweilan. Death comes to us all. Many in this world are stronger than you. They may try to take your life, and they may succeed. But you must never *give* it to them. Make them pay, Hweilan. Make them pay."

Hweilan sat on the ground near her father's tomb, thinking on these things.

The final resting places of the family of the High Warden were high above the fortress. The cemetery was on a wide shelf of rock that looked down upon Highwatch. Boulders and tough bushes, their thick leaves green year round, were the only wall. Rugged, scraggly pines, their gnarled roots clinging like talons to the broken rock, lined the path to the graveyard before spreading out into a small grove that separated the tombs from the path. Rather than digging into the hard rock to bury the dead, thick stone coffins lay in the yard in even rows. Over two score in all, and only four of them empty. They were simple in design, unadorned save for the inscription bearing the name of the deceased and a few words of devotion to Torm. Of all the bodies laid to rest here, her father was the only one she'd known.

That had been the darkest day of her life, but her mother had given her hope and courage to face a world that had suddenly seemed uncertain and decidedly cruel. But she had still been a girl then. A girl who needed her mother. And now, her mother was part of that cruel world. Had it always been so? Was that realization what it meant to become an adult?

You're not a little girl anymore. Your childhood is over. You must find your fate, or it will find you. Her mother's words.

Hweilan reached under her leather jerkin and pulled out a braided leather thong, old and weathered with age. The *kishkoman* hung from it. She seldom went without it, and even after all these years, the point was still sharp. Once, while hunting with Scith on the open steppe, she had fallen down an ice-slick slope, landed hard, and the *kishkoman* had given her a nasty cut.

Scith . . .

Of the Var tribe, he had served the High Warden as his chief advisor and ambassador to the Nar tribes. But after the death of Hweilan's father, Scith had been much more than that to her. Hweilan had taken to following Scith when he went onto the steppe to meet with the tribes or to hunt. The first few times, she had sneaked away, and after being caught, she had been punished. But her mother—and much to her surprise, her grandfather—had spoken for her. It would be good for one of the family to learn the ways of the land and the native people.

The priests taught her to read and write, and instructed her in history and the faith. But it was Scith who gave her the education she loved. How to speak the native tongue of the Nar. How to track both beasts and men. How to find shelter and survive the harsh Nar winters. How to hunt and live off the land. He was a good teacher. Hweilan loved him like a beloved uncle, both mentor and confidant.

Hweilan missed their closeness, and the division that had grown between them hurt like a thorn under the skin.

Hweilan had not been the only one in need, not the only one with a hole left by her father's death. As one of the chief servants of the house and Hweilan's teacher, Scith spent much time with the family. He and Merah had grown close. Many whispered that they had grown too close. Hweilan had even heard it said in Kistrad that Scith the Var had found enough favor in Highwatch that he now shared the Lady Merah's bed. The looks that some in the household gave her mother told Hweilan that the rumors were not isolated to the common folk. Had they been lies, Hweilan would have known how to deal with them. But the plain fact was that Hweilan feared there might be some truth to the rumors.

It had soured her friendship with Scith. She still took lessons from him, still sometimes accompanied him among the tribes, but their once warm affection had turned cold. He had not said anything to her. A Nar warrior did not speak of such things. But she sometimes saw the regret in his eyes.

"Find your fate, or it will find you," Hweilan muttered to herself. She looked at the stone coffin that held her father's body. Sometimes, no matter what choices you made, fate found you anyway. Found you, smashed you to the ground like some great wheel, then just kept on rolling, merciless and uncaring.

Swift shadows passed over the ground. Hweilan looked up. The sun was no more than a blurry disk in the gray murk of the sky, and beneath it several winged shapes circled. Even as she watched, one of them tucked its wings and dropped.

Scythe wings were not graceful fliers like hawks or the great mountain eagles, who rode the skies like a fine ship might ride the waves. Scythe wings conquered the sky by brute strength and ferocity. Called *orethren* by the priests and scholars, the beasts looked like some sort of unholy combination of a monkey, bear, and bat. But they were loyal mounts for the Knights of Ondrahar. The Nar held them in superstitious dread, and the goblin tribes in the Giantspires were absolutely terrified of them. The wing of the *orethren*— jointed like a bat's, the final spur of which curved forward in a sharp bone—gave them their more common name "scythe wings."

The beast spread its wings just in time, its free fall turning into a glide that swept the graveyard with a harsh wind as it passed overhead. The pennant whipping behind the rider's back bore the standard of an open gauntlet flanked by two golden wings. It was Soran's standard.

Hweilan stuffed the *kishkoman* back under her jerkin.

The scythe wing circled back around and settled on

the rocks above the tombs. It sniffed the air and glared at Hweilan. Even from the distance of forty feet or more, Hweilan could feel the ground trembling at the roar building deep in its chest.

Horses could not abide Hweilan's presence, nor her mother's. No horses would bear them, and the knights' scythe wings were even worse. A horse would merely roll its eyes and run, only kicking and biting if she inadvertently cornered it. But the scythe wings . . .

The one time Hweilan had come near, the great beast had tried to swipe her with the great wing bone that earned them their name. Had her Uncle Soran not had the beast under tight rein, Hweilan would have died.

"Easy, Arvund," said Soran. He climbed out of the saddle and stroked the scythe wing to calm him. The creature kept its gaze locked on Hweilan, but its growl changed into something more like a purr, and it lowered its head to rest on a snow-covered rock.

Soran was the single most imposing man Hweilan had ever seen. His elder brother Vandalar, High Warden and Hweilan's grandfather, was taller, but not by much, and Soran's frame was wrapped in thick muscle. Middle age softened many men. Soran had only grown harder, like old oak. And now that even middle age was passing, he was harder still. The Chief Priest of Torm at Highwatch, Commander of the Knights of Ondrahar, Soran was one of the most feared and respected men within five hundred miles. No one who met him ever forgot him. He was solemn to the point of grimness, but he was also the most fair, just, and uncompromising man Hweilan knew. He demanded much from his men and his family, but he demanded the most from himself.

Soran hadn't chosen the best landing place, not that there were many to come by up here, and it took him awhile to get down. He walked up to Hweilan, not removing his helmet, but loosening the straps on the face mask so that it slapped against his chest as he walked. His cheeks were flushed, his eyes bright from exertion, and his face set in their usual deep lines.

"Well met, Hweilan," he said.

"Why are you here?" said Hweilan.

Soran did not smile, but she saw a gleam of mirth in his eye. "Is that how you greet your uncle?"

"Well met and all hail," she said in a flat voice. "Now why are you here?"

"My brother's wife is convinced that you've run off to marry a Nar chieftain. She has guards searching every cranny of the castle and servants searching Kistrad. Even Guric's men are hounding the fortress for you."

"She rousted the Captain of the Guard?"

"You know your grandmother."

Hweilan looked up at the other knights circling above. They were so high that she just barely made out the wings. "How did she persuade you to send the knights out after me?"

Soran snorted. "Don't flatter yourself. You are a stop along the way. We have other troubles."

"The Nar?"

"Yes."

It was not unusual for many clans to camp in Nar-sek Qu'istrade for the winter. But come spring, most went back into the open steppe to hunt, tend their herds, and feud. It had been much the same this year, but a great many had not moved on. In fact, more had come and were camping just beyond the main gates of the Shadowed Path.

"Your mother told me where she thought you might be," Soran said. "She asked me to come here and ask you to come back."

"Ask me or command me?"

"If this were a command, she'd have come herself."

"Hmph."

Soran opened his mouth to say something, but then his eyes settled on the thing leaning against the stone coffin beside Hweilan: a bow. Unstrung, it was almost as long as Hweilan was tall. Of the finest yew, it had many runes of power etched along its surface—all inscriptions sacred to Torm and the Knights. Seeing it, Soran's jaw tightened, and his nostrils flared. "That isn't a toy, girl."

"I know," she said. She wrapped her hand around the bow. "It was my father's. It's . . . it's the only thing I have left of him. That and memories. I bring it with me when I come here."

The anger melted out of Soran. "You've never used it?"

Hweilan snorted. "Used it? I can't even string it."

"Why do you carry it now?" said Soran.

She looked down at the bow. "It helps me remember him. He's been gone so long. My memories of him aren't as clear as they used to be. I come here. To remember. To think. To . . ."

"Honor the dead?"

"Something like that."

From far above them came a cry, harsh and guttural. One of the scythe wings circling overhead. Arvund, still perched on the ledge nearby, snorted and flapped his wings, raising a cloud of frost and grit.

Soran looked up, scowled, then said, "Would you like some advice from your older and much wiser uncle?"

"Not particularly."

His scowl deepened. "Very well, then. How about a request? Don't be so hard on your mother."

"She's sending me away!"

"Don't be foolish," said Soran. "Of course she isn't. That's your grandmother's doing, and you know it. I've met Duke Vittamar's son. I like him. But that wasn't what I meant about being hard on your mother. I meant Scith."

Hweilan flinched as if he'd slapped her. "You've heard? You . . . *approve*?"

"Hweilan . . ." said Soran. "Your mother is a woman. Your father has been dead for seven years. You can't expect her to spend the rest of her life alone. I would have thought that you'd be the first to defend her. Scith is a good man. And you know that better than anyone. He devoted his life to our family before you were born. He loved your father as a brother, and your father loved him."

"Then why is he rutting his brother's wife?"

Soran stood very still, not even blinking. All the flush drained from his face, and his white skin was almost pale as his short hair. "You will never speak so of your mother again," he said. "If you do so in my hearing, you will regret it the rest of your days." He stood there a moment, looking down at her, then said, "I'm surprised you listen to those nattering hens."

"You don't?"

"If you'd stop thinking about yourself for half a moment, you'd see," said Soran. Scith loves your mother and she him. That's plain. But they can do nothing about it. For one reason."

Hweilan snorted. "What?"

"You."

"What?" Hweilan realized she was shaking. She hugged herself but couldn't make it stop.

"Think," said Soran. "She has long since passed her time of mourning. But you know how things are in this house. Vandalar loves your mother like his own daughter. But your grandmother rules the house, and you know how she feels about your mother—how she's always felt. Your mother's only status in the household is as the widow of the High Warden's son. If she takes a lover or a husband, it'll be the end of any power she holds—and right now, you stupid, ungrateful, little girl—the *only* reason she's clinging to that is you."

"Me?" The tears were falling now, and Hweilan scrubbed them away with her sleeve before they could freeze.

"Think. If you're your mother actually took Scith into her bed, married him, if she allowed herself one night of being happy and not being lonely, she could no longer protect you. Your grandmother could marry you off to whomever she pleased—and there are a lot of duke's sons out there *much* less appealing than Vittamar's."

Hweilan turned her back to him. She couldn't stop the tears, and she hated appearing weak. Especially in front of Soran, who had nothing weak in his entire being. Everything he said made perfect sense. She felt furious at herself for not realizing the blazing obvious sooner. Shame welled in her at her own selfishness. She had been behaving like a little girl. But that still didn't change one simple fact.

Her shame melted before her anger, and she whirled on her uncle. "Highwatch is my home. I won't go!"

Soran took two steps forward, glaring down on her as he did so. "You're going if I have to tie you up and throw you in the wagon myself."

Hweilan opened her mouth to reply, but before she could get a word out, the sound of a horn drifted down from the sky. Arvund let out something between a bark and a roar and flapped his wings.

Soran looked up. One of the riders had come down about half the distance from the others. Hweilan could not make out the details of his pennant, but by the colors—white on gray—she knew it was Soran's second.

"We'll talk later," said Soran as he began to strap the faceplate back to his helmet. "Go home."

CHAPTER FOUR

HWEILAN SAT FOR A WHILE AFTER SORAN HAD LEFT. She was still angry. She wasn't going to prance off to some western court, dress in gowns, curtsy, and fawn over some spoiled lordling.

But she knew her uncle was right. Her mother was doing her best for her. Or at least what she thought was best.

And so it went, round and round in her head, going nowhere.

Something tingled on the back of her neck.

Something was watching her.

Hweilan looked around. Nothing but row after row of stone coffins, the mountain rising behind them, and the scraggly winter-bare trees that managed to burrow their roots into the rock. Overhead, the scythe wings were long out of sight. Even the blurry eye of the sun, resting on the tip of the peaks, had dimmed behind thickening clouds. No birds. No breeze. Nothing.

But Hweilan knew the feeling. A hunter developed it. Scith said that all beasts had this sense, though it seemed to have gone to sleep among humanity. But those men who spent much time in the wild, who knew the land and became part of it, learned the old ways, the flow of the blood from ancient times . . . it would waken in them. And like any tool, it could be honed with use.

Hweilan took up her father's bow and headed home, but she decided to take a different path—another of Scith's lessons. The Nar learned to hunt by watching the wolf packs. Wolves knew the ways of the swiftstags, for the large deer were creatures of habit, always following the same paths. A predictable creature was easy prey.

So Hweilan took another path that led her round a shoulder of the mountain and into deeper woods. The feeling of being watched did not lessen.

The sun fell behind the peaks, and the woods dimmed. Shadows fell together and deepened, like a convergence of streams.

Hweilan's new path took her through another graveyard—the one used by the Damarans of Highwatch who were not of the High Warden's family. Situated on broader, more level ground, this yard housed real graves. Gravestones, ranging from small slabs set level with the ground to marble pillars taller than Hweilan, marked each resting place.

Statues of Torm in all his manifestations—a young warrior, a knight mounted on a golden dragon, a venerable knight, and an armored warrior with the head of a lion—stood watch at the four corners of the graveyard, all looking outward. Black iron rails fenced the graveyard between the statues, and the path ran between two gates, one on each end.

Hweilan passed through the first, quickening her pace. The feeling of being watched pressed on her.

She smelled it before she saw it.

The aroma of freshly turned soil. Thick and loamy. Rich. But something else. Beyond smell really. More of a heaviness on the brain. Something . . . foul.

Then she saw it. An open grave.

No one had died recently. Why would there be a freshly dug grave? Hweilan's throat had gone very dry. She tried to swallow.

Just go, she told herself. Run back. Tell someone.

She lifted one foot to do just that. Then stopped. She'd feel ten times the fool going back without at least having a closer look.

She left the path and took a few steps toward the fresh hole. It was not a new grave. It was an old one. Hweilan read the inscription upon the rectangular pillar of stone at the far end of the wounded ground:

VALIA

BELOVED

Guric's wife. Her death had scarred him deeply.

Hweilan took another two steps. Just enough to peer down.

The soil was almost black, and darkness welled thick inside the open grave. But there was no mistaking what was down there.

The grave was empty.

Hweilan could not look away. She felt locked in time and place. The scent of fresh earth, overlaid by the foul stench, drowned out all other smells. Far away she could hear the wind howling over the peaks, but down here in the steep valleys, the air was still. Not even a breeze. The air, cold though it was, felt heavy and close on the exposed skin of her face.

The open grave, filled with shadow—something about it seemed to pull at her, as if she stood in the midst of water being sucked down into a fissure. Her chin began to fall, and she lurched forward, the open hole seeming to spread out.

Hweilan screamed and stepped back, the spell broken.

Her scream came back at her, faintly, echoing off the mountainsides, which suddenly seemed very close.

A harsh caw came from behind her.

She whirled.

A tall figure stood under the trees, draped in shadows. Man-shaped, but antlers protruded from his skull. A raven sat upon his shoulder.

Hweilan took in a breath—to scream or call for help, she didn't know—and the raven took wing, crying out again and again as it left the graveyard. But her eyes were fixed on the antlered figure.

The shadows thinned under her scrutiny, and she saw that it wasn't a man at all. Just an old stump of a lightning-blasted tree. Another smaller tree behind it, its branches winter gaunt, gave the illusion of antlers. Just a trick of light and shadow.

She let out her breath with relief. Her heart hammered so hard she could feel its pulse in her ears.

Foolish, she told herself. Jumping at shadows.

"Better step away from there. You'll hurt yourself."

Hweilan turned at the voice. Jatara.

Jatara and her brother were the personal bodyguards of Argalath, a spellscarred shaman who had managed to worm his way into the service of Captain Guric. She stood just inside the gate, another man at her back. The woman was dressed in assorted animal skins and untreated leathers. She wore no cloak against the cold, and her pale skin told why.

She was one of the Frost Folk—a people of the far, far north, said to be distant relations of the Sossrim. They had a dark reputation among the Nar and were rarely seen south of the ice fields. Her hair—a blonde so pale that it was only a glimmer away from white—hung almost to her waist, but she shaved the front of her head completely bald. The man behind Jatara was a Nar that Hweilan didn't recognize, though she suspected he was another of Argalath's sycophants. Who else would take company with Jatara?

"What are you doing here?" said Hweilan.

Jatara walked into the graveyard, the Nar at her heels. Sheathed swords bumped against their legs as they walked.

"Many in the fortress search for you," said Jatara. Her

command of Damaran was not flawless, but very precise and lightly accented.

"I've been told," said Hweilan. "Have you been following me?"

Jatara stopped at the edge of the path. She cocked her head to the side, almost birdlike, no sign of deference, amusement, or any emotion whatsoever on her face. Just . . . coldness.

"Why are you here, woman?" Hweilan said again.

"Why are *you* here, little girl?" said Jatara. The Nar behind her chuckled.

"How dare you!" said Hweilan. "I am the daughter of—"

"I know who you are," said Jatara, her voice still low, calm, completely unaffected by Hweilan's rage. "You will come with me now."

Hweilan was so struck by the woman's casual command, her sheer confidence, that for a long moment she could think of nothing to say.

Jatara motioned to the man, and he walked toward Hweilan.

"Do not give Oruk any trouble," said Jatara. "It makes him . . . unpleasant."

In that moment Hweilan knew something was very, very wrong. She was in real danger. Servants of the Captain of the Guard did not give orders to the High Warden's granddaughter.

As Hweilan's foot came down, her heel dipped low. She'd come up against the edge of the open grave.

She held her father's unstrung bow in front of her. "Keep away from me."

The Nar's grin widened.

Hweilan turned and leaped over the grave, landing in the pile of freshly turned soil.

She heard the Nar grunt in mild surprise at her move.

On her hands and knees in the grave soil, her father's bow still clutched in one hand, Hweilan turned to look at them. Jatara had still not moved. But the Nar was coming around the foot of the grave, his smile gone. He reached out one hand to grab her.

Hweilan turned and threw a handful of dirt in his face.

He stood back, sputtering and rubbing at his eyes.

Hweilan rose to her knees and swung the bow at his head. It connected about two-thirds of the way down the shaft. The Nar stumbled from surprise more than any real pain. But it put him off balance.

Scith had taught Hweilan to fight. Nar methods were neither graceful nor fair—at least by Damaran standards. The Nar were brawlers and completely unashamed in fighting with fists, feet, elbows, knees, and teeth.

Pivoting on one knee, Hweilan brought her other leg around in a wide swipe. The thick, flat toe of her boot connected with the side of the Nar's knee.

He cried out—in real pain this time—and crumpled. One leg slid into the open grave. Overbalanced and caught completely by surprise, he tumbled in.

Jatara still had not moved. The woman crossed her arms beneath her breasts, blinked once, and said, "Impressive. But you are still coming with me."

Hweilan came to her feet running, leaping gravestones and dodging monuments. She threw her father's bow between the iron rails of the fence, then leaped atop it.

"Hweilan!"

Jatara's voice, raised for the first time, stopped Hweilan cold. She turned. The Nar was struggling to climb out of the open grave. Jatara stood over him, but her eyes were on Hweilan.

"My orders," said Jatara, "are to bring you to the fortress. Alive. But I was not told 'unscathed.' Force me to chase you, girl, and I promise you, you will be . . . scathed."

Hweilan tumbled over the fence, grabbed her father's bow, and ran.

• • ⊚ • •

Raised in Damara among formidable citadels, Guric had come east to foster relations between his family and the High Warden. He expected these colonials to dwell in hovels of stone, scarcely finer than swept-out caves. How wrong he had been. Highwatch was not the most beautiful fortress he had seen, but in terms of martial defense, there was none finer.

From the watchtowers on a clear day one could see for a hundred miles into the open grassland. At Highwatch's feet, surrounded on all sides by cliffs, was the bowl-shaped valley of grass the Nar named Nar-sek Qu'istrade. The only way through the cliff wall was the narrow way of the Shadowed Path, where only a few horsemen could ride abreast. Even if half the Nar in existence had laid siege outside the Shield Wall, no large-scale charge could make it through the Shadowed Path, and with the Knights' scythe wings able to bring in supplies or drop flaming pitch on any besiegers, no army in Narfell could siege the fortress. As a knight, Guric had admired the fortress, perhaps even envied those who dwelled there, but it had not been home.

Until he met Valia.

Her family had fallen out of favor with King Yarin. Forced to flee their ancestral home with only what possessions they could carry, Valia's father had taken them into the Gap, deciding to take his chances against the goblin and ogre tribes of the mountains rather than wait for Yarin's forces to catch up with them. A third of their company died before they made it halfway, and they lost more daily to raids and the cold. Had Soran and his knights not found them and come to their aid, they would never have made it.

Homeless, branded traitors, with no wealth save what they had carried, Valia's family had begged protection from Vandalar. He granted it.

Guric, still in his first year at Highwatch, had been among the soldiers sent into the Gap to bring the refugees to Highwatch. Never had he seen such a pitiful sight. Frightened out of their minds, freezing, and half-starved, there was nothing aristocratic about the sorry company. It was hard to tell noble from servant. But one look at Valia, and Guric had eyes for no other. His heart was hers.

Later that year, when the storms lessened and messenger hawks could again make it across the mountains, Guric had written to his father, begging his blessing to marry Valia. His father had refused. Not just refused. Forbidden. His son and heir would not marry some vagabond outlaw's daughter. Their family could not afford such an affront to Yarin's authority. He demanded his son return at once.

Guric's final reply was short and to the point. He withdrew all claims to inheritance, lands, and titles. He would marry Valia and live, with honor, in Highwatch. The High Warden had not encouraged the decision, but he had accepted it and given Guric a place in the household.

Guric never heard from his father again.

He and Valia married, and for over a year, Guric had never known such happiness. He had something he had never felt before: a home and hope. He knew his place in the world and loved it.

But then came the fever. Most thought it had first started among the Nar, who lived in such scattered groups that it did little damage. But then people began to sicken in Kistrad. The healers and priests did what they could, and many recovered. But in the close confines of the village, it spread beyond their control. All the medicines of the healers and prayers of the priests could not stop it. Many graves were dug and pyres lit that year.

Valia's father's spirits had never recovered from the loss of his household. He was the first to sicken in Highwatch itself. And the first to die. The disease spread. There seemed to be no pattern. No distinction. The fever struck servants, soldiers, knights, and even the Warden's household. As in Kistrad, some recovered and some did not. To some, the prayers of the priests brought an almost instant recovery. To others, no amount of prayers, litanies, sacrifices, or medicines brought relief. The High Warden's wife was one of the lucky ones. Valia was not.

She sickened not long after her father. It struck lightly at first, and for a while the fever lessened. She was even able to leave her bed at times and sit with Guric upon their balcony that overlooked the little garden. But when her father died, the grief weakened her. Her mother had not survived their journey out of Damara. Her older brother had died defending them in the Gap. With her father gone . . .

"You're all I have left," she told Guric. Tears came at her words, and that night the fever returned with a vengeance.

She died nine days later.

Soran himself had prayed at her bedside, had offered sacrifices on her behalf, but all to no avail.

"I'm sorry," she said. The last words she spoke to Guric. She closed her eyes and fell into some dark dream from which she never woke.

Guric begged for Soran to perform the rites to raise her, but Soran refused, saying that if his prayers had failed to heal her, it could only be the will of Torm.

"Damn Torm's will!" Guric said.

"That's your grief talking," said Soran. "I forgive you. But don't do it again."

And then Guric had understood. He had thought Highwatch his home. He had thought himself a valued member of a proud and noble house. If not a son, then at least a beloved liege. But in that moment he saw it all for the sham it was. How could he have been so wrong? The Knights spoke of honor and truth and loyalty, of fidelity. But when it really mattered, when nothing else mattered more, it was all empty platitudes.

Guric could not return to Damara. He'd severed those ties. If he went back, he'd return as a beggar. And Guric would beg no more. He would seize what he wanted, and gods help anyone who stepped in his way.

It was Argalath, his favored counselor in his dealings with the Nar, who had first told him of other means to bring Valia back to him. Ways that the Knights would not smile upon. Older ways. Rites that the Nar had performed when they were a great people. But there would have to be sacrifices.

Guric had not balked and, in fact, seized on the notion. He began gathering Damarans who were disaffected with the rule of Highwatch, who felt themselves wronged at one time, or those who simply wanted more. Argalath found allies among the Nar.

Guric had placed his men well. Inside the fortress, they weren't many. The Damarans he could trust numbered less than a score. The Nar, mostly Creel gathered by Argalath, numbered almost a thousand. But they were camped outside the Shield Wall. Just as Guric had planned.

It brought the Knights out of the fortress. A third of the knights or more were out on their usual patrols. A scarce few remained at Highwatch. But the others, led by Soran himself, went to confront the Nar, whom they believed to be the usual winter bands who simply lingered too long. That many Nar gathered this late in the season . . .

Highwatch, which had once struck Guric with such awe, which he had once believed to be the most formidable fortress within a thousand miles, fell in a single afternoon.

• • ⊚ • •

"What are they doing?"

Guric heard the guard's question as he approached the main gate. Before the Damarans had come, this bit of the Shadowed Path had been unworked walls of solid stone. But in the years since, Damaran and dwarf craftsmen had hollowed out tunnels, halls, raised a thick wall at the entrance and exit, and built parapets along the cliff wall, both inside and outside.

The gate guards were all gathered around the doors, both the large main gates and the smaller postern door. Three of the ten had their faces pressed up against the small peepholes. None of the men turned at Guric's approach.

"It'll be over soon," said one. He was taller, older, the beginnings of a paunch straining under his mail. "You just watch."

"Took you long enough," said the first at hearing footsteps behind them. "A man could die of thirst waiting on you."

Guric cleared his throat.

The men whirled. Upon seeing their captain and four armored soldiers before them, all the guards whirled and stood straight, their eyes forward.

"Your companion," said Guric, "has others duties now."

"Yes, Captain," said the chief guard.

He let them stew a moment. Then he motioned to the gates. "Anything to report?"

"Lord Soran is circling them now," said the older guard. "The Nar are scattering. Lord Soran will land soon, I expect."

Guric paced in front of the guards, inspecting each one. All stared straight ahead, none daring to meet his gaze. Good. He needed them pliable.

He stopped before the chief guard and said, "I want both main gates opened and an honor guard lined up outside. Now."

The chief guard's eyes went wide. "M-my lord? I . . . I don't understand."

"The Knights are about to get most of that rabble on the move," said Guric, "but their chiefs are going to come inside to meet with the High Warden. For a good tongue lashing, I expect."

"My lord," said the chief guard, "we were not told of any—"

"I am telling you now," said Guric. He took a step forward, putting his nose only inches from the guard's forehead. "Are you questioning my orders?"

The guard swallowed. "Of course not, captain."

Guric turned and stepped away. "Then do it."

"You heard him," said the chief. "Double quick! Get those

gates open. I want Hailac near the winch. Everyone else, a line on each side, just inside the gate."

"Make that just outside," said Guric, loud enough for all to hear.

The chief guard frowned. "*Outside* the gate, captain?"

"The Knights are just outside," said Guric. "Are you really concerned about a half-dozen old men riding past?"

The eight men selected to line up outside the gates all looked decidedly paler, but they gripped their spears in steady hands as the large double doors swung open with a creak of frosty hinges and rattling chains.

Light poured inside the path, and Guric got his first good look of the scene playing out before him.

It had still not warmed enough for the winter snows to melt, but most of it had been trampled by the thousand or more Nar camped before the main gates. Tents, rope palisades, fires—all laid out with no semblance of order. Each tribe staked its claim and camped. When the next came along, they found a place and did the same.

A few hundred feet above the plain nine scythe wings circled and swooped like a monstrous murder of crows. One of them let out a roar, and even from the great height it hit the ears with an almost physical force. Guric could hear horses in the Nar camp neighing in panic, and over them the shouts of their masters as they tried to get their mounts back under control. Three scythe wings descended in a wide spiral. Guric saw that Soran led them.

"Good," said Guric. "Here it comes, you bastard."

"Captain?" said the chief guard. He was looking at Guric with wide eyes.

Guric smiled. "The Nar. Soran will give it to them. Won't he?"

The chief gave a nervous laugh. "As you say, my lord."

The guards had lined up facing each other, forming a path leading into the gate. Guric and the chief walked between them. The four soldiers Guric had brought remained just inside the gate.

The nearest edge of the Nar encampment was a few hundred yards away. Even as Guric and the chief guard stepped past the last of the guards and stopped, a large company of horsemen galloped out of camp and headed right for them.

"That doesn't look like a half-dozen old men," said one of the guards behind them.

Guric said nothing. The man was right. He counted a score and one horsemen, all hardened warriors, all holding bows.

"Captain . . . ?" said the chief guard.

"Rest easy," said Guric. "This will all be over soon."

The Nar rode at an easy canter, not hurrying. Beyond them, Soran had landed his scythe wing, and his rear guardsmen were about to do the same. The ground shook with the approach of the horses.

"Those don't look like chiefs either," said the chief guard.

"No?" said Guric. He smiled and stepped forward, raising a hand to halt the warriors' advance.

The horsemen reined in their mounts and spread into a wide arc. Guric had to give the guardsmen credit. They kept their posts. The chief guard looked on the Nar surrounding them with dismay, but he stood his ground and kept his mouth shut.

It wasn't until the Nar reached over their shoulders for their arrows that the Damaran guards broke and ran.

"Captain!" the chief guard screamed, then the first arrow struck his throat.

Guric stood unmoving as arrows flew past him, some close enough that he felt the wind of their passage. He closed his eyes and listened to the dying shrieks of his men. Arrows found their marks, and the four soldiers he'd left inside the gates did their duty with swords and daggers. Some small part of Guric cringed at the sounds. But then he thought of

Valia. He remembered feeling the life slip out of her as he held her hand. He could still feel the cold emptiness of her dead flesh as he held her until dawn. The screams of dying Damarans didn't mean as much anymore.

• • ◎ • •

Something wasn't right. Soran's hackles were already up as he landed his mount, and when he saw the Creel, he understood why. Even in the cold, the Creel was naked from the waist up, and every bit of exposed skin had been painted with arcane symbols. On shoulders, chest, and forehead, the symbols had been cut directly into his flesh, and blood ran down his face. A shaman at the least. But by the wild look in the man's eyes, Soran feared he might be one of the demon binders.

Soran called upon the Loyal Fury.

The Creel, chanting a litany in some language that was not any tongue of the Nar, raised one hand, and a tiny ember of light shot out. But as it flew it seemed to feed on the air, tumbling and growing into a ball of flame.

Soran raised his own hand, and the sigils etched into his gauntlet flared. Holy light engulfed him and his guardsmen, and as a river swallows a stream, so the power of Torm swallowed the dark magic of the Creel.

Then the arrows began to fall.

CHAPTER FIVE

H WEILAN TOOK TO THE TREES AND DID NOT LOOK BACK, weaving through the trunks and stumbling over roots hidden under the snow.

When the ground began to slope under her feet, she realized she'd made a poor choice. These woods ran along the arm of the mountain for a ways, then ended on a rocky escarpment. No paths and far too steep to climb.

Hweilan stopped, realizing she had to make it back to the path.

Then she heard sounds of someone coming through the woods, right on her trail. She couldn't see who it was. Among the pine and spruce that stood like silent sentinels on the hillside, she could discern little more than snow under her feet and dark shapes all around.

Hweilan turned, following the grade of the hill in hopes of the graveyard and finding the path again.

Sounds of pursuit grew closer, and she forsook stealth for speed.

"Stop!" said a voice behind her. A man's voice. She risked a glance behind her. It was the Nar. Oruk. Still a ways behind her, lurching over the uneven ground and favoring one leg, but the look of fury on his face . . .

Hweilan turned and ran, leaping roots and rocks and

ducking under branches. She veered uphill, hoping to find the path again.

She saw it, no more than a few dozen paces ahead of her. Risking a glance back, she saw that Oruk had fallen behind but was still coming on.

Hweilan bolted out of the trees and onto the path. A sort of ululating hiss in the air was all the warning she had.

Something struck the back of her leg, right behind the knee, then pulled round both legs. Hweilan went down, throwing both hands in front of her to break the fall. Her father's bow flew out of grasp. She hit the ground hard, her breath forced out of her, and her face skidded over the thin snow on the path.

"Thank you," Jatara's voice came from behind her. "Had you stayed in the trees that never would have worked."

Hweilan rolled over and forced air into her lungs. A thin braided cord, weighted on both ends by round stones, was tangled around her legs. Jatara was walking down the path toward her.

"Stay away from me!"

Jatara reached back and pulled a coil of rope from her belt.

Hweilan let out a long, wordless scream, hoping that someone—anyone—would hear.

Jatara laughed. Only a few paces away, she stopped and her eyes hardened. "Take that knife and toss it aside. Then be still and I won't make this too tight."

Hweilan tried to scream but it came out more of a sob.

Think, she told herself. Jatara had the sword at her hip, and if even half the things Hweilan had heard were true, the woman knew how to use it. Hweilan's knife would be no match, not unless she could get in close. And then it came to her.

Hweilan sat up and reached for the cord round her knees.

"Ah-ah!" said Jatara, her hand going to her sword. "Knife first."

Scowling and doing her best to keep back the tears, Hweilan pulled her knife from the sheath at her belt and tossed it to the side of the path.

"Good," said Jatara. "Now on your knees and turn around."

Hweilan could hear Oruk getting closer. She'd have to make this quick. She turned around, putting her back to Jatara, got up on her knees, and clasped her hands in front of her, as if in prayer.

"Arms at your sides," said Jatara, as she leaned in close, the rope held out before her.

Hweilan reached inside her coat with her right hand and moved her left arm down to her side.

"*Both* arms," said Jatara. Almost close enough.

Almost—

"I said—"

—close enough.

Hweilan's fist closed around the *kishkoman*, the sharp spike protruding from between her middle fingers, and brought it out of her coat. She turned and punched.

Jatara saw it too late. Her eyes widened in the instant before the sharpened antler went into the right one. She shrieked and fell back, dropping the rope and both hands going to her face.

Hweilan scrambled away, her legs kicking, trying to loosen the cord around her legs. It only made it tighter.

The sounds of Oruk breaking through the brush were very close now. Hweilan lunged to the side of the path, grabbed her knife, and raked its sharp edge down the cord. The tight braided leather parted like spidersilk before her blade.

Oruk crashed through a pine branch, sending needles loose in a shower, and stared at the scene before him— Hweilan on the path, knife in hand, Jatara writhing on the path, blood leaking from between the fingers she held to her face.

"Whuh——?" said the Nar, and then Hweilan was on the move. She snatched her father's bow in one hand, keeping the knife in the other.

"Never mind me!" Jatara shouted. "Get! Her! *Now!*"

Hweilan ran.

· · ◎ · ·

She kept to the path. Many times she slipped or skidded in the frost or through the carpet of pine needles, but she kept her feet, knowing that a bad fall or twist of her ankle would be the end of her. She'd walked this path more times than she could remember. She knew every twist and curve, every tree and stone. Hweilan ran, swift as a hart. Never able to ride a horse, Hweilan had walked or run her entire life, and there were few in Highwatch or Kistrad who could outrun her. Once Scith had even said that in a long distance race between her and any horse in Highwatch, he would have laid his coin on her.

Although the sounds of pursuit grew farther behind, they did not cease. Oruk was still following. If she fell, if she stopped to rest, he'd be on her in moments.

She knew that once she reached the fortress, found the first guards, a knight, or even a servant, she'd be safe. One word in the right ear and Hweilan could have every soldier in the fortress out after Jatara and Oruk. Argalath himself would be hauled before her grandfather. A deep and vindictive part of Hweilan's heart warmed to the thought of what her Uncle Soran would do when he heard of this.

Then she saw the smoke.

A smear in the sky. Not the usual haze of evening cookfires or wood burning against the early spring cold. A thick, gray smoke.

Hweilan rounded a bend in the path. The trees fell away and she had a clear view of Nar-sek Qu'istrade, the distant cliff walls, the fortress of Highwatch, and Kistrad huddling at its feet. At the bottom of tall columns of smoke she saw the angry glimmer of flames. Kistrad was burning. Thousands of Nar filled the valley. Some moving toward the fortress, but a great many not moving at all.

Shocked, Hweilan stopped, her breath coming in great heaves, her heart hammering against her ribs. But even over the sound of her own breathing and her frightened heartbeat, her sharp eyes caught other sounds—faint, but still clear, even over the distance.

Steel ringing against steel. The bellow of a scythe wing. The screams of the dying.

Highwatch was under attack.

● ● ◉ ● ●

Much to Guric's fury, Soran had survived the ambush. The powers of his god had protected him from the Creel spellcasters—though his guardsman had not been so fortunate—and the poisoned arrows, if they had even managed to pierce the scythe wing's thick coat and skin, had no effect.

The fiercest fighting took place in the valley between the village and the Shield Wall. Once the Knights saw Nar pouring through the Shadowed Path toward the fortress, they regrouped and attacked. Just as Guric knew they would.

He knew the tactics of the Knights, and he placed his men well. In the first wave, the scythe wings came in low, roaring and sending the Nar horses into a panic. They landed, and as the Knight set to work with bow and arrow, the scythe wing waded into the Nar. Each sweep of its wing wreaked carnage among warriors and horses alike.

It worked once, as Guric ordered. It made the Knights bold.

The second wave was a feint, and as the scythe wings landed, Creel spellcasters struck, throwing fire and lightning at the great beasts. One knight died screaming as his mail suddenly blazed, burning through the padding and clothes beneath. Had the Knights been prepared, had they not rushed in, thinking they were putting down a mere rabble of bloodthirsty raiders, most would have been able to repel the attacks. But their panic combined with Guric's feint killed all but four of them before they could take to the air again.

Seeing that this was no mere rebellion, the surviving Knights took to the air and returned to the fortress.

But again, Guric had his men well placed.

Three years ago, when relations with King Yarin had grown particularly sour, Guric had appealed to the High Warden to install several large mounted crossbows around the eyries. The Knights of Ondrahar were the only aerial cavalry within five hundred miles, yes, but they were hardly the only ones in Faerûn. Should their enemies ever decide to take Highwatch, mercenaries on other aerial mounts could be found, and should the Knights be on patrol or in battle, the eyries could prove a weak spot for the fortress. Vandalar had relented.

Guric's men in Highwatch did their work even as the battle began on the plain below. The Knights were well trained for open battle and learned in the tactics of Nar warfare. But treachery from within caught them completely by surprise. Some died in their beds. Others by ambush. And those scythe wings still in the eyries died by poison and spear.

When Soran led his survivors back to the fortress, Guric's men were ready for them. They let the scythe wings come in close, wings spread, soft undersides exposed as they prepared to land. Then the crossbowmen went to work.

• • ◉ • •

High in the fortress, in the courtyard known as the Horizon Garden, the surviving defenders of Highwatch made their final stand. Guric and his men—mostly Creel, but with a few Damarans guarding his back—pursued them. The fighting in the valley, through the streets of Kistrad, and into the fortress itself had been fierce. But this day had been long in the planning, and when the final fight began, Guric's men outnumbered the defenders three to one.

The Creel fanned out, facing the defenders, Guric and his guards several paces behind. The Creel held bows and spears, the soldiers of Highwatch only swords. Two still had shields. This would be a short fight.

"Listen!" Guric called. "Lay down your arms, and you will all be spared! Your comrades have done so. Even now, their wounds are being treated. Any who wish to return to their homes will be given arms and food to go."

One of the soldiers with a shield called out, "*This* is our home, you treasonous bastard!"

"Lay down your arms now," said Guric, "and you can go in peace. Or stay here and serve me."

"I'd rather die."

A few of his fellows exchanged nervous glances, but none stepped forward.

"No one?" Guric called.

"The Nine Hells take you!" the shield man called.

Guric ignored him and looked to one of the nervous fellows. "You stand no chance against my archers. Last chance . . ."

One of the Highwatch soldiers opened his mouth to respond.

The Creel cried out.

But it was too late. The great beast landed in the middle of the Creel, crushing three underneath its massive bulk. Guric felt the ground shudder beneath his feet. A scythe wing, the bulk of its body at least four times the size of a warhorse, its wings the size of sails. The knight on the creature's back let fly an arrow, and another Nar fell. The pennant at his back whipped in the wind. It was Soran.

Guric had thought all the Knights dealt with. He himself had passed two scythe wing corpses on his way to the higher towers. If Soran had survived . . .

"Fall back!" Guric shouted.

It was a needless order. His men were already scrambling away. But some were too slow.

The scythe wing swept one wing outward, and the hard, sharp bone along its length plowed through his men. Two went flying, and one went flying in two pieces. Another arrow from the knight took out yet another.

"Regroup!" Guric roared to his men. "Turn and loose! Turn and loose, damn you!"

The Creel obeyed. Turning, they loosed arrows and lobbed spears at Soran and his mount. One arrow bounced off the knight's armor, and the others struck the scythe wing. They only seemed to enrage the creature. It bellowed, spittle flying from its mouth, the roar drowning out all other sound.

Guric's men drew arrows for another volley. The scythe wing lumbered forward and drew back one wing. Half the archers managed to loose before the wing mowed them down.

"Fall back!" Guric called. He ran backward, not daring to turn his back on Soran and the huge beast. The archers were the first to retreat. They turned and ran. The spearmen backed away, keeping their sharp iron barbs between them and the great beast.

The scythe wing did not pursue, but let out a great bellow. The men cowered, and a few even dropped their spears to cover their ears. The sound echoed off the mountain. Guric had always imagined it might sound like that if a wall of strong steel were ripped in half.

Soran loosed another arrow, taking down another Nar, then turned his attention to the Damarans behind them. Knowing it might be only a lull in the carnage, Guric seized the moment.

"Soran!" he called. "Soran, hear me!"

Soran returned his attention to Guric but said nothing.

"It's over, Soran," Guric said. "Lay down your arms, and on my oath all of you will be spared."

"On your oath?" Even behind the face mask, Guric could hear the ragged edge to Soran's voice. There would be no surrender. "You swore oaths to serve the High Warden. Your life for his and for his people."

"I did what I had to do," said Guric. "I took no pleasure in it. Let the bloodshed end here. Save your men. Save yourself."

"Listen to your new lord," said a voice from behind Guric. Argalath had arrived. He stepped forward to stand beside Guric, Kadrigul a pale shape just behind him. "Highwatch is fallen."

Argalath raised one hand and let the cloth of his robe fall back to reveal his hand and forearm. The red light of the fires from the village below made the pale waves and pools of his skin between the bruises seem to burn like the flames themselves. The deeper blotches of his spellscar shone blue. He took a deep breath, closed his eyes, and pulled down his cowl.

The scythe wing let out a low growl that sounded like tumbling river stones. Argalath kept his eyes closed. Guric could feel the ground shaking as the creature approached.

The blue patches marring Argalath's skin flared with a cold, blue light, and when he opened his eyes, the same light burned in his gaze. The scythe wing stopped its approach and snorted in surprise.

Around him, Guric heard the Nar gasp, taking in a collective breath of superstitious fear. Soran was close enough now that Guric could see his eyes widen with surprise.

"No!" Soran called out.

The scythe wing opened its jaws and roared, its fangs long as daggers. The sound echoed off the cliffs and towers, and Guric could smell its fetid breath washing over him. But he stood his ground.

The blue glow emanating from Argalath flared.

The scythe wing's roar cut off, ending in something like a whimper. Its jaws snapped shut, and it shook its head. A tremor passed through its entire body, and for a moment it stood stock still. Guric was watching when the first real pain hit it. He saw it as a flash in the creature's eyes and a dilation of its nostrils. It gathered its strength for one final lunge.

But halfway its muscles lost all strength. The scythe wing collapsed and slid forward, its head coming to rest almost at Guric's feet. Its breath washed out of it, ruffling the hem of Argalath's robes, but it was only the great creature's dead weight pushing the air out of lifeless lungs.

The Creel cheered.

Argalath let his arm drop. Guric could see it trembling. It had been a long night.

Soran roared in grief and fury. He threw aside his bow and drew the sword from the sheath at his back as he leaped from the saddle.

CHAPTER SIX

THIS CAN'T BE HAPPENING—
—can't be happening—
—can't be—

The thoughts tumbled through Hweilan's mind as she ran.

She was no stranger to bloodshed. Narfell was a hard land. Outside of Nar-sek Qu'istrade, the tribes fought all the time. A warrior culture based on honor and status . . . bloodshed was inevitable. Most were little more than skirmishes, but now and then entire clans would feud.

Never—not once—had anyone dared to assault Highwatch.

But the smoke, the screams, the clang of steel, the harsh bellows of scythe wings . . .

Spring rains had not yet come, and it had been too cold for the snows to melt. Fire could spread among the dry wooden buildings of the Kistrad. An unfortunate accident. That had to be it. A spilled lantern in someone's stable. It would spread fast. Scythe wings hated fire. That explained their cries. Perhaps the horde of Nar she'd seen flooding the valley were merely coming to help.

Hweilan clung to these hopes. Tried to convince herself of them.

Then she found the bodies.

She rounded the hill and descended the final slope to the back walls of the fortress, still at least a quarter mile away. As fast as she was running, she was in the midst of corpses before her panicked mind registered them. She stopped so quickly that she skidded on the frosty ground, caught her boot on a bump in the path, and fell forward. She landed only inches from the staring eyes of a dead soldier. He lay on his stomach in the middle of the path. Two arrows sprouted from his back. Hweilan's eyes seemed drawn to them—anything but looking into the soldier's sightless stare.

The shafts were of a dark brown wood. Shallow grooves had been etched lengthwise down the shaft. Called "wind sleeves," they supposedly kept the shaft from warping. The fletching was the dark gray and brown feathers of pheasant. Nar arrows. Creel or Qu'ima.

Not a nightmare then. Real. Nar were attacking Highwatch.

Hweilan pushed herself to her feet and looked around. Three bodies were soldiers. Men of the Highwatch guard. But the rest were servants—older men and women in thick homespun clothes. Hweilan looked away, not wanting to see their faces, afraid she might recognize one.

A man stood up from behind a bush next to the path. His dark hair pulled back in a topknot. Clothes of animal hide and furs. His face impassive, a mask, almost of boredom. But his eyes were hard, and his breath steamed in long plumes.

"You were right," he said in Nar, "someone was coming down the path."

"Fresh little doe, isn't she?" said another voice from behind her. "Good thing we lingered after all."

Hweilan whirled. Another man stepped out of the brush on the other side of the path. Each man held a bow, and a sword hung from their belts. They came at her. Not hurrying. Nice and easy. Obviously not wanting to spook her, but utterly confident.

From behind her, Hweilan could hear Oruk blundering down the path.

The two Nar—both Creel by their accents—glanced that way.

"Your friend comes?" the first one said, obviously struggling over the Damaran words.

Hweilan tightened the grip on her knife. She didn't brandish it. No need to provoke them.

"Let me pass," she said in Nar. "I—" She almost said, I am the High Warden's granddaughter, but instinct stopped her at the last moment. "I serve the High Warden. Let me pass, and I will not remember your faces."

The Nar's brows rose as she spoke in perfect Nar, but he laughed. "Remember all you want," he said. "Vandalar feeds the crows."

Hweilan felt as if she'd just been punched in the stomach.

The sounds of Oruk's approach were very close now. She could hear his ragged breathing as well as his footsteps.

The other two Nar were only a few paces away now. They had dismissed the bow she held, unstrung as it was. But both eyed her knife.

"Drop the blade," said one. He had an arrow fitted on the string of his bow. He pulled a little tension into the string. "Drop and we have no trouble."

"Stop! Argalath wants her alive!"

The two Nar looked up the path, where Oruk, red-faced and panting, was stumbling toward them.

Hweilan ran. The distraction gave her a head start.

"Stop her!"

She jumped over a corpse in the path, and when she came down, her boot slipped on the uneven, frosty ground. She stumbled—

And it saved her life. An arrow hissed past, so close that she felt it tug loose a few stray strands of hair.

"Alive, you whoreson! Argalath wants her alive!"

Hweilan regained her balance and ran on. She could hear the men right behind her.

"Stop! No!" Oruk screamed.

Pain erupted from the back of Hweilan's skull.

• • ⊚ • •

The next thing of which she was aware was voices.

"It was a fowling arrow," said a man in Nar. "No point. I always keep one handy for birds and pretty girls."

"Still might have cracked her skull," said Oruk. "She dies, Argalath will kill you."

The voices were close. Hweilan tried to open her eyes. Her left wouldn't open at all. It hurt to open her right. She realized half her face was planted on the ground, and her hair had fallen across the other half of her face, some of it right across her eyelid.

She felt a hand against her throat. "She's not dead."

Full awareness seeped back in. She was lying on the path, one hand—the one that had held the bow—outstretched. The other, the one still holding the knife, was under her. It was a blessed miracle she hadn't fallen on the blade.

"Find something to tie her," said Oruk. "She took Jatara's eye and I chased the little *kûjend* over half the damned mountain."

"She took Jatara's eye?" one of the men asked.

"Gouged it right out," said Oruk.

The voice nearest her laughed and said, "I would not want—"

Hweilan rolled away from her pinned arm and brought her blade around in a fierce swipe. Her hair still covered her face, and she forsook a good aim for speed. The Nar screamed and jumped back, the tip of the knife slicing through his arm.

"Get her!" said Oruk, who was standing only a few feet away, the other Nar by his side. "Don't let her—"

An arrow struck him in the neck. It hit with such force that Hweilan heard the *snap!* of breaking bone. Oruk went down. The Nar beside him reached for his sword, then his eyes widened at the sight of something behind Hweilan, and he decided on flight rather than fight. He turned and made it all of two steps before an arrow hit him in the back. Screaming, he fell facedown into the brush.

The man Hweilan had cut was scrambling away, trying to put distance between them as he struggled to his feet.

Hweilan pushed herself to her feet, intending to run the final distance to the fortress, but when she looked up she found herself facing another Nar. He held a thick horn bow in front of him—Hweilan could hear it creaking with tension—and an arrow against his cheek. Blood covered the man—a spattering over his face, but shining wet gore, almost black, from his fists almost to his shoulders. His topknot was awry, and strands of hair made thick by sweat and blood draped his face. His eyes shone with a fury Hweilan had seen only in cornered beasts. There was nothing human in that gaze.

But then she recognized the face.

Scith.

"Hweilan, down!" he said.

She dived to the side of the path. She heard the twang of Scith's bow and the flight of the arrow over her, followed by the hard slap sound of the shaft striking flesh and bone. Men were screaming, but her heart beat so loudly in her ears that the sounds of dying men seemed thick and far away.

She lay at the base of a thicket, thick with green, waxy leaves and wire-strong branches. She looked up to see Scith walking calmly past her. He dropped the bow on the path and drew his knife. Hweilan knew that blade well. Scith's hunting knife. Made of black iron, its single edge honed razor sharp, with it Scith could gut and dress a swiftstag in moments.

Several paces away, the Nar Hweilan had cut was trying to crawl away, but the arrow protruding from his back seemed to be keeping his legs from working properly. Scith didn't hesitate or increase his pace. He walked steadily, patient and sure.

Just before he reached the man, he turned and looked at Hweilan. "You should look away now."

She didn't.

Vandalar feeds the crows.

That had been the man who said it.

Hweilan watched the whole thing. Before it was over, she was smiling.

WHAT IS THIS PLACE, MY LORD?" BORAN SPOKE IN A
reverent whisper as they passed through the
stone arch and into the open air of the holy place.
Something about it seemed to call for soft voices.

The other men left their torches on sconces just inside
the arch, but the snow on the ground outside reflected
the star and moonlight, so that even without torches
they could take in the entire scene. They stood on a
great shelf of rock. Where it met the wall of the mountain
behind them, it was broad as the fortress's inner bailey, but
it narrowed to a point a stone's throw away before ending in
a sharp precipice. The rock wall behind them showed many
additions—elegant borders and runes carved in the dwarf
fashion, Dethek runes praising Torm the Loyal Fury, and
over the door itself a graven image of an open gauntlet. All
of it displayed master craftsmanship.

Most of the area beyond was empty space, open to wind
and sky. Guric could see how its starkness appealed to
Soran and the man's understanding of proper worship. But in
the middle was a stone altar, about waist high, and before it a
wide basin set in the ground, now filled with snow. Argalath
stood there, a half dozen of his acolytes around him.

"My lord . . . ?" said Boran.

"This place is sacred to the Knights of Ondrahar," said

Guric. He took a deep breath of the mountain air and let it out in a great plume that turned to frost before it hit the ground. The snowstorm had blown over, the clouds had broken, and the air was almost painfully cold.

Argalath walked over and bowed before Guric. "Well met, my lord," he said.

"All is ready?" said Guric.

"It is."

"And she . . . ?"

"My servants have tended her well, my lord. Soon, you shall have her back."

Guric thought that at those words a feeling of profound relief would have flooded him. He'd done so much to come to this moment. But now that it was done, all he could feel was dark apprehension.

Argalath cleared his throat. "My lord, the sacrifice . . . ?"

"On its way," said Guric.

"Very good, my lord," said Argalath. He bowed again and returned to his acolytes.

"My lord," said Boran, his voice pitched not to carry. "What sacrifice?"

Guric swallowed hard, then turned to his men. "I . . . I need a few moments. You men, go back down and help the others with their burden."

The four guards bowed—Boran with a frown—then turned and disappeared back into the tunnel. Once the glow of their torchlight was gone, Guric walked over to Argalath and his acolytes. Closer, he could see their tracks in the snow, and the bundle they had laid in the very middle of the basin. Guric approached, slowly at first, but gaining speed so that when he fell to his knees before the shroud, he slid in the snow. Five years in the frozen ground had made the outer layers of the linen wrappings deteriorate. The runes written on them had faded to bruiselike splotches. Guric reached forward, reverently, and touched the shroud. The weakened fabric crumbled beneath his touch, but beneath, the linen seemed almost new, barely even stained from its burial. Wrapped in thick linens and bound with braided ribbons, it was still obvious what lay within. The head lay back, turned slightly to the side. Guric swallowed hard. She used to lie that way when in deep sleep. He remembered lying there, watching her as the lamp burned low, the low flame off the red tapestries of their chamber making her pale skin seem warm and soft, like summer sunset through thin clouds.

Guric tore his gaze from the bundle and looked to Argalath. He knew four of Argalath's acolytes—three Creel and one Qu'ima, the oldest of them no more than twenty. But two he didn't recognize. They wore the same robes of swiftstag hides and had shaved all but the topknot of their hair. But they had the bearing and hard build of seasoned warriors.

Argalath stepped to the side and presented them. "Durel and Gued. My acolytes."

"I don't know them."

"They begin their disciplines tonight, my lord."

Guric grunted. He'd been with Argalath long enough to recognize that more was going on here.

"Your spells worked?" said Guric.

"Perfectly, my lord," said Argalath behind him. "She has not changed since the day we put her in the ground."

"I . . ." Guric gulped, part of him recoiling at what he was about to do. He hadn't seen his wife in five years, except in memory. "I must see her."

"The outer wrappings must be removed for the rite," said Argalath. "If you will stand back, I will have my man remove the linens. He is most skilled with a blade."

"No!" Guric looked up at Argalath. "No one touches her but me."

Argalath closed his eyes and bowed. "As you wish, my lord. But I urge utmost caution. Cut away layer by layer. We must not damage the——"

"I know!" Guric drew the dagger from the sheath at his

belt, then peeled off his gloves with his teeth. His hands were trembling, and not from the cold.

Using only his thumb and one finger, he gently peeled up the top layer of linen, set his blade under it, and pushed upward, slicing through the cloth. Rather than going layer by layer down the length of the shroud, he pressed into the lower layers with his fingers, pulled the cloth up and well away from the treasure beneath, and cut away all the upper layers, peeling them back like the pages of a book. Layer by layer he cut, his heart hammering faster with each layer. After five layers, the thick cloth was completely dry, and he thought he could still smell a faint waft of the burial oils.

That sudden scent brought the memory back, stronger and more vivid than he had experienced in years. Even in the depths of his grief, he had not allowed others to handle Valia's corpse in those final moments. After Argalath had performed the rituals to preserve his wife's body and the servants lowered her into the grave, Guric had ordered everyone away. He had filled in the hole himself. Every last grain of soil and the rocks over it. In the moment when the black soil covered the last glimpse of the linen shroud, Guric's grief had almost overwhelmed him. Even his thirst for vengeance—no, for *justice*—had not been enough. It had been the promise of Argalath's words that held him.

I can bring her back. I can give her back to you.

Guric breathed in the scent and kept cutting away, layer by layer, until he could feel something beneath the cloth. Hard and unyielding. Cold. Dead. Nothing in that touch held any hint of life. Guric's gorge rose, and he had to force himself to lift that final layer, pierce it with his dagger, and cut it away.

Silk. The finest silk. Guric knew the wine red cloth had three layers, joined by intricate embroidery. The gown in which his wife had been wrapped in her shroud. Guric knew it because he had been the one to put it on her. Part of him longed to touch it, to feel the flesh beneath, but another part of him recoiled in horror at the thought, knowing that the flesh was cold, heavy, and lifeless.

Guric swallowed and took in deep breaths through his nose.

"Are you well, my lord?" said Argalath.

He couldn't respond.

Argalath knelt on the other side of the shroud and said, "Shall I do the rest, my lord?"

"No," said Guric, with much more force than he'd intended. "Make your preparations, Argalath. I do this alone. No one touches her but me."

When Guric peeled back the last scrap of shroud, Valia lay before him, her wrists bound by red ribbon under her breasts. A gold scarf—it looked off-white in the reflected moonlight, but Guric knew it was gold, for he'd chosen it himself, almost five years ago—had been wrapped around her eyes to keep them closed. Above the fabric, strands of her hair wafted in the breeze off the mountain. Her flesh was pale as the snow around her, and just as cold. Her lips were gray and lifeless. That they were slightly parted was the worst of all. He could see the rim of her teeth, and even in the dim light he could see the tip of her tongue, cold and colorless like a slug creeping out of a crevice. There was nothing of the softness and warmth he remembered. The sight revolted Guric, but he could not look away.

"Lord Guric," said Argalath, and Guric realized that his counselor stood beside him, hand on his shoulder, shaking him. How long had he been there? "Your men return with the sacrifice. Be strong, my lord. Soon now, you shall have your reward. But now your men must see their lord, commanding and sure. Be strong."

Guric looked up. He saw the red hue of torchlight flickering on the snow. He turned.

Boran, his five other personal guards, the closest Guric had to friends, and five other soldiers whose names he did not even know were coming out of the stone doorway. His personal guard and one other bore torches. The other four carried a man between them—taller than any of them, but bound at wrists and knees so that he had to be carried. Soran. Tough leather ropes at elbows and wrists bound his arms behind his back, and a stick was wedged in his jaws and bound with a thick strap to keep him quiet. He wasn't struggling, but the men carrying him panted from the exertion of carrying the large man up thousands of steps.

At the sight of the once-proud knight, a cold dread built in Guric. The old Guric, the one who had known life and laughter, who had been Valia's lover and husband and given up his inheritance for her, seemed to rouse and whisper, *After this, there's no going back. Before was battle. This is murder.*

He turned to Argalath. "You're sure this is the only way?"

"Yes," said Argalath. "If you still want Valia back, this is the only way. If you wish to let her rest in peace, to lose her forever, then—"

"No!" Guric said, so loudly that it echoed off the mountainside. He lowered his voice then for only Argalath to hear. "If this is the only way, so be it. Soran denied her life. Let him answer to his god tonight. Face to face."

Argalath bowed his head. "So be it." He turned to the guards. "Bring forth the sacrifice!"

• • ◉ • •

Guric sent the extra guards back into the tunnel, with strict orders to go down at least two hundred steps and remain there, no matter what they heard. His personal bodyguard stood with the acolytes and Guric himself, forming a ring of thirteen around the rim of the basin. Guric had not told his men exactly what to expect, but when it became obvious what was about to happen, they had not flinched. Their loyalty filled Guric with pride and love for them.

Soran lay next to Valia. He still moaned and struggled, but his bonds kept him from getting away, and the tight rope going from his elbow bindings to the loop round his throat kept his thrashings to a minimum. Too much movement and he could not breathe. Guric's men knew their business.

"Ignore his noise, my lord," Argalath said. "Soon, it will no longer matter."

"It doesn't matter now." Guric took his place on the rim of the basin.

They waited. Argalath paced the inner ring of the basin, muttering various incantations and sprinkling a dark powder of who-knew-what into the snow. It had a charnel stink, but Guric did not care. He'd bathe in the reek if it would bring Valia back to him.

After what seemed his hundredth journey round the circle, Argalath stopped over the two prone figures, one still thrashing weakly, the other cold and still. He lifted one hand to the eastern horizon and pointed at a gathering of stars.

"Behold," he said, his voice low and rasping. "H'Catha rises over the rim of the world. Korvun the Stone of Sacrifice bears witness above."

He lowered his arm and began a new incantation. At first Guric thought it was in one of his native tongues—Argalath's mother was of the Nar, but his father had come from Frost Folk, like Kadrigul and Jatara. But Guric knew much of the Nar speech, and he had listened to Argalath over the years to pick up the flavor, if not the precise meaning, of the language of the Frost Folk, and this was neither. The words were sharper, harsher, and seemed to speak of malice, hunger, and things that lurk in the dark.

Argalath lurched to a halt, wavering, and for a moment Guric feared his counselor was going to fall over in the snow. But then a great shudder passed through Argalath, he threw his head back, and Guric saw that his eyes had rolled back in his head. The voice that spoke was deeper and rougher than Guric had ever heard his counselor speak, and it held a timbre of malicious glee.

Argalath looked down on the figures lying in the snow, one dead and still, the other watching him with wide eyes.

Argalath reached inside his robes and withdrew a knife, not long but curved and of such pure steel that it caught every fragment of starlight.

Soran renewed his struggles, but in so doing pulled the noose tight around his neck. He thrashed even harder, and when he struck Valia, Guric growled and stepped forward.

"No!" said Argalath, still in that alien voice. "You must not break the circle."

Soran lay there panting, his eyes closed. Guric stepped back onto the rim of the basin.

Argalath resumed his pace, walking in a tight circle around Soran and Valia. Something in the way he moved set Guric's teeth on edge. He moved with an unusual, even beautiful, grace. But one that was decidedly inhuman. He raised the knife, resuming his chant, and Guric saw that more than starlight reflected off the blade. The edge of the curve blade glowed red, as if it had been sheathed in hot embers.

Argalath's incantation grew in volume, echoing off the mountainside, and took on a repetitive rhythm, almost like an incessant pounding upon a locked door. The words were still gibberish to Guric, but he picked up one phrase often repeated:

"*Jagun Ghen* . . ."

" . . . *resh Jagun Ghen'ye* . . ."

" . . . *Jagun Ghen!*"

Argalath's eyes rolled back in his head again, and he seemed rapt in a fit of ecstasy. The hand holding the knife trembled and shook.

Soran began screaming again. His jaws ground into the stick wedged between his jaws. Guric heard a cracking sound, and he didn't know if it was the wood or the man's teeth.

The knife flashed down.

Guric had known what was coming. He'd expected a slash to the throat, as a butcher might put down a young bull or goat. A quick slice. A few moments of pain followed by a rush of euphoria, then death.

No.

The knife plunged up to the hilt just below Soran's navel, then Argalath pulled, opening up a wide gash until the blade struck bone and stopped. Dark blood and pale blue offal welled out, steaming in the cold air. Soran screamed, a wail of agony that Guric had never heard even on the most brutal battlefields. It drowned out Argalath's final words.

Soran thrashed like a live fish thrown onto hot coals. Blood flew outward to stain the surrounding snow black. From the corner of his eye, Guric saw all but one of his guards turn away.

With his free hand Argalath grabbed Soran's head and pressed it into the snow. He brought the dagger to his throat at last, but not a quick slash. He pressed the point inward, almost lovingly, and slowly twisted open a jagged wound. Soran's screams died away in a wet gurgle, and he coughed with such power that a mist of blood shot out of his nose and around the wood still wedged in his jaw.

Guric opened his mouth to scream, *Enough!*

But then Valia moved.

The words died in Guric's throat.

Guric's stared at his wife's corpse. It had been the slightest movement, her left arm pulling against the binding ribbon. Soran's struggles caused her arm to move, he told himself. He watched for it again. So much blood had darkened the scene, covering both Valia and Soran, that it was hard to—

Valia's back arched, her jaw opened, and she took in a great breath, so much air rushing through her throat that she let out a sort of reverse howl. Her arms tensed, straining at the ribbon around her wrists, then the soft fabric snapped. Her back hit the ground again. Violent tremors shook her body, and she thrashed with hands and feet, sending bloody slush flying over the onlookers. Her gown ripped open, exposing one shoulder and breast.

"Argalath—!" Guric called, but he was too frightened to move.

"Be still!" Argalath said.

The tremors ceased. Both Soran and Valia lay still. For one instant, no one moved, and not even a whisper of steam came from anyone's mouth. No one dared to breathe.

Valia sat up. Even though she moved, there seemed to be no warmth about her. And even as he watched, Guric saw her cheeks sink, the skin stretch tight around her hands, like some half-starved refugee. For the first time that night, Guric felt suddenly and terribly cold. Chilled to his core.

With one hand, Valia reached up and removed the bit of cloth blindfold. She threw it away and looked at Guric. Looked him right in the eyes.

There was no welcome there. No love. No recognition. Not even confusion. What Guric saw in those eyes was hunger.

Snarling, Valia scrambled to her feet and lunged at Guric.

But Argalath stepped between them, brandishing the still glowing blade. Valia flinched and drew back at the sight of the knife.

"Ru!" Argalath said. *"A shyen. A kyet!"*

Valia threw back her head and screamed. There was nothing human in that sound. It was the cry of something that knew only cold, dark, and hunger.

Still brandishing the knife at Valia, Argalath turned to one of his acolytes and nodded.

The young man stepped to the acolyte standing next to him—one of the new ones; Durel?—grabbed both his shoulders, and shoved him at Valia. The man was too surprised to resist.

The man stumbled in the snow, and Valia fell on him, her teeth tearing into his throat.

That broke Guric out of his shock. He screamed and rushed forward, part of him wanting to pull Valia away and plead for her to stop and part of him wanting to pummel the life out of Argalath for allowing this to happen. Damn him, he had *promised!*

But before he'd made it three steps, two of Argalath's acolytes tackled him. Guric screamed and thrashed and called for his guards.

"Stop this!" Argalath roared, and his eyes and the dark splotches of his skin began to glow blue. "Stop this madness now!"

Unable to break free, Guric looked up at his counselor. "You promised I'd have her back. You promised!"

"You shall, my lord," said Argalath. "You—"

"Defiler!" said a new voice, as cruel and lacking in warmth as the winter. It was Valia. She crouched over the dead acolyte, fresh blood steaming in the cold, soaking them both. The man's throat had been torn to shreds. "You break the pact."

"No!" said Argalath. "The line of the House of Highwatch is ended." He pointed at Soran' corpse. "This man's blood—"

"Lies!" she screamed, and bloody spittle flew from her mouth.

The meaning of the conversation began to sink in to Guric's mind. Something had gone wrong. Terribly, horribly wrong. Whatever was speaking through his beloved's body now . . . it was not Valia.

"You lie!" she said. "One still lives. The House of Highwatch still walks this world. Still breathes. Her blood runs hot."

"Who?" said Argalath.

"The youngest. The girl."

"Hweilan," said Guric, and all the strength left his body.

Argalath had sent Jatara to retrieve the girl. But Jatara had come back missing an eye, claiming that the girl had tricked her and run away. The Creel sent after her had only managed to chase her back into the fighting. She'd been killed. Looking for her family, she'd made it all the way to the middle bailey, where the dogs had found her. Creel hunting hounds that had been used to sniff out anyone hiding, they'd gone mad at the scent of the girl. By the time their masters had pulled them off, her features were mangled beyond recognition. Guric remembered the torn and bloody corpse on the flagstones. No way to tell who it might have been, save for the word of the men chasing her. Guric had trusted the competence of the damned Creel. What a fool he'd been. His own eagerness to see this done had blinded him.

"We . . . we did not know," said Argalath. "I swear it!"

"Swear . . ." said the thing in Valia. "Vow, promise, mock, bleed. Call it what you like. You did not honor the pact. Our agreement is ended."

Guric took a breath to speak, but Argalath beat him to it.

"No! Please. Our utmost desire is to honor the pact. Grant us another chance to appease you."

The thing sat there, watching Argalath through narrowed eyes. Guric noticed that no steam of breath issued from Valia's mouth or nose. The thing seemed to take air only to speak. Guric squeezed his eyes shut, fighting back tears. His beloved was truly dead then. All this had been for nothing. He had damned himself for nothing.

"What do you propose?" said the thing.

"Remain in this body until a more suitable replacement can be found. Accept—"

"*No!*" Guric surged to his feet, catching the acolytes by surprise and breaking free. But two more stepped forward and grabbed him. Guric punched one, but the others grabbed his arms and held firm. "No, Argalath! I'll kill you myself if you do this!"

After such a spectacular failure, Guric would kill him anyway. But he had to get away from the damned warlock's brutes first.

"Boran!" Guric called to his guards. "Gods damn you, men, help me!"

Argalath's spellscar flared, briefly illuminating the holy

site, then fading to a dull glow again, and all five of Guric's guards dropped senseless into the snow. Guric screamed in wordless fury and despair.

"My lord, please," said Argalath. "Your men are sleeping, not dead. Please listen to me."

Left with no other choice, Guric stopped his struggles and glared at Argalath.

"Please, my lord," said Argalath, and Guric saw the compassion and sincerity in his counselor's eyes. "All is not lost. Trust me. Please. Allow me to salvage this before it is too late."

Guric took a deep breath and gave one swift nod. "Your life if you do not."

Argalath returned his attention to the thing in Valia's body. "The sacrifice"—he motioned to Soran's corpse—"was the most honored knight of Highwatch, and one of the most feared warriors of this realm. I beg you, take this body. Such a great warrior . . . would he not be a fine host?"

The thing smiled. "The rite is unfinished. What you began cannot be undone. If I leave this body, it dies."

"No!" Guric screamed. "Argalath, no! Do not—"

The thing's laughter cut him off. "You love this one, don't you? This body?"

"Y-yes."

"Then I propose a new pact."

"A new pact?" said Argalath.

"That one"—the thing motioned to Soran's mutilated corpse—"was a formidable warrior in this world, yes?"

"Yes."

"Then here is my offer. We summon another of my brothers to take this warrior's body. This warrior will hunt down the last scion of Highwatch and bring her back to complete the rite. When Highwatch lives no more, when the girl's blood slakes this circle, this pact shall be fulfilled. I will leave this body and complete the rite. She will be restored to you."

"But what of my wife until then?" said Guric.

"I keep her, and you keep me. A show of good faith on both sides, yes?"

Argalath turned to Guric. "My lord?"

"This is the only way?" said Guric.

Argalath lowered in his head. "For now, my lord. Given time—"

"No! No, damn it all. I agree. Let it be done."

The thing looked to Soran's corpse, at the mangled throat and spilled entrails. "This vessel will need some repair."

"It shall be done," said Argalath.

"And my brother will be hungry when he arrives."

Argalath smiled. "That should not be a problem."

CHAPTER EIGHT

Y OUR MOTHER IS DEAD.
Your grandparents
. . . the household . . .
. . . servants . . .
. . . dead.

After rescuing her, Scith had dragged her into the woods and told her. He hadn't wanted to. He'd stopped only to clean his knife, rob the corpses of their arrows, and then he was off, dragging her away.

And then he'd told her.

"They're all dead, Hweilan. You are the last. The last scion of Highwatch."

She couldn't remember much after that. Only running away from Highwatch, the secret way that only a few knew. Back up into the mountains and through passages cut into the rock. Up and up and up. Hweilan remembered darkness and cold. Darkness of tunnels, and darkness of the woods as night fell.

When dawn came, still they ran, the smoke-filled sky at their back. When the first rim of the sun finally peeked over the hills to their right, Scith found a brush-choked hollow and made a small fire. It smelled clean. Not like the black burning behind them.

Hweilan sat in front of the fire, her eyes fixed on the

narrow plume of smoke but her mind registering little. Scith had been standing behind her, looking down and chewing his lip for a long time.

He walked around and sat across the fire from her. "Hweilan, I . . . must go back."

She didn't answer.

"To Highwatch. You understand? I must . . ." He looked away, squeezed his eyes shut, and took very deep breaths.

This more than anything brought Hweilan out of her stupor. She had *never* seen Scith cry.

"Find out who did this," said Hweilan.

He looked back at her. "What?"

"You said you're going back. It isn't to save anyone. Our family is dead." It all came out of her in a toneless rush. "You said so yourself. You saw my mother die trying to save her maidservants. The others were dead when you found them. If Creel were able to storm the fortress, that means that the Knights are dead or fled. Any of the servants or villagers who survived are either captives or sworn to new masters. We have tools for food and fire. We can make shelter. If you're going back, there's only one reason: to find out who did this, and why. We must know so that we can hunt them down and kill every last one of them. That's the only reason to go back. And I'm going with you."

Scith sat there in stunned silence for a long time. Finally, he said, "No, you will not come. Think. You heard those Creel *golol*. They wanted you. Not as spoils. They wanted you. They knew *you*. They had orders for you. You are being hunted."

"Why?"

"I do not know," said Scith. "But we need to know. Our best hope now, I think, is to go west to your family's allies in Damara. The Creel are savage and cunning, but they could not have done this without help. That they were hunting you specifically . . ." He scowled and added a bit of wood to the fire. The blood soaking his arms had frozen black, and his sleeves creaked as he moved. "If their help came from the west, then we must know from where, or we could be seeking shelter from wolves in a lion's den."

"And you want me to . . . what? Sit here and tend the fire?"

His scowl deepened, but part of Hweilan took great comfort in it. This was far better than tears. This was the Scith she knew. "If those *golol* were hunting you, if *Jatara* was hunting you, then by now whoever gave those orders knows you escaped. They'll still be hunting. Every Creel and ally will probably be watching for you. But I am Nar. Change my hair, maybe even take some clothes off a corpse, and I can blend in. I can walk among them if I am careful. You cannot. You will stay here, because you are not a little girl anymore. You are a hunter. And after last night, you are a warrior. You must *think*. You'll never bring vengeance to your enemies if you hand yourself to them."

And so he left. He took his bow and all the arrows. The thick horn was too strong for her to draw, and even if she'd had a string for her father's bow—and she didn't—she couldn't draw it either. Scith told her to wait one day. If he had not returned by dawn the following day, Hweilan was to leave without him. North at first. Returning to the Gap would take her too close to Highwatch, and the lesser passes wouldn't be safe for a woman alone. Her best hope would be to go north around the Giantspires, then turn west for Damara. A long, cold road.

Exhausted, Hweilan tried to sleep, but she only dozed fitfully. She lay curled under her cloak beside the fire, and as sleep came upon her, so did the memories—

Vandalar feeds the crows.

No one can help you.

Your mother is dead.

But under them all was a deeper rhythm, like the sound of distant drums. With them, a sense of fear and dread seized her, and in the final moments before she clawed her way out of sleep, she thought she could hear words in the beat.

Jagun Ghen . . .

She woke shivering. The fire had burned low. Lying still on the ground, her body had soaked up the chill. She sat up and fed the fire, careful not to add too much. With the solid ceiling of low clouds—some wisping along the tops of the surrounding hills—she knew it would take a miracle for the smoke to be seen more than a few hundred feet away. But if Scith didn't return soon, she'd need all the wood to get through the night.

Sitting there, hunched near the fire, she dozed off again, and again the memories came, and the distant beat.

Jagun Ghen . . .

Jagun Ghen . . .

She coughed. In her doze, she'd leaned in too close to the fire. The smoke was choking her. She took in a ragged breath and wiped tears on the back of her glove. Through the haze of smoke and tears, she saw the man, just at the edge of the trees, watching her. He crouched, elbows resting on his knees, a massive spear laid across them. Standing, he would have looked down on Uncle Soran. But it was his eyes that drew her. They burned with a hot, green fire, like looking at the sunset through an emerald. So bright that their glow hid his face in darkness. Beyond the darkness massive antlers protruded from his head, melding with the twisting branches of the wood.

"Jagun Ghen . . ."

The sound didn't seem to come from the antlered man, but from the woods beyond him.

Hweilan came fully awake and took in a breath to scream.

The man was gone. Another trick of shadows and branches seen through the haze of smoke and tears. Probably mixed with exhaustion and nightmare as well.

Heart hammering in her chest, Hweilan looked around.

Evening was drawing nigh. The sky had taken on the deep gray color of heavy snow on the way. She was utterly alone. Ravens cawed in the distance, but nothing more.

Night fell, and still Scith did not return. Hweilan kept the fire going. Alone in the dark, it struck Hweilan how utterly and completely alone she really was. Before, in the wild she had always had Scith with her—and usually a great many guards besides. And there was always a home to which she could return. No more. The sounds of the hills at night, sounds that Hweilan had always loved on hunting trips—the breeze through the branches, stronger gusts seeming to sigh over the hilltops, night birds in the trees, small animals rustling through the brush, now and then the hoot of an owl—seemed almost furtive. Even sinister.

Hweilan found herself shivering. She added more wood to the fire. Her rational mind knew it was foolish. Nothing she heard was anything she had not heard dozens of times before. Nevertheless, a sense of dread grew within her.

She hugged herself to try to still the shivering, and her hands caused something sharp to poke her chest. Her *kishkoman,* still under her coat and jerkin. It brought her mother's words back to her—

. . . our people, Hweilan, we are . . . not like others. If you find yourself in danger, if you need help, blow this, and we will hear.

Hweilan pulled on the leather cord around her neck until she held the *kishkoman* with her frost-tinted gloves. She set the small horn whistle to her lips and blew, long and hard, again and again and again.

She lost count of how many times she blew. But she forced herself to stop when lights began to dance before her eyes. Her head felt light and airy. Clutching the *kishkoman* in one fist with the sharp point protruding from her fist, Hweilan lay down again and tried to sleep.

Just before she dozed off, a wolf howled in the distance.

● ● ◉ ● ●

When she woke the next morning, her sense of unease had not lessened. If anything, it seemed stronger.

Dawn had come, and Scith had not returned. Hweilan stood, kicked snow and dirt over the smoldering remains of the fire, and looked northward. Down in the wooded valley, she couldn't see far, but she knew what lay that way. Mile after mile, mountain, hills, and steppe. Even if the gods smiled on her, she had a journey of many tendays ahead of her.

"Alone." Her voice seemed very loud in the morning stillness.

But that one word made her decision for her. Everyone she knew and loved was dead. Everyone but Scith. She could go off alone, and if she was very, very lucky, find herself a beggar on some lord's doorstep. Or she could go after her friend.

Hweilan turned and headed south. Scith had trained her well, and his trail was easy to follow. She took her time. She knew that even if the invaders were sitting secure in Highwatch, feasting on their bounty, they would have scouts and guards out. Especially if Scith was right, and the invaders were hunting her.

With every mile, her sense of unease grew, so much so that she felt as if she were pushing her way up an invisible stream.

Shortly before midday, she was skirting her way around a clearing—she didn't want to be out in the open—when she saw it. A wolf, watching her from the shadows of the deeper wood. She might not have seen it had it not been for its pale fur. A silver so pale to be just shy of white, like starlight on new snow. Nothing unusual about that. Narfell was thick with wolves—especially near the hills, where the swiftstag herds came to forage and take advantage of the mountain streams in summer.

But less than a mile later, she saw it again. The same wolf. With that pale fur, there was no mistaking it.

She kept going.

The last time she saw it, it was standing on a treeless slope above her, looking down. Very strange behavior, especially for a lone wolf. Giving its position away like that for anyone to see. It let out a short yip that melted into a whining howl, then turned tail and disappeared over the hill.

She smelled them before she saw anything. Wood smoke. A campfire, most likely.

Hweilan crouched low, kept to the deep brush, and chose each step with the utmost care.

There, in a small valley next to a frozen pool, she found Scith.

Hweilan counted five men with him—all Creel as near as she could tell. They had picketed their horses under the nearest trees and built their fire in a basin formed by the crater left behind from an old treefall. The tree still lay next to it, its large root system gnarled and probably hard as iron. The Creel had tied Scith to the upended roots of an old tree, his arms spread, the coat and clothes covering his upper torso cut away. His skin was bloody with fresh cuts. The men were laughing as they knelt over the fire.

One of them stood. In his hand he held a long stick, the far end glowing hot and smoking. His laughter stopped, and he stepped toward Scith.

CHAPTER NINE

76

"HOW IS THE EYE?"

Jatara's jaw tightened and she breathed heavily through her nose. Guric saw the fury in her remaining eye, and it warmed his heart. A strip of gray cloth around her forehead bound a linen bandage over her right eye. Lord Guric, two guards behind him, faced Jatara, who stood guard outside the door of Argalath's chamber.

Jatara bared her teeth. Perhaps it was supposed to be a smile, but it seemed more snarl to Guric. "Which eye, my lord?"

"Why the only one you have left, of course. I was told you lost the other in failing at the one task given you yesterday."

No mistaking it. He could definitely hear her teeth grinding.

"It won't happen again, my lord."

"I should hope not. Only one eye left. Tell your master I wish to speak with him. Now."

Jatara bowed and stepped inside the room.

Guric suppressed a shudder. He didn't care for any of Argalath's bodyguards, but Jatara in particular made his skin crawl. It wasn't the too-pale skin of her people, nor the odd way she shaved off the front half of her hair. She had never shown Guric anything but the utmost deference and obedience, but he sensed no genuine respect in her. She honored Guric because Argalath wished it, and no more. What hold his chief counselor held over the woman and her twin brother, Guric neither knew nor cared. As long as they did as they were told.

He could hear whispered voices beyond the door. Jatara and one other. Probably Vazhad, Argalath's Nar bodyguard.

His patience gone, Guric told his guards, "Wait here," pushed the door open with his fist, and stepped inside. A low fire burned in the hearth, more for heat than light, since bright light pained Argalath. Jatara stood a few paces away. Vazhad was beyond the bed, helping his master into his robes. Both were scowling at Guric for barging in.

"Out," Guric ordered them. "I wish to speak to your master alone."

Both waited for Argalath's nod before obeying, which only fueled Guric's fury. He slammed the door behind them.

"How may I serve you, my lord?" said Argalath.

"I want to see her. Now."

"My lord?"

"You know who I mean, Argalath. Don't vacillate with me. I haven't the patience for it."

"My lord, I . . . I don't think that wise."

"Your *wisdom* brought this upon me, counselor. After last night, you'll forgive me if your counsel holds less weight with me."

Argalath looked at the floor. "You wound me. I did my best. If you will remember, my lord, I did warn you that in . . . these matters, nothing is certain."

"Damn you! *What have you done with my wife?*"

Argalath started at Guric's shout, then bowed low and did not rise again. "She is being well cared for, I swear. I beg you, my lord, heed my counsel."

Guric ground his teeth together and took a deep breath. "Stand straight and look at me."

Argalath straightened but still did not look him in the eye. "My lord, please. Listen to me. Your wife's body is being given the utmost care, under the watch of the best guards. But you must understand: The body moves, speaks, sees, hears . . . but whatever is inside the body, that is not Valia."

"You think I don't know?" Guric could feel his fury rising again, but he kept his voice low. "I was there, Argalath. I saw what she . . . *it* did. I looked into its eyes. But—"

"It is not too late. Do not despair, my lord. The rite did not fail."

"Did not fail? Are you mad? I—"

"The rite worked perfectly. It was our knowledge that failed. The Nar sent after Hweilan were mistaken. They swore that the body we saw was hers, that the House of Highwatch was gone from the world. They were wrong. Once that error is rectified, your wife will be restored to you. I swear it."

Guric winced and turned away. "She's just a girl, Argalath."

"You regret our actions?"

"No! What was done two days ago, that was justice. That was battle, and innocent lives are sometimes lost in battle. But this . . . this feels like murder."

"And murder it is." Guric felt Argalath's hand on his shoulder. He hadn't even heard his counselor cross the room. "But it is the only way to return your beloved Valia to you."

They stood in silence a moment, the only sounds Guric's heavy breathing and a slight crackling from the low fire in the hearth.

"It is not too late," said Argalath. "Kadrigul leads the hunters. If you find this whole business too distasteful, we can call them off, exorcise the . . . thing from Valia's body, and set her to rest. But if we do that, there is no going back. She will be beyond my powers to restore."

Guric swiped Argalath's hand off his shoulder and said, "Where is my wife?"

Argalath sighed. "My lord, nothing has changed. I fear seeing her will only bring you further pain."

Guric looked down on Argalath with the full weight of his authority. "Pain is part of the price of leadership. Take me to her. Now."

After crossing several courtyards and many stairs to one of the upper sections of the fortress, they had climbed well over two hundred steps to the top of one of the northern towers. At Guric's insistence, they had left their guards behind. Guric cursed the time it had taken. Argalath leaning on him was no burden, but the man was damnably slow.

Guric looked down at Argalath. His chief counselor's cheeks were even more sunken than usual, and lines of fatigue creased the corners of his eyes. Still . . . Guric's anger and frustration at Argalath's failure—no matter how the man painted it or placed blame elsewhere, the rite had failed; spectacularly so—were strong enough that they drowned out any feelings of remorse or pity. After last night, Argalath deserved to feel a little pain.

A door stood along the right wall and two more guards, both Nar, stood before it. The men showed no emotion whatsoever. No deference at the sign of the two most powerful men of Highwatch suddenly appearing at their post.

Still leaning on Guric, Argalath took a moment to catch his breath, then said something to the men in their own tongue. Guric had only a basic understanding of the Nar language, and this one had a different sound to the words, the accent strange. He caught only *trouble* and the word signifying a question.

"*Nyekh,*" said the guard on the right, followed by a short string of words.

"What did he say?" Guric asked.

"I asked if she had given them any trouble," said Argalath. "He replied that she has not, that she has not even spoken."

Both guards bowed, then one stepped aside while the other removed a long iron key from a chain around his neck. He fitted it into the lock, twisted—the old mechanisms tumbled with a creak that set Guric's teeth on edge—then stepped back.

Guric stepped to the door and pushed it open. Beyond, all was darkness.

"It's black as pitch in there," said Guric.

"We don't mind," said a voice from the darkness, and Guric stepped back. The voice was strong but cold, and although it was utterly inhuman, there was a timbre to it that still held hints of Valia's voice. Guric felt a shiver go up his spine, and his mouth suddenly felt very dry.

"Here, my lord." Argalath had lit a torch from a brazier the guards used for warmth. He stepped around Guric into the room, holding the torch high and averting his eyes.

The light pushed back the shadows, revealing a small cell of stone walls and floor, with old clumps of dirty straw the only flooring. The roof was old timber beams and planking of the roof.

The creature—one glance and Guric could not think of it as Valia—was on the far side of the cell. She crouched against the far wall, still in the fine robes of her burial, though the skirt had been torn to shreds. The skin of her legs and one arm was pale as bone, but blood covered her other arm and face, for in one hand she held a rat, its legs dangling and entrails spilling from where she had torn out its underside with her teeth.

Guric felt his gorge rise. He clamped one hand over his mouth and took deep breaths through his nose. But that only made it worse, for he could smell the reek of blood and offal—and all around it, something worse. It reminded Guric of an animal stench. An animal of the cold and dark places.

"Where is my brother?" she said, then buried her face in the rat's entrails for another mouthful.

"He has other duties now," said Argalath. "As we agreed."

She swallowed and smiled. There was nothing human or even bestial in the expression. It was merely a movement of muscles and dead skin pulled tight over the teeth. "And what are my . . . *duties?*"

"Your time has not yet come," said Argalath.

"And when will my time come?"

"When your brother has fulfilled his promise."

"Hm." She looked down at the dead rat in her hand. "That might take some time. The tall one there . . . this one's body means something to him?"

"It does. We must take great care of it."

"Then I must be fed, or this shell will decay. This"—she dropped the rat and stood—"dulled the edge off my hunger. But if I have to feed off vermin, the tall one here will not like what it does to this body, I think. I will require more fitting food."

Guric fled the room.

Outside the cell, the door shut and locked once again, Argalath put a hand on Guric's shoulder. The lord of Highwatch leaned against the wall, stared out the window, and took in deep draughts of air.

"I'm sorry, my lord," said Argalath.

"Did I . . . did I take her—" Guric shook his head and cursed. "Its. Did I take *its* meaning correctly?"

"I fear so, my lord."

Guric groaned. He swallowed and took in another deep breath before turning to face his chief counselor. "There is no other way?"

Argalath shook his head. "She will not need to be fed often. We could withhold as much as possible, but I fear the damage that might do to your wife's body. The body itself—forgive my bluntness, my lord—is still dead, animated only by the spirit occupying her flesh. That . . . life-force must be fed, lest the body decay."

"Fed . . . people?"

"Yes. But is the return of your beloved Valia not worth the sacrifice?"

"This is not sacrifice," said Guric. "If it were me, that would be sacrifice. To take another's life . . . that is murder. Again. More murder."

Argalath shrugged and at least had the good sense to try to appear uneasy. "I know of no other way, my lord."

Guric turned back to the window. His voice hardened with resolve. "You are certain this hunting party of Kadrigul's can find the girl?"

"Quite certain," said Argalath. "We have one who will find her for us."

Remembering Soran's eviscerated corpse and that horror's talk of summoning her brother, Guric shuddered.

"Show me."

Argalath leaned on Guric for their descent down the stairs. As they took their first steps, Guric said, "You said this happened because a few of our Nar lied about killing Hweilan?"

"Five of them, my lord," said Argalath. "And I do not know that they lied. They might have been mistaken."

"Find those five, Argalath. They will be that thing's first dinner guests."

"As you command, my lord."

CHAPTER TEN

H WEILAN KNEW THE PREFERRED TORTURE METHODS of the Creel. Scith himself had taught her. If they wanted a victim to take days dying, their favorite method was to bury the victim up to his neck, then slice off the eyelids. But digging a hole in the frozen earth was hard work, and Creel were notoriously lazy. Thus, this was their so-called "summer torture."

The rest of the year, their favorite method was to hamstring the victim, sever the tendons at elbows and shoulders, cauterize the wounds, then wait for the wolves to do the rest. Seeing Scith covered in blood and the Creel heating sticks in the fire, Hweilan feared the worst. Feared she might be too late.

The only bow she had, she could not draw, and she had no arrows. Only her knife and the *kishkoman*. And there were five Creel down there.

Then it came to her. Creel, for all their faults, were still Nar, and the life of any Nar warrior was his horse.

Get the horses.

She knew the beasts would go mad near her. Horses always did. But that might help. It would certainly take the Creels' attention off Scith. If she could get close enough to cut the lines, the horses would flee. If she could keep out of sight, most of the Creel would go after the horses.

If . . .

She stashed her father's bow under the thick leaves of a bush, then set off. She was within a short bowshot of the horses when they began to snort, stamp, and pull at their picket line.

One of the Creel said, "What is that?"

Hweilan pulled her knife and ran. Crouching low, she pushed her way through the brush. The horses went mad, screaming and pulling at the single line of rope to which they'd been tethered.

She could hear the Creel even over the screaming of the horses.

". . . horses!"

"What is it?"

"If that wolf is back . . ."

Hweilan reached the tree around which the picket line had been tied. The horses reared and pulled, their eyes rolling back in their heads.

From where she stood, she was in full view of the Creel, all of whom had turned to see to their horses. They saw her.

"Hey!"

She leaped forward and brought her blade across the picket line in a swift swipe. It snapped, and the horses surged away.

"Charge!" Hweilan screamed. "Loose arrows! Get them! Get them!"

Her ruse worked. Every Creel reached for weapons, their eyes scanning the trees.

Hweilan turned and ran. It worked. She couldn't believe it. But it worked.

Creel knew the open grasslands better than the castle chambermaids knew every cell and hallway of Highwatch. But they didn't know these hills. Not like Hweilan. And they were unused to the trees and thick underbrush.

Tired, cold, and hungry as she was, Hweilan still managed to lose them. By the time the Creel realized that there were no arrows hissing from the trees and no soldiers bearing down upon them, Hweilan was up in the rocks again, where there was little grass, but lots of the thick bushes whose roots cracked the stone and grew branches tough and pliable as wire. They left few tracks but gave good cover. The first place to hide she found, she took. She couldn't see their camp, burrowed as she was among the thick evergreen leaves. But she could hear them shouting, some apparently going after the horses while others came after her. None came close.

Hweilan took deep, careful breaths, slowing her hammering heart. She listened to them arguing which way to chase.

After awhile, she heard horses galloping away, following the gap between this hill and the next. When the hoofbeats had faded, Hweilan waited, listening. Ravens in the distance. An intermittent breeze rattling the leaves higher up the hill. Nothing more.

Knife still in hand, Hweilan made her way back down the hill.

Nothing moved in the camp. All the horses were gone. Not a Creel in sight. Scith lay against the roots of the fallen tree, his chin resting on his blood-spattered chest.

Hweilan ran to him. It was even worse than she'd feared. The Creel had cut both of Scith's ankles and sliced through the thick tendons that ran from his shoulders to chest. To keep him from bleeding to death, they'd burned him from heels to halfway up each calf. His left side had been scalded so badly that his shoulder was a blackened husk that faded into red blisters and peeling skin to the center of his chest. But the right shoulder had only been singed and was still leaking blood. The weak pulse of red fluid was the only sign Scith was still alive. Hweilan had seen worse. But the smell . . . a sickly sweet reek; it caused her stomach to wrench and brought bile up to the back of her throat.

"Oh, Scith . . ."

She reached out but could not bring herself to touch him.

He'd never walk. Not without a healer.

Scith lifted his head. Scith was the strongest man she had ever known. Even more than Soran, whose strength lay in his unyielding rigidity. Scith's strength was deeper. Both kinder and crueler. Primal. But now, his head wobbled with no more strength than an infant's. His jaw hung slack, and bits of bloody drool ran from the corner of his mouth.

He took a ragged breath and said, "Behind you!"

Hweilan whirled.

One of the Creel was coming out of the brush, a long, curved knife in hand. Watching her watching him, he froze. Neither of them moved. Neither breathed. Then the Creel straightened and smiled.

"You . . . no moving," he said in Damaran. Then he screamed in Nar, "Back! Come back! She's here!"

"No!" Hweilan said.

"You no worry," the man said. His lips peeled back in what he obviously intended as a smile, but emerged more of a leer. "You beautiful. No cutting for you."

"Run," Scith rasped.

Hweilan kept her eyes fixed on the Creel. "I'm not leaving you."

The Creel's leer melted away and his eyes hardened. "You drop knife now."

She raised it. "No."

The Creel tossed his own knife from hand to hand, then twirled it in his right. He began taking slow steps toward her. "You drop it. Or I make you drop it."

"Run!" Scith said.

Hoofbeats in the distance. The other Creel returning. It had all been a ruse to draw her in, and she'd fallen for it.

The Creel flipped his knife, caught the blade, then flipped it again. The leather-wrapped hilt slapped his naked palm. "Last chance, girl."

Hweilan lowered her knife. "I will. Just . . . just don't hurt me."

Scith let out a long, low groan. "Run," he whispered.

Keeping her gaze fixed on the Creel, who was still slowly advancing, Hweilan crouched and set her knife on the ground. Right next to the campfire.

"Good," said the Creel. "Good, girl. Step back. Now. By your friend."

Hweilan's hand grasped one of the rocks the Creel had used to surround their fire. The outside of her glove was wet, and it sizzled against the hot stone.

"What—?" said the man. The sound of hoofbeats was very close now.

Hweilan stood and threw the rock as hard as she could. Wearing the thick gloves, her aim wasn't perfect, but the man was only a few paces away now. She aimed for his forehead, but the stone smashed into his mouth. He fell screaming.

She kicked the contents of the fire over him, then went for her knife. She was shaking all over, and her hand, encumbered by the thick leather of the glove, fumbled around the handle. As she scrambled for it, her eyes met Scith's.

In that moment of frozen time, that one brief instant between one heartbeat and the next, she saw it. Scith was dying. Each beat of his heart weaker than the last. Each breath a struggle. Every thought a battle. One he would soon fight no more.

Her fingers closed around the knife, and she turned.

The Creel was already on his feet, knife in hand. His eyes looked more shocked than hurt or angry. The burning coals she'd kicked on him had singed his outer clothes in spots but done no real harm. He spat a black glob of saliva and blood. Hweilan thought she saw a small chip of white—a tooth—in it.

"Stupid girl," he said in Nar. "Maybe I cut you anyway."

A rider broke through the brush and reined in his mount

on the edge of the campsite. Three others came in behind him, the last leading the fifth horse. They took in the scene, and all but one of them erupted in laughter.

"Seems we're just in time," the leader in Nar. "Lucky she didn't kill you."

The man on the ground spit another gob of blood and said, "She tricked me."

"It's her," the man said.

Everyone looked to who had spoken. It was the rider leading the extra horse. The one who hadn't shared in the laughter. He was studying Hweilan intently. "The one Argalath wants. The one who hurt Jatara. That's her."

The Creel all returned their attention to Hweilan. None were laughing now, and the man on the ground looked more apprehensive than angry. The riders fanned out, and the unsmiling one let go of the riderless horse. The beast tossed its head, snorted, then trotted back into the woods.

Hweilan waved her knife. "Stay back!" she said in Nar.

The nearest rider was only a few dozen paces away now, but he was having trouble getting his horse to come farther. His mount pranced and fought at the reins. Two other riders had gone back to the brush, and Hweilan could hear them trying to circle in behind her.

Hweilan couldn't gather her thoughts. Everything in her screamed at her to run, but she knew that even if she could get away—and that seemed very unlikely—she couldn't leave Scith. Not like this.

The man with the knife began to creep forward again. He gave her a bloody smile. "We'll be rich."

"You need to catch her first," said the leader. He'd brought his horse in behind the man on the ground and was trying to bring it around to her left, but the beast seemed reluctant to get too close. "Put the knife down, girl. We'll get the fire going again, have some hot food, then go back to your home. We'll even see what we can do for your friend."

"Home?" Hweilan had a hard time spitting out the word.

She remembered the smoke, the glow of fires in the distance. The corpses outside the wall.

Vandalar feeds the crows. . . .

Your mother is dead. . . .

She screamed, more grief than fury, and charged.

The leader's horse shrieked and bucked away, its rider cursing as he tried to get it under control. Part of Hweilan's mind heard the other horses charging, but she focused all her attention on the man with the knife.

She made her attack clumsy. A feint, bringing the open edge of her knife around in a wide arc aimed for the man's face. He stepped back, caught her wrist easily, and squeezed.

"Now," he said. "Drop the kn—"

All breath shot out of his body as the toe of Hweilan's boot hit him between the legs. His grip on her wrist melted away. She yanked her hand free and felt the edge of her knife slice through his glove and into flesh. He tried to scream and lurch away at the same time, but his knees collapsed beneath him.

Hweilan raised the knife and lunged.

Something hard struck her in the back. Pain flared through both shoulders and she fell, the Creel she'd kicked scrambling away. She rolled over to see the man who had first recognized her. He'd forsaken his horse and was running toward her on foot. A few paces away, Hweilan saw the spear that had hit her. He'd thrown it shaft first.

"Got her!"

Another Creel fell on her right arm, both his hands locked around her wrist.

Hweilan shrieked and punched at him with her free hand, but he held on. She got in four good hits before another man grabbed her arm.

"No!" Hweilan screamed and kicked and twisted, but the men were too strong. "Let me go!" Hweilan looked up. The leader was standing nearby, a spear in hand.

"You *will* drop the knife," he said. "Hard way or easy. You w——"

He stumbled, his jaw went slack, and he fell face forward. An arrow—pale shaft, black feathers—sprouted from his back. It had pierced his heart.

The men holding her let go and scrambled to their feet. Another arrow hit the man on her right. He screamed and went down. The other ran for the woods. He was only a few paces away from the nearest trees when another arrow took him in the back. He went down and did not move again.

The second man to be hit was still screaming as he struggled to his feet. The arrow protruded from his side, just above his hip. His face was a grimace of agony, but he held a spear in one hand and knife in the other as he faced the woods.

"Face me!" he screamed. "Come out and——"

Hweilan took three quick steps toward him and buried her knife in his throat. The shock of the steel hitting bone traveled up her arm. The man stumbled back, staring at her, his eyes wide with shock. His mouth moved, trying to speak, then he fell. The knife was caught in bone, and she could not keep hold of it. The man's legs kicked once, the breath went out of him, and for a moment only, all was silence.

She could not look away. The world around her seemed to stop, everything focused on the dead man at her feet. She had killed him. Killed a man. She had killed many animals in her life. But this was the first time she had killed another thinking being. He would never love or laugh or cry again. Never breathe. Because of what she had done.

But she was not sorry. In fact, something deep inside her, some smoldering rage, exulted in it. She had to resist the urge to throw back her head and bellow.

Then she heard the horses galloping away. Somewhere in the woods, a man was screaming. There was the brief growl of an animal, then the man screamed no more.

Hweilan heard movement behind her and turned. The

only surviving Creel, the one who had first confronted her, was standing in a sort of crouch, his knees still trembling. Blood streaked down his chin. He held his knife again, but his hand was shaking.

"You . . ." he said.

Hweilan spun and grabbed the hilt of her knife. She pulled, twisted, and pulled again, but the knife would not come free.

"You!" The man was coming for her.

"Stop!" said a new voice, speaking Damaran.

Both of them turned in the direction of the voice. A figure stood just at the edge of the trees. Tall, lean, dressed all in skins and furs. The bits of skin showing between his coat and fur cap were pale as the snow, but intricate inks twisted vinelike patterns across his cheeks and round his eyes, making them seem very bright. One was a blue pale as winter sky, but the left eye was a vibrant green. His hair was light as his skin and gossamer fine. The slightest breeze set the long locks wisping around his face, save for two thick braids knotted before each ear. And those ears rose into sharp points. An elf.

The newcomer held a thick bow of some pale wood, an arrow nocked and ready, though he held it low, with only the slightest tension on the string.

The elf looked to Hweilan. "Get your knife," he said.

"I kill you!" said the Creel. "Kill you both!"

"She is unarmed," said the elf. "You will wait, or I will feather you where you stand." He fixed those eyes on Hweilan. "Get your knife. Now."

She tugged and twisted. The blade moved, making a mangled mess of the dead man's throat, but the point was lodged deep in bone.

"Put your boot on his throat and pull," said the elf. "But take care not to slice your foot when the blade comes free."

She looked at him. Who was this stranger, and why was

he helping her? Or was he? Was he only waiting until she had steel in hand to turn the bow on her? He raised an eyebrow in question.

Hweilan planted her left boot on the corpse's throat, grabbed the knife with both hands, and pulled. A moment's resistance, and the blade came free. Hweilan fell hard on her rump, and a line of blood—still warm and steaming—splattered across her face.

The Creel was looking back and forth between her and the elf. He was panting, and by the look in his eyes, Hweilan knew he was barely holding back panic.

"Crooked Knife!" the Creel shrieked, a ragged edge to his voice. "Help!"

"Your friend is dead," said the elf. "Your horses are gone." He looked to Hweilan again. "I can kill him now, or you can. By rights, he is yours. But you seem rather . . ." He shrugged. "Out of sorts."

"You want *me* to kill him?"

The elf relaxed the tension on his bow, then slid the arrow into a quiver on his belt. He scowled, seeming a little puzzled, then said, "I ask what *you* want. His life is yours, by right."

The Creel screamed and charged the elf.

The elf looked up, almost casually, and drew a sword from a scabbard he wore on his back. It was somewhere between a short and long sword, sharp only on one edge, and slightly curved near the end. A long tassel of braided leather and bits of fur dangled from the end of the leather-wrapped hilt.

Several paces away from the elf, the Creel threw the spear. The elf leaped aside, and the shaft sailed past him to land in the bushes.

The Creel looked at the elf's sword, looked at the knife in his hand, then turned and ran. He made it into the trees, and the elf did nothing.

"You aren't—?" she said, then she heard the growling of an animal, followed by the shrieks of the Creel. He didn't scream long.

"He is . . . taken care of," said the elf.

He sheathed his sword and walked over to stand before her. Still holding his bow in one hand, he spread the other in an open gesture and said, "I am called Lendri. You are Hweilan, daughter of Merah, are you not?"

ONE OF THE GREAT DISADVANTAGES, IN GURIC'S mind, of a fortress the size of Highwatch was that it took so damnably long to get from one place to the next. All the winding stairways and halls of the outer fortress were bad enough, but Vandalar's dwarves had burrowed dozens of tunnels through the western cliffs. It was into these that Argalath, after retrieving Jatara and Guric's two guards, led them. Into the deep dark of the mountain itself.

The tunnel was tall enough for Guric to walk upright, but the walls and ceiling were still unfinished stone, broken only by occasional support beams.

Argalath had buried his face deep in his crimson cowl. Even now, he kept it up, for both of Guric's guards—one leading, one trailing—held lamps, and in the close confines of the tunnel, their light was very bright.

"What is this place?" the lead guard asked, his voice little more than a whisper.

"A mine at first," said Argalath.

He spoke like a host giving his guests a tour. The patronizing tone rekindled Guric's anger. How could the man seem so damnably content when their plans had gone so wrong?

"When the mine turned up nothing," Argalath continued,

"the burrowers began expanding it for storage and future dwellings. See there."

They passed a doorway on their right. A stout frame of worked stone supported the arch, but there was no door, and beyond the stone floor had been smoothed only a few feet. The rest of chamber was raw rock.

"See," said Argalath. "Very new."

"Enough talk," said Guric. "Get this done."

They passed two more such chambers when they saw light before them. In the middle of the floor, a large lamp filled the tunnel with yellow light and the strong scent of oil. More light glowed from a doorway to the left. This one showed no stonework whatsoever, beyond the cutting of the tunnel itself.

Argalath stopped. "My lord," he said, "our men should wait here."

Guric nodded at his own men and gave Jatara a look that told her that "our men" included her. He reached out for Argalath to lean upon him.

One of the strange Nar with the shaven head and single topknot stepped into the doorway. One quick glance took in their procession. His eyes settled on Guric and Argalath, and he gave a slight bow. The man and Argalath exchanged a series of words, then the Nar stepped aside.

"Ah," said Argalath. "It seems we are just in time. Our hound is ready for the hunt."

Another Nar stepped out of the doorway and into the tunnel. A third man followed. He was bare from the waist up, his chest and stomach smeared and spattered with blood, and his hands and forearms were covered with blackish gore.

Kadrigul emerged from the room, whispered, "It is done, master," to Argalath, and then he too stepped aside.

Another figure stepped into the doorway, and all the breath escaped Guric in a gasp of utter shock.

The newcomer had to stoop to get through the doorway.

He was taller even than Guric, who looked down on everyone else in the tunnel. The figure was naked, save for a ragged loincloth. His pale skin had a sickly yellow cast in the soft lamplight.

It was Soran. No mistaking that carved-from-granite visage, the square jaw and deep-set eyes. But now the eyes were black, whether from the unnatural light in the tunnel or something else, Guric could not determine. And the wounds that had killed him—he'd been gutted like a deer—were completely healed.

"Gods, Argalath," said Guric. "What have we done?"

"What all strong leaders must do," said Argalath. "What is necessary."

• • ◉ • •

Later that morning, Guric and Argalath, their guards keeping a respectful distance, stood behind the parapet of the outer bailey wall, watching the hunting party disappear in the distance.

"You're certain it can find her?" Guric asked Argalath.

"Yes, my lord."

"How?"

Argalath thought a moment before replying. "Soran's flesh is dead. Still the flesh is of Hweilan's family. His blood runs in her veins through Vandalar. What's inside Soran can use that. He will be able to sense her."

"Like a hound."

"Something like that, yes. Furthermore, seeing her uncle riding after her, the girl might not flee. She might even run to his arms."

Guric grunted. "Once she's close enough . . . she'd never mistake that thing for Soran."

Argalath smiled. "Once she's close enough, it won't much matter."

CHAPTER TWELVE

"H-HOW DO YOU KNOW MY NAME?" SAID HWEILAN.

"I heard the *kishkoman*," said the elf. "Yesterday. In these lands, a human with a *kishkoman* . . . there's only two people you could be. Hweilan or Merah. You are too young to be Merah."

Her mother's words came back to her.

The whistle is beyond the hearing of most folk. But our people, Hweilan, we are . . . not like others. If you find yourself in danger, if you need help, blow this, and we will hear.

"You . . . you're Vil Adanrath," she said.

The elf cocked his head, and his brows narrowed. "Of course. What did you think?"

"I . . ." She didn't know what to say.

"We should see to this one." The elf waved in Scith's direction.

Hweilan stumbled over to Scith. Her heartbeat was calming, and her knees suddenly felt weak. She dropped her bloody knife and sat beside him. His head had fallen again, his chin resting on his chest. But a faint trickle of blood still leaked from his shoulder wound.

The elf knelt on the other side of Scith. He frowned.

"I am no priest," said the elf. "His wounds are beyond my skills." He looked to Hweilan and set a hand to the knife at his belt. "I could ease his passing."

97

"No!"

At her shout, Scith's eyes fluttered. He tried to raise his head but failed.

Fighting back tears, Hweilan took his face in her hands and lifted his head. She eased it back against the frost-encrusted soil between the fallen tree's roots. His eyes opened, focused on Hweilan, then looked to the elf.

"You!" he gasped.

"You know each other?" said Hweilan.

"You . . ." Scith said, his voice scarcely more than a whisper. "Stay . . . away. From. *Her!*"

"I have done as the lady asked," said the elf. "I have honored her wishes."

"What are you talking about?" said Hweilan.

Scith's gazed returned to Hweilan. She saw his pupils flare, then his eyes rolled back in his head. His entire body trembled as he exhaled his last breath. Blood no longer flowed from his open wound.

"Scith?" said Hweilan. *"Scith?"* She shook him. His head flopped forward and struck his chest, causing his jaw to snap shut. Lifeless as a canvas doll. "Scith!"

"I am sorry," said the elf.

She squeezed her eyes shut, and the tears spilled, freezing on her cheeks. She scrubbed at them with the back of her glove.

"Hweilan—"

She grabbed her knife with both hands and pointed it at the elf. "Who are you, and *how* do you know my name?"

The elf looked down, seemingly unconcerned at the blood-smeared steel trembling only a few inches from his nose. "I have told you my name," he said. "Lendri."

A growl, so deep that Hweilan felt it rattling her gut, came from behind her. Still holding the knife, she turned her head and saw a wolf standing on the edge of the campsite. The largest wolf she had ever seen, it easily outweighed her. One paw stood off the ground, as if frozen in midstep. Every gray hair on its body stood on end, it held its ears erect and forward, and its lips—still smeared with blood—were peeled back from long teeth.

"Lower your knife," said Lendri. "You're making me uneasy. Hechin doesn't like it when I'm uneasy."

Hweilan remembered the sounds of the men screaming in the woods and how they had suddenly cut off. Seeing the wolf's bloody muzzle . . .

She lowered the knife.

The wolf opened its jaws wide, almost in a yawn, then padded over to nuzzle the elf, a low whine emanating from its throat.

"A friend of yours?" said Hweilan.

The elf smiled. "More of a cousin."

"I want some answers."

The smile melted off Lendri's face, and he pushed the wolf away. "We should see to your friend first."

Lendri spoke as he worked. He drew his knife—a long flat piece of silvery steel, shining like ice, etched with runes, hilt bound in thin strips of some dark leather—and cut the thick coils of horsehair rope around Scith's wrists.

"I am Vil Adanrath," he said as he sliced. Scith's right hand fell limp to the ground. "As was your mother—or half so, anyway. Her mother was Thewari, of the Red Horizon band. Her father . . . well, that's another tale. Thewari's grandfather"—he reached over and sliced the rope binding Scith's left hand; it fell, limp as a wet coil, onto Hweilan's knee, and she recoiled—"was Gyaidun, who was *rathla* to me."

"*Rathla,*" said Hweilan. "I . . . I know this word. My . . . my mother told me. Told me stories. It means . . ." She searched her memory for the right words.

"Blood-bound, in your tongue," said Lendri. He opened his right hand and pretended to draw his blade across it. There, bisecting his palm, was an old scar, almost blue against his pale white skin. "Brothers of the same mother are *yachinehra,* 'milk-brothers.' It is said that the gods choose your *yachinehra,* but *rathla* choose each other. Brothers in blood."

"I . . . I don't know what that means," said Hweilan.

"It means that I swore an oath to your grandmother's grandfather. Blood to blood. His blood binds me still. To you and to your mother."

"My mother is dead." Hweilan couldn't believe how easily it came out. After the horror of this day, it already seemed distant. But saying the words, her next breath caught in her throat and threatened to come out a sob.

The elf's eyebrows shot up. The wolf, sensing his tension, let out another low growl. "Merah is . . . dead?"

"Yesterday," said Hweilan. She took a deep, calming breath. "Creel sacked Highwatch. Vandalar, the Knights . . . my mother. All dead."

"All the Creel in Narfell could not have taken Highwatch," said Lendri. "Not without—"

"Treachery. I know."

"Who?"

"I don't know. I was . . . away when it happened. But on my way back, I ran into servants of Argalath, sent to find me. Scith"—she had to stop and breathe deeply to keep from crying—"saved me."

"Who is this Argalath?"

"A Nar shaman," said Hweilan. "Or half-Nar maybe. I've heard stories . . . But he wormed his way into the confidence of Guric, Highwatch's Captain of the Guard."

Lendri nodded and sheathed his knife. "Captain of the Guard? Yes, he could plan such an attack."

"I'll kill them." Hweilan had not even thought it until the words were out of her mouth. But she didn't regret them. She looked over to the man she had stabbed. The open wound at his throat was still steaming a little. "Just like that one."

"A trained soldier and a Nar shaman—perhaps even a demonbinder? You will walk up to them and stab them?

When at least one of them—probably both—are looking for you? And how will you do this?"

Hweilan suddenly felt weary to her bones, as if she could crawl off into the nearest tree shadows and sleep for a tenday. "I don't know."

Lendri looked down on Scith. The wolf nudged under his arm, sniffed at the corpse, then let out a long, low whine. Lendri took the tattered remains of Scith's shirt and coat and folded them over his cut and bruised torso. "This one—Scith you called him—he was a friend to you?"

Hweilan could hardly believe that the lifeless shell before her was the Scith she knew, the man who had been the closest thing to a father she had known since her real father's death. Scith had been dead only a few moments— she knew if she reached out and touched him with her naked skin, he wouldn't even be cold yet—but already there was something *other* about him. Still in every feature the man she knew, but in every way that truly mattered, something altogether separate from her. Only a shell. A lifeless image.

And so she simply said, "He was."

"Then we must do him honor." Lendri stood and inspected the old tree against which Scith lay. "This will do."

"Do for what?"

"A pyre. We will use this tree. The wood is old and will burn well."

Hweilan stood and looked at it. "It's covered with ice."

Lendri slid a steel-headed hatchet out of his belt and handed it to her. "Get the ice off first, then hack out a bed in the wood. Save the kindling."

She hefted the hatchet, testing its weight. "You'll never get that wood to burn."

"I will. Get to work."

With that, he turned away and headed back into the woods, his wolf at his heels.

"Where are you going?" she called after him.

"To look for an *uskeche tet*." He melted into the shadows of the wood.

Hweilan walked to the side of the tree, purposefully not looking at Scith. She knew that if she did, she might not be able to hold back the tears anymore.

She set to work.

● ● ⊚ ● ●

Lendri returned before she finished. She had cleared off most of the ice—taking a great deal of old bark with it—and had begun hollowing out a bed. The more she worked, the more it began to look like a coffin.

The elf was carrying a straight piece of wood, slightly longer than his forearm. He had stripped off the bark. He sat down next to the cold fire bed and, using what to Hweilan looked like a long iron nail, began carving the stick.

"What are you doing?"

He answered without looking up. "Making the *uskeche tet*."

"The what?"

"It means . . . 'ghost stick,' " said Lendri. "But also 'fire stick.' The *uskeche tet* is for both fire and ghosts to our people."

Our people. Hweilan's mind was still wrestling with that one. She found no fault in the elf's story. It matched with things that her mother had told her over the years. But Lendri seemed so . . . different, so *other* from what she had always imagined her mother's people to be like.

"Where are the others?" Hweilan said.

Lendri did look up at that. "Others?"

"Your people," she said. "Vil Adanrath."

He frowned and set back to work. "I am the last."

"What?"

He looked to the log and frowned. "The pyre is ready?"

Hweilan began chopping again. "I can listen while I work."

"Our people were exiles in this world for many

generations," said Lendri. "But it was never home. They have returned to the Hunting Lands. Your mother had the choice. To return with her people or stay here with your father and you. She chose you. Now, all that remains of their blood in Faerûn is me—and you."

Hweilan stuck the hatchet in the side of the log, then scooped out all the loose kindling and dropped it onto her already considerable pile. "Why?" she said.

"That is a long, long tale," said Lendri.

"No. I mean why are they gone but you are . . . not?"

"Another tale, though not quite so long. But in short, because of my oaths to your forefather." Lendri's lips compressed and he thought a moment before continuing. "*Rathla* . . . the most sacred of oaths, save marriage. *Rathla* live, die, and kill for one another. Understand: To harm my *rathla* is to harm me. To bless my *rathla* is to bless me. Gyaidun and I were brothers, and long were the shadows we cast. But he was a man, and I am Vil Adanrath. Long after I lit his pyre and mourned his passing, still my oaths bound me to his children. And his grandchildren. And to you, Hweilan inle Merah."

"You and I," said Hweilan, "we are this . . . *rathla?*"

"No," he said. "Your forefather was my *rathla*. But the Vil Adanrath walk the world far longer than the children of men. And my oath to him binds me to you."

"But I'm not . . . like you. I am not Vil Adanrath. My mother—"

"Loved a Damaran, yes," said Lendri. "Bound herself to him in marriage. She was not the first to find love outside the people. Her own mother did so. But my *rathla's* blood ran in her still. And it runs in you. My dearest sister was your foremother, Hweilan. We are *k'che*. We are family, you and I."

Her distant foremother's brother. That made Lendri her uncle. Of sorts. Hweilan retrieved the hatchet and went back to work, considering the elf's words. Some of his tale she knew already. She knew her mother was not Damaran, not even fully human by the sharp curve of her ears and her slightly offset eyes. Her mother had been born among some "barbarian" people to the east. Everyone in Highwatch knew that. Hweilan had even heard the name Vil Adanrath pass her mother's lips from time to time. But she had never known that she had family beyond her aunts, uncles, and grandsires—the Damarans. Now . . . the dead.

"Why have I never heard of you?" she said. "Never seen you? My mother never—"

"Merah put the ways of her people behind her," said Lendri. "Not without reason."

"Then why are you here?" said Hweilan. It came out harsh. Accusing. But she didn't care. Her mother and her entire family lay dead in the ruins of their home, and this buckskin-clad brute whom she'd never met or even been told about sat across from her, calm as a summer morning, telling her that they were family while he whittled on a stick. "Why now?" she said. "Scith recognized you, and he didn't seem happy about it."

Sadness passed over Lendri's face, and he set back to work on the stick. "I came. Once. Not too many years ago. But your mother would not have me. She honored her people, but her life was among the Damarans now. And I think she did not want me influencing you. She told me to leave. I honored her wishes."

Hweilan attacked the fallen tree with sudden savagery, sending bits of wood flying. "Doesn't death release you from your oaths?"

"I am not dead."

"But Gyaidun. Your . . . *rathla*. And my mother—"

"The oaths were mine," said Lendri. "Only my death will free me."

"You said you heard my whistle-knife," she said. "But why were you here at all? The Vil Adanrath dwelled far to the east."

"I am . . . looking for someone."

"Who?"

"I am . . . not sure yet."

Hweilan stopped her work and stared. The elf was so damnably *odd*. "What does that mean?"

"Later," said Lendri. "We see to Scith, then we must decide what to do with you. Now work."

• • ◎ • •

Once Lendri had finished, he set the *uskeche tet* carefully aside, then used his heavy knife to help Hweilan finish her work. Once it was done, they stood and looked down at the corpse. Ravens had begun circling overhead, and Hweilan could hear more off in the woods, already eating. Together she and Lendri stood over Scith. In the short time they had worked, his skin had taken on a grayish cast, and frost now caked him.

"I can't do this," Hweilan whispered, more to herself than Lendri.

"You must. I cannot lift him in by myself. Honor your friend. Would you leave him as carrion?"

She did it. Hweilan cried the entire time, but she helped Lendri lift Scith into the shell they had hollowed out inside the tree. A heavy, completely dead weight. They covered him with the kindling.

"It will never burn," said Hweilan. "Too wet."

"Stand back," said Lendri. He peeled the glove off his right hand and curled it into a fist. A small ring, a dull yellow like brass, circled one finger. He pointed it at the log and said, *"Lamathris!"*

The air round his fist ignited, and a gout of flame shot outward, striking the tree and enveloping it in bright orange fire. A hot gale swept over Hweilan as the fire heated and pushed back the air. Flames rose, tumbling over one another and sending up thick clouds of gray smoke. Somewhere out in the woods, Hechin howled.

Lendri retrieved the stick he had spent so much time

carving. He handed it to Hweilan. She examined it by the light of Scith's pyre. Into the pale wood, Lendri had etched many Dethek runes in a spiral down the length of the shaft, and within the carving he had rubbed some sort of resin. Turning the stick, she read them.

MERAH INLE THEWARI
SORAN OF HIGHWATCH
VANDALAR OF HIGHWATCH
SCITH OF THE VAR
KNIGHTS OF ONDRAHAR
PEOPLE OF HIGHWATCH

"Your honored dead," said Lendri. "I will sing. Add your own prayers if you wish."

Lendri sang. More of a whispered chant really, like a soft breeze through dry branches. At first he sang in his own tongue. Hweilan listened, understanding nothing but the names.

"Sing with me," he said.

"I . . . I don't know the words," said Hweilan.

"We will sing them in the tongue of the Damarans."

And so they did, Lendri chanting one line, Hweilan following.

Flames of this world, bear this flame to our ancestors
Our family burned bright
Our family . . .

Lendri took the stick back from her. Holding one end with both hands, he stepped forward and thrust it into the middle of the fire, sending a great shower of sparks fluttering amid the smoke. He held it there as long as he could bear to be near the flames, then he stepped back. The end of the stick was black, but the resin pressed into the runes burned a hot red.

Merah daughter of Thewari burned bright,
Soran of Highwatch burned bright,
Vandalar of Highwatch burned bright,
Scith of the Var burned bright,
The Knights of Ondrahar burned bright,
The people of Highwatch burned bright.
Their exile is ended, their rest assured.

Lendri looked up to the sky and sang in his native tongue, but this time loud—more of a shout than a chant. Then he looked down at Hweilan. His eyes seemed hard, not with any sort of religious passion. More in expectation.

"You still wish to bring justice to your family's murderers?" he said.

"Yes." No hesitation.

"Then do as I do. Take off your gloves."

She did.

He raised his right hand, long fingers outstretched, and he sang, "Our family burned bright. Those who robbed the world of their light will rest no more."

She repeated his words, not singing but speaking them clearly.

Lendri brought his open palm down on the top of the stick. Hweilan heard skin and flesh sizzle, a sharp intake of breath from Lendri, then he pulled his hand away. She looked at him with wide eyes.

"Hurry," he said, "before the fire consumes the wood."

She hesitated. What kind of fool put his naked hand on burning wood? But Lendri's gaze on her was fierce and unwavering. She raised her right hand. It trembled.

"Do it, Hweilan!"

In her mind, she saw Scith's last moments. She saw the last look her mother had given her, heard their last words, spoken in anger. She heard again her father's parting words to her on the day he'd ridden out of the fortress—*Listen to your mother, Hweilan. She does what is best for you. Make me proud.*

The next time she'd seen him, his face had been pale and cold, more like lifeless stone than the always-quick-to-smile face of her father.

Hweilan slapped her hand down and grabbed the stick. Pain seized her entire arm. She gasped and tried to let go, but the muscles in her hand convulsed, squeezing tighter. She could feel the skin of her palm and the insides of her fingers burning away, her flesh fusing to the wood.

Control returned. She let go, flesh that did not want to come away from the hot wood tearing and peeling away. She stumbled back and landed hard on the icy ground. The world seemed to spin around her, going black, and she could hear nothing but a roar.

When the world cleared again, she could see the great cloud of her breath mixing with Lendri's. The elf knelt over her, his brows creased in concern.

"Can you hear me?" he asked.

"Yes."

"Foolish girl," he said, and it was then that Hweilan first noticed that he held her burned hand between his own. He was pressing snow into her palm. She couldn't feel the cold. Everything from her wrist down was only pain. "You were supposed to touch the stick, not grasp it. Why?"

She smiled weakly. "It felt like a good idea at the time. My family . . ." Tears began to well in her eyes again.

Lendri held her gaze a long time, then nodded. "Grieve for them, Hweilan. Honor them. But do not punish yourself. Punish those who killed them. I will help you."

"When do we start?"

CHAPTER THIRTEEN

HWEILAN'S HAND WAS STILL IN AGONY, BUT THE COLD snow she held helped. Now that all of her attention was not focused on her arm, she felt a pounding headache coming on. Not like others she'd had in the past—pain behind her eyes or her forehead. This was a nagging pulse right at the base of her skull. Almost like a drumbeat.

"Try to open it," said Lendri.

Clenching her teeth against the pain, Hweilan opened her hand slowly. Pain shot up her forearm. She turned her palm down and dropped the snow. She could feel tiny tugs as bits of skin came away with the ice.

"I have some salve," said Lendri. He gently turned her hand and opened his mouth as if to say more. He gasped and his grip tightened, pulling her closer.

Hweilan winced and tried to pull away. "You're hurting me!"

He let go and looked at her, his eyes wide and his mouth hanging open.

Hweilan looked down at her hand. Most of the skin was gone, the flesh beneath burned. But across her palm, three of the letters from the names that Lendri had carved into the stick were clearly visible, branded right into the flesh of her hand in raised, puffy red flesh:

"Kan?" said Hweilan.

Lendri closed his mouth and looked down at the brand again.

"What?" said Hweilan. "What does it mean?"

"Death . . ." he said, though his eyes were distant, and he seemed to be talking to himself. "She carries death in her right hand."

"What are you talking about? Lendri?"

He shook his head, almost as if waking from a dream. His haunted eyes focused on her, and he said, "That word . . . it means 'death' in our people's language."

Hweilan studied the scar. "Maybe it is a good sign?" she said. "I swore to bring vengeance to those who killed my family. Now I have 'death' branded on my right hand. A sign?"

"Perhaps." Lendri's looked away. "Rub some clean snow on it. I will put on some salve and a clean bandage. Then we must leave. Quickly."

"Wait," said Hweilan. "Go? Go where?"

Lendri pointed at the fire, and his upper lip curled over his teeth in a very wolflike snarl. "That smoke will draw any Nar within ten miles. You want to be here when they come for a look?"

Hweilan looked away. The pounding in her skull was getting worse. She knelt and rubbed snow on her hand. "What makes you think I'm going anywhere with you? You come out of nowhere claiming—"

A shrill sound cut the air, bringing a sharp pain to her ears. She looked up. Lendri was holding a *kishkoman* to his lips, much like her own, but brown with age.

He dropped it back into his shirt and walked over to her. He loomed over her and said, "I am Vil Adanrath. I am blood to you, by oaths and birth." He crouched and leaned in close, his nose only inches from hers. "But if that is not enough, I am the only hope you have."

• • ◎ • •

They were getting close.

Soran, riding out front, had set an unrelenting pace. Almost dangerously so, since the ground was not only uneven and rocky, but covered with snow and ice.

Argalath had been forced to ensorcel all their horses before they would tolerate the Soran-thing's presence. But it had worked, and their "hound" never hesitated in his chosen path. He led, and they followed—Kadrigul and eight Nar behind him. He thought all were Creel, but it didn't matter to him. Nar were all alike.

They crossed a slight rise—a thickly forested saddle between two hills—and Soran disappeared between the trees. Kadrigul reached for the amulet Argalath had given him and whispered the words to activate it. Through the cured leather of his glove, he felt the metal tingle.

He followed the tracks through the snow and soon found Soran sitting on his horse, glaring at him. The Nar stopped their own horses well behind Kadrigul.

Soran drew in a deep breath to speak. "She is close."

They set off again, and when they next left the trees, Kadrigul could see a thick column of smoke in the near distance. A mile away or less.

Soran spurred his horse, and Kadrigul followed.

• • ◎ • •

Lendri finished bandaging Hweilan's hand, then helped fit her glove back over it. The salve helped. The pain in her hand was already fading to a throbbing ache, but the pounding in her head was so bad that she thought she could feel her skull rattling.

Scith's pyre still burned, but the flames had lessened considerably, and the smoke had gone from thick white plumes to wisps of gray. With almost no breeze, the pyre had filled the little valley with an eye-burning haze.

"The pain is very bad?" said Lendri. He was studying her intently.

"My head worse than my hand. Where will we go?" Hweilan asked.

"North for now."

"The people who killed my family are sitting in my home right now, at Highwatch. To the south."

Lendri looked at her with that unnerving gaze of his. The ice blue right eye reminded her of the strange Sossrim who occasionally came to Highwatch to trade. But the green left eye . . . there was something unnatural about it. "Our oaths bind us, yes, but we need help."

"What kind of help? Where?"

"To answer that to your satisfaction will be a long tale. For now, we must run."

"Why won't you tell me?"

"I will tell you!" Lendri's lip curled over his teeth and she heard the beginning of a growl in his voice. She stepped back.

Seeing her fear, Lendri's expression softened. "I'm sorry. I will tell you. I promise. I have . . . so much to tell you. But to explain everything will take time. Time we don't have now. We are still too close to Highwatch. Now, let's move."

Hweilan turned and went the other way.

"*Where* are you going?"

She stopped and glared at him. "I left my father's bow up the hill. I'm not leaving without it."

Lendri thought a moment, then nodded. "Be quick."

She pushed through the brush and made her way up the hill, finding the bow with little problem. She retrieved it, stood, and looked down into the camp. Lendri was rummaging through the supplies of the dead Nar, discarding most of what he found, but pocketing an item here or there.

I could go . . .

The thought hit her. She could turn, keep going up the hill. Lendri wasn't looking her way. She could be over the rise and be long gone before he suspected anything. Hweilan gripped her father's bow in a tight fist and turned uphill—

To come face to face with a wolf, standing on a ledge no more than a few paces away. Hechin. The huge gray wolf's yellow eyes, unblinking, fixed on her. He didn't snarl, didn't growl, did nothing whatsoever to threaten her. But his very stillness spoke volumes.

"Hweilan?" Lendri called from below.

"Coming."

By the time Hweilan walked back into camp, Lendri had his supplies—two thick bundles, bound with leather cords—secured on his back. Ravens sat thick in the trees, and more were circling overhead, their cries a raucous counterpoint to the crackle of the pyre's dying flames. Only a shell remained of the log. Everything within was gray ash and red coals. Nothing left of Scith but what the gods had taken.

Lendri walked over to Hweilan and held out a thick bundle. "Here. You'll need this in the coming days."

It was a thick Creel cloak, make of swiftstag hide and rimmed with fur. Her head fit through the middle of it, and it flared in the front, covering her when needed but easily thrown back in case she needed to free her hands. It even had deep pockets along the inside.

"Did you . . . did you find this in their packs or take it off . . ." Off a dead man? She couldn't speak the words.

"Does it matter?" said Lendri.

She shook her head and settled into the cloak. Hweilan looked at the Nar corpses. "What about them?"

"A feast for the crows," said Lendri. "Let's leave them to it. Come."

He set off, setting a brisk pace through the woods, following frost-covered deer trails along the bottom of a steep escarpment.

But they made it no more than a quarter mile out of the camp before Hechin barked from behind them.

Lendri stopped and raised a hand to signal quiet.

The wolf bounded out of the thick brush. Even Hweilan, who had studied wolves only from a distance, could see that he was agitated. His ears lay flat against his head, and his tail pointed straight out.

"What's wrong?" said Hweilan.

"We're being followed," said Lendri. "Keep moving." Lendri shrugged out of his pack and handed it to her. "Here."

"What? What do you mean?"

"You keep going. I'm going back to see who it is."

She set the bow on the ground so she could settle the packs on her back. "Probably other Nar, coming to investigate the smoke. Why not keep moving?"

"*You* will."

He fitted an arrow to his bowstring and headed back the way they'd come, Hechin at his heels. Hweilan watched them go, then watched a while longer. Finally, she turned her back and headed north, fast as she could. If the elf never came back . . . well, at least she had the supplies.

Her trail led her away from the escarpment. The hills reared up into a wall before her, blocking the north, while the trail bent eastward. Hweilan knew of a pass several miles farther that way. With Lendri not there to tell her otherwise, she headed east.

The ground soon smoothed out, becoming less rocky, and the tall woods gave way to a scrubland of thick brush and squat trees, their branches still winter bare.

Hweilan fell into a steady jog, and her long legs ate up the ground. The pulse at the back of her head was still there, but it was no longer a hammering pain. More of a tingling just under her skin, an itch, a buzzing on the brain. Very much like the feeling of being watched she'd experienced on her way back to Highwatch the day before. But this feeling had an undertone of anger, sharp and hot. It didn't make her want to look around to see who might be watching. And even though there was a hint of danger, it didn't make her want to run or hide. It made her angry

Hweilan suddenly found herself with the urge to hit something. To pound it again and again until it couldn't move any more. Standing here in the cold afternoon, Hweilan felt positively hot with fury.

A wolf howled behind her, the sound beginning low, rising high, then dropping again to fade into something just shy of a growl. Brief silence, then the same howl. Hweilan had learned enough from Scith to guess at what it meant. Wolves howled for a reason. Usually to communicate with the pack over vast distances, and sometimes just for fun when the pack was gathered. But when one pack encroached on another's territory, the lead male would sometimes howl like the sound she'd just heard. It was meant to warn off the invaders.

Hweilan stopped to listen, and she heard something else. At first she thought it was just her own heartbeat, but as she stood there in the path, taking deep, steady breaths, there was no mistaking it. Hoofbeats. Coming up behind her. That could only mean Nar.

Her hand seemed to search for her knife of its own accord. The anger in her was seething to come out. But her rational mind forced that down. Had she been able to use the bow, had she even a few arrows . . . maybe. But on her own, with a knife, against mounted men . . . no.

She looked around, searching for a place to hide. Squat trees and bushes everywhere. If she could take care not to leave any tracks . . .

The hoofbeats were getting closer. At least three horses. Perhaps more. And moving just shy of a gallop. The fools were risking breaking their mounts' legs on the icy ground, which meant they were pursuing something.

Hweilan leaped off the path, going from rock to rock or the thickest ice as best she could. Only once did her boot crack the frost. She passed the first bushes and trees, fearing they were too close to the path. When she had put at least a dozen yards between herself and the path, she threw her father's bow under a large bank of scrub brush, then wriggled under it. With the thick Nar cloak and both packs still riding her back, it was no easy task.

Lying on her belly under the bush, she pushed herself up just enough to bend back an outer branch and peer out on the path. Other foliage was in the way, but between them, she caught her first glimpse of the rider.

A large horse—larger even than that of a Nar chieftain's war mount. One of the huge Carmathan stallions that Damaran traders sometimes rode through the Gap in summer.

Trees hid the rider a moment, and when he came back into view, he had slowed his horse to a canter as he cast his gaze about. Hweilan's breath caught in her throat.

"Soran!" she cried. "Uncle Soran!"

Grabbing her father's bow in one hand, she scrambled out of her hiding place as quickly as she could, heedless of the branches scraping her face. The rider reined in his horse with such ferocity that it screamed and skidded to a halt on the frosty ground.

Hweilan ran to him, but the first good look at Soran stopped her in her tracks. She wasn't sure what she'd expected to see on his face. A look of utter relief perhaps. Joy. Grief that they were the last of their family. Or maybe even anger that she was all the way out here while the good people of Highwatch and Kistrad were suffering. But there was nothing. Not even a sign of recognition. The look that he turned on her was completely blank, like . . .

Just like Scith had looked after he took his last breath. Soran looked dead.

Perhaps it was a trick of the light, or maybe only a sign of Hweilan's exhaustion and frayed nerves, but as Soran turned his horse toward her, she thought she saw a flicker of red in his eyes.

"Uncle Soran?"

More riders came into view. All were Nar, save one. Kadrigul. One of Argalath's lackeys—and Jatara's brother.

Kadrigul followed Soran's gaze, saw Hweilan, and reined in his own mount. The Nar behind him did the same. The other riders urged their horses off the path, right for her. All were reaching for weapons.

The tingling in Hweilan's head suddenly spread through her body, like being woken from deep sleep by a splash of cold water. The anger was no longer just an emotion. It was a physical force, making her muscles tremble with a sudden irresistible urge to *hurt* all the men before her. The world around her became sharp and clear, perfectly focused, every sound sharp and distinct. Every sensation, every breath, every beat of her heart screamed at her to lash and rend and kill. So sharp were her senses that she thought she could hear the beating hearts of the horses and the men on them—though not Soran's.

A blur of gray ran among the Nar horses, barking and snapping at them. Hechin! The horses screamed and tried to scatter, but their riders reined them around and brought their weapons to bear against the wolf. But he was too quick, evading their spears and the swipes of their swords.

Soran reached over his shoulder and drew a sword—a huge, ugly thing of black iron—then urged his mount forward. Hweilan could feel the ground shaking as the huge horse surged toward her.

"Soran!" It was Kadrigul, calling out as he spurred his horse toward her. "Soran, no! We need her alive!"

Hweilan couldn't move.

An arrow struck Soran in the back. He didn't even flinch.

"Run, you stupid girl!" It was Lendri, reaching for another arrow as he ran from cover on the far side of the trail.

"Soran!" she shouted. "Uncle, please!"

Still no recognition in his face, and then her mind caught up with what her instinct had known all along. This was not her uncle. She didn't know why and could not fathom how, but this horror bearing down upon her was not her uncle.

Hweilan screamed in defiance and charged.

She heard Lendri scream, "No!" and another arrow hit Soran.

Hweilan was less than five or six steps from the horse when it screamed and reared. Whatever it was about her that spooked horses—some effect of her Vil Adanrath heritage, she now suspected—it worked on Soran's horse. The stallion's eyes rolled back in its head as it fought to scramble away. In its panic, its hooves slipped on the uneven, icy ground, and the horse fell, smashing Soran's leg. Even over the noise of Hechin's barking and the screaming of men and horses, Hweilan heard a *crunch* of shattering bone.

Soran's mount fought its way to its feet, then bounded away. Soran tried to push himself to his feet, but his right leg folded beneath him.

"Hweilan, run!"

Lendri stood his ground just this side of the trail. He dodged a spear from one of the Nar, planted an arrow in his attacker, knocking the man from his horse, then reached for another arrow.

Soran regained his feet, and he lumbered toward Hweilan, leaning on the sword like a cane and dragging his shattered leg.

The breeze shifted, just for a moment, and the thing's scent washed over her. Worse than a charnel house, it made Hweilan's gorge rise to the back of her throat.

Hweilan's hand fumbled for the knife at her belt.

"Run!" Lendri called. "These aren't the only—!"

Another arrow hit the Soran-thing, lodging in his good leg. A pure white arrow—shaft and fletching all white as snow, and smaller than Lendri's arrows. Where had it—?

Soran didn't slow. Didn't even seem to notice the arrows sprouting from his body. Only a few paces away now.

Hweilan couldn't get her knife free. The thick glove

over the bandages robbed her fingers of all nimbleness. She stumbled backward, her heel struck a rock or root, and she fell.

Soran stood over her. This close, she got her first good look at his eyes. Black eyes. Dark as polished stones. Not a fleck of white or color remained. And they seemed too wide, as if something mean and hungry were trapped in his skull, trying to press its way out. When those eyes looked down on her, it woke something deep inside Hweilan, like a spark catching in dry tinder. Her anger flared, and she had to push down a sudden urge to snarl.

The Soran-thing lunged. Hweilan scrambled backward, but the uneven ground was slick, and pain shot up her injured arm. The creature's iron-hard fist locked round her ankle.

Hweilain's uninjured hand found a rock and closed around it. She smashed it into the side of his face. He didn't even flinch. She hit him again. And again. On the fourth strike, she gouged off a long strip of skin and heard bone crack.

He released his hold on his sword and caught her next strike. Hweilan screamed and tried to pull free. She felt the cloth of her coat and shirt slipping under his grip, but then the fist tightened.

"Let me go!" She planted her free leg and pulled with all her strength. The fabric between her arm and his hand slipped again, and for an instant, they touched, skin to skin.

Something passed between them, sizzling, like cold water tossed on hot steel. The thing's black eyes locked on her, and she could feel them penetrating skin, flesh, and bone, gazing upon something she had only felt in her dreams.

Soran's face twisted into a scowl. Pure malice.

"I can smell him on you, girl." It was a hollow voice. Nothing like Soran's. All malice and hunger. His mouth opened wide, and he took in a deep breath, as if tasting the air. Dead lips pulled back over his teeth in mockery of a smile. "You reek of—"

A black cloud washed over him. Hundreds of ravens

hit the Soran-thing, cawing and screaming, burying him beneath flapping wings as their sharp beaks pecked at him. The wind of their wings buffeted Hweilan, and she felt their feathers brush her cheeks, but they passed over her to attack the Soran-thing. Soran released Hweilan and swiped at the birds with both hands, but for every one he hit, ten or more descended on him.

Soran stood, his sword in one hand, his other continuing to swipe at the birds. But his eyes locked on Hweilan as he shambled toward her.

A huge, shaggy shape hit the ground between Hweilan and her pursuers. Kadrigul's horse screamed and reared, and then the roars filled the valley, one after another, pounding through the air like thunder off the mountains. The trees shook with the sound. Hweilan felt their force like a punch in the gut, and the marrow in her bones trembled.

Tundra tigers. One swiped at Kadrigul's horse, and two more ran among the Nar.

Soran, still covered in ravens and hampered by his shattered leg, lurched toward her. Just beyond him, Kadrigul, upon his horse, was bearing down upon her. Beyond them, two tigers were pressing the attack against the Nar. Only the long spears of the Nar warriors held them at bay.

Hweilan's eyes widened, and she scrambled to her feet. One of those tigers carried a rider. Small as a ten-year-old child, clothed in furs and a snug blue material. She had no idea who or what it could be. Even as she watched, she saw more of the little people emerging from the trees, spears in their hands.

Where was Lendri? Where——?

Run, girl . . .

Hweilan wasn't sure where the voice came from. It seemed to pass her ears entirely and speak in her mind.

Run! Run! Run!

Hweilan ran.

CHAPTER FOURTEEN

BROKEN BRANCHES SNAGGED HWEILAN'S CLOAK AND scraped her face, roots beneath the carpet of snow tripping her. Again and again she fell, but each time she pushed herself up and kept going. Before long she could discern little but the lingering blue glow in the snow set amid the deeper black of the surrounding brush and heavy sky.

The sound of the fighting grew fainter with each step, and bit by bit, reason began to return to Hweilan. She knew she was making an awful racket, blundering through the timber, her feet crunching through new snow and old frost. But she didn't care. Every beat of her heart screamed at her to get away from the *thing* that wore Soran's face. And the ravens . . .

She pushed through a thick patch of darkness—some thick bush or scrub that kept its thick, waxy leaves throughout the winter—and the ground fell away beneath her feet.

She tumbled, striking hard ground beneath the snow and sliding down a steep enough slope that her stomach seemed to jump up her throat.

She hit level ground. It drove what little air she had left from her body, and for a long moment, all she could do was lie there, half her face in the snow, trying to draw breath back into her chest as bright orbs of light danced in her vision. With each breath, the lights winked and faded a little more.

She'd managed to keep a grip on her father's bow during the fall. She still held it, her right fist locked around it. Something else was poking her in the chest, just below the soft part of her neck. Something under her shirt. The *kishkoman*.

Hweilan pushed herself up to her knees and pulled the bone whistle from her shirt. She put it to her lips, took in a deep breath, and blew a shrill note, as loud and as long as she could. The sound cut through the night, hurting her ears.

She sat, holding her breath, straining to hear an answering call. Nothing. Only a breeze rattling winter-brittle branches. She tried again, holding the note as long as she could. Still nothing.

Now that she was no longer running, her body began to shiver, and she could feel her own breath beginning to freeze against her face.

A thick darkness loomed before her. It was one of the great pines, but fallen ages ago. Most of the trunk had probably gone to rot, but the thicker wood of the roots had gone iron hard, and the years of brush that grew up and around them formed a sort of woody cleft. It would do. She dared not risk a fire, not with that Soran-thing maybe still out there, but she had to keep the wind off her and find someplace close to keep in her own body heat.

Hweilan threw herself into the cleft, branches and nettles and thorns ripping her clothes and skin. There was no wide way through, but her body found the path of least resistance, and she pushed and pushed, turning herself sideways to squeeze through the crack. She hit a wall of tangled brush, rotted wood, and soil, all frozen hard as stone. Exhausted, terrified, and cold, Hweilan wept.

• • ◎ • •

She had no idea how much time passed, wedged between old roots and frozen soil. Her body shivered so badly that the roots and frost around her were rattling. She could no longer feel her fingers, toes, or face.

One clear thought rose in her mind: You have to move, or you're going to die.

Hweilan moved, the roots digging into her clothes again. She thought they were most likely scraping her face, as well, but she could no longer feel her exposed skin. The farther she went, the easier it became.

She was nearly out when she heard it: something coming through the brush.

Hweilan held her breath and kept her body perfectly still.

The sounds came closer, and besides the crunching of branches and snow, she heard something sniffing.

Hweilan took a chance. With fingers she could no longer feel, she brought the *kishkoman* to her numb lips and blew one note—very softly, scarcely above a whisper.

A plaintive whine came from the darkness.

"Hechin?" she called out.

But whatever it had been was running away.

Hweilan waited, counting to a hundred, listening. If anything was out there, it wasn't moving. Never in her life had she been so cold. Lendri's packs still rode her back. Surely he had flint and steel. Maybe even dry grass for kindling. But she could not get the image of Soran out of her mind—

The dead face.

The implacable approach.

The red fire, all malice and hunger, flashing behind the dead eyes.

And she knew that any fire would be seen, even if she could muster the will to gather dry wood.

Her teeth would not stop chattering, and she was shaking so hard that her jaw ached. Gooseflesh prickled her from head to toe, and she felt as if every hair on her head was standing straight up. She had to keep closing her eyes to keep the moisture on them from freezing. Each time, she had to force her eyelids open again. Her body cried out for rest, but she feared that if she slept, she'd never wake again.

She knew her only two choices were to build a fire and risk being seen by the Nar and . . . that thing. Or freeze to death. Given the two fates . . .

Scith had once told her that freezing to death became painless after a certain point. One even began to feel warm again, before the end came.

Hweilan closed her eyes, and remembering that moment, the thing she cherished the most was the fire that had burned merrily between her and Scith, wafting long, slow breaths of warmth over her open hands.

Just thinking of it, Hweilan felt warm again.

● ● ⊚ ● ●

She stood on black rocks, looking down on clouds and listening to the roar of the world. Above her, a clear night sky rimmed the horizon. There was no moon, but the stars burned like fresh-cut diamonds set on velvet tapestry. One star just topping the horizon burned bright as a small sun, though it shone blue and cold.

Behind her, a great wall of mountains pushed up against the sky. Their heights dwarfed any mountains she had ever seen. Fully half their slopes were draped in snow, and even the nearer foothills were taller than the Giantspires near her home.

She stood on the fingertip of the mountains' last grasp, and the world fell away at her feet. Miles away to her right, a river thundered over the chasm, its voice so powerful that it shook the rocks beneath her. Hweilan had no way to fathom the depth of the valley, for it was all a mass of starlit mist stirred by the cataract. Woods covered the lower slopes of the mountains and the distant lowlands, and they were black amid the trails of mist winding through their boughs.

Turning her back on the valley, she faced the woods of the mountainside. Mists curled through the trunks, and here and there she could see birds or small animals flitting from branch to branch.

She relaxed her eyes and took it all in, not focusing on any one spot. Just the way Scith had taught her. *Let your eyes drink every dreg of light. In the darkness or in thick cover, watch for movement. If you see something, do not focus on it. Keep it at the edge of your sight. That part of your eye takes in more light than looking at it straight on.*

There it was. Pale shapes moving amid the boughs. Just a shade paler than the mists themselves. They moved without haste, and now and then one or more would stop, and Hweilan knew they were watching her.

She looked to each side. A broken, uneven chasm all around. To her left, climbing up again to the mountain's heights. To her right, sloping down and finally curving to the edge of the falls. No paths anywhere, and the few protruding rocks that might serve as holds or even the occasional shelf to rest upon . . . all were slick with spray from the falls. One slip, and Hweilan would soon find out how deep the valley was inside the mists.

Howling wafted down the mountainside, and when she turned back, the shapes had come much closer. Dozens of them at least. Maybe a hundred or more, and the nearest ones were only a stone's throw away. She could see that although most were pale as ghosts, some were a darker gray, some brown, and one was black as dreamless sleep.

She reached for her knife, only to discover that she had no knife. No belt. In fact, she wore no clothes at all, and it wasn't until that realization that she felt cold. Goosebumps shot up all over her, her hair standing on end.

The first wolf—a beautiful thing, white as new snow— was almost upon her. Hweilan crouched and raised her arms to protect her throat.

But the wolf rushed right past her, so close that its fur brushed her leg. The final step it leaped into the air and plummeted into the mist. Another wolf followed it, then another, then three more. In moments it seemed an entire river of wolves rushed past her, their claws clicking on the rocks, and their panting breaths enveloping her in thick, warm fog. Every one leaped into the open air and fell without a sound, the mist swallowing them.

Only the black wolf remained. It stood a few paces in front of Hweilan, watching her for a moment, then turning back to look into the woods. A low whine escaped it, and she could see tension in its movements. Fear. What could have—?

Then she sensed it.

It had not been the wolves' eyes intent upon her. Something from the woods was watching her, from up there in the dark where she couldn't see it. And it was getting closer. She could sense it, like a sudden lightness to the summer air that meant a storm was on the way.

She heard rustling and shrieking in the woods, and as she watched a great cloud of birds erupted from the trees for miles around. They flew every which way, most seeking the heights and speeding away, but she saw some of the stragglers stop their fluttering midair and fall back to the ground as if dead. More creatures ran past her—mice, squirrels, bears, and many strange creatures that she'd never seen. Those who could scrambled down the cliffside. The others leaped, much like the wolves had done. Even the insects were leaving the shelter of the woods.

Most of the breeze had been coming up from the valley itself, pushed upward by the great fall of water. But now the wind shifted, coming from the woods itself, and Hweilan smelled something putrid and foul.

The black wolf gave her a final look that seemed to shout—*Run!*—then it too leaped off the cliff.

Hweilan coughed at the foul stench coming from the woods. What could make such a foul reek?

Then she heard laughter and singing. The voices were sweet, but in the laughter she sensed hot malice, and even though she could not understand the words of the song, she sensed blasphemy in the words.

Whatever it was, it was getting closer.

Time to choose, said a voice from behind her. Something about it reminded her of her mother.

She turned, but no one was there. Only the distant falls and a long, long drop.

She turned back to the woods. *Death,* said the voice again. *Death comes from that way. Be sure of it.* Hweilan faced the chasm again. *And that way . . .*

The voice trailed off. Death? Something worse? The animals had leaped that way, without hesitation, choosing the drop into nothingness over whatever approached from the dark.

Choose, Hweilan.

She took a deep breath, gagging on the reek, then took two quick steps and leaped, pushing as far as she could in hopes of clearing the cliffside rocks below.

Her mind swirled, her body took in one great gulp of air.

She plunged into the mist, the wetness hitting her naked skin like a cold slap. Her whole world went gray, she took in another breath to scream—

It came out a cough. Water sprayed out of her nose and throat, and she found herself on her hands and knees on a rock floor, bits of grit and sand raking into her skin. Her hair hung in heavy, dripping clumps, and water streamed off her, as if she'd just been dumped from a bath.

A cold bath. She was shivering, and her breath clouded in front of her face.

Still on her hands and knees, she looked up.

She was in a cavern. Bigger than any she'd ever been in. Her grandfather's hall could have fit inside with room to spare. Great columns of stone went from floor to ceiling in no particular order. In other places, long cones of stone hung from the ceiling or pushed up from the floor. A red glow lit the cavern, making the damp stone seem almost bloody. But she couldn't see where the glow was coming from. It certainly gave no heat.

Still shivering, Hweilan stood.

Cold, said a voice. The same one that had spoken to her on the cliffside. *But this is a lifeless place now. I am gone. Empty dens, dead hearts . . . cold.*

"Who are you?" said Hweilan. "What is this place?"

Hweilan heard a light splashing behind her and turned. A pool took up the back half of the cavern, its water almost black in the dim light. Emerging from the pool was a tall figure, moving with a bestial grace, all willful intent commanding smooth movement. Not a wasted motion, as if the body were more raiment than flesh.

A woman's body, but Hweilan could not put the word *woman* to this figure. She was far too . . . other. Her frame was thin, but there was no hint of weakness or want in her limbs. Hweilan could not discern the exact color of her skin, for a slick wetness covered the woman from forehead to toes. The wetness was too thick and dark for water; the figure before her was covered with blood.

Although she was wet in it from head to toe, the woman's hair was stainless, woven into scores of tight braids that hung to her waist. Amid the locks were smooth stones, bits of bone, feathers, and dozens upon dozens of tiny flowers. Even through the strong, metallic scent of the blood, Hweilan could smell the flowers, almost as if they were newly bloomed and still growing.

The figure stopped upon the shore and looked down on Hweilan. Her Uncle Soran had been the tallest man she'd ever known, but even he would have looked up to this woman's chin.

Hweilan swallowed and said, "Wh-who are you?"

The woman cocked her head, almost birdlike. Her lips did not move, but Hweilan heard the words, *My name holds no more power in your world. For generations I guarded and guided your people like a mother to her cubs. But the cubs have gone home. All but two. And you do not need a mother. Time to grow up, Hweilan inle Merah. Time to hunt.*

"I . . . I don't understand."

You do not need understanding. You need to choose. Understanding will come later . . . if you survive.

"Hweilan!"

She jumped, and her eyes snapped open. How long——?

"Hweilan!"

It was Lendri. Whispering, but most definitely Lendri. And close.

"H-h-here!" she called out, and was surprised at the weak rasp of her voice.

She sensed movement outside her shelter, but she didn't have the strength to look up. Strong hands helped her out.

"You're freezing," Lendri said.

"It's . . . not s-so bad . . . nuh-n-n-ow."

Lendri muttered something in his own language, then said, "Do your hands and feet hurt?"

She shook her head again, and managed, "H-haven't . . . f-felt 'em, f-f-for a w-while."

Lendri rummaged through the one pouch on his belt. "I have something," he said. "Not a permanent solution, but we can't risk fire just yet. This will help."

He held out a small, dark something to her.

"Kanishta," said Lendri. "A root that has been . . . treated. It will give you some strength back and keep you warm. For a while." Gently, he opened her mouth and shoved the root between her cheek and teeth. "Chew."

At first, she could barely open her mouth wide enough to wedge the root between her teeth. But whatever the root was, the tissue in her mouth responded to it almost immediately, flooding her cheek with fresh spit. The taste of the root hit then, and she almost gagged, but one swallow and a tingling warmth spread from her mouth and throat to her head. She managed to chew, coaxing more juice out of the root. It was beyond bitter, but with each swallow, she felt warm, and vigor began to work its way back into her limbs.

"Better?" Lendri asked.

"Much," she said. "Tastes like garden soil, but it's . . . warm. Oh, that's magical."

"Only somewhat. Are you hurt?"

"Scrapes and bruises," she said.

Now that she could feel her limbs again—and feel something besides cold—her mind seized on . . .

"The Nar, the tigers, are they . . . ?"

"I killed two Nar," said Lendri. "And Hechin scattered their horses. But they are still out there. Can you walk?"

"If they're still out there, I can run."

Lendri let out a short bark of a laugh, then said, "*Besthunit nenle* will do."

"What?"

"A proverb," he said. " 'Hurry up slowly.' We need to move fast, but not so fast that we announce our presence to anyone within a half mile." He took their packs from her and fit them on his back. "Now let's move."

He turned and headed off into the dark.

Hweilan followed. "But, Lendri . . oh, gods, what was . . . that . . . that *thing*? It looked like my uncle. My uncle! But it wasn't. I swear it wasn't. It—"

He didn't turn or slow. "I know."

"What was it?" she whispered.

"I do not know. But I could feel its . . ."

"Wrongness."

"Yes." Lendri stopped on the trail and turned to her.

"Like the taste of meat gone bad," she said. "Yet somehow still . . ."

"Yes. I know. It's—"

"And those . . . those other . . . th-things?" She was having a hard time catching her breath. She could hear herself beginning to babble, but she couldn't stop. "I-I-I s-saw them! Like children! But one of them was riding a tundra tiger. *Riding!* No one rides tundra tigers. And the ravens . . . when Kadrigul was after me."

"Kadrigul?" said Lendri. "The *Siksin Nene?*"

"*Siksin* what?"

"The pale one. Frost Folk your people name them. This Kadrigul . . . ?"

"Yes, that's him," said Hweilan. "You saw. Didn't you see? Ravens . . . hit him. Dozens of them. Hundreds maybe. That was . . . you?"

"No," said Lendri. He had gone very still, save for his head, which he turned this way and that as if listening. She could hear him sniffing the air. His voice dropped to a whisper. "That was . . . I don't know what that was."

"What is it?" she whispered.

"Shht!" Lendri stepped forward—more of a pounce really—and grabbed her arm in a painful grip. She looked down. Too dark to see clearly, but she could see that his glove and much of his sleeve was smeared with something dark. The scent hit her. Blood. He still had the blood of dead men on his hands.

"Lendri?"

He drew an arrow from his quiver and placed it on the string of his bow. "Run!"

He pulled the arrow to his cheek, and in that instant the moon peeked out from a rent in the clouds. In the new light, Hweilan saw that Lendri had nocked a fowling arrow—no arrowhead, just a hardened tip of wood, meant to stun birds without spoiling the meat.

"What are you—?"

"Run, girl!"

A bone-shaking roar came out of the woods behind them, followed by another off to the side.

"Run!"

She ran. Behind her, she heard the twang of Lendri's bow, followed by a sharp cry, then the sounds of Lendri following.

The woods around them erupted in a riot of sound—many shapes blundering through the brush, high-pitched cries, and above her on the left, the roar of a tiger. The sound washed over her, a physical force, and for three steps her knees weakened, threatening to buckle beneath her.

Lendri grabbed her above the elbow, pulled her back up, and dragged her behind him. A huge shape hit the ground several paces in front of them, stirring up a cloud of snow and spraying branches everywhere. Though she couldn't see it clearly through the snow, she knew it was a tiger.

Lendri pulled her to the right, but too quickly. Her feet tangled over an exposed root or branch, and she went down, breaking Lendri's grip. She scrambled to her feet. Several feet away, Lendri was standing still again, one hand reaching over his shoulder, fingering the nock of another arrow in his quiver.

In front of them crouched two tigers.

And one of them bore a rider. A small rider, to be sure, child-sized, but the long spear it held looked lethal. In the dim light, the rider's eyes gave off a pale luminescence.

That was when the smell hit her. Flowery almost. But not quite. It had the sharp tinge of cold, like the autumn winds off the Giantspires—the breezes that promised the first storm of the season, bringing days of howling winds, bitter cold, and darkness even at midday.

Another tiger had come in behind them, and in the woods all around, more glowing eyes watched them. The nearest was no more than five or six paces away—two pale diamonds seeming to float in the air. But even as Hweilan watched, a form materialized around the eyes—whatever magic had hidden the creature dismissed. This one held a sword, but not like any she had ever seen. It drank in the little light off the snow and seemed to amplify it, so that the cold steel seemed a shard of ice. Jagged edges and protrusions angled off the blade near the hilt, giving it a thorny appearance. And although the creature would have had to stretch up on tiptoes to reach Hweilan's head, it held the sword with an easy confidence.

"Lendri," Hweilan rasped, "what do we do?"

"Do not reach for a weapon," he said. "Don't even move."

"Very good advice," said a voice from the darkness, "coming from a fool such as you, Lendri."

A fierce gust swept down the hillside, rattling branches and snow into a stinging tide that washed over them. The air caught and swirled next to the little swordsman, forming a small cyclone of snow and shadow. When it settled, another figure stood there, much taller than the hunter, snow and frost wafting off his armor like tiny cataracts. The armor itself was more elegant than anything Hweilan had seen—a breastplate, spaulders, and tassets made of many layers of fitted metal, which gave off their own unearthly sheen. A long cloak hung from the spaulders, and in the dark it rippled like a living shadow as the wind died away. The man wore no helmet, and his long hair played in the breeze. He rested one hand on the head of a tundra tiger and scratched it between the ears, as if it were a favorite lap cat.

Lendri still hadn't lowered his hand from his quiver. "Your skills have improved, Menduarthis."

"Your sense has not." The man spoke in Common, though with enough of an accent that Hweilan could tell it was not his native tongue. "I always hoped you'd come back. But I never actually believed you so stupid. I must say, I am most pleased to have been proven wrong. You and your friend are going to surrender your weapons now." He motioned to the little warriors all around them. "*Valdi sin yolen.*"

CHAPTER FIFTEEN

134

HWEILAN STOOD DUMBFOUNDED. HAD LENDRI JUST called the man by name? The man had definitely called Lendri by name. But was he a man? His skin was pale as Lendri's, but his breath wasn't steaming in the frigid air, and he seemed quite comfortable in the cold, with no cloak, coat, or hood.

Two of the little hunters came toward her, weapons held ready in one hand, the other reaching out to take her bow.

She pulled back. "No!"

The hunters stepped back, and a dozen spears lowered in her direction.

"Voi!" Lendri shouted. *"Ele vahat sun!"* He had already been disarmed. Even his quiver was gone.

"Now, now, Lendri, you don't give orders to the Ujaiyen," said the armored man. He sounded amused. "Not anymore."

He walked off the slope, pushing his way through the brush and past the hunters to approach Hweilan. She stiffened and stood her ground.

The man looked her up and down, and reached one gloved hand toward her.

She stepped back, raising the bow before her and reaching for her knife.

"Easy, easy," said the man. "Don't be skittish. You've got nowhere to skit."

Hweilan risked a glance over her shoulder and saw two of the little hunters behind her, both holding spears.

"Menduarthis, please—" said Lendri.

"I'm not going to hurt your friend," Menduarthis told Lendri, though he kept his eyes fixed on Hweilan. He smiled. "Not yet, anyway."

Before Hweilan could react, Menduarthis's hand shot forward and pushed down her hood.

"Well!" His eyebrows shot upward and he smiled. "I go out for a night of hunting beasts and instead happen upon a rare flower."

He stroked her cheek with the back of one finger. Hweilan stepped back and brought her knife out and forward in a quick swipe. Menduarthis pulled back in time, her blade barely missing his finger.

"Ho!" Menduarthis laughed. "This flower has thorns, I see! Don't worry, little one. I'm not out to peel your petals."

"Leave me alone," she said.

Menduarthis chuckled. "Not tonight. Why so unfriendly?"

"Menduarthis, please!" Lendri called. "Allow me to explain!"

Still watching Hweilan—she couldn't tell if his gaze was lecherous, curious, or simply amused; a little of all three she suspected—he called out something in a tongue she didn't recognize. Two hunters lowered their spears at Lendri, and all around her Hweilan heard many blades leaving their scabbards.

"Know what I told them?" said Menduarthis.

"No," Hweilan replied.

"I told them that if *your* friend over there opens his mouth again, *my* friends are to kill him." He pushed at the inside of one cheek with his tongue, thinking, then said, "A shame, really. Truth be told I always liked Lendri. I don't suppose you've seen his little wolf friend around, have you? What's its name? 'Itching'?"

Hweilan glared at him. "Hechin."

"No matter. Let's talk about you. What's *your* name?"

Hweilan's glare deepened to a scowl. She didn't lower the knife.

"Not very friendly, is she, Lendri?" Menduarthis called out. When Lendri didn't answer, he looked over his shoulder at the elf and said, "Oh, yes. You aren't to speak. So glad you're paying attention."

When Menduarthis turned back to Hweilan, his gaze had hardened. The hint of lechery and curiosity was gone. The amusement was still there, but it was peeking from behind a very dark curtain.

"Let me tell you something, little flower," he said. "The world is not a nice place. Fools say it's unforgiving, but that's why they're fools. The world doesn't forgive because it doesn't blame. And the world doesn't blame because it doesn't care. So here's my little lesson for you tonight: You can name yourself, or others will name you. And you might not like what they call you. So I'll ask you one more time." He leaned in closer, just beyond the point of her knife. "What's your name?"

Hweilan's grip tightened around her knife, but her hand was shaking. Something about the tone in Menduarthis's voice—she felt as if Kelemvor had just placed her in his scale, and her next words would decide which way she swung.

She licked her lips and said, "H-Hweilan. My name is Hweilan."

Menduarthis straightened, closed his eyes, and breathed in deep through his nose. "Ah . . . Hweilan," he said, pronouncing it very carefully, savoring each syllable. "A flower indeed. And I even like the thorns." He bowed. "Well met. My hunters tell me that a band of frantic Nar ride not a half-mile from here, and one of the Frost Folk leads them. Friends of yours?"

"No! They attacked us."

"And what do you know of the thing that rides with them? Big brute with black eyes."

"I know it attacked us."

"And the ravens? A whole murder of them coming to your rescue?"

She shuddered at the memory. "I don't know."

Menduarthis held her gaze. "Don't know or won't tell?"

"Ravens hit the man. I ran. We ran. Lendri and me. We thought we'd lost them, and then you arrived."

"And here we are, yes?"

Hweilan shrugged.

"Back to the matter at hand, then," said Menduarthis. "You were about to hand over your weapons."

Hweilan looked to Lendri. The elf kept his jaw clenched, but he gave her a careful nod.

"No," she said.

"No?" said Menduarthis.

"I'll surrender the knife," she said. "But the bow belonged to my father. It's all I have left of him. I'll give my life before I give the bow."

"Hm." Menduarthis peeled off his gloves with his teeth, then tucked them into his belt. "Dear Father is dead, I take it?"

Hweilan's scowl deepened.

"Don't take offense," said Menduarthis, his tone light and mocking again. "My father is dead too. At least I think he is. But I assure you, Hweilan, I am no thief. I don't even want to keep your little steel thorn there, though I do appreciate the offer. I simply don't want you causing any trouble on the way. The Ujaiyen's tigers can be a bit . . . ill-tempered."

"On the way to where?"

"To where we're taking you."

She waited for more explanation. It didn't come, and she knew it wouldn't. "I promise I won't cause any trouble," she said.

"Well, I do appreciate that. But we hardly know each other. How do I know I can trust you?"

"How do I know I can trust you?"

"What makes you think you have a choice?" He waved his fingers at the hunters surrounding them. "Unless you have more ravens up your sleeve . . . well, I'm afraid I have the advantage, yes?"

"I don't have any arrows," said Hweilan. "I can't even bend the thing enough to string it—much less use it!"

"Then why hang on to it?"

"Because it was my father's!"

"Anything else of his you'd like to hang on to?"

"J-just the bow."

"Hm." Menduarthis folded his hands in front of his face and hummed while he considered it. He looked around at the little hunters, then back to Hweilan and said, "No."

"Why?"

"Because," he said, and his voice went hard and cold again, "although you do seem like a most trustworthy little flower, right now, you need to understand who is in command here. *Me*. Hand over the bow."

"No. You'll have to kill me first."

"Will I?" Menduarthis laughed and looked to Lendri. "Is she really that foolish?"

Lendri said nothing.

"Oh, yes," said Menduarthis. "Can't speak." He let out an exaggerated sigh—Hweilan noticed that his breath still didn't steam, even in the cold. He raised his voice and said, "The elf can answer this question. Nobody kill him."

Lendri fixed him with a cold glare, then looked around at the hunters.

"Ah, yes," said Menduarthis. "They don't speak the language. Can't understand what I just said. You *are* paying attention! I guess you'd better keep quiet after all." He turned back to Hweilan. "Last chance. Give me the bow and knife, or I take them."

"No."

He clucked his tongue inside his cheek. "You like magic, Hweilan?"

"Not really."

"Hm. Pity." Menduarthis planted both his heels together, stood very straight, and waved both hands in an intricate pattern. "You probably aren't going to like this, then."

Menduarthis's hands shot forward, and with them came a wind with the force of a dozen winter gales—but focused in one thick stream that flowed around him. His cape billowed out like a pennant. Storm and darkness hit Hweilan, then swallowed her.

CHAPTER SIXTEEN

HOWLS HAUNTED HWEILAN'S DREAMS. PAIN TINGED these howls. Remorse. Fear.

Everything around her was cold. Cold and hard. Mountains covered with snow and ice that had not melted in a thousand generations of men. Jagged, broken peaks that bit through gray clouds lined by moonlight. At the mountains' feet, forests of pine older than the kingdoms of men filled valleys—some so deep that they never saw sun or moonlight.

Cold as it was, still the land felt alive. Not merely filled with living things—though that was true; thousands of animals and birds singing, playing, sleeping, waking, hunting and being hunted . . . dying; even flowers bloomed amid the frost—the land itself and the air around it possessed . . . a . . .

Livingness. A steady pulse ran through everything. A breathing. Almost like a song, though one not so much heard with the ears as felt in the blood.

But that blood ran cold.

• • ◎ • •

Her eyes opened, the memory of the dream already fading. She couldn't see. Shadows masked everything.

She tried to sit up, but something held her back. For an instant, she panicked, but then she found she'd been wrapped—more snug than tight—in blankets, then lain upon a thick fur and wrapped again, some of the outer fur blanket folded over her head like a hood.

Wriggling like a caterpillar escaping its cocoon, Hweilan managed to free her arms, sit up, and pull the blanket off her face.

She was surrounded by bones.

She was in a sort of domed tent, made from bent poles of wood—some so green that leaves and verdant moss still clung to them. A small fire in the center of the room cast everything in orange light. Hanging from the tent frame were dozens and dozens of bones. Leg bones, ribs, sections of backbone strung through braided thread like the macabre necklace of a giant. But worst were the skulls. Swiftstags, some with antlers and some without. Tundra tigers, their daggerlike teeth painted in swirls of red and yellow. Many smaller animals—badgers, squirrels, voles—and many birds. And here and there were even a few human skulls, some bare and yellowed with age, painted in many curved and branched patterns, and others still brown and glistening fresh.

The last thing she remembered was Menduarthis on the mountain, then a great gust of wind, hitting her like a felled tree. Her body still ached from the impact, but it was a dull ache. Either a healer had seen to her, or she had slept for many days while her body healed. Perhaps both.

Her stomach felt empty and her throat dry enough to make her believe she had slept for a day at least.

Feeling her body and looking down inside the blankets, she saw that her own clothes were gone. She had been washed and now wore a sort of shift. It felt soft and warm as doeskin but looked fibrous. Someone had washed and clothed her. Hweilan shivered.

She looked down at her right hand. The bandages were gone, and the skin almost healed. The new skin had a too-smooth sheen, but the scabs were gone. The letters were still there, though, a puffy scar: KAN. "Death." She wiggled her fingers, then clenched her hand in a tight fist. The new skin felt tender, but there was no pain.

The flap of the tent opened, admitting a breath of frigid air and one of the little hunters. He ducked inside, pulled the door shut, and his eyes widened at seeing her awake.

They locked gazes for a long moment, then he placed one hand to his chest and said, "Nikle."

In the light of the fire, Hweilan got her first good look at one of these strange hunters.

Her first impression of a halfling had not been far off, at least in height. But there the resemblance ended. He was very thin, and his skin had the tint of a cloudless winter sky. And so much skin showing for such cold weather! It made Hweilan shiver even in her blankets. The little hunter wore a sleeveless tunic of some cured animal hide, belted at the waist. Its fur fringe hung just above his bare knees. He wore no boots, gloves, or coat. Just a very strange hat. It, too, was made from some sort of animal skin, fur around the edge of the cap, tied around a rim of dark wood, or perhaps horn. On the left side, a single antler spike protruded from the rim, and bits of leather lacing tied it to the long cap, so that the hat rose to sort of a curved cone over his head. A tiny skull—from a squirrel or small badger perhaps—dangled from a tassel attached to the top of the hat. The ears protruding from under the rim of the hat were very pointed—sharper and taller than even Lendri's—and the green eyes had the look of elfkind. By the warm light of the fire, they did not quite glow, but they seemed very bright, like flawless emeralds.

Hweilan shook her head. "Nikle?"

The hunter nodded and motioned to her with one hand. *"Nu thrastulet?"*

The door opened again, letting in more cold air, and Menduarthis entered.

"He's telling you his name," said Menduarthis, "and asking for yours." He rattled off something in the same language she'd heard them speak on the mountainside. Nikle smiled and shuffled out of the way.

Menduarthis shut the flap and sat across the fire from her.

"He knows your name already," he said. "But the uldra insist on propriety and good manners to a guest."

Hweilan looked to Nikle, who was watching them both. If he understood Menduarthis's words or sensed his flippant tone, the little hunter gave no sign.

"Uldra?" Hweilan asked.

Menduarthis waved one hand at the little hunter. "Nikle here. He's an uldra."

Hweilan took in her first good look at Menduarthis. She'd only been able to get a few details on the dark mountainside. He wore no armor now—trousers and shirt of a simple cut, an unbuttoned coat that fell to his knees, and boots laced up to his knees. Nothing unusual in his manner of dress, but his physical appearance was something else. His skin was not simply pale. It was bone white. Which made his hair seem all the darker—the blackest black she had ever seen. It scarcely reflected the firelight. He wore it long, well past his shoulders, and it didn't look as if a brush had visited it in many days. Her first thought was that his eyes were silver, but upon closer inspection she saw that they were very light blue flecked with many darker shades, and he had no pupils.

"You are eladrin?" she said.

Menduarthis gave her a sly smile. "Among other things."

"What does that mean?"

Menduarthis chuckled, but he had a dangerous glint in his eye. "And what are *you?* Hmm?"

"Human," said Hweilan. "Though I have elf blood through my mother."

Menduarthis sat up straight, closed his eyes, and leaned his head back, almost as if in meditation. A breeze came from somewhere behind her, tossing her hair in her face and causing the fire to lie low. But when she turned, there was no gap or tear in the walls. Just the wooden tent frame and wall of animal skin.

When she turned back around, Menduarthis had not moved, but he breathed in deep through his nostrils.

"Ah," he said, and looked down at her. "Human with some elf blood, she says. True enough. True enough. But what *else* runs in your veins? Hmm?"

"You never answered my question."

"I didn't come to answer your questions, girl. I came to fetch you. You have an audience. With the queen."

"Queen? There are no queens in the Giantspires."

"Oh, you *are* a sharp one. Now, get dressed or I'll have to take you in your blankets, and that is hardly a way to make a good first impression."

"Where are my clothes?"

He leaned back, opened the door just enough to reach one hand out, then brought it back inside holding a thick bundle of cloth tied crossways with a cord.

"*Your* clothes, I'm afraid, are gone." He glanced at Nikle. "Those rags you had on were not suitable for an audience with the queen."

"They were no worse than what you're wearing."

Menduarthis chuckled. "Yes, but I'm a loyal subject. You? Well, you were found running with that *sivat,* so I suggest you wear what you're told and mind your manners. At the moment, you're a guest, but you can join your little elf friend if you aren't careful."

"Where is Lendri?"

"Taken care of."

Hweilan took the bundle and undid the knot of cord. Opening it, she found fine linen smallclothes, a shirt of the same fibrous material as the shift she was wearing, a leather belt, and trousers and a coat that seemed to be made of swiftstag skin. Soft rabbit fur lined the coat. Nothing fancy, but all very well made.

Nikle rattled off something in his own language, and Menduarthis responded in kind. The little hunter poked his head outside, spoke to someone out there, then reached out and came back in holding a large sack. Menduarthis was watching her intently, an amused glint in his eye.

"What is it?" said Hweilan.

"Nikle has a gift for you," said Menduarthis.

She looked at the sack. As Nikle moved back to sit beside the fire, she could hear something rattling inside. "What kind of gift?"

Menduarthis said something to Nikle. The little hunter smiled and emptied the sack beside Hweilan.

Five skulls rattled out. Dark brown and glistening wet, bits of tissue and blood still clinging to them. The stench of death caught in the warm air of the fire and filled the tent, making Hweilan's stomach clench.

Nikle spread his hands over the gift and said something.

Menduarthis translated. "Nikle wishes to tell you that those Nar who hunted you will trouble you no more. Whatever grievance they had against you died with them. Though in truth, I do believe that your elf friend killed two of them, and a good many more got away—including that Frost Folk brute and that . . . whatever it was."

She looked down at the grisly pile. "What am I supposed to do with them?"

Menduarthis threw back his head and laughed. "Nikle here would be happy to treat and paint them for you. You can use them to adorn your . . . well, wherever you might end up. But that is for another day."

He said something to Nikle, and the little hunter began tossing the skulls back in the sack.

"I'll give you a moment to dress," said Menduarthis. "A quick moment. We must be off. Not wise to keep the queen waiting."

Menduarthis waved to Nikle, and they turned to leave.

"Where are my things?" said Hweilan. "My bone whistle? My father's bow?"

"I told you," Menduarthis said over his shoulder, "you had to give those up. Don't worry. They're in safe keeping. But until we're sure you aren't going to cause any trouble, I'll just keep them safe."

"I am not going anywhere without them."

"I could make you come."

"And I could make that very difficult for you."

Menduarthis stared at her a long time, those pupilless eyes seeming to weigh her. Finally, the left side of his mouth curled up in a grin. "You could, I think. Hmm. Well, as much as I might enjoy that, our time is short. Shall we compromise?"

"What?"

He reached inside a pocket sewn on the inside of his coat and pulled out her *kishkoman*. "I give you back your *kishkoman*, and you come along with no trouble."

"How . . . how do you know what that is?"

"Let's just say it isn't the first I've seen."

He tossed it to her, and she caught it.

"Know this," said Menduarthis. "Blow it all you like. No one here will answer. You'll only annoy the locals, and I don't recommend that. Try anything with the pointy end, and you'll never see dear Mother's *kishkoman* again. Get dressed."

Menduarthis crawled back outside and held the door open for Nikle. The air that rushed inside was absolutely frigid. Nikle turned and faced her, gave a small bow, then walked out. The door shut after him.

Hweilan crawled out of the blankets. Even with the fire nearby, the air inside the tent was cold, and she shivered.

She was halfway finished donning the smallclothes when the door flew open, and Menduarthis leaned inside. Hweilan shrieked and grabbed the blankets to cover herself.

"I almost forgot this," he said, and threw in a pair of

fur-lined boots, gloves, hat, and a fur cloak. The door slammed shut. "Hurry, girl!"

Knowing what nights in the mountains could feel like, Hweilan put the shift back on over her smallclothes and tucked it into the trousers. Every little bit of clothing would help.

Once she was fully dressed, she hung the *kishkoman* round her neck and stuffed it between her smallclothes and shift.

Give me the bow and knife or I take them. Menduarthis had said that right before he'd done . . . whatever he'd done. And he'd taken the bow and knife. Damn him.

Hweilan's fear subsided as her anger returned. She'd been chased and threatened, and Menduarthis had taken away her weapons with ease. She'd have to find a less direct way of beating him if his magic could summon the winds like that.

Hweilan crouched and threw the door open. Menduarthis stood a few paces away, scuffing the toes of his boots through the snow. Nikle and a few other uldra chattered among themselves. Beyond them—

Hweilan stepped outside and got her first good look around. Her jaw dropped, and her eyes went wide. There were dome tents all around—some clustered around large firepits where cauldrons bubbled, others alone between the roots of trees.

And such trees. Hweilan craned her head upward. Pines of some sort, branches powdered in snow and trunks coated with frost, their lowest branches far overhead. The bases of the trees were larger than the topmost towers of Highwatch, and several had roots that broke up through the soil and twisted in arches that under which she could have walked upright.

She could only assume it was daytime, for soft gray light filtered down from the pines, but she could not see the sky through their branches. Most of the light came from the campfires.

Flowers grew amid the frost—in the dim light their petals looked silver, their leaves dark blue. Above she heard the songs of birds and cries of animals, but none she recognized.

All this she absorbed in one glance, then pain broke her concentration.

Cold hit her like a slap. Hard enough that she gasped. The sharp intake of breath froze the insides of her nostrils and slid like a razor down her throat. Her exhale plumed like a geyser in front of her, froze into a miniature storm of frost, and fell with a whisper on the ground. The skin on her face tightened, and she thought she could feel the blood just under her skin freeze solid. Both eyes seemed to turn to round stones of ice in her head. She squeezed them shut.

She'd lived in snow-covered, ice-bound Narfell all her life, where winter winds howled down the mountainsides like tormented dragons. But she had *never* felt cold like this.

"Bit of a chill in the air this morning, isn't there?" said Menduarthis, and when Hweilan opened her eyes a crack, she could see he was looking at her with that insolent smile. How could he be standing there bare-faced, no hat or hood, and seem so at ease?

He rattled off a string of words in the lilting language of the uldra, and Nikle proffered a small wooden bottle.

"Let me help you," Menduarthis told Hweilan. He upended the bottle on his thumb and reached for her face.

She flinched back out of reach.

"Easy. This is *halbdol*. A bit scenty, but the fumes will keep your eyes from freezing in your skull."

"Why aren't you wearing any?"

"I don't need it. Take it or not. You can walk around all squint-eyed and grow icicles off your nose if you like. Yes or no?"

She gave him a curt nod and stepped forward. He smeared a thick coating of the black paste over each eyelid, coated the skin around her eye, and smeared a line below each eye. Then he drew a stripe down her nose and around each nostril, and coated her lips, chin, and cheeks. "Scenty" had been an understatement. The *halbdol* gave off wonderfully warm fumes, enabling her to open her eyes fully and breathe without pain. It had a heady scent of mint, flowers, and . . . something she couldn't quite place.

"What is that made of?"

Menduarthis chuckled. "Probably best you not know. There!"

He stepped back and his chuckle turned into a laugh. Even Nikle and the other uldra smiled.

"You look like a very sad skull," he said

Hweilan scowled.

"Forgive me," said Menduarthis. He handed the bottle back to Nikle, then bent and cleaned off his thumb in the snow. "It's quite becoming on you. The *halbdol,* I mean. Not the scowl." He turned on his heel and began walking away. "We must be off. Mustn't keep our lady waiting."

Hweilan stood her ground. The uldra behind her crowded in close. Even Nikle scowled, and the others had taken tighter grips on their spears.

When Menduarthis noticed he was walking alone, he turned and raised his eyebrows. "Problem?"

"Where am I?" she asked.

"You'll be in the bad graces of your hostess if you don't come along."

"I'm not going anywhere until I get some answers."

Menduarthis grimaced. "We shall talk while we walk, yes?"

Hweilan spared the uldra another glance. The look in their eyes made the decision for her.

"Very well," she said, and followed Menduarthis.

• • ◉ • •

"This isn't the Giantspires," Hweilan said as they threaded their way through the scattering of tents and fires amid the trees.

"Very good," said Menduarthis. "You have a talent for noting the obvious."

They passed into a part of the camp where the fires were fewer, the trees closer, and all around her the world was a mixture of snow amid dark blue shadow. The trees seemed an army of towers that disappeared into a foggy murk overhead. But amid the murk, Hweilan caught glimpses of glowing eyes. More uldra? Perhaps. But if so, they could climb like monkeys.

"So where are we?"

"Frightened?"

"No," she told Menduarthis, and was surprised to realize it was true. Everything around her looked, smelled, and sounded completely . . . other. Completely foreign to everything she knew. Still, something about it seemed right. Not quite comfortable exactly, but . . .

"Home," said Menduarthis.

"What?"

"The short answer to your question. This is home. I've lived here many years. The uldra call it *Isan Meidan,* which in their tongue means 'our land.' " He chuckled. "Very imaginative folk, the uldra. But those people in your world who know enough to know of this place, they call it the Feywild."

Hweilan's heart skipped a beat, and she gasped before she could catch herself.

The Feywild.

She'd heard bards' songs of the place, and Dorim's stories. Of all the dwarves who lived in Highwatch, Dorim was the only one to whom Hweilan had ever been close. Master craftsmen, his family crafted the bows for the Knights, and Dorim himself had crafted her father's bow. But more than a master of weaponry, Dorim fancied himself a loremaster—though Hweilan's grandmother had always called them "foolish dwarf nonsense." But Hweilan had loved his stories—the ones he'd tell her over a fire on the coldest winter nights, his bare feet propped next to the fire, his favorite pipe dangling between his lips.

All the lore and songs and fireside stories agreed on one thing—the Feywild was a place of peril, of beauties that would break your heart and horrors that would eat it. Some who wandered into the Feywild returned to the real world half-mad. And some never returned at all.

She didn't know what to think. Her senses couldn't deny her present location, no matter how much her reason tried to fight it. She'd somehow stumbled into a bard's tale.

"Where is Lendri?" she asked.

Behind her, the uldra hissed. She turned and saw the hunters staring at her through narrowed eyes.

"Hmm," said Menduarthis, and though his back was to her, she could hear the frown in his tone. "Best not mention that name around our little friends. Your pale pet doesn't have the best reputation 'round here."

"Where is he? He isn't . . . dead?"

"No." He cast a sly eye over his shoulder and winked at her. "But the day's not over yet."

The darkness pressed down on them. Even with her keen eyesight, Hweilan could make out little except pale swathes of snow amid patches of shadow. They passed under a great arch of a tree root, icicles and silvery moss drooping from it like a ragged tapestry, before she saw the tundra tiger lounging atop the root, watching them.

Menduarthis caught her wide-eyed stare and said, "You behave yourself and so will the uldra's playthings."

She hurried under and past the root. The tiger watched them leave but did not follow.

"Why am I here?" she asked. "Why have you brought me to this place?"

"You'd rather we left you in the Giantspires to freeze or starve?"

"Of course not. But why bring me here?"

Menduarthis was silent a while. Long enough that Hweilan

was beginning to think he wouldn't answer. But then he sighed and said, "I was bored."

"You brought me here because you're *bored?*"

"You were found in the company of an elf that the queen swore to kill if she ever found. A little exciting, yes? That makes you a candidate for . . . well, a few questions, at the very least. What happens to you next"—he turned and smiled at her, but it was the smile of a wolf finding a lamb all alone on the hillside—"depends very much on your answers." He looked around at their surroundings, and his voice dropped to a whisper. "Best we not talk through this little bit of our stroll."

"Why?" she whispered back. "You said the tigers would behave themselves."

"There's more than tigers in these woods. Quiet now. And stay close."

They wound their way farther down into the valley. They left the giant trees behind and entered woods that seemed more familiar to Hweilan—at least in size. Set amid the frost and snow, their bark seemed just a shade above black, and their trunks and branches leaned and twisted every which way. Even though they were seemingly still in the grip of winter, leaves filled their branches. The leaves, some as large as her hand, seemed like an oak's—though the blade had far too many points and their veins looked silver, even seeming to glow if she looked at them just right. Silver moss and icicles hung from them, and undergrowth, aside from the occasional bit of the strange flowers, was sparse.

Their path disappeared, and Menduarthis led them into the trees.

The air became much quieter. There were no more songs of birds or cries of animals. Their footfalls crunching through the snow seemed muted, and even the uldra appeared uneasy. They gripped their spears in tight fists, and their oddly glowing eyes kept careful watch.

A rift in the earth blocked their path. It was only four or

five paces across, but so deep that Hweilan could not see its bottom. Ice-covered stone and soil fell away at her feet into shadow. Definitely too far to jump. Hweilan looked both ways, searching for a bridge. Then she saw somthing on the other side of the ravine.

"That is the strangest tree I have ever seen," she said in an almost reverent whisper. The thing had two trunks that joined together about a third of the way up, then sprouted outward again just below the crown. It had an unsettlingly human shape. Hundreds, perhaps thousands, of smaller branches, vines, and thorns sprouted from its limbs.

At the sound of Hweilan's voice, the tree moved, the thick cluster of branches that Hweilan could only describe as a "head" turning toward them, and two eyes regarded her. They glowed like the uldras' eyes, verdant green, and the look was decidedly baleful.

Menduarthis turned to her. He put a thin finger across his lips and whispered, "I said quiet."

She stepped as close to him as she could without actually touching and whispered, "If this place is so dangerous and your queen wishes to see me, why has she not provided an escort?" Her words came out in a plume of frost that coated Menduarthis's shoulder.

He smiled, but taut anger lay behind it. "What do you think I am?"

She opened her mouth to reply, but he placed his hand over her mouth and shushed her. His skin was shockingly cool—far colder than any man's ought to be. She wondered how he could stand being outside without gloves.

They continued on. The tree thing across the canyon followed them for a while, keeping pace and watching them from the opposite side. But the rift grew no narrower, and the thing made no effort to cross. Finally it gave up but stood there watching them as they continued. When they were almost out of sight, the thing threw back its head and let out a long, mournful sound that seemed part howl and part trumpet.

It sent a chill down Hweilan's spine—and when other calls answered, in the distance, her chill grew into a full-fledged shudder. The sounds stopped them all in their tracks.

"How many of those things are out there?" she said.

Menduarthis turned and said, "We might just find out if you don't keep quiet. If I have to tell you again, I'm going to have Nikle gag you."

They walked on, always downslope, and at a much faster pace.

• • ◎ • •

The rift widened the farther they went. The slope on which they trod grew steeper, the trees sparser, and more rocks began to peek through the snow. But Menduarthis seemed to know his way, and Hweilan followed his footsteps almost exactly.

Walking near the cliff's edge, Hweilan looked down and was surprised to see something: the bottom of the canyon. Its flatness made her suspect it was a river or lake where the water flowed right up to the cliff's edge, for there were no trees or brush of any sort. Just a flawless sheet of snow, blue and sparkling in the faint light.

"What—"

"Best not to talk just yet," Menduarthis interrupted, and he motioned to the path in front of them. "The walls have ears."

Looking where Menduarthis had pointed, Hweilan saw that the woods were coming to an end, and they were nearing a wall.

As their little company passed out of the shelter of the wood, they walked into snowfall. Large heavy flakes that seemed to whisper as they fell. They came to the wall, and Hweilan saw that it was not a wall at all, but a huge hedge, comprising many thousands of dark-green-leafed branches, each armored in an array of thorns. No frost of ice covered it, and there was movement within the branches. Furtive shapes that must have been very small to work their way through the tangle. Hweilan saw tiny pairs of eyes glowing from the shadows, but if they caught her watching, one blink and they were gone.

"Menduarthis," Hweilan whispered, "what is in the hedge?"

"Locals. Don't worry. They know you're with me."

"That last local didn't seem to like you much," she said, thinking of the tree things.

He shrugged. "Most of the locals don't. But they know I'm here at the queen's behest. No one will interfere with that. Now be quiet."

Hweilan scowled, but the place seemed to call for quiet, almost as if the sound of snowfall was a constant *shush*. She turned to look at the uldra. The little hunters, all of whom seemed perfectly at ease around tundra tigers, were as wary as she'd ever seen them. They kept looking around, their eyes wide and movements skittish as birds.

She saw no more eyes in the depths of the hedge, but she did notice that even the snowflakes would not settle upon it. Most flew away at the last instant, as if stirred by a puff of air. But a few did manage to hit an outstretched branch or leaf, whereupon the flake sizzled away into a tiny mist that fell to the ground.

Menduarthis walked a few paces left, then back to the right, leaning in close and passing one hand over the hedge. The leaves and branches rasped and rattled as his hand passed over them.

"What are you looking for?" she asked.

He stopped and stood ramrod straight, heels together, head back, arms outstretched slightly. Almost exactly the same pose he'd taken that night on the mountain before——

Hweilan gasped and stepped back. She could feel the power building.

Menduarthis leaned his head back, his eyes closed, but his nostrils flaring as he took in deep draughts of air.

The ground shook. Just a trembling at first, like the feeling in the air during thunder. But then everything underfoot shuddered with such force that Hweilan fell forward into the snow. She looked up.

Before Menduarthis, a shard of ice came up from the ground, splitting the hedge like shears through cloth. The shard was knife thin at first, but as it rose it thickened. By the time it stopped some ten feet or more above them, its base was wider than she was tall.

Still holding his pose, Menduarthis flicked his fingers forward, and the ice shard split with a *crack!* that sent a gout of frigid air and frost spewing over him. He brought his palms together with a flourish, then waved them apart. The split shard molded outward into an arch, then melted away into a heavy frost, much like the snowflakes had on the leaves. When it was gone, all that remained was a tunnel through the hedge, blue-silver mist falling down the sides and swirling along the bottom.

Hweilan pushed herself to her feet and brushed herself off. "What are you?" she said.

Menduarthis dropped his pose and turned to her. The frost that had coated him melted before her eyes, falling away in that same strange mist that the snowflakes had. He looked down on her with the strangest expression. Curiosity? Bewilderment? A little of both, and something else. Something that bordered on affection. That made her more uncomfortable than all the rest.

"You behave yourself, you survive your meeting with the queen, and I'll tell you all about me."

"Survive?"

"Too late to worry about that now," he said. He turned and walked into the tunnel. "Come along!"

Hweilan followed. Looking over her shoulder, she saw that the uldra did not. Nikle motioned at her—it seemed more of a benediction than a wave—then he and his companions turned and fled.

CHAPTER SEVENTEEN

WHEN THEY EMERGED FROM THE TUNNEL, HWEILAN and Menduarthis were in a field that sloped gently downward, filled with trees that she could not name. Their branches sprouted not needles but thick and vibrant leaves—some larger than her hand. Whether it was their true color or simply a trick of the dim light, the leaves had a bluish tint, the color of evening clouds, thick with snow. Among them were waist-high bushes, their small, waxy leaves dark green and sprouting tiny flowers that seemed black against the falling snow that would soon hide them. The brush had a tangled look, but paths wound between them. The only sound was the falling of the snow and their own footsteps.

Many side trails branched off their path. Hweilan stopped counting them after thirty. Theirs were the only prints in the snow. Occasionally their path took them beneath the boughs of the strange trees, and the ground was more frost than snow. Still, the ground sloped ever downward, as if the garden were set on a shallow hill.

The woods ended on the lip of a steep bank. The snow was falling too fast and thick for her to see more than thirty or forty feet, but beyond the bank was a flat field of white. A lake or river, then.

Menduarthis stopped in the shadow of the last tree.

Hweilan stopped beside him and was about to ask why when she sensed it. Nothing tangible that touched her five senses. This tickled an older, more primal sense in the very core of her mind. Something was different here. The sense of the entire land being not only alive but *aware*. That awareness seemed focused, like the summer sunlight through the window glass of her grandmother's shrine.

Menduarthis didn't turn but looked at her sidelong. "Are you ready?"

"I've never met a queen before," said Hweilan, and she realized that her heart was beating twice as fast.

"It wouldn't help you if you had. There are no queens like Kunin Gatar."

"Is that good or bad?"

"She is what she is," said Menduarthis. "If you're the praying sort, now is the time."

He stepped forward and slid sidelong down the bank.

Hweilan did the same, though as she hit the soft snow at the bottom, she wondered why. The part of Hweilan that loved the wild seemed to have gone numb out of sheer bewilderment. But the very small part of her that was still the pampered castle girl was wide-eyed awake, and she was screaming at Hweilan to run.

● ● ◉ ● ●

She followed Menduarthis over the snow-covered ice, and the storm swallowed them. The trees behind them became indistinct, soft blue shadows watching over them from above. The last look over her shoulder showed them as little more than fading shapes in the snowfall. Then they were gone.

But there were other shadows.

Hweilan saw them out of the corners of her eyes—shapes watching them from the storm. But when she turned to face them, she saw only snow, heard only a whisper of footfalls that might have been the snow settling all around them. She couldn't smell anything over the *halbdol* paint on her face.

A terrible power emanated from some place in front of

her, like an invisible sun. It touched the very marrow of her bones, but not with warmth. This sun burned cold.

Still she followed Menduarthis.

Thinking on it, it came down to simple choices. Her family was dead. Murdered. Her friends too. Even people she hadn't much liked. Slaughtered. And what she would have given to see them now. Lendri . . . Dead? Alive? Did it matter? He wasn't here. It all boiled down to one simple fact:

"I have nowhere else to go."

"Ah, now that's not true, little flower," said Menduarthis, and it wasn't until he did that she realized she'd spoken her thoughts aloud. "We always have a choice."

Another shadow loomed to her left. She turned with a gasp, but it was gone.

"Don't mind them," said Menduarthis. He stopped for a moment, until she was beside him, then he put an arm around her shoulder and led her on. "Hmm. Choices, choices. Everyone has choices." He chewed on his lip, made a clicking sound in his cheek, then said, "Not always good ones, though. Damned on left or right. Story of my life."

"Are you saying I can choose to turn around?" said Hweilan. "Go back? Not face your queen?"

Menduarthis chuckled, though there was no humor in it. "Afraid not."

"You said—"

"I said there are always choices. I didn't say there are always good ones. And that one, I'm afraid, is beyond you. You've been summoned. You will answer to Kunin Gatar."

"So I have no choice, then?"

His voice dropped to a whisper. "Oh, but you do. You can go in there all weak-kneed and scared. Maybe even blubber a little. Fall on your knees and beg mercy. You won't get it. Kunin Gatar's heart is as cold as her . . . well, let's just say I don't recommend that choice. Or you can go in there and face her. Tell the truth. Don't lie, I warn you. She'll know if you do." He looked away, and she detected a slight trace of his mocking manner returning, though there was a sadness to it now. "I speak from experience."

"You're saying I should—"

"Don't misunderstand me," he said. "I'd say there's a decent chance you're about to die. But I've been wrong before. I would have bet my left eye Lendri would be dead by now, and I would have lost that bet. Though I can't say he's any better off. But you can do one thing. Face your fate standing up. Look her in the eye. Tell her the truth. If you die . . . well, at least do it without shame. No one likes a coward."

A great shadow loomed out of the storm before them. At first, Hweilan thought it was simply an errant breeze swirling the snow. But with each step, the shadow loomed larger and grew more distinct. It took up the entire sky before them.

At first she thought it was the most magnificent sculpture she'd ever seen—taller than the outer wall of Highwatch by far, but elegant beyond anything she'd ever imagined. All curves and eddies, like . . .

A waterfall. The largest she'd ever seen. A river falling off a precipice that had to be at least a thousand feet high. But the entire waterfall was frozen. Not slowly, like the usual winter grip of the Giantspires. This great cataract had been locked in ice in an instant of glory, thundering fall and tumbling waves and spray. The fall seemed a great multifaceted curtain, shaped in every shade of blue, white, and purple. The waves at the bottom large as houses, no two alike, all curves and swirls that melted into one another before freezing forever. All beautiful beyond description. But the frozen spray . . . it reached out at jagged angles, like thorns or curving blades. Sharp as razors.

"The palace of Kunin Gatar," said Menduarthis. "*Ellestharn*. Snowthorn."

Hweilan suddenly felt very small. She'd always taken great pride in Highwatch, even though in her heart of hearts she'd never really loved the place. Carved onto the mountain's face, crafted from the bones of the earth, it rose above the steppe, the tallest dwelling for hundreds of miles. A great house of stone in a land where most people lived in hide tents. Shaped by the hands of master stoneworkers, it demanded awe. But this . . .

The crude buildings of men, dwarves, their mightiest works . . . they seemed ugly, crude, the scratchings of petulant children in comparison to this. Ellestharn was a work of magnificent, terrible beauty.

"How could . . . this"—she gestured at the frozen palace—"be?"

"Kunin Gatar," said Menduarthis. "The Queen."

• • ⊚ • •

Hweilan heard the raven before she saw it—a harsh *caw! caw!* that broke through the reverent silence of the storm. She turned and saw the bird circling them.

Menduarthis kept walking, ignoring the bird. Hweilan followed, though she kept a wary eye on the newcomer. It faded in and out of the storm behind them.

They stopped just in front of the nearest walls of the ice palace—a great wave of ice shards that curved over them, almost like a reaching hand.

The raven alighted on the nearest column of ice. It regarded them with one eye, then flapped its wings furiously. Feathers flew about it, mingling with the snow, and the bird's form blurred, seeming to suffuse like a droplet of blood in clear water. Its black feathers became smokelike, spreading then swirling amid the snow. The swirls coalesced and reformed into a more human shape.

At first Hweilan thought it was some sort of twisted elf child—small, thin, all loose angles connecting lanky limbs. Black eyes set in gray skin beneath an unruly shock of black hair that still had the look of feathers. His entire body, crouched on the ice, seemed to be letting off a faint black steam, but it fell around him rather than rising.

"*Govuled,* Menduarthis," he said, and Hweilan was shocked

at the deep voice that emanated from such a small frame.

"Well met, Roakh," said Menduarthis. "You should speak so that our guest might understand."

Roakh cocked his head sideways and looked at Hweilan. A shiver went down her spine, and she felt suddenly very helpless. One of her Uncle Soran's knights had once told her stories of great battles, how the corpses might lie for days under a sun broken by clouds of ravens. The dead were lucky. Those who were too wounded to move had to wait for one of the healers to find them—if there were any combing the battlefield, and many times, there weren't. That, or the youngest squires whose job it was to wander the battlefield with a knife and slit the throat of any living too far gone to heal.

Those who were found by neither waited for the ravens. As little Hweilan, no more than six or seven at the time, had listened, she had imagined lying there helpless, surrounding by corpses and buzzing flies, having only the strength to breathe and close her mouth to keep out the flies. A rustle of feathers, and she'd look up to see the pitiless black eye of a raven and the long beak the instant before it jabbed right into her eye.

The raven, hopping among the corpses, looking for a tasty morsel . . . that was the look that this Roakh gave her now.

"And what is our guest's name?" he said.

Hweilan stood there staring.

"No one likes a coward," Menduarthis whispered.

"Hweilan," she said. "Of Highwatch."

"Highwatch," said Roakh. He closed his eyes, leaned his head back, and smiled. "Stone houses in the mountains. Damarans so far from home. Nar at their feet. Dwarves dig-dig-digging deeper at Damarans' demands. Ahh . . . Hweilan. Hweilan is not a Damaran name."

Hweilan returned his stare. He hadn't asked a question, and something about his manner was stirring Hweilan's anger.

"Haven't brought us another liar, have you, Menduarthis?" said Roakh.

Menduarthis gave the silence no chance to become uncomfortable. He looked down at Hweilan and said, "Answer him."

Hweilan kept her gaze fixed on Roakh. "He didn't ask me anything."

Roakh threw back his head and laughed—a raucous guffaw in which Hweilan heard the sound of a corpse-hungry raven. "Oh, I like this one! I can't quite decide which way my hopes should go."

Hweilan gave him a quizzical look.

"It is my honor to take you to our queen," Roakh said. "If you please her, it will be my job to take you back out again. If not . . . well, Kunin Gatar is a most kind and benevolent ruler, and she usually allows me to eat unpleasant guests." He smiled, and Hweilan saw that his tiny teeth were very sharp. "After she's done with them, that is. But alas. I've just eaten, and I'm not at all hungry. So you see, I'm not quite sure whether I should be hoping you live or die."

"That's enough, Roakh," send Menduarthis.

Roakh slipped off the shard of ice and stepped toward them. He had a hunched way of walking, his arms and head both thrust forward, but even standing up straight he would have had to look up at Hweilan's shoulder.

"True enough," he said. "If things don't go my way today, there's always tomorrow. Let's test fortune's favor, shall we?"

He held one hand toward the wall, and Hweilan saw a yawning passageway through the ice. It hadn't been there a moment ago. It was higher than the main gates of Highwatch, and wide enough for four horsemen to have ridden in side by side. A few steps led upward—either ice or a pale marble, she couldn't be sure. But beyond that, the light failed.

Roakh leading, Menduarthis following, they entered the palace of Kunin Gatar.

Inside the palace, the cold pressed in, making the air heavy. As the light, dim as it was, of the outside world faded, the darkness took them. Menduarthis stepped beside Hweilan, took her arm, and led her onward. The stairs were shallow and widely spaced. Even in the dark Hweilan had no trouble despite their gentle curve. The only sounds were their footsteps, their breathing, and the frost of Hweilan's breath whispering to the ground in a fine frost.

"Can we not have some light, Roakh?" said Menduarthis.

In front of her, a raven cawed, followed by the flap of wings. Instinctively, Hweilan squeezed her eyes shut. But the bird was moving away.

She opened her eyes and could see. Set along the wall at every dozen paces or so were misshapen pillars, black as onyx but gleaming as if wet. From the top, a sort of waterfall of frost and fog, its stream no wider than her hand, fell away into a basin. The frost and fog glowed with blue light, dimmer than lamplight, but the walls seemed made entirely of ice, and they caught the glow and reflected it back a thousand times.

The stairway ended a dozen steps above them. They stepped onto a landing, broader than a tourney field. It was lit in the same manner as the stairway. Hweilan could not see the ceiling. The walls went up and up until they were swallowed by darkness. Many doorways lined the walls. Some led into halls, others to stairs leading down. But to their left, a passage opened large enough for a parade, and more steps led up.

"That is our way," said Menduarthis.

From the stairway came a raucous cry. Hweilan could not tell if it was the caw of a raven or words. "Come! Come! Come!" A bit of both, she decided.

The wide stairs straightened for a while, then wound back and forth, passing more landings lit by the little falls of glowing frost. Not even a candle burned in the entire palace, much less torches or lamps. It was entirely bereft of flame and warmth, and as near as Hweilan could tell, she, Menduarthis, and Roakh were the only living things in the palace.

They passed through an arch, and the wall to their right disappeared into nothingness. The stair clung to the wall of a huge chamber of ice. It was about as far across as the inner bailey of Highwatch, but the drop . . .

Fifty or sixty feet down, the light failed. It might well have been bottomless. And there was no rail. One wrong step . . .

Looking up, the walls of the chamber glowed cold blue, lit by more of the little falls of frost. Hweilan could see that the stairs ended at a landing some hundred feet or more above them on the opposite wall of the chamber.

"Almost there," said Menduarthis.

They kept going, and when Hweilan heard the flutter of wings, she looked up. A raven was flying back and forth across the chamber. It dipped close a few times, then flapped up to the landing.

When they reached it, Roakh was sitting upon the top step, elbows on his knees, chin on his crossed arms. When his eyes were level with Hweilan's, he said, "You never answered my question."

She stopped a few steps beneath him. "Which question was that?"

"You say you are from Highwatch," he said. "Highwatch founded by Damarans, populated by Nar, a few score of dwarves, and whatever draped-in-rags wanderers find a place to feather a nest. Yet your name, Hweilan, is neither Damaran nor Nar. So are you one of the draped-in-rags wanderers? Or was it your mother, buying a warm bed by sharing it?"

Hweilan lunged at him, one fist cocked back.

Menduarthis caught her wrist before she could pummel him.

"Oh, I like this one!" said Roakh. He hopped to his feet and backed out of Hweilan's reach. "She'll do well, I think.

A pity? A grace? Could be either, 'specially in this place."

Hweilan jerked her arm out of Menduarthis's grip and glared at him.

"Roakh asks a discourteous question," said Menduarthis. "Don't give him a discourteous answer. That can only harm you here."

Hweilan held her glare a moment more, grinding her teeth, then she looked back at Roakh and said, "My father was Damaran. My mother was not. I was given a name of my mother's people."

Roakh smiled, showing his sharp teeth. "And those would be . . . ?"

"Vil Adanrath."

All glee melted from Roakh's eyes. When his smile returned, it was pure malice. "Well," he said. "Looks like we know which way this is going to go after all."

"What do you mean?"

Roakh looked at Menduarthis. "You can see to things from here?"

"Yes," said Menduarthis. He sounded subdued, like a man who had just gotten back to his feet after a strong punch to the gut. "Where are you going?"

"To work up an appetite," said Roakh. He ran to the ledge and jumped. He fell out of sight, but a moment later a black raven rose through the air. It circled the chamber a few times, cawing raucously, then dived into the darkness.

• • ◎ • •

The hall was wide enough for several wagons, but the ceiling low enough that Menduarthis probably could have reached up and trailed his fingers along it as they walked. It gave their footfalls an odd echo.

The hall was unlit, but Hweilan could see light not too far ahead. She walked beside Menduarthis rather than letting him lead.

They emerged into a domed room. The floor was black and smooth as the bottom of a deep well. The ice walls curved around, and they held inside them ancient trees, their trunks and branches black and hard. Only a slight curve of the trunks protruded from the walls, but their bare branches spread out into a low ceiling, and cold white globes of light dangled from their clawlike branches. They gave off no heat, so Hweilan assumed they were lit by magic. Their glow reflected off the flawless blackness of the floor, giving Hweilan the sense of walking on the night sky.

Across from Hweilan and Menduarthis, two of the trees framed tall double doors, which seemed to have been crafted from the same wood as the trees. To the right of the door, a pale figure hung from the branches of one of the trees.

"Lendri!"

Hweilan ran to him, and Menduarthis did nothing to stop her.

Lendri had been stripped naked. Cuts, welts, and bruises covered his face, legs, and torso. Ugly blue bruises covered his forearms like fresh tattoos where he had obviously tried to ward off blows. Dozens of black cords bound his upper arms. The other ends had been tied to the limb so that he hung like some lifeless puppet. He could have stood if he tried, but he hung limp, his knees bent beneath him, and for one moment Hweilan was sure he was dead.

She fell to her knees in front of him and lifted his face in both her hands. Through her gloves, she couldn't feel for warmth, but she could see that his skin tone, abnormally pale to begin with, had taken on a sickly, grayish cast. Something had taken a few small bites out of his left cheek. A raven's beak. Roakh's beak. Her stomach turned.

Lendri's eyes beneath the lids had sunk into his skull. She shook him and whispered his name.

His eyelids fluttered open. He licked his lips and tried to say something, but all that came out was a soft rasp.

She looked over her shoulder to Menduarthis, who stood a few paces away, arms crossed over his chest and looking down on them. Given what little he'd told her about Lendri, she expected to see disapproval on his features. But instead his face was a stone mask. Only the slight softening around his eyes told her that he was masking profound disapproval.

"Do you have anything for him to drink?" said Hweilan.

Menduarthis shook his head. "No. And even if I did, I wouldn't give it to him. His fate is up to the queen now."

Hweilan looked back to Lendri. Something nagged in the back of her mind. "His skin."

Before, tattoos had covered Lendri, most old with age. Every bit of skin she'd seen had been decorated in some sort of design, with scars overlapping many of them. They were gone now, his pale skin decorated only by the rents caused by the thorns.

"Flayed off him," said Menduarthis, "then grown back by Kunin Gatar's healers."

"That's monstrous!"

"It is," said Menduarthis. "But unless you'd like that confirmed firsthand, we need to be out of here."

"Can we do nothing for him?"

"I don't know about we. But my counsel to *you* is the same as it was before. Be strong. Don't cower. Tell the truth. You won't be any help to anyone if you end up there beside him."

She turned back to Lendri and bent down so that she looked him in the eye. "I'll do what I can for you. I promise."

She stood and turned away. Menduarthis spared Lendri a final glance, shook his head, then led Hweilan over to the double doors. She could see no handles, and the crack between them would not have fit a razor.

"Is there no one to announce our presence?" Hweilan asked.

"She knows we're here," Menduarthis whispered.

The doors flew open toward them, pushed by a gust of frigid wind. The branches of the trees caught them, like the hands of eager attendants.

The wind swirled around the room in a furious vortex. Beyond the open doorway, all Hweilan could see was impenetrable white, like the heart of a blizzard.

She tried to back away, but the air seemed to solidify and push them both forward. Hweilan forced her legs to move, fearing that if she didn't the gale would simply bowl her over and shove her along like a dry leaf across a snowfield. They staggered through the doors, and in the great rush of wind, Hweilan thought she could hear a cold, feminine laughter.

The doors slammed shut behind them, and the fierceness of the wind began to abate. The whiteness surrounding them flowed and swirled in a hundred streams, condensing more and more tightly, until they joined into a single cyclone

In an instant, it stopped. Snow and frost fell to the ground with a million tiny rattles.

Hweilan found herself in a wide room, with walls made of towering columns of ice in every shade of blue. They gave off a faint light.

Before them, no more than five paces away, Queen Kunin Gatar stood in the midst of the last of the snowfall. Hweilan gasped at the sight of her.

She'd expected a woman of her mother's age at the least, perhaps even her grandmother's. But the woman looking down upon her seemed scarcely past girlhood, her pale skin flawless, her hair swept back off her high forehead. Tight braids so black that the light reflecting off them shone blue were tucked behind high, pointed ears, and a hundred tiny diamonds—or perhaps they were bits of ice—sparkled in her hair. The queen's eyes were a blue so pale that the color simply seemed to fade into the whiteness beyond—and like Menduarthis's, they had no pupils. The fabric of her gown was gossamer fine, and the long strands of cloth dangling from her bodice and sleeves rippled and flowed in the eddying air currents of the room.

"Well met," said Kunin Gatar. Her voice was light but had a hoarse edge, like new snow blown over hard frost.

"W-well met, my lady."

"My lady?" the corner of the queen's mouth curled up in a sardonic grin. "Not yet. But we shall see."

CHAPTER EIGHTEEN

"THE SCOUTS HAVE RETURNED, MY LORD," SAID Argalath. "The Gap is passable. Not easy, mind you, but passable. Our forces should depart within four days, as planned."

"They will be ready," said Guric.

Guric looked up at the archway in front of him. Dwarvish runes ran from the floor, over the curve of the arch, and down again. The splintered remains of the oak door still littered the floor inside the archway. Guric could count on one hand the number of times he'd been down in the parts of the fortress where the dwarves made their homes—and he had never been down this deep.

"But," Guric continued, "we're not leaving Highwatch before I see Valia alive again. You must complete the rite."

"My lord," said Argalath, "it is possible that the girl *might* be returned to us within four days." A moment's silence, then, "But she might not."

"You heard me, counselor. I won't leave Highwatch until this is done."

"Forgive me, my lord, but you must. To solidify your rule here, those houses sympathetic to Vandalar *must* be subdued before they have the chance to rally. And you must show your strength to the king. To allow our enemies to array against us—"

"I didn't do this to be king," said Guric, and he had to press down the urge to shove Argalath into the stone wall, again and again until he heard bones crack. "I did this for her. Without her, none of the rest matters."

"Valia *will* be restored to you. But unless we secure your rule here, you may find yourself branded an outlaw by summer. What kind of life will you be able to give her then?"

"I don't care how much faith you place in your acolytes. Jatara has already failed us. I won't leave Valia's fate in the hands of those savages."

"Of course not, my lord. You must lead your army into Damara, but I will stay here to finish the rite. Once Valia is alive——"

"That was not the plan!" Guric stopped walking and faced Argalath.

His plan had been simple in its brilliance. Secure Highwatch, then lead his forces through the Gap to Damara. Ride up to a city or fort with an army at his back, then come forward under flag of truce to discuss terms, with Argalath and his guard as escorts. When the city's delegation came out under flag of truce, Argalath would use his spellscar to kill all but one of them. The conniving fops would simply topple dead from their horses. Guric would then smile and inform the lone survivor that if the city surrendered and swore loyalty to him, everyone would be spared. But any who resisted would be instantly killed, just like these poor fellows.

Absurd, of course. Argalath's spellscar actually held very little power. Using it, he could move objects with his mind. But only very small objects. Anything much larger than a flagon pained him. Put wine in the flagon and it could leave him bedridden and blind for days. But he had discovered something about the human body. A blood vessel below the brain was far, far smaller than a flagon——and much more flexible. Squeeze it shut, and a man would fall senseless in moments. Keep it closed and he would soon be quite dead.

A simple trick. It took very little power. But power carefully applied could prove deadly. Still, using it against even a half-dozen people at once tired him greatly. The threat of using it against an entire populace . . . impossible. Argalath would be hard-pressed to use it against twenty people at once, and never at a great distance. Afterward, he might well be blind for days, and scarcely able to move. But the good people of Damara did not know that. Reality and perception were two different things. As long as their ruse remained a secret—and none knew beyond Guric and Argalath's bodyguards—it gave his counselor a dreaded reputation. One they hoped to use to subdue Guric's enemies with very little bloodshed.

Guric wouldn't begin with the great castles or larger cities, of course, which were likely to have several wizards among their defenders. He'd take the smaller, outlying places at first. Those forts that surrendered would be left in peace—provided that their soldiers joined Guric's army. Those who refused . . . well, Argalath had other gifts besides his spellscar, and their strategy assured that the first forts they attacked could be taken with Guric's army if necessary.

The conquered would first serve him out of fear, but soon out of love. He would rule with justice and a fair hand. He would free them from the oppressive incompetence of Yarin Frostmantle and make Damara the jewel of the north, Valia by his side.

But without Argalath, it would be bloody battle after bloody battle. Guric would not be seen as a proud liberator. He'd be loathed more than Frostmantle. And if the Damarans did manage to rally quickly—not likely, but not impossible—his plan might fail altogether. If it failed, Guric could probably still lick the proper boot heels, and if fortune favored him he might come out as the new Duke of Highwatch. But Guric was done licking boots to get what he wanted.

"Our plan is secure, my lord," said Argalath. "Though I fear we must make one small change."

"What change?"

Enough of Argalath's face showed within his hood that Guric saw his smile. "Follow me, my lord."

They passed through an archway, decorated with dwarven runes. Beyond, the halls became rougher, their walls only minimally worked stone, save for the occasional rune etched into a wall or burned into a wood beam. But Guric and Argalath had left even those behind some time ago, passing through tunnels of round stone where Guric had to walk hunched over, holding the torch well away from him. No matter how he held it, the oily fumes seemed to gather around his head, as they walked into a natural cave, carved by time and water rather than hands. It was narrow, but high enough that Guric could walk upright again, and sometimes the roof rose out of reach of the torchlight. The air felt close and damp.

The tunnel spread into a large chamber, points of stone dripping water from a high ceiling, and warped mounds of age-old rock, wet with condensation, reflecting Guric's torchlight into a thousand motes of light. A path snaked its away among the rocks, and when Guric looked down he saw that it was not gravel on which he trod, but the dust from precious stones—rubies, emeralds, sapphires, diamonds, and bloodstone. They were walking on the treasure of a dozen lords.

The path ended at a stone arch set amid the opposite wall. Hundreds of runes and images decorated the cut stones of the arch support, and on either side were two statues, each twice his own height. Their bodies were stout, their hands large. Guric thought they might have once been dwarves, but their features had been defaced, the stone hacked away, and newer runes painted in a dark substance covered them. Guric could read none of them, but he recognized the style of these new runes from some of Argalath's rites in which he had taken part.

"What was this place?" said Guric.

"A temple of sorts, I gather." Argalath turned, and the

smile he gave Guric sent a chill down his spine. He motioned for Guric to go inside. "We have found better uses for it."

Beyond the archway, all was darkness. Guric held his torch in front as he ducked into the tunnel. The ceiling was several feet above his head, but something about the feel of the darkness made Guric instinctively hunch over.

Jewels of every color sparkled along the walls and ceiling. Gold, silver, and other precious metals had been inlaid into the stone, highlighting sculptures of dwarf heroes. But on the floor, rats squealed and scurried away from the torchlight, bugs crunched under Guric's boots, and with every step he waded through a thickening stench. He could hear Argalath following, but he kept his eyes forward, afraid that at any moment a cloud of bats might surge out of the darkness or the stream of rats might decide to brave the torchlight.

"Not much farther, my lord," said Argalath.

Guric ground his teeth. How many times had the man said that already?

"Gods, Argalath, what is that reek? It smells like—"

The light washed over a demon, standing in the middle of the tunnel, and Guric started. The thing stepped forward, and Guric saw that it was not a demon after all, but one of Argalath's special Nar. The man's head was shaved in a fashion uncommon to the Nar: completely bald save for a topknot, in which were knotted bones and teeth. His face had all the expression of a death mask. Bare from the waist up, his torso and arms were covered with inks and scars of leering eyes and tongues slathering around sharp teeth. The red and green inks had looked very much like scales in the torchlight, which was why Guric had first taken him for a demon.

The Nar bowed and said, *"Kâ bâr khorluk."*

Shielding his eyes from the torch, Argalath stopped beside Guric and said, *"Kâ bâr khor,"* followed by a long string of words that Guric could not follow.

The Nar answered, then turned away, the darkness swallowing him.

"All is ready, my lord," said Argalath.

They walked on, and within a dozen steps Guric could see light ahead. Low and purplish, like the dying light of evening. Another scent mixed among the stench. Smoke that smelled of spices.

The tunnel turned to the right, and beyond, Guric's torch was no longer necessary. The tunnel ended and opened into a vast stone chamber, lit by coals burning in braziers so large that he could have bathed in one. The coals piled high within them glowed sickly purple and gave off a scent that seemed sweet but still tickled the back of Guric's throat, threatening to make him gag.

But the light they cast, though it seemed weak—so much so that even Argalath did not flinch—went very far, lighting up a chamber in which a hundred people could have milled with room to spare. Carvings and symbols decorated every wall, and the five columns of natural stone that joined the floor to the ceiling at least fifty feet above them had been left unmarred, though fine bits of gold wire had been wound around them in intricate, interlocking patterns so that they seemed to have been dressed in metal lace.

On the far side of the room was an altar half the size of Guric's council table. Two dwarf-sized statues flanked it, and one three times the height of a man looked down from behind, but all three had been hacked, defaced, and smeared with soot and a darker, wetter substance.

The Nar guard that had startled Guric stood just inside the room with four others that might have been brothers to the first. So alike were they in dress, build, and the designs etched into their skin that Guric would not have been able to tell one from the other.

Beyond the Nar, the stone floor sloped down into a sort of bowl, and Guric gasped at the sight. It was a charnel house. Bodies had been torn and spread apart. All of them human. Broken bones, shredded skin, flesh, and offal lay everywhere. Rats and other vermin crawled over the remains.

But other corpses, whole corpses, stood among them, looking at Guric.

"Behold your new army," said Argalath.

CHAPTER NINETEEN

THE QUEEN STEPPED TOWARD HWEILAN. THE RUSTLE of her robes reminded Hweilan of the sound of Deadwinter wind in the eaves outside her window at Highwatch. Looking into the eyes of the queen, Hweilan felt a *presence* rattling around in her mind, any barriers she might have had against it long since ripped away and discarded.

Kunin Gatar stopped, leaned in close and Hweilan heard a deep intake of breath. The queen pulled away, her head back and eyes closed, her nostrils flaring as she took in Hweilan's scent. The presence in her mind did not leave but seemed to settle in. Quiet. Lurking, watching like a predator in tall grass.

"Hweilan, is it?" said the queen.

"It is . . . uh, Queen." The last word ended in the tone of a question.

Kunin Gatar gave her a tight smile, showing no teeth. "Address me with only the truth," she said. "We are not so caught up in titles as you mortals. Your petty lords . . . they drape themselves in titles like face paint on a whore, hoping it will make her a lady. *I* know who I am. What you name me says more about you than me."

Kunin Gatar turned and walked away, and Hweilan saw that a throne now sat in the middle of the room. Had it been there before? She could not remember. It was like no chair she had ever seen, all jagged angles and sharp protrusions, save for the seat, back, and armrests, which were smooth as polished glass.

While the queen's back was turned, Hweilan took the opportunity to risk a glance at Menduarthis. He stood several feet behind her, watching and waiting. He gave her nothing but a small raise of an eyebrow.

The queen sat and said, "Would you sit?"

Hweilan turned and saw that a chair of sorts now rested behind her. She was quite certain it had not been there a moment ago. It looked very much like an arm rising from the floor, made completely of ice, the hand bent back flat so that the palm formed a sort of seat, the fingers curling up into a backrest.

"N-no. Thank you," said Hweilan. She could imagine those icy fingers closing into a fist all too easily.

"As you wish," said the queen. She regarded Hweilan a moment, glanced at Menduarthis, then continued. "You are Hweilan, daughter of Ardan of the Damarans and Merah of the Vil Adanrath. Yes?"

"Yes." Hweilan could not recall telling anyone the names of her parents. Had they beaten it out of Lendri?

"I know of Highwatch," said the queen. "A pile of stone set on the mountains' last grasp. Nar used to winter there like cockroaches scuttling away from the light. Then came the Damarans, hoping to rape riches from the rock. Your fathers sat in their houses of stone and scattered favor to any too weak or stupid to seize it for themselves. And for this, they fancy themselves lords. You mortals know little of true power."

Hweilan said nothing. The queen's words poked at the fire of her anger, but mostly because Hweilan, as a girl, had often thought the very things Kunin Gatar had just spoken. Hearing them come from her, Hweilan felt shame and anger.

"I care not for the Damarans," the queen continued, and

Hweilan saw a girlish glee in Kunin Gatar's eyes. "Like flies in the Melting days, they will serve their purpose, then die. And not even the stones will remember them. I will remain, and I will remember them as no more than an occasional itch I was forced to scratch."

The queen gripped the arms of her throne with a sudden fierceness, and Hweilan thought she heard cracks running through the ice.

"But these"——the queen's lips twisted into a snarl——"Vil Adanrath they name themselves. That itch is long since scratched, save for one. So I would hear it from your own lovely lips, little Hweilan. *Why* are you running with that *kus itaan sut?*"

"You mean Lendri?"

Gale force wind shook the chamber, knocking Hweilan onto her hands and knees. Frost and ice stung her exposed skin, and through the howling air she heard the queen's voice, seeming to come from all directions at once.

"I mean that murdering traitor! That——" the queen's words fell into a stream of words in a language Hweilan did not know.

The wind abated as the queen's tirade died away, and when Hweilan ventured to look up, Kunin Gatar was standing again, her throne gone. Hweilan looked behind her as she pushed herself to her feet. Menduarthis was standing in the same place, covered with frost. But it didn't seem to bother him. He rolled his eyes and brushed it off his face.

"Answer me, girl," said the queen, and when Hweilan turned, Kunin Gatar stood only inches away, cold radiating off her like heat from a forge. Hweilan hadn't heard her approach.

"H-he found me," said Hweilan.

The queen did not move. Her gaze did not falter. Did not soften. So Hweilan ventured on. The words tumbled out of her.

"Highwatch . . . is gone. Fallen. By treachery, I think. I

escaped." A sob shook her. But one look at the queen, and she did not even consider stopping. "I ran. Lendri found me. Promised to help me."

Hweilan searched for more words to say. But there were none. The presence in her mind held her in its grip, and she found she could do nothing but look into the eyes of the queen.

"Hear me, Hweilan," said the queen. "You would do well not to trust the words of that one. He holds them only as long as they seem comfortable to him."

With that, the queen turned away. Her throne was back, and she sat again.

"I . . . I don't know what you mean," said Hweilan.

The queen had lowered her gaze and seemed to be staring off into nowhere. She motioned to Menduarthis with a flick of one finger.

"Tell her," she said.

Menduarthis bowed, then began to pace the room, circling Hweilan like a bird searching for a safe place to roost.

"Your Lendri is not the most reputable of pups around here. We found him, years ago, wandering the valleys where our people hunt when it suits them. Our lord, uh . . ." He seemed at a loss for words, and looked to Kunin Gatar.

"You may say his name," said the queen, still not looking up.

"Our lord at the time, Miel Edellon"—he stopped his pacing a moment and bowed to Kunin Gatar—"our lady's beloved, decided to hunt your friend. But Lendri . . . a tricksy little cur that one. He evaded the hunt again and again, and when it became clear he could not get away, he turned on the hunters. Lord Edellon was so impressed that after he caught Lendri—for he did catch him at last—rather than take his tail for a pennant, he brought him home and offered him a place among our people. An offer that Lendri accepted."

"He swore oaths," said Kunin Gatar.

"So he did," said Menduarthis. "Loyalty, keeping our

secrets, preserving our ways—all that. But . . . well, it seemed his heart wasn't in it."

"Wh-what do you mean?" said Hweilan.

"Faithless cur, he——" The queen stopped, and Hweilan was shocked to see a glimmering tear fall down one cheek. For a moment, she really did seem a bereft girl, no more than Hweilan's age, heartbroken and alone.

"Understand," said Menduarthis. "Our world, our society . . . it isn't like the outside world. The mortal world . . . your so-called lords and kings, they swear oaths and vows like they wear clothes—easily sloughed off when they become uncomfortable. Here, that isn't so. Here, once you are one of us, the only way out is death. There is no . . ." He chewed the inside of his cheek, considering. "There is no change of heart. Here, you change your heart, we'll feed it to you."

Hweilan swallowed. The *halbdol* must be wearing off, she thought, for her face suddenly felt very cold, almost too chilled to move, to speak. "You're saying . . . Lendri left?"

"Left?" the queen shrieked. "That whorespawn murdered my beloved!"

Hweilan looked to Menduarthis, who nodded. "Killed our lord, yes. That he did. Killed our beloved Lord Miel Edellon and ran."

A murderer . . . no. Worse. A traitor. Someone who killed his own lord . . . among the Damarans, even trying that meant hanging. Among the Nar, they were even less merciful. They slit open a traitor's stomach, tied the entrails to his own horse, then slapped the beast into a gallop. Once the traitor stopped screaming, his own family would hack him to pieces and leave the remains for wolves and ravens.

"I don't believe you," said Hweilan.

"You doubt me?" Menduarthis frowned, but it was a theatrical gesture. Mocking. "After all I've done for you?"

"Roakh!" the queen called. "Bring him!"

Hweilan heard a *snap!* like someone breaking a dry stick, then turned to see Roakh entering the room, leaning away from a series of black cords, dragging Lendri behind him. Lendri didn't resist. Didn't even move.

As Roakh passed Hweilan, he grinned at her and said, "Heavy, your friend. Dragging him makes me . . . peckish."

He stopped halfway between Hweilan and the throne, then stepped back beside Menduarthis, who frowned down on the smaller figure. But Roakh didn't notice. His hungry eyes never left Hweilan.

Kunin Gatar flicked her hand, and shards of ice shot up under Lendri, encasing his torso, arms, and lifting him off the floor. She walked over, grabbed a fistful of his hair, and pulled up his head. Hweilan saw icicles forming around her grip.

She shook him. "Wake!"

A groan escaped Lendri, but his eyes did not open.

The queen looked to Roakh and spat an order in her strange language. Roakh shuffled forward and pulled a black phial from inside his jerkin. He pulled what looked like a wet wad of leaves from the mouth, then dumped the contents into Lendri's mouth.

Lendri coughed, spraying Roakh and the floor between them with the green liquid. Roakh poured more, and clamped the elf's jaw shut. Lendri swallowed, and his eyes opened. Roakh shuffled back to stand beside Menduarthis.

"Look at me," said Kunin Gatar, and she gave Lendri's hair a cruel twist.

Lendri glanced at Hweilan, a look of sadness passing between them, then up at the queen.

"Your new pet here," said the queen, "thinks Menduarthis a liar. Tell her. Tell her what you are. What you did."

Lendri swallowed and licked his lips. "That would be a long tale."

Kunin Gatar looked down on him, stood absolutely still for a long moment, then brought her free hand around, one finger pointing. Hweilan heard a crackling, almost like the sound of water thrown on a hot rock, and Lendri's mouth opened. But as Hweilan watched, his jaw kept opening, and Hweilan saw the ice forming there, growing, pushing his jaws apart. It was past the point of comfort, then kept going, into pain, and Hweilan feared at any moment she'd hear tendons breaking, skin tearing.

When Lendri cried out at last, Kunin Gatar stopped and leaned down so that her face was only inches from Lendri. "I can send that all the way down your throat. I can freeze the blood in your veins and keep you alive. I can think of ways to kill you that will take days and nights and days again. But you'll be begging for mercy in the first few moments."

The queen released him, whirled, and stomped away. The ice in Lendri's mouth shattered, and he breathed out in a great cloud of steam.

Kunin Gatar stood in front of her throne and pointed an accusing finger at Lendri. "You killed him! You *murdered* Miel!"

Lendri swallowed, flexed his jaw and seemed to bite back pain, then looked up at the queen. "He would have killed me."

The queen's hand dropped back to her side. "Oathbreakers die," she said. "He did only his duty."

"It was him or me," said Lendri. "I chose me."

Kunin Gatar chuckled, but there was no mirth in it. "You chose poorly. Miel might have killed you. He might have even skinned you for a rug. But it would have been quick. Not at all what I'm going to do to you."

Lendri said nothing. His head fell again, and his hair hid his face. Hweilan couldn't tell if it was from resignation, or if he simply no longer had the strength to look up.

"Which brings us to you," said the queen, returning her attention to Hweilan. "What to do with you . . ." She sat and let her fingers play over the sharp shards of her throne. "You are kin to this one. Do you deny it?"

"No," said Hweilan.

"You share his blood," said the queen. "Would you share his fate?"

"She does not share his crime, my lady," said Menduarthis. Both Hweilan and the queen looked to Menduarthis. Roakh was scowling up at him.

"What is she to you, Menduarthis?" said the queen.

He shrugged. "Interesting."

The queen laughed. "You jest."

"No, my lady. I knew it the moment I saw her. Human? Yes. And Vil Adanrath? Some, yes. But the other . . . can you not smell it in her?"

Menduarthis smiled. Roakh looked from his queen to Menduarthis, and his scowl deepened.

"Menduarthis is a liar and conniver," said Kunin Gatar. "And many troublesome things besides. But in this, I think he is telling the truth."

"What is that supposed to mean?" Hweilan said.

The queen looked to Menduarthis, and again Hweilan was struck by the girlish expression on a being of such power. She'd never had an older sister, but if she had, one who perhaps liked to torment her younger siblings, she would have very much expected to see a look on her face like the queen had now.

"She really doesn't know?" said the queen.

"So it would seem, my queen," said Menduarthis.

"What is this?" said Hweilan, looking back to Menduarthis.

"Yes!" said Roakh, a look of utter bewilderment on his face. "What——?"

"Oh, flutter off," said Menduarthis.

Roakh stood to his full height, which was still well below that of Menduarthis, and shouted, "I demand to know what——!"

"Be silent, crow," said the queen, barely more than a whisper.

Roakh snapped his mouth shut and glared at Hweilan.

"Hweilan," said the queen, and Hweilan turned to look at her. "Child of Damarans and Vil Adanrath. And what else, I wonder?"

"I have no idea what you're talking about." It was true.

The queen stood from her throne, and the seat crumpled to frost behind her. She walked to Hweilan, and it was all Hweilan could do to keep from backing away.

"Let's have a look, shall we?" said the queen.

There was a hiss in the air around her, and before Hweilan could move she found herself encased in ice, much like Lendri, only her hands and head free. She could not move, and she could feel the cold swiftly seeping through her heavy clothes.

Kunin Gatar took Hweilan's right hand in both of her own, and very gently opened her fingers. Hweilan was too shocked to resist.

"What is this?" said the queen, studying the scar.

"Curious, isn't it?" said Menduarthis.

"What does it mean?" the queen asked.

"I don't know," Menduarthis said, and at the same time, Hweilan said—

"Death."

The queen looked up, and Hweilan felt the Presence in her mind flex its claws. "What?"

"S-so Lendri told me," said Hweilan. "K-A-N. The runes are Dethek. But Lendri says it is a word of the Vil Adanrath for 'death.' "

"Hm," said Menduarthis. "Curiouser and curiouser. You are a mystery, little flower."

Hweilan felt a sharp pain in her palm. She gasped and looked down. A thin shard of ice pierced the middle of her palm. The queen held the other end, and even as she watched, the ice turned red with blood.

The queen pulled it out and held the red icicle in front of Hweilan's eyes. "We shall see."

Kunin Gatar closed her eyes, her lips parted, just slightly, and slid the frozen blood into her mouth. She leaned her head back and swallowed. A slight, almost ecstatic tremor passed through her, and the queen sighed, long and low.

"Oh, Menduarthis," she said, "you *are* a liar." The queen lowered her head and looked Hweilan in the eye. "But not today."

The ice holding Hweilan disappeared, and she fell at the queen's feet.

She heard the queen say, "Menduarthis, what is the word mortals use?"

"See?" Menduarthis laughed softly . "In her blood. Something . . . other."

The threads of Hweilan's emotions had been pulled as far they would stretch, and finally they snapped. She sat on her knees in the chamber of the fey queen and broke into an uncontrolled laughter until her gut ached and tears made it halfway down her cheeks before freezing solid.

When she was able to gain control of herself at last, she looked up. The queen was sitting upon her throne, looking down on her with an amused expression. Menduarthis was still circling her like a cat considering what to do with a mouse.

"You're mad," she told him.

"You wouldn't be the first to say so," he said. "But even a madman can tell you which way the wind blows."

"What game is this?" said Hweilan. "You capture me and drag me off to this godsforsaken wasteland, and now——"

"Now you find out you're one of us," said Menduarthis. He stopped his pacing, stood before her, and gave an exaggerated bow worthy of a drunken bard. He spared a glance to Roakh and the queen. "A mortal nature? Yes. But also . . . something else. Something *magical*."

"I'm not like you," she said.

Menduarthis laughed and said, "Well, there's like and there's like. I was born eladrin, as was Our Lady Queen. But we have . . . improved ourselves, yes?"

Kunin Gatar smiled.

"Your parents were your parents," Menduarthis continued. "I'm not suggesting otherwise. But your father's father? Your mother's father? Or your grandmother's grandfather's grandmother? Who knows? The blood runs thin in you, perhaps, but it runs true. Someone from . . . well, *somewhere else* planted a seed in your family garden. You're Damaran, to be sure. If you say you're kin to Lendri there . . . well, I have no reason to doubt you. But make no mistake. You're something else too. Something . . . *more*."

"I don't believe you!"

"Believe what you like." Menduarthis rolled his eyes. "Believe Toril is flat and dragons lurk past the edges of the map. Believe a lie, but it won't stop the world from turning. And it won't stop you from being a god walking over ants."

"Shall we find out, Menduarthis?" Kunin Gatar rose from her throne and walked past him. She had a most eager look in her eyes. Hweilan had once seen that same look in the eyes of two Nar boys after they'd pulled the wings off a grasshopper and headed for the nearest anthill.

Menduarthis scowled. "Find out . . . ?"

"Find out whose seed went into whose garden."

Menduarthis blinked twice, very quickly. It was the first time Hweilan could remember seeing him shaken. "Wh-why?" he said, and gave what even Hweilan could see was a false smile. "We see the flower in bloom before us. Does it matter who planted it?"

"Ah, Menduarthis, you forget. This particular flower may need plucking. It would be wise to make sure we aren't trampling in the wrong garden."

Roakh made a noise that was something between the clearing of his throat and the caw of a raven. "Does this mean you won't be needing me further, my queen?"

Kunin Gatar kept her eyes fixed on Hweilan as she answered, "No one likes a glutton, Roakh. Haven't I already fed you today?"

There was no reply, and Hweilan could not tear her eyes away from the queen to look at Roakh.

"Careful, Ro," Menduarthis called to him. "If she is Vil Adanrath, she might eat *you*."

The queen stepped in front of Hweilan and looked down on her. Had she grown taller? It seemed—

Kunin Gatar placed a finger under Hweilan's chin and pulled her gaze up so that she stared right into the queen's eyes. Hweilan could feel the sharp nail pressing into her skin. So cold.

"Let's see what we can see."

Hweilan could not break her gaze from the queen. Close up, she thought herself a fool for believing there was any blue in those eyes at all. They were two orbs of white, cold and pitiless as winter. They grew in Hweilan's mind, and she fell into them.

The Presence in her mind was no longer the tiger lurking in the grass. The tiger had pounced and was devouring her, raking through her mind, taking great bites out of her, swallowing, tearing, then digging deeper, digesting every morsel. But then the Presence came to a deep part of Hweilan's mind, a tiny spark. And where the queen was cold incarnate, this spark burned hot. When the Presence bit down, something bit back.

Kunin Gatar gasped and fell back as if struck. She and Hweilan hit the floor at the same time. Menduarthis simply stood there with his mouth hanging open.

The queen rose first. Hweilan lay on the black floor, watching, but unable to move. She felt like a wineskin that had been filled to the point of bursting, then emptied completely.

Kunin Gatar pushed herself to her feet and swayed a moment. Hweilan saw something strange. The queen had been the very image of cold, all whiteness like frost, broken only by cool shades of blue, gray, and black. But no more. A trickle of red ran out one side of the queen's nose. Blood.

"Wh-what just happened?" said Menduarthis.

"Get this creature out of my sight," said the queen, and she turned away.

"She is to live, then?"

The queen laughed, but it was a mirthless sound. "I very much doubt it, Menduarthis. But she isn't mine to kill. Someone else has a claim on her."

Someone else? Hweilan's vision began to blur. She could no longer see Kunin Gatar. The queen was fading into a whiteness that seemed to be overtaking everything. Even the floor was more gray than black now. Menduarthis remained the only bit of color in the world, and his voice cut through the steadily building hum in her mind.

"What would you have me to do with her?"

"I told you. Get her out of my sight! Use your imagination, Menduarthis."

Hweilan heard a raven cawing.

Then Menduarthis shouting.

Then nothing.

CHAPTER TWENTY

"BEHOLD YOUR NEW ARMY," SAID ARGALATH.

Guric swallowed hard. He had to take careful breaths through his nose to keep the contents of his stomach from coming up. The stench in the enclosed cavern was overpowering.

"Not an army proper, perhaps," said Argalath. "But the troops at your back will be only for show. These"—he motioned to the standing corpses, still starting at them—"will be all the army you need, once the Damarans see what they do."

Their eyes had the same look as his beloved Valia's, that horror staring from the black eyes of her lovely face.

Before becoming a squire, Guric had studied with the clerics of Torm in Damara, and he knew of demonic possession. He'd never seen an exorcism himself, but his fellow students had told him that their teacher had once been famed in his crusades against evil spirits. Whatever profane pacts Argalath worked with his northern devil-gods, it was nothing like any possession Guric had ever heard of.

"What is this abomination?" said Guric.

Argalath frowned. "Not an abomination, my lord. When the rite to restore your beloved Valia . . . did not go as planned, well, we seem to have stumbled upon this rather happy accident."

"Accident?" Guric seized Argalath's robes in both his fists and shook him so hard that his hood fell back. "Happy *accident!*"

The acolytes began to approach, weaponless but fists clenched tight, but Argalath shook his head, and they stopped.

Guric lifted Argalath off the ground until their noses were only inches apart. "Give me one reason I shouldn't snap your neck right now."

He saw no fear in Argalath's eyes. Only a little surprise, but he buried it in what Guric was suddenly sure was an entirely false deference.

"I have three, my lord. The first and most immediate are your new troops. Killing me would rather upset my acolytes, I fear, and they might not be able to control our new creations."

"Without Valia, I don't care."

"Which brings me to my second reason, my lord," said Argalath, and the bastard even had the boldness to smile. "The forces we are dealing with . . . they do not know pity or remorse or fear. Only hunger. Their only delight is in death. The power is great, but the pacts we make with them . . . they are not bargains or alliances. We force them to bend to our will by words of power and deeds of blood. But they hate it. *Hate* it. It only fuels their hunger and malice. That thing up in the castle? The being using your beloved Valia's body like new clothes? Do you really think it will give her up unless we *force* it? It is trapped, my lord. We called it forth—"

"You!" Guric said, and shook him again. "*You* did this!"

"At your behest! At your *command.*"

"Because you said it would bring her back."

"And it will! It will, my lord. But not without sacrifice. These things you see before you. Abominations, you named them. They are . . . an experiment of sorts. And it worked. It worked, my lord!"

Guric's resolve fractured. He kept a tight hold on Argalath's robes, but he lowered the man's feet back to the ground. "Explain."

"That thing in your wife, I do not think it will leave as promised. Its hunger is insatiable, and now that it has come into the world, surrounded by so much life, it will not go back willingly. And truth be told, it is beyond my skills to force back. But we can send it elsewhere. Give it a new home. A new body. A body we can control."

Guric looked to the creatures, none of which had moved during this confrontation. "We can control them?"

"A new army, my lord. One that does not know fear or feel pain or cold. One that can endure injuries that would kill the hardiest soldier. We were forced to allow such a being in Soran. But I realized, if this can be done once, why not twice? Or thrice? Or a hundred times? Yet with even one of them at your side, you will not need me to take the cities and forts of Damara. We will need to devise a new ruse, to be sure. So there are my three reasons." Argalath's voice softened. "All true. And all give you your heart's desire."

Guric let it sink it. "Yet every one requires murder."

Argalath sighed and looked away. "So it does, my lord. But if you will look"—he pointed to the first of the creatures on the left—"there is Lakan, one of the Creel responsible for the mishap with Valia's rite. The man you ordered slain, as you'll recall. Next to him is another of the same order. That hulking brute beyond him was found raping the hostler's wife in Kistrad—which was strictly forbidden, and by your orders punishable by death. You see my point. Is it murder if we use those deserving death anyway? This is Narfell, my lord. There will be no shortage of such men."

Had it really come to this? Guric had told himself that the death of the house of Highwatch was only justice for what they had done to Valia—and a small price to pay to get her back. But this . . .

Still, if it was the only way to get her back . . .

"Show me," he said.

"My lord?"

"You ask me to put great faith in these things. Show me what they can do for me. Show me now."

Argalath smiled. "As you command."

Guric let him go. Argalath pointed at the creatures and said something in a language Guric did not understand. All but one of the creatures walked out of the bowl, stepping through the body parts and vermin with no reaction. The one who remained had once been a Nar warrior—average height for his people, but this one was unusually muscular. He was dressed only in a ragged loincloth that fell to his knees. The strike that had killed him—a precise thrust of a knife between the ribs and into the heart, had been expertly stitched over.

Argalath turned to his acolytes. "Bring them."

Three of the Nar walked around the edge of the room and disappeared behind the altar. Guric looked to Argalath.

"A storage area below the altar, my lord," said Argalath. "Quite sizeable."

"What are they doing?"

Argalath nodded in the direction of the altar, and Guric looked. The Nar were returning, one leading and two following a procession of five men, all with arms bound and joined by a chain that ran through a collar around their necks. All of them were Nar—Creel as near as Guric could tell—but they were a dejected, disheveled lot.

"Criminals, my lord," said Argalath.

"Nar deal with their own criminals."

"Ah," said Argalath. "These five did not break any laws of their own people. They violated *your* commands, my lord."

Guric grunted in response. He knew what those were likely to be. He had very few commands enforced on his Nar allies. During the taking of Highwatch, they had killed and pillaged at his command. Everything in the village and every weapon taken in battle was theirs for the taking. He placed only two restrictions upon them. Women and children were to be spared, and raping was strictly forbidden. Breaking either of these commands was a death sentence.

The prisoners were led into the bowl. Their eyes went wide at the sight of the carnage, and their steps faltered, but the Nar pulled them on. At the sight of the creature standing amid the charnel and more of his fellows looking down upon them, two dropped to their knees and screamed for mercy. The others tried to run.

"Be still!" Argalath shouted. He raised one arm, and the sleeve of his robe fell back. The mottled blue patches of skin along his arm and head began to glow. His reputation among the Creel was well known, and the prisoners stopped. "Hear me," Argalath continued. "You men are condemned to death for crimes against Lord Guric. But your lord is not without mercy. Among his people of the west, his gods of justice allow trial by combat. This man"—Argalath pointed to the creature, still standing motionless several feet from the prisoners—"is Lord Guric's champion. Kill him and prove your innocence. Stay alive, and you will leave here free men."

Argalath stepped away and called to one of the Nar. The man untied the prisoners and removed the collars from their necks, then he and the other Nar stepped back. The prisoners still looked scared, but they were warriors. The thought of leaving this place had enlivened them, and the promise of a fight seemed to have given them strength. But as they rubbed blood back into their arms, every one of them kept looking at the torn body parts all around them. Guric knew such a sight would have completely unmanned one of his own knights.

"Argalath?" said Guric. "You said this . . . experiment was a success."

"Yes, my lord."

"Then whose are the body parts?" He pointed at the carnage in the bowl. "And why are they . . . in pieces?"

Argalath shrugged. "The end result was a success. But I fear it took . . . several attempts."

"Criminals all?"

"Of course."

Guric didn't believe it. But he realized that he no longer cared. They were Nar after all, and Creel—the lowest of a low people. If killing a few of them brought Valia back, he would lose no sleep over it.

Two of the acolytes stepped to the edge of the bowl. They had long wedges of sharp steel that Guric supposed were some sort of swords, though they seemed to him more like cleavers. The Nar tossed the blades down to the prisoners. They picked them up, dropped into defensive crouches, and surrounded the creature.

The man directly in front screamed and charged, while the man behind him came in quietly, but just as quick.

The creature didn't move. Didn't even flinch.

The Creel prisoners knew their business. The one charging head-on brought his blade around in an arc and buried it in the flesh between the creature's neck and right shoulder. Guric heard bone snap, but the creature did not fall, barely even stumbled at the blow. The man coming in from behind showed less skill, but put much more strength into his blow, aiming for the creature's back.

The creature moved at last, with a quickness beyond anything human. He turned to the man behind him. The one in front still had hold of his blade and was dragged along, apparently so surprised that he didn't think to let go. The second man's blade fell, but the creature's arm shot up and caught the man's wrists. The creature squeezed, and even over the man's screams Guric heard bones crumbling. The first man still hadn't let go.

The creature brought the second man around, smashing him into his companion. Both went down. The creature stepped over the second man's discarded sword and reached up to grab the handle of the blade still embedded in his shoulder. As the blade came free, the men at his feet screamed and scrambled in different directions.

Swinging the blade sideways, more like a paddle than a blade, the creature swatted the nearest man onto his back. The prisoner raised his arms to ward off the next strike, but the creature threw the blade aside—with such strength that one of the Nar acolytes standing on the rim had to jump out of the way—and leaped on the man. It reminded Guric of the time he'd seen one of the local tundra tigers take down a swiftstag.

Guric looked away, but he could still hear the man screaming as if he were being flayed.

"Forgive me, my lord," said Argalath, "but you should see this."

Guric clamped his jaw shut, took a deep breath through his nose, and looked up. The man was quite dead, his head hanging limply from the remains of his savaged neck. The creature standing over him—still chewing, Guric noticed with a grimace—was black with blood from his face down to his waist. But even as Guric watched, the creature's grievous wound closed. A stunned silence had filled the room so that Guric was able to hear the broken bone snap back into place.

"You see," said Argalath, "the spirits inside are able to keep their bodies alive by feeding on living flesh. They can heal from the most savage wounds—though the greater the wound the more . . . um . . ."

"Food?"

"Very good, my lord. The more *food* required to repair the damage."

The four remaining prisoners—one of them now weaponless—were not fools. They saw the hopelessness of their cause. All it took was one to make the first move— turning and charging the rim in hopes of escape—and his fellows followed. Each chose a different spot to try to escape, but each met with the same fate. One of Argalath's monsters simply grabbed the man and tossed him back into the bowl.

Guric did not need to see the rest. He turned his back on his counselor and walked out.

THE SUN WOULD BE DOWN SOON. KADRIGUL CURSED his luck. After the fight with the tundra tigers and whatever those little monsters were—a fight in which he'd lost almost half his Nar—it had taken the survivors most of the day to regroup and find their mounts. He supposed it was a small blessing that those Creel who survived the fight had fled the scene. Had they seen what Soran had done in order to heal his wounds, Kadrigul never would have been able to rally them again. As it was, they'd crept back like beaten dogs, skittish and uncertain.

They'd followed Hweilan's trail yesterday, deeper and deeper into the mountains, until it was too dark to see. They made a cold camp where they stopped. Back at it at first light, and now with the day dying around them, they still hadn't found her.

Not long after finding the trail yesterday, the two sets of tracks they'd been following had been overtaken by many others—tundra tigers, and the smaller, stranger tracks that even the Creel could not identify. It was obvious that Hweilan and whoever was with her had been captured. It went a long way to explaining why Soran could no longer sense the girl. If she had been killed . . .

But by whom?

The Creel were frightened to the point of breaking. They

held these hills in a superstitious dread, and fighting the tigers and those little hunters had pushed their loyalty to its bounds. The only thing keeping them here now was that they were still more afraid of Soran and Kadrigul than whatever might be lurking in the hills.

If the girl had been killed, whoever had done it had left no trace of a body. Tigers might have eaten most of a dead body. They might even have broken the bones to get at the marrow, but they would have left the bones. There would have been signs. And Soran and Kadrigul had found none.

The sun slipped behind the mountains as their company left the treeline. They were in a high, rocky country now, walking in mountain twilight, sometimes passing beside deep ravines or under high cliffs. The thick snowfall made following their quarry easy, but it also hid rocks and cracks in the ground. They could not run the horses for fear of breaking a leg.

Their company skirted the edge of a bare, snow-covered hill, the heights of the Giantspires looming beyond. The Creel snaked out in a long line behind him, every man leading his horse. Soran was just ahead, dragging his mount behind him. He'd taken the lead early that morning, and Kadrigul let him have it. The Creel seemed more than eager to put as much distance between themselves and Soran as Kadrigul would allow.

There was a silent sharpness to the air that raised Kadrigul's hackles. He took his scabbard from where it hung off his saddle, slid it under his belt, then loosened the knot on his cloak so that he could throw it off quickly if need be.

They continued on, rounding the shoulder of the hill. Below them, in a round hollow between the hill and the next, were a jumble of shapes that at first glance Kadrigul thought was some sort of building, long fallen to ruin. The trail they followed headed in that direction.

As they grew closer, he saw it wasn't a ruin at all, but a series of standing stones, some fallen at haphazard angles.

When they closed to within a hundred feet or so, he saw that he'd been wrong yet again. If the shapes were standing stones, they were like none he'd ever seen before. They looked more like broken shards of ice thrust up from the ground. Some almost straight up, but most at varying angles, no two seemingly alike, and in no discernible pattern that he could see. The bases of most were far enough apart that three men could have walked between them, side by side, but the way many leaned past one another formed odd pathways, some open to the sky, and some covered by leaning pillars of ice.

Soran stopped in front of the nearest, its pinnacle leaning over him.

Kadrigul stopped behind him. "What is it?"

"I do not know," said Soran, no emotion in his voice whatsoever. His gaze seemed to strain at the deep blue shadows between the great shards, and his nostrils flared as he took in a great lungful of air. But Kadrigul could see it was an effort for him to do so. It wouldn't be long now.

"Anything?" said Kadrigul.

"She was here."

"But no longer?"

Soran gave a strong wrench on his mount's reins and began pacing around the structure, circling it.

Shifting his own horse's reins from one hand to the other, Kadrigul turned to the Creel, who had stopped several feet away. They were staring at the strange structure, and Kadrigul saw one of them clutching some sort of talisman.

"You men," he called in their own tongue, "do you know this place?"

"No, lord," said one of them.

One of the Creel in the back of the group called out, "We must leave this unclean place!"

The first said, "It is getting dark, lord. Should we not find a place to camp for the night? Some place else?"

Kadrigul looked up. The eastern sky, mantling the arm

of the mountains as it stretched out onto the steppe, was already a muted purple, and the first stars peeked out. The western sky, where the mountains piled up against the sky, still held a blue glow of evening. Even if they left now, they wouldn't get far before full night fell, and the breeze off the mountains was getting colder by the moment.

"We'll camp here," Kadrigul told the Creel. "Get the tents up and sort out the last of the fuel. We'll need a fire tonight. Picket the horses nearby. They'll need the warmth as well."

None of the Creel moved, other than to exchange nervous glances.

"We can't sleep here, my lord," one said.

Kadrigul walked over to them, leading his horse behind. He walked up to the Creel who had been doing most of the talking. He didn't get too close. Kadrigul wasn't one of those blustering fools who counted on intimidation to win his fights. He acted or didn't. If he did, better let it come as a surprise.

"And why is that?" he asked. He pitched his voice for all to hear, but he kept his gaze on the nearest man.

"L-look at this place, my lord." The man pointed at the structure. "That . . . not right. Not natural. We've come too close as it is. The girl isn't here, lord! This place is *lakhôt!*"

Kadrigul wasn't sure of the exact meaning there. *Unholy* perhaps, though not in the way most thought of it. Many of the Creel had returned to their ancestors' devil worship and demon binding, so the concept of *holy* was not really in their thinking. *Lakhôt* meant something older, some *other* than mortal men—and best left alone.

He pulled his left glove off with his teeth and was about to reach for his sword—perhaps killing this mouthy one would put the rest back in line—when he heard hoofbeats. They all turned to see Soran coming around from the opposite side of the structure from which he'd departed. He was riding his horse now, the great beast billowing out clouds of steam in the cold. Soran had a tight hold on the reins, but he rode hunched over, as if wounded or sick. Kadrigul knew it wouldn't be long now. Better to leave all the Creel alive in case they were needed for other purposes.

"You've found something?" Kadrigul called.

Soran pulled up beside the Creel and stopped his mount just in time. He looked down at Kadrigul and said, "Their trail leads into that structure. It doesn't come out again. Whoever took the girl took her in there and didn't come out again."

"Then in we go," said Kadrigul.

"My lord, please!" said the Creel. "At least wait for the sun. Please, I beg you."

"We look now," said Kadrigul. "She's in there, or she isn't. Either way, our hunt ends here tonight. If she isn't there, we head home with the sun."

"You swear?"

Kadrigul ground his teeth.

"Come," he said. "It shouldn't take long. But we'll need light."

• • ◎ • •

Weaving through the leaning shards of ice, the horses would have been more hindrance than help, so Kadrigul chose two of the Creel to stay behind with their horses and supplies. The other five, three holding torches, gathered with Kadrigul and Soran at the edge of the structure.

Soran led the way, plunging in without a torch. Kadrigul drew his sword and motioned the Creel after him.

The boldest of them licked his lips and said, "After you, my lord."

"You men get in there now," said Kadrigul, "or I'll have Soran come back and hold two of you by the neck. Which two will it be?"

The men exchanged nervous glances, and every one of them either looked at Kadrigul's naked blade—or pointedly did not look. One of the torch bearers said, "Sooner in, sooner out," and plunged in after Soran. The others followed, and Kadrigul came after.

He prodded the rearmost man with the point of his sword and said loud for all of them, "Catch up with Soran."

The trail was easy enough to follow. Most places inside the structure were still open to the sky, and snow lay thick on the ground.

"Ai, *lakhôt!*" one of the men ahead said. The others stopped and stood in a tight group. The path was just wide enough for all of them to gather. Kadrigul saw why. The light from their torches hit the great shards of ice and refracted back in dozens of colors. In the thicker parts of the ice—and this close, Kadrigul was no longer certain it even was ice—the light seemed to catch, spark, and glimmer in tiny motes at times very deep within the shards, and at other times just below the surface.

"What is it?" said another.

"It doesn't matter," said Kadrigul. "Move along. Quickly!"

The men looked at one another. The one who had called out was trembling with fear. He placed a hand on the hilt of his knife.

"Soran!" Kadrigul called.

That got them moving again, though all of them had hands on weapons now.

Paths veered off in every direction between the shards. Three times out of four, they veered left at one of these branches. The trail remained clear, but they still hadn't caught up to Soran.

Night fell outside, and as darkness pressed in, the glow from their three torches seemed all the brighter, refracting off snow and shards in a dozen shades of blue, green, and red. Gold, silver, and bright white flared in the depths of the shards. At least two of the men muttered frightened prayers.

The Creel with the torch leading the way stopped again.

He turned to look past his companions to Kadrigul. There was no insolence or rebellion in his face. Just fear. "Shouldn't we have come to the other side by now?"

Kadrigul remembered seeing the structure from the hillside above and how Soran had circled it on horseback in a short time. The man was right. They should have come out by now. Even the few forks in the path had not bent them around enough to walk in a circle. Something was wrong.

"Keep going," he told them.

The man who had spoken looked to the other Creel. The others all seemed to look to the man nearest Kadrigul, the one holding the other torch. He swallowed and stood straight. "No, my lord. We go no further. This is madness."

Kadrigul swept his sword out and forward in an arc aimed for the man's belly, but he was ready for it and jumped back. Kadrigul's blade glanced off the wall in a small shower of blue sparks.

All the Creel had swords drawn now. They fanned across the path three across, with the two torchbearers behind.

"Please lord!" their leader called out. "Not this! I beg you. We mean no disrespect. But this . . . this is madness. This is no place for men. Can you not feel it?"

The wind had picked up. Not strong, but a good steady breeze. As it cut its way through the shards, the entire structure whistled, and damned if Kadrigul couldn't hear a music in it—a soft, sad song, almost a lament, that sang of cold and ice and the darkness between the stars.

"We go on," Kadrigul said.

"Please, lord . . ."

The man in front of him, the only one holding his sword with a steady hand, dropped his eyes and said, "Please."

Kadrigul heard a *swiiisht,* like someone swinging a green twig through the air, then one of the torchbearers fell backward screaming. His torch went down fire first into the snow and snuffed out in a small cloud of hissing steam.

The other Creel screamed and leaped away. Kadrigul

saw something long, thin, and dark wrapped around him, snaking across one shoulder near his neck then under the opposite arm. Curved thorns, some half as long as a man's finger, sprouted from it, shredding the Creel's thick clothes and biting into the flesh beneath.

Kadrigul's gaze followed the line of the vine through the snow beyond. Just where the light from the last torch and glowing shards ended, Kadrigul saw a small figure, no taller than a halfling, but scantily dressed in strips of fur and leather. One of the hunters that had attacked them in the hills. It held the vine in gloved fists and watched them through eyes that glowed with a feral light. A long cap festooned with bones and feathers dangled from one shoulder. The creature saw Kadrigul watching him, then hissed, dropped the vine, and fled back into the dark. But rather than going slack, the vine tightened.

The Creel screamed in agony, his cries drowning out those of his terrified companions, as he was dragged away into the dark, leaving a trail of bloody snow behind him. There was no way such a little creature as that hunter could pull away a full-grown man. Something else was in the dark.

The roar of a tiger hit them, so loud that Kadrigul felt his teeth rattle.

Still screaming, the Creel scattered, two heading off together down a side path, one going down another, and the remaining torchbearer bounding past Kadrigul. He let him go. The more distractions the better.

But the man had taken the light with him.

Kadrigul was alone in the dark.

Kadrigul had lived most of his life in the far north, in lands where summer came colder than most winters in southern lands. In winter, night could last for months. To stay alive, to thrive in lands that would kill even the hardiest of Nar, his people had learned to survive the cold and hunt the dark.

Once his eyes adjusted, he found that he could see quite

well. In this high country, the stars seemed very close, and their stark light reflected off the snow and the great shards that thrust up from the ground like fallen watchtowers. It was the shadows between that gave him pause.

He followed the trail of the two Creel, but he took his time, not rushing around corners or past a crossing where anything could be hiding behind the shards. The screams of the men had continued for a long time as they ran. The ones in front of him soon grew weak with distance. But Kadrigul distinctly heard one from behind him cut off abruptly. The tiger did not roar again; he had no idea where it was.

Kadrigul rounded a corner and saw that the snow in front of him was scattered all the way across the path and stained dark. Steam rose from it. Blood. He could smell it. Pushed up against the bottom of one of the shards was a wet, grayish pile that, by the smell, Kadrigul knew were entrails. But no body.

One set of tracks continued beyond. Two other pathways led off to either side, but there were no tracks. The snow was pure and untouched.

Kadrigul heard a skittering overhead and looked up. He saw a dark shape against the sky, a quick glimpse of two glowing eyes, and then they shot out of sight.

He leaped over the blood—no sense in picking up its scent—and took the left path, his feet trudging through the unbroken snow.

He took the first path to the left he found, then two more to the right, hoping to throw off pursuit but still moving away from where the first Creel had been taken.

Kadrigul sheathed his sword and went to the shard leaning at the greatest angle. He went to the back of it and tried to climb. No luck. It was dry as bone, but slick. He could make it no more than a few feet off the ground before sliding back down.

A tiger roared. Kadrigul froze. It was some distance away, but still loud enough that he could feel the shard vibrating under his hands. It was the deep, bone-rattling roar that tigers used to stun their enemies. It roared again, but this time the roar ended in a fierce growl. The tiger had caught whatever it was after. Time to move.

Kadrigul forsook the path and began to weave through the shards themselves, but he soon regretted his decision. In places, the bases of the shards ran together at odd angles, making it hard to find proper footing. In open ground between them, the snow was often knee deep. Either way, he'd be at a disadvantage if it came to a fight.

As soon as he found a path again, he took it.

He heard the tiger again. Not roaring or growling this time. It was a great scream of anguish, high-pitched and almost pitiful. But it was still behind him. He moved on.

Kadrigul soon came to a wide part in the path, where the great shards all leaned away, forming a fence in the shape of a long V. The moon had not yet risen over the mountains, but the stars shone down, their light reflecting off the snow and shards so brightly that Kadrigul cast a long blue shadow at his feet.

Ahead, the path took a sharp turn to the right. He was halfway there when a small figure stepped out from between the shards, blocking his path. One of the little hunters. The creature's eyes glowed with a frosty light.

Kadrigul stopped a half-dozen paces from the creature. Even in the starlight, he could see its skin had a bluish tint, and the ears protruding from the rim of the cap were far too sharp. The creature spread both hands outward, almost as if proffering himself, and Kadrigul saw that something was wrapped around him, from his fingertips all the way to his shoulders.

The creature smiled, showing sharp teeth, and flicked both wrists. A length of vine fell and coiled in the snow at his feet, and as it hit the ground, soft tendrils along its length stiffened into sharp thorns. The same whiplike weapon that had taken the first Creel.

Kadrigul turned. Another of the creatures was blocking the path behind him—this one holding a spear that was twice his own height. He heard rustling above and looked. More of the creatures were perched on the shards above, like birds on a ship's rigging, looking down on him with their glowing eyes. He counted four on one side and three on the other. Nine in all.

"So be it," Kadrigul said, and drew his sword.

The creature who had first blocked his path began swinging the thorn-covered vines, one in each hand, twirling them in intricate patterns to each side and over his head, cutting the air and sending up clouds of snow as they hissed over the ground. Kadrigul had no shield, so he held his empty scabbard in his off hand, ready to block the vines.

The creature advanced, twirling the vines faster and faster, still smiling his feral grin. So far, the others seemed content to watch.

The creature leaped forward and one vine shot out in a vertical swipe. Kadrigul danced to the side, the vine missing him by a foot or more, but the other was already coming across at his midsection.

He hit it with his scabbard, and the vine whipped around it, cutting through Kadrigul's coat, shredding it but missing the skin beneath. With the vine tangled around his scabbard, Kadrigul struck the length of it with his sword, hoping to sever it.

His blade, which he sharpened to a razor's edge every night, nicked a long strip of bark off the vine, then bounced away.

The creature yanked on the vine, trying to pull the scabbard from Kadrigul's hand, but he used the added force to his own advantage, stepping in to the pull, within striking range, and bringing his sword around in a long swipe aimed for the creature's throat.

The creature dropped so quickly that the tassel of his cap flew up and Kadrigul's sword sliced it off. The creature snarled and backed away out of reach of the blade. His vine was still tangled around Kadrigul's scabbard, but he let out enough slack to pull away. Kadrigul twirled the scabbard in an attempt to dislodge the vine, but the thorns held their grip.

The onlookers hissed, whether in delight or consternation Kadrigul could not tell. They slapped the great shards with bare feet and hands, all in unison, and began a whispering chant. The wind picked up, howling through the structure and setting a mournful tune to counter the creatures' song.

Kadrigul's opponent brought his arm back in a swift yank, hoping to dislodge the scabbard from Kadrigul's grip. Kadrigul let him take it, but he directed the pull, throwing the scabbard at the creature's head, using his own momentum against him. It struck the creature full in the face, causing him to stumble back.

Kadrigul was on him, forsaking good form for brute strength, aiming the point of his sword for the creature's midsection.

But the creature twisted away from the blade, the edge of Kadrigul's sword scraping his side, and brought the other vine around in a diagonal strike. Kadrigul had to fall into a crouch and roll to keep from being caught, but the thorns still raked along the back of one shoulder, tearing through clothes and skin as they passed.

He came back to his feet, bloodied. The creature had a wicked cut along his side, and the thorns from his own weapon had pulled a great deal of skin off the left side of his face where the vine-covered scabbard had hit him. Kadrigul could feel blood soaking his side, and his left shoulder burned as if a thousand ants were biting their way through his veins. Poison.

"Niista! Niista!" The onlookers chanted.

Kadrigul shot a quick glance over his shoulder. The creature behind him held his spear ready, but so far he was still guarding the way, not joining in the fight.

He had to end this quick.

With one vine still tangled around Kadrigul's scabbard, the creature let it go and set his remaining weapon twirling over his head. He advanced, not charging, but step by careful step, a dance in time with the onlookers' chant. He struck diagonally, three quick swipes, spraying snow. Kadrigul backpedaled, taking him near the spearman.

The onlookers were standing now, perched on the great shards and stamping their feet. More had come. At least twice as many as had been there before. Perhaps more.

The vine came across in a horizontal swipe, Kadrigul dropped beneath, but this time rather than rolling to the side, he rolled back, under the spear, and brought his sword around in a backhand strike. It struck the spearman's knee, cutting all the way through one leg and halfway through the next. The spearman hit the snow and let out a long, keening wail.

Kadrigul came up, buried the point of his sword in the spearman's midsection, and snatched the haft of his weapon with the other. The onlookers screamed, and the creature with the vines charged. Kadrigul stood and threw the spear at the creature with the vine. The little hunter jumped to the side, his charge spoiled, and the spear flew past him.

Kadrigul took up a guard position, holding his sword in both hands, as the creature charged again.

Strike and swipe and thrust. Again and again the two combatants struck at each other, drawing more blood, ripping more skin and clothes, but doing no permanent damage.

The creature backed into the spear and seemed to stumble. Kadrigul struck, but it was a feint. The creature righted himself, hissed through bared teeth, and brought his weapon around, swift as an adder, aiming for Kadrigul's head.

Kadrigul had to give up his attack and bring the blade up to block the vine. It whipped around the blade, and the creature pulled, yanking the sword from Kadrigul's grip. Vine and sword flew away into the snow.

Kadrigul stood before him, blood leaking from a dozen cuts.

The creature reached behind his back, and his hand emerged holding what looked like an antler, one long spike sharpened to a glistening point.

"Niista! Niista!" the onlookers called.

Kadrigul kept his gaze fixed on the antler.

That was his mistake.

The creature leaped into the air—surprisingly high for one so small—and kicked Kadrigul in the chest. He'd been hit much harder before, but it caught him off guard, and he fell back in the snow. The creature landed on top of him, straddling Kadrigul's stomach, his weapon held high.

"Niista!"

The creature over Kadrigul screamed, tensed the arm holding his weapon—

Kadrigul pushed up, easily dislodging the creature's light weight. He seized the creature's head in both hands, gripped like a falling man grasping that last ledge, and twisted. The creature's head went around with a sharp *snap!* of breaking bone and torn muscle.

The onlookers went silent at once. The only sound was that of the howling wind.

Kadrigul threw off the dead weight, jumped for his sword, grabbed it, and ran, the sound of dozens of pursuers right behind him.

TWENTY-TWO

CHAPTER

SOMEONE ELSE HAS CLAIM TO HER.

Time to grow up, Hweilan inle Merah.

The blood runs thin in you, perhaps, but it runs true.

Time to hunt.

—Jagun Ghen—

A dozen voices vied for Hweilan's attention. A hundred. Some she knew. Many she did not. Some were altogether strange, more beast than human. Others spoke in tongues she had never heard, but she felt a kinship to these. Like a wolf pup raised by hounds, who hears howling in the distance, she longed to reach out to them.

But others—many others—filled her with a cold terror, awakening in her every instinct to flee.

Death comes from that way. Be sure of it.

You're something else, too. Something . . . more.

Time to choose.

—Jagun Ghen—

None shouted. None needed to. Hweilan couldn't move, couldn't reply, couldn't shout for them to quiet. Couldn't even cover her ears to block out the voices.

You do listen, then. But do you understand?

Someone else has claim . . .

. . . something else . . .

—Jagun Ghen—

. . . if you survive.

Someone else . . .

. . . consumer . . .

—Jagun Ghen—

. . . despoiler . . .

I require one who is of this world.

Time to choose.

. . . the Hand of the Hunter.

She saw the great waterfall again. The animals fleeing an approaching darkness. The black wolf. Heard and felt the cackling malice in the dark. The pool, deep and dark, comforting like sleep. The woman covered in living blood.

Something getting closer. She couldn't see it or hear it. But she could sense it, like a blind man can feel the heat of fire.

She heard the bells of Highwatch. For years they had called the people to shelter, the warriors to arms, and the Knights of Ondrahar to battle. But that night, they were the death knell of Hweilan the High Warden's granddaughter, and they were the herald of Hweilan the . . .

What?

Time to grow up, Hweilan.

Time to choose.

Time to hunt.

Time to—

• • ◎ • •

"Wake up, Hweilan."

She opened her eyes and saw a haggard-looking Menduarthis leaning over her.

Hweilan pushed him away and sat up. She was upon a pallet of many furs, with more on top of her. The bed was set on a large shelf in an alcove. Beyond was a room that seemed equal parts living quarters, kitchen, and dining area. A table covered in the cured skin of some animal dominated the middle of the room, and four chairs sat around it, one to each side. A large goblet in the midst of the table bubbled over with what looked to be a vaporous frost, but it gave off a strong blue light, much like the little falls in Ellestharn. In the hearth on the other side of the table, a fire burned under a large kettle. Long drapes, set in the colors of snow and sky, hid what she assumed was a door, and opposite that were two windows, both oval, both shuttered. The ceiling stretched low, and Hweilan noticed it was uneven. It seemed to undulate, almost like low waves. In fact, the entire room seemed not to have been built or even cut so much as shaped.

"Where am I?" she said.

"My humble abode," said Menduarthis. Stepping away from the bed, he extended his hands and twirled in a little circle. For all his bluster and power, there was still very much the element of a little boy about him. A mischievous little boy.

She kicked away the blankets and set her feet on the floor. Her coat, gloves, and boots were gone, but she still had on her lighter clothes. "And where is . . . here?"

"You are still in the realm of Kunin Gatar. We're in the mountains between her palace and the camp where we first took you."

Hweilan remembered the walk from the uldra's camp to the palace. She looked around at the walls and ceiling, wondering how strong they were, and said, "Those moving tree things . . ."

"Won't bother us." He smiled, and when she scowled in return, his smile broadened. "You hungry?"

She was. Starving. When had she last had a good meal?

"Yes," she said.

"Good! Good!" Menduarthis clapped and sauntered over to the hearth. "Have a seat at the table—any place you like. I'll get the food."

Hweilan sat. Menduarthis hummed tunelessly as he set wooden bowls and spoons on the table, then stirred whatever was cooking in the kettle.

Hweilan watched the glow bubbling up out of the goblet. She could see no light source. The liquid simply seemed to bubble up and glow as it spilled over the rim of the goblet. But it never ran out, and the vapor simply evaporated on the skin cloaking the table. She reached out and passed her fingers through the vapor. It was cool and tingling, almost pleasantly so, and when she pulled out her hand, the bits of whatever it was glowed on her hand a moment before evaporating.

"Here we are," said Menduarthis. He set the kettle on the table and filled Hweilan's bowl with a thick brown stew.

The smell of the food wafted over her, and her stomach gave a low growl. Hweilan blushed.

Menduarthis chuckled. "Your compliments to the cook, eh?"

"I'm starving," said Hweilan.

Menduarthis sat in the chair to her right and filled his own bowl. "Then eat," he said.

She did. With a vengeance. The stew was wonderfully warm, but not too hot to eat. And it was delicious, sprinkled with small chunks of meat, vegetables, and herbs.

"You like it?" said Menduarthis after his first few swallows.

"Mm," said Hweilan. "Very much. What is it?"

"Raven stew."

Hweilan coughed, spraying stew back into her bowl.

Menduarthis erupted into laughter. "Ah, you're too easy! Don't worry. Even if this were raven stew—and it isn't—I'd never eat that old bird, Roakh. Never know what he's had in his mouth. This meat is simply a plump rabbit."

Hweilan studied his face for any sign of deception, then resumed eating. After two more bites, she said, "I've never tasted rabbit this good."

"You warm my heart, little flower."

"My name is Hweilan."

"Yes, I know."

"So stop calling me 'little flower.'"

He grinned as he swallowed, then said, "Why does it bother you so?"

"It isn't my name."

"Menduarthis isn't my name."

Hweilan scowled. "But . . . but Lendri called you Menduarthis. I heard him. And Roakh. And the queen."

His smile faded. He left his spoon in the bowl and left the table. For a moment, Hweilan thought she'd offended him, but he merely went to a cabinet near the hearth, retrieved a black bottle and two glasses, then said, "So they did. But remember, Hweilan." He placed a glass beside Hweilan's bowl. A tapered cylinder the length of her forearm, it seemed made of finest crystal. "Remember what I told you on the night we met: 'You can name yourself, or others will name you.' I spoke from experience."

He tipped the bottle over her glass and filled it with a dark red liquid.

"Wine," he said, and filled his own before sitting down again.

"What is your name, then?" she asked.

"Ah, Hweilan, I don't think we're close enough yet for such intimacies."

Hweilan scowled again. "Well then, why Menduarthis? Does it mean something?"

He took a sip of the wine, then said, "My black hound."

"What?" Hweilan snorted.

"Well," he said, "the short of it is that my coming to live here, among the queen's people, had a less than wise beginning. Perhaps even a bit foolhardy, you might say."

"You? I'm shocked."

"The flower's thorn doth prick me," he said and took another swallow of wine. "To tell the long tale short, I killed the queen's most prized hunting hound—a vicious black monster named Venom. To be fair, I did not know it was the queen's hound at the time—or even that there was a queen. She was furious at Venom's loss, but intrigued that a . . . well, a person such as I had stumbled into her domain. Very much in the fashion of Kunin Gatar, she told me that she was going to kill me unless I could give her good reason not to do so. Seeing her power—not to mention the score of hunters and half-dozen guards she had with her—I told her that I would take her hound's place. She laughed and accepted my offer, naming me *My Black Hound* in her language."

Hweilan finished the last of her stew and decided to try the wine. It was delicious, but the fumes hit her throat like fire. She choked it down and coughed. "What kind of wine is this?"

"The strong kind. Do you like it?"

A very pleasant warmth was spreading through her, but unlike the wines she'd taken at her grandfather's table, this did not dull her senses. In fact, sounds and smells seem to hit her with sharper clarity, and the light seemed richer.

She took another drink and managed to swallow this time without choking. "What's going to happen to me?" she said.

Menduarthis leaned back in his chair, took a slow drink, watching her over the rim of his goblet the entire time. He swallowed and said, "What do you mean?"

"What the queen did . . . what she said . . ."

Menduarthis let the silence build until it was becoming uncomfortable, then he set his almost empty goblet beside his bowl and said, "How much do you remember?"

Hweilan shuddered, and her stomach clenched. Suddenly, she didn't seem that hungry anymore. "I could feel her . . . inside me. In my mind."

She took another long drink of the wine. The queen had scraped through Hweilan's most intimate secrets, and she still sat up there in her palace, smug with victory. But still, something had happened, something . . .

"You surprised her," said Menduarthis, breaking Hweilan's reverie. He sounded more serious, more solemn, than she had ever heard him, and when she looked up, he was scowling into the depths of his wine. "The last person who surprised

Kunin Gatar . . . well, he's been through a hellish day, and he might not survive another."

"You mean Lendri," said Hweilan. She'd seen what the queen had done to Lendri. Or had others do for her.

The solemnity in his gaze dropped, and for a moment he looked . . . not contrite. Something told Hweilan that this one probably wasn't capable of such an emotion. But perhaps . . . sad?

"Hweilan, I must ask your forgiveness. Perhaps if I had warned you what to expect, things might not have . . . gone as they did. You must understand, I wasn't sure of you. Why you were traveling with an outlaw, why despite your rugged clothing you obviously had not lived a hard life in the wilderness, and you being . . . Other."

"I'm not like that!"

Menduarthis didn't flinch at her shout. Instead, he locked eyes with her and said, "You are. I'm sorry if that is upsetting for you, but it's the truth. Somewhere—some way back, I suspect—you have an ancestor who was . . . well, let's say, from beyond."

"You're mad."

"Mad, bad, glad, sad—all boiled into one. That's me. But it doesn't change the truth." He put his elbows on the table and leaned forward. "All your life, you have dreamed, but not like others. Sometimes—not always—you dream true, of things past, things yet to be, and things far away. You can sense the truth—and the lie—in people. And your eyes itch."

Hweilan snorted. "My eyes itch?"

"An expression of the uldra. It means you are discontented. Always. No matter how happy your surroundings, how much you are getting everything you want and need, you're never satisfied. Your eyes are always on the horizon, wondering what might lie beyond. Others might see rain coming to water the grass. You wonder from what distant seas the clouds came. Others wonder at the beauty of sunset.

You wonder on what lands it is rising. Others fear the moon and the night. You lie awake, wondering if there is a way to make them fear you." Menduarthis smiled. "Am I close?"

Hweilan took a long, slow sip from her goblet, then looked away. "I'm not like you."

Menduarthis chuckled. "Well, you aren't nearly as good a liar as I am, that's for certain."

"You never answered my question."

"I have yet to answer many of your questions, as I recall. Which one do you mean?"

"What's going to happen to me?"

"I'm no seer, but if you mean what is Kunin Gatar going to do about you . . . I don't know. When she was . . ." Menduarthis cleared his throat and looked down, obviously finding the subject uncomfortable. "When she was *sifting* your mind, she found something . . ."

"Something that surprised her, you said."

"Hmm, yes, well . . . I'm not sure 'surprise' is the best word. Truth be told, you scared the frost out of her tightest orifice." Menduarthis pushed his bowl and goblet aside, leaned forward, and dropped his voice almost to a whisper. "She was sifting your mind, Hweilan, like a miser might sift through an old sack of coins, hoping for gold. Like dwarves dig through dirt, hoping for shiny rocks. And she found something. Something that knocked her on her arse." His voice dropped further so that she had to strain to hear it. "What was it?"

"I don't know. Why should anything in my mind scare her?"

Menduarthis stared into her eyes, and she could sense him searching her for the slightest flinch, the barest sign of an evasion. "Hm," he said at last. "Well, that is why you aren't sharing your friend's fate, I expect. 'Someone else has a claim to her,' she said. No idea what that means?"

Hweilan looked away and searched her memory. "They wanted me for some reason," she said.

"Who?"

"On . . . on the day Highwatch fell, the traitors sent someone after me. A horrid slug named Jatara. I don't know why. But the other day in the woods, that pale man who came after me——"

"The Frost Folk?"

"Yes. Kadrigul. That was Jatara's brother, and he was screaming at the . . . the other thing, screaming at him that he wanted me alive."

"Why do you suppose that is? You'd be easier to carry off dead."

"I have no idea. Kadrigul and Jatara serve Argalath. Some sort of half-Nar shaman. Spellscarred. Makes my skin crawl. But he somehow wormed his way into the good graces of the captain of the Highwatch guard. I . . . I have reason to believe that they were the ones responsible for . . ." Hweilan took a deep breath, choking back tears. "For Highwatch."

"Hm," said Menduarthis. "Well, it does sound as if this Argalath is up to something. But a Nar shaman? That wouldn't even make the queen twitch. She'd give him no more thought than a horse brushing a fly off its rump."

She could sense the truth in much of what he was saying, but still . . .

Someone else has a claim to her.

But that wasn't all that had been said.

She is to live, then?

I very much doubt it. But she isn't mine to kill.

"Who is Nendawen?" said Menduarthis. He was watching her intently, and he grinned when her eyes widened at the name.

"I don't know," she said. "Is that a riddle?"

Menduarthis sat there a long time, staring at her, then said, "I was wrong. You are a better liar than I thought."

"It's no lie! I don't know who Nendawen is. Where did you hear it?"

"You talk in your sleep." His grin widened.

"I . . ." *Never heard of him,* she'd meant to say, but something stopped her. Some feeling like an unremembered dream.

"What?"

"I . . . don't know. Can't remember."

"Lendri never mentioned Nendawen? Never?"

She thought a moment, then said, "No," sure of it.

Menduarthis chuckled, but it sounded more in disgust. "That flea-bitten little bastard," he said. "How much do you know about your friend Lendri?"

"I just met him. He . . . he saved me. Told me that he is some sort of blood brother to one of my grandsires. He offered to help me."

"Help you?" Menduarthis snorted. "Help you what?"

"Bring vengeance to those who killed my family."

"So you went with Lendri, hoping he would help you kill several hundred Creel and Damarans?" Menduarthis shook his head.

Hweilan scowled. "Well, for one who used to lie awake wondering of ways to make the moon and night fear her, several hundred Creel doesn't seem like much."

Menduarthis threw back his head and laughed. "Ah, Hweilan, I *did* misjudge you! Ah, well, the gods favor children and fools, they say. Why not both in one?"

Hweilan stood so fast that her chair fell over behind her. "I'm no fool, and I am *no child!*"

All jollity left Menduarthis's face. He pursed his lips, and for just an instant, he reminded Hweilan of her Uncle Soran, disapproving and in the midst of a scolding. "You've called me mad several times," he said. "Do you know the true madness of a madman?"

"What?"

"He thinks he's the only sane man in the room. The truly sane? They know we're all a little mad, deep down. So pick up your chair and sit down. There's a few things you need to know about your little elf friend."

Hweilan stood there, glaring down at Menduarthis,

wanting nothing more than to smash that smug look off his face. Her chair still lay on the floor behind her.

"Why should I believe anything you say?" she said.

Menduarthis spread his hands and rolled his eyes. "Why should you believe anything Lendri says? You listen, try to understand, then you make up your own mind. You don't want to believe me? As you wish. But at least hear what I have to say. Now, please, sit. I like to sit while I drink, and I hate looking up at someone when I talk."

Hweilan picked up the chair, though she placed it back up a few feet from the table and sat with her legs in front of her and her arms crossed.

"Your . . . friend"—Menduarthis twisted his lips round the word—"Lendri. Well, I'd call Kunin Gatar warm and cuddly before I'd call that pup a liar. He holds the truth like a dwarf holds his last copper. But he has a talent for telling you only what he wants you to know and holding back more. A lot more."

"He admitted he killed . . ." She couldn't recall the name.

"Miel Edellon. Bah." Menduarthis waved his hand as if shooing a fly. "Good riddance to that one. I told you Lendri's no liar. He did us all a favor when he ripped that throat—though I'll admit our beloved queen hasn't been in the best of moods since. But that isn't what he's hiding from you."

"What then?"

"What's he told you of Nendawen? What's he told you *exactly?*"

"Nothing. Never mentioned it."

"No?" Menduarthis's brow creased. "You said his name in your sleep, Hweilan. More than once. If Lendri has never told you, let me tell you now. The Vil Adanrath call Nendawen the Hunter. He's some sort of demigod or some such to them. Not a greater god, but he is . . . what you might call a very, *very* powerful spirit. Something primal."

"A powerful spirit . . . hunter?" Hweilan snorted. "Sounds like a bard's tale."

"Nendawen is a hunter, girl. But not only of swiftstags or bear. Nendawen's favorite prey walks on two legs."

"He hunts men?"

"Men, elves, dwarves . . . whomever finds his disfavor, or sometimes whomever just happens to fall in his path. I've heard stories . . ." Menduarthis shuddered, though to Hweilan it seemed affected.

"You're saying he's evil?"

"Evil? No. I don't know that Nendawen even thinks in those terms. No. Nendawen is . . . primeval."

Hweilan smirked. "He's old and woodsy?"

"You have to understand, Hweilan, your world . . . your cities and walls and castles and fires that keep out the night. Your wizards waving their wands and warriors strutting with their swords on their hips . . . they think they've tamed the world. Made it serve them. And maybe in their little cities and towers they have. They've tamed it by keeping it out. By hiding. But there are powers in the world that were ancient when the greatest grandfathers of men still huddled in caves by their fires and prayed for the gods to keep out the night. These older powers . . . they don't fear the dark or the things that stalk in it. They *revel* in the dark. They *are* the things that stalk it. You speak of good and evil. When a wolf pack takes down a doe, are they evil? When a falcon takes a young rabbit, is it evil? Or are they merely reveling in their nature?"

"You're saying Nendawen is some sort of beast?"

"Nendawen is to beasts what Kunin Gatar is to snowballs."

Hweilan laughed, but Menduarthis did not join in her mirth. He simply sat there, looking at her, as grave and solemn as she had ever seen him.

"How do you know all this?" she said.

He shrugged. "I've been around awhile. A long while. I

was here when little Lendri came here like a little lost puppy. I was here before he and Miel Edellon had their falling out, and I used to have to listen to Lendri pine away." Menduarthis rolled his eyes, very much the mischievous little boy again, and did a very impressive imitation of Lendri's accent. " 'O, I'll never see my people again. I'm so alone. Woe is me!' "

Hweilan scowled. "You shouldn't mock him."

"I know him," said Menduarthis, "better than you, most likely. He's earned a little mockery from me. And I know all about his people. Your people, too, you Vil Adanrath. An impressive lot of savages, I'll grant you. And that's saying something, considering the company I keep. Lendri could be the most impressive savage of the lot when he set his mind to it. But I'll tell you this. In the entire time I knew him, Lendri only mentioned Nendawen a few times. But every time Lendri spoke of Nendawen—*every* time, Hweilan—he sounded fearful as a scarecrow dancing round a bonfire. I'll say it plain: Lendri is using you."

"Using me?" She looked at Menduarthis. He was an admitted liar, but she could see no sign of it in him now. "Using me how?"

"I'm not sure. But I do know that the lands sacred to Nendawen were less than a tenday's walk from where we found you. If Lendri is taking you to this Nendawen— someone that terrifies him, and gives even Kunin Gatar serious pause—it can't be good."

"I could use powerful friends right now." Hweilan said it barely above a whisper, more to herself than him, but he heard it.

"I'm sure. But are you sure this Nendawen is a friend? Kunin Gatar . . ."

She watched him, waiting for him to finish, but he simply looked away and took another drink.

"What?"

"You heard her."

" 'She isn't mine to kill,' " said Hweilan, and then she

and Menduarthis said at the same time, " 'Someone else has a claim on her.' "

They sat in silence for a while, listening to the fire crackle in the hearth.

"You think . . ." Hweilan said at last. "You think this Nendawen has a . . . a claim on me? What does that even mean?"

"I don't know," said Menduarthis. "But I know someone who does."

"The queen?"

"Lendri."

Hweilan's eyes went wide, and she stared at Menduarthis. He wasn't joking, wasn't playing with her mind. At least not that she could see.

"You still haven't answered the one question I most need answered," she said. "What does the queen intend to do to me?"

"At the moment, nothing. She told me to get you out of her sight and left it at that. I think she'd be quite content if I took you back where we found you and left you to freeze or starve. But the more tormenting Lendri riles her up, the more time she has to think about it . . ." He pursed his lips and stared into his empty glass. "You want my advice? Let me take you out of here. Tonight. Right now. Take you far away from the queen, far away from Lendri."

"To where?"

"Wherever you want."

She sat, watching him, looking for the slightest hint of insincerity or double meaning. She saw none. But that didn't mean it wasn't there.

"Why are you helping me?" she said.

"Truth be told?" He chuckled. "I'm bored."

"You're bored."

"As a river stone. I've been here too long. People like you and me, Hweilan . . . we're like the wind, never happy unless we're passing on. Put the breeze in a bottle and it's just dead air. I'm starting to feel dead. The queen gives me a long leash, to be sure. But a hound on a long leash is still leashed, and mine has been chafing a long time now."

"Then why haven't you left?"

"I'm sworn to the queen. Her hound, remember."

"The queen would release you from your oath? You, her faithful hound?"

He leaned over the table again, his voice dropping to a whisper. "Well," he said, "I did say *far away from the queen*. And, I might add, fast. If we're going to go, best we go quickly. Her arm is strong, but her reach isn't infinite. Besides, I know a few tricks." He shrugged. "And the uldra like me. If she ordered the Ujaiyen after me, they'd scamper off. But I don't think they'd look very hard."

"Ujaiyen?"

"Kunin Gatar's scouts and hunters. Mostly uldra and their tiger mounts. A few eladrin besides. Bunch of simpering, high-nosed frill shirts. They'd be glad to be rid of me."

"So why now?" said Hweilan "Why . . . me? Why break your oath to help me? I can't believe it's just boredom."

"You're the best chance I have," he said.

"What does that mean?"

"I told you. I think our dear queen is just a little bit afraid of you. At least right now. Give her time to get over it . . . well, as I said, best go soon. And now would be best." He gave her the mischievous boy smile again. "Before I change *my* mind."

Hweilan put her elbows on the table and stared into the glowing vapor fuming out of the goblet. She made a show of considering it, but in truth her mind was already made up. A fool's plan, perhaps. But that might be the only type of plan that stood a chance of working.

"One thing," said Hweilan.

"Only one? You're easy."

"I'm not leaving without my father's bow."

K ADRIGUL STOPPED, HIS CHEST HEAVING, HIS BREATH pluming out from him in a spray of frost. Cold as it was, sweat drenched him, and his heart was beating like war drums.

No sounds of pursuit.

Had he lost them?

After the duel, he had run back the way he came, then begun zigzagging every which way. Taking paths at random. Leaving the paths and squeezing his way between the great shards. Fearing at any moment to feel one of the thorn-covered vines tightening around his throat.

The little creatures had pursued him, the sounds of their footfalls like a small stampede. But they hadn't called out. Not in fury at seeing their companions killed, or even to signal one another. They ran in silence. Like animals. That was the worst.

But he'd lost them. So it seemed.

Kadrigul's left shoulder was still bloodied and sore from the fight, but none of the cuts were deep. He slowed to a careful walk, his eyes searching every shadow. The snow before him was unmarred, and none of the creatures' glowing eyes watched him from the dark.

He was hopelessly lost. Fleeing the creatures, he felt sure he'd run at least half a mile. But from the outside, the entire structure had seemed half that size at most. Much as he hated to admit it, he regretted not heeding the Creel's warnings. Sometimes cowards feared for a reason.

The path widened, but unlike the wide area where he'd fought the creature, the spires did not lean outward, open to the sky. They leaned inward, forming a haphazard roof, and as the path began a gentle slope downward, Kadrigul felt as if he were walking down a hallway.

The path ended at a strange archway. It was tall and wide enough for an entire column of cavalry to have ridden through, but here the great shards looked almost like thorn-covered trees, twisting and turning into the archway.

Beyond was an open area, a sort of hollow in the midst of the structure, only slightly larger than the main hall of Highwatch. More arches covered other paths across the way. In the midst of the open ground was a pool of sorts, but rather than water or ice, it seemed to boil over with a sort of frosty vapor that gave off a bluish glow—bright enough that it muted the light from the stars above.

At the edge of the pool, right where the glowing vapors evaporated, a tundra tiger lay in a frozen pool of its own blood. Its limbs twitched feebly, and it let out a horrible mewling sound. Its bottom jaw had been broken and ripped open. In fact, it had been damned near ripped off. Only a few bits of bloody skin still held it to the head.

Kadrigul walked up to it. The tiger's eye rolled to watch him, but its claws did no more than twitch. Closer up, Kadrigul could see where its back had been broken just above its back legs. The pain had to be so great that Kadrigul couldn't understand how the beast was still conscious.

Before he could change his mind, Kadrigul brought his blade around and down, plunging the sharp point deep into the tiger's throat. He twisted and yanked down, opening a deep gash, then removed the steel. Blood streamed out, and the tiger was dead in moments.

Kadrigul stepped back and knelt to clean the blood from his sword in the snow.

"You have killed my favorite pet," said a voice behind him.

Kadrigul stood and whirled, his blade held before him. A tall figure stepped out of one of the passageways. He was dressed all in black, loose-fitting clothing and a long cloak of ermine. A crown of twisted leather held long, black hair back from pale skin. His features were lean and sharp, and pointed ears emerged from the locks of hair. An elf or eladrin. At this distance, Kadrigul couldn't tell for sure.

Another stood behind him, so alike in appearance and manner that the two might have been brothers.

"Thrana was my best hunting cat," said the first.

"Where is your friend?" said the second. "The big one?"

Kadrigul said nothing.

Four of the little blue-skinned creatures emerged from the passage behind them. Between them, they dragged one of the Creel, tangled in at least four of the thorned vines and bleeding from dozens of cuts and scrapes. His eyes were wide and seemed to stare into nothing, but he was still alive. His entire body trembled, and by the smell, Kadrigul could tell he'd soiled himself.

"I'll ask you once more," said the second elf. "Where is the big one?"

Kadrigul wished he knew.

"Take him," said the elf.

The four creatures dropped their hold on the vines and charged. They held no weapons that Kadrigul could see.

Kadrigul brought his sword back to strike.

The elf pointed at the blade, shouted, "*Saet tua!*" and the sword flew out of Kadrigul's grip as if snatched by an invisible giant. It struck one of the great shards and bounced off.

Then the creatures were on him, bearing him to the ground and tearing with tooth and claw. Like rats.

The thick hide of Kadrigul's coat and the tough fabric of

his clothes were no help against the creatures' sharp teeth. They shredded through them and into the flesh beneath. Their fingernails were tough as claws and raked at his face and the skin of his ungloved hand. He had to squeeze his eyes shut to protect them from their ravages.

Then he heard shouting. From the elves, he thought.

And part of the biting, clawing weight left him. The creatures cried out, and more weight was gone.

Kadrigul dared to open his eyes.

Soran stood over him, grabbing the creatures one by one and throwing them. Even as Kadrigul watched, he grabbed another. The creature snarled and bit into Soran's wrist, but it didn't save him. Soran whirled and hurled the creature. It flew through the air and smashed into the nearest archway with a bone-crunching smash.

The remaining creature leaped off Kadrigul and at Soran.

Soran's fist caught him in midair. The creature hit the snow and did not move again. But Soran did. He brought his boot down on the creature's skull, smashing it.

The elves spread out. One held a long, silver sword in one hand. Green light rippled along its curved edge. The other was waving his hands in an intricate pattern and chanting an incantation.

Soran went for them, approaching relentlessly like a rising tide.

The first elf twirled his hand in a final flourish, then balled his fist and struck the air in front of him.

Hundreds of shards of white light erupted around Soran, whirling and striking him again and again like a cloud of fiery wasps. Skin, flesh, and bits of gray hair were torn from Soran's face. He growled, but he did not slow his approach.

The other elf stepped between his fellow and Soran. He screamed something in his own language, then charged, running Soran through with half the length of his blade. Soran coughed up a great gout of black blood—the elf smiled in grim satisfaction—and then Soran grabbed the elf's sword arm. Even from the distance, Kadrigul could hear the bone crumbling like shale as Soran squeezed. The elf shrieked. Soran reached forward with his other hand, grabbed the elf's throat, and ripped. The elf fell soundlessly to the ground.

The remaining elf turned to run, but Soran was too close now. He leaped over the dead elf, the sword still protruding from him, and bore the sole survivor to the ground.

"No, Soran!" Kadrigul called. "We need him alive!"

Sitting on the elf's back, Soran looked over his shoulder, growled, "Very well," then turned and dislocated both the elf's arms.

The elf screamed and writhed, and Soran got off him. Brutal as it was, it was effective. They needed the elf alive—at least for now—but they couldn't have him casting any more spells.

Kadrigul's limbs ached from the bites and claw marks he'd endured. He retrieved his sword from the far side of the pool, and when he returned, Soran was removing the last of the vines from the Creel.

The man seemed to have come back to his senses somewhat. He was looking back and forth from Soran to Kadrigul. But the sword still protruding from Soran's stomach seemed to have him very disconcerted.

Soran looked very much like the corpse Kadrigul knew him to be. His skin was dry and gray as shale. The wounds he'd endured from the elf's spell would have sent any normal man to the ground, screaming in agony. Soran's didn't even bleed. The thorns from the vines had shredded most of the skin from his fingers and palms, but he didn't seem to care.

"Ah, gods," said the Creel. He pointedly looked away from Soran and up at Kadrigul. "Th-thank you. Oh, thank you."

"Don't thank me," said Kadrigul.

Soran threw away the last vine and buried his teeth in the man's throat. The Creel kicked and screamed. But not for long. Soran savaged the man's throat like a tiger on a deer. Blood sprayed. The sight of it, Kadrigul could take. But the sound of Soran gulping it down like a deprived drunkard turned his stomach.

Kadrigul turned away. He walked over to the elf, lying on his back near his dead companion. Both his arms hung at crooked angles, and the elf was weeping with the pain.

Behind him, Kadrigul heard breaking bone and tearing flesh. The elf cried out and shut his eyes. Kadrigul wasn't sure if it was from terror or pain. Probably both.

When Soran joined them, he had the Creel's heart in one bloody fist and was still chewing from where he'd bitten a large chunk. Most of the wounds on his face and hands were gone. With his other hand, he removed the sword from his midsection, spraying the prone elf with dark, stinking blood, then threw the blade away.

"I feel much better," said Soran. He took another bite from the heart, chewed, and swallowed.

The elf cried out something in his own language.

Wincing at the pain from his many cuts, Kadrigul knelt beside him and said, "Now. You are going to tell us where the girl is."

• • ◉ • •

The patrol had still not returned. Jijoku, whose task it was to remain by the portal and watch, had expected them long ago. After the capture of the exile and the girl, the Ujaiyen had suspected there might be more lurking in the valleys. The Nar never came close to their hills. Where two mortals did come, there were sure to be more. No one came that close to their lands unless they were up to something. So the Ujaiyen had continued their hunt.

But they should have been back by now.

The storm's fury had begun shortly after dawn. Jijoku relished the fresh cold and the beauty that the snowfall brought to his home. But it was falling so heavily now that he could no longer see the portal.

If it had just been Jijoku's brothers and the tiger, it might have not been so worrisome. The uldra often reveled in their hunts too long when game—two-legged or four-legged—was plentiful. But the eladrin Amarhan and Teirel had been leading the company. They were never late.

Unless they'd found something.

"They should have been back by now," Jijoku muttered to himself.

It was snowing even harder. He'd waited longer than he should have. A sentry who could no longer see what he was supposed to be watching wasn't much of a sentry. Time to move.

Jijoku retrieved his spears and hopped down from the outcropping of rocks where he'd been hiding. His bare feet had no trouble finding traction in the snow as he hopped and slid down the incline.

Even as the ancient tree, bowed over as if forever frozen in the wind, came back into sight, Jijoku thought he saw the last of telltale shimmer fading from its branches. Had something just come through?

He gripped his spears—one ready in one hand, two held loosely in the other—and advanced more cautiously.

Something was leaning against the bole of the ancient tree. It didn't move of its own accord, but the gusting wind caused something to ripple. Some sort of fabric.

Jijoku raised his spear and approached.

It was Amarhan. Both of his arms hung at twisted angles that made Jijoku wince. The eladrin's eyes were wide with panic, and he panted like a deer brought to ground by wolves.

Amarhan's eyes locked on Jijoku, and his mouth moved. Jijoku stepped closer. "What?"

"Run!" Amarhan gasped.

Jijoku turned in time to see the sword descending. Then he saw no more.

"No," Kadrigul said, as he knelt to clean his sword. "Don't."

Soran emerged from the swirling snow like a ship through a storm.

"Are there more guards?" Kadrigul asked him.

"Not anymore." Soran closed his eyes and leaned his head back, like a man might bask in the sun. A smile spread across his lips, but it was the most inhuman thing Kadrigul had ever seen. No joy. Not even malice. Just the pulling of lips back over the teeth.

"You can sense her again?" said Kadrigul.

"Oh, yes. She burns like sun's first light. So much brighter here."

Kadrigul scowled. He had no idea what that meant. "You can find her? You're certain?"

"Quite certain," said Soran.

Kadrigul stood and walked over to the eladrin. They wouldn't be needing him any longer.

TWENTY-FOUR

CHAPTER

"I'M NOT LEAVING WITHOUT MY FATHER'S BOW," SAID Hweilan.

Menduarthis frowned. The warm light from the hearth fire burned low, setting a flamelike halo around his hair. But the blue light from the goblet on the table lit his pale face, setting his eyes and the folds of his frown in deep shadows. All in all, it gave him a maniacal aspect.

"Hmm," he said. "That could be difficult, I'm afraid. I may be the queen's hound, but Roakh is her main meddler. Your things are with him."

"Then we go see Roakh."

"You think he's just going to hand over your things?"

"We ask nicely," said Hweilan. "If he refuses, we take them. Less than nicely if necessary."

"You're ready to cross that bridge?" Menduarthis said. "Once you do, there's no coming back."

"I'm not leaving without my father's bow. It's all I have left of him."

"You have your blood. If you rouse the queen's ire, she'll take that as well."

"Not without a fight."

Menduarthis watched her in silence. She returned his gaze without flinching.

"How far are you prepared to go?" he asked.

"As far as necessary."

"Have you ever killed anyone before, Hweilan? I mean a person—not a beast, not something intended for your table."

She remembered her first day on the run. The Creel chasing her down. The fear and anger in the man's voice— *Face me! Come out and*—

If she tried, she could still feel the shock going up her arms as she plunged her knife into the man's throat. She had killed him. No doubt.

But that had been different. The man had been hurting her, and she'd struck out. This would be different. This would be going after what she wanted and being faced with the stark reality of killing whoever got in her way.

"Are you a killer, Hweilan?" Menduarthis asked.

"Not . . . not like this," she said. "But I have to start some time."

• • ⊚ • •

Menduarthis donned the armor he had worn the first time she'd seen him then donned a blue cloak over it. Had his wild, black hair not spoiled the image, he would have looked every inch the prince.

He disappeared into the hallway again and returned with a large bundle. Fresh clothes for Hweilan. Not the leather and animal hides Lendri had provided for her, but fine clothing of an excellent cut. The material felt soft as fine linen over her skin, but it was thick as tent cloth and, he assured her, would keep her warm. Loose trousers and tunic, a jerkin that fell past her hips, all a dark gray that would fade into shadows, snow, and stone. Over that a sort of sleeveless robe with a deep cowl, rimmed in fur, all black, as were the belt, gloves, and boots he gave her. And over that a thick cloak made from the white fur of some animal. He even had the grace to turn his back while she changed.

"How do I look?" she asked when all was done.

"You don't look like you," he said, "and that's the important thing. Keep the hood up, and you'll pass a casual glance for one of the eladrin. Just pretend everyone is beneath you. Also very eladrin."

He turned and rummaged through a chest of black wood set against the wall. Peeking over his shoulder, Hweilan could see only more clothes, but when he stood and extended his hands, a long knife in a scabbard rested across both his palms.

"In case we run into trouble before . . . well, before."

She took it from him and drew the blade. It was single-edged, the point ending in a slight curve. The blade alone was as long as her forearm, and the silver steel was etched in curving designs that seemed to evoke wind and clouds.

"It's beautiful," she said. "Thank you."

"Keep it under the cloak," he said. "No sense in asking for trouble." He reached inside his own jacket and pulled out a small phial. "One more thing."

"*Halbdol?*"

"You're still in Kunin Gatar's realm, and it's still very cold. You'll want it. Trust me."

"Why don't you need it?"

"A long tale. For another day."

She closed her eyes, and Menduarthis applied a thick coat all around her eyes, painting a sort of mask. But her hair kept falling in the way. Her eyes still closed, she felt him brushing the hair back behind her ear, very gently with the backs of his fingers. His touch lingered a bit too long, and she pulled away.

"Let me do something about my hair," she said. Feeling her face flush, she turned away.

"Here," said Menduarthis. "Try this."

She turned back around. He was holding out a long silk scarf, a dark red, like heart's blood.

"It's lovely," she said. As she took it, the scent of a feminine perfume wafted out from it—fading, but still there. She gave him a wicked smile. "Something tells me I'm not the first lady to enjoy your hospitality."

He grinned back. "So you *are* enjoying me, then?"

Hweilan took the scarf, swept her hair back off her head, and bound the cloth atop her head.

She held out her hand for the phial. "I can do the rest."

"As you wish," said Menduarthis.

Rather than another death mask, Hweilan smeared the *halbdol* on one finger and covered most of her face, neck and ears.

"Most fearsome," said Menduarthis. "Let's do this."

He walked over to an open space on the floor between the shuttered windows and motioned toward the floor with one fist. With a rush of air, a door flew up from the floor and banged against the wall.

Remembering the night she'd first met Menduarthis, and being reminded of his powers now, Hweilan asked, "You're a sorcerer?"

"Nothing so droll," he said. "Let's get today over with, then we can get to know each other properly."

Hweilan felt herself blushing again and was grateful for the black paste covering her face.

● ● ◎ ● ●

They stepped outside, into a gust of frigid air and snow. The cold hit like a slap, and Hweilan cried out.

"Hmm," said Menduarthis. "Good thing you painted yourself with the *halbdol* after all. Looks as if Kunin Gatar's in a mood today."

They stood on the broad ledge of a cliff. How far it ascended over the ledge and fell below, she couldn't tell, for the snow hid everything beyond a few dozen feet. She saw another round door and shuttered window peeking through the snow. Whether they were other dwellings or more of Menduarthis's, it didn't much matter now. Hweilan knew she'd either be dead or gone from this place before the day was done.

Menduarthis led her down more steps—none with rails, and she walked as close as she could to the rock wall—along more paths along cliffside ledges, and across stone bridges where the wind seemed determined to push her over the edge. She clutched at the insides of her cloak to keep it near her body, not just for warmth, for she feared if the wind caught it, it would fill like a sail and throw her into depths where she might fall forever.

Only the *halbdol* kept her face and eyes from freezing, but her breath came out in great clouds that froze into snow only inches from her face before being swept away by the gale.

Hweilan saw no other living creatures, but she could sense things watching them from the storm. Sometimes with only simple curiosity. But once, as they passed underneath an overhang of black rock, she could feel malice washing over her, like a foul stench, and Menduarthis called over the shriek of the wind, "Best stay close here!"

She didn't ask why, and the feeling soon passed.

They continued on, rounding a bend in the mountain and walking into the face of the wind. Every step brought them closer to the palace. They were walking into the heart of the storm.

By the time they reached the frozen river, the light was beginning its slow fade to evening, and the new snow was up to Hweilan's knees. With no snowshoes, they had to wade through it. But Menduarthis had spoken truly about the clothes he'd given her: even walking into the wind, Hweilan wasn't cold.

Menduarthis kept near the base of the cliff, for out on the snow-covered ice, uldra were racing down the river in sleds affixed with large sails. They moved incredibly fast, and although Hweilan caught only glimpses of them through the snow, she thought by the snatches of laughter she heard that most of the sailors were children.

As they neared the section of the cliff, on the other side of which lay the main gate, two uldra passed them riding on the back of a great swiftstag. Menduarthis spoke to them in their language—Hweilan tense and looking elsewhere the whole time—then they rode off. She watched them go until the great beast was lost to the storm.

"I thought they rode tigers," Hweilan said to Menduarthis.

"Only the Ujaiyen," he said, "the queen's scouts. Other uldra ride swiftstags, wolves, rams. I've heard rumors there's one old fellow a ways upriver who has tamed a bear. But on the rivers and fields, they love their sailsleds. Not much good up in the mountains and woods, though."

Another sailsled raced by, just a swift shadow passed through the swirling snow. The sound of laughter lingered after the sled was lost to sight.

"Who said there are no benefits to a queen's wrath?" said Menduarthis

He led Hweilan to the cliffside. Under the snow, Hweilan could feel her boots cracking on something that felt like dry branches—many of them too thick to break and simply threatening to trip her.

She knelt in the snow and rummaged under it until her glove brushed up against one of the branches. She grabbed it and pulled it out. It wasn't a branch. It was a bone. A leg bone by the looks of it. She was no expert on such things, but its narrow length looked very much like a human leg bone. She tossed it aside, then found another. Definitely a rib. When her other hand brushed up against something more round, she closed her eyes and swallowed hard, fearing what it was. Her fears proved true. Her hand emerged from the snow with the upper half of a human skull.

She looked up at Menduarthis. "What is this?"

He pointed up. "We're here."

Hweilan looked up. The falling snow obscured everything above a few dozen feet. But she could just make out where the wall of the cliff began to lean out a little.

"We're where?" she asked.

"You said you wanted your things back."

"Roakh lives here?" Hweilan looked back down at the skull in her hand and remembered her meeting with Roakh in the palace. Memory of the old nightmare came to her again, of ravens on the battlefield, their dead, black eyes eager for hers.

"For the moment," said Menduarthis, and it took Hweilan a moment to catch his meaning.

She reached behind her back and drew the knife that Menduarthis had given her. "I'm ready," she said.

Menduarthis extended his hand. "Very well," he said. "Come here."

Hweilan walked to him, the knife held loosely at her side, and stopped just shy of his hand.

"Don't you trust me?" said Menduarthis.

"I'm here, am I not?"

"That's not what I meant. Roakh's up there." He pointed to the cliff wall above them. "I can get us there, but not like this. You must suffer my embrace for a few moments."

Hweilan scowled. "Suffer your—?"

Menduarthis lunged, adder-quick, taking her in a tight embrace, his arms pinning her own. She stiffened as she felt his cool skin press against her cheek, but he only held her tighter. Then the breath of his whisper in her ear. "No one likes a coward. Trust me."

Before she could react, she felt a great rush of air—not the storm, this gale was narrow, concentrated, and under the control of strong will. She almost panicked and tried to fight her way free, but she remembered exactly how Menduarthis had captured her in the first place, and she decided to trust him. Just this once. She could always use the knife once he let her go.

The wind swirled around them, so fast and fierce that it felt almost solid. Menduarthis held her very tight, and she suddenly found it hard to breathe.

The air hit them, a physical blow that knocked them off their feet.

No, Hweilan realized. It was lifting them. They had lurched, but not down. The cyclone was lifting them up, faster and faster each moment.

Hweilan felt a scream building in her chest, and just when she could contain it no more, the cyclone was gone, the wind simply dissipating. Still in Menduarthis's tight embrace, Hweilan fell. Not far, but enough to clamp her teeth together.

They hit a snow-covered ledge of rock and rolled. When they stopped, Hweilan was on her back, Menduarthis on top of her.

He pulled the upper half of his body up and looked down on her. He had a dark smear of *halbdol* across one cheek where he had rubbed against her. "Do you trust me now?"

She pushed him away with her free hand. "A lot less than I did a moment ago."

They got up. Hweilan found herself on a curving lip of rock several feet wide. Up here, the wind from the storm was stronger, and less snow had gathered. The litter of bones was much more evident. Four skulls—one of which still had bits of flesh and hair clinging to the scalp—and countless random bones strewn about. Even in the wind, the ledge reeked.

Set amid the cliffside was a round window, closed by a thick shutter. It hadn't been crafted by planks of wood, but seemed rather to have been grown or molded, almost like the parchmentlike outer wall of a wasp's nest.

"Follow my lead," said Menduarthis. He walked over to the shutter and raised a fist.

The shutter flew outward, barely missing Menduarthis and revealing the upper half of Roakh, standing on a lower floor just inside the window. Snowflakes sprinkled him, laying against his gray skin and black hair in stark contrast.

"*Govuled,* Menduarthis," he said. "I thought I heard——" His gaze found Hweilan. She felt it, almost like a physical touch, those black eyes, void of all warmth and emotion save one. Hunger. "What have we here? Brought me a gift, have you?"

Roakh's eyes flicked to the naked blade in Hweilan's hand. His eager gaze was just turning to a scowl when—

Menduarthis said, "I have."

"And what is the precious gift's name?"

"Boot."

"Boot?" Roakh looked up at Menduarthis—

—and Menduarthis kicked him in the face.

Roakh fell backward into the room, and Menduarthis jumped in after him. Hweilan's eyes, accustomed to the glare of the snowstorm—fading as it was to evening, it was still bright compared to the gloom beyond the window—could not see the two men, but she could hear Roakh's surprised croak, followed by the sound of more blows landing.

Inside her gloves, Hweilan's palms felt hot and slick. She tightened her grip on the knife and approached the window. Closer up, she could see bits of the room beyond. A hallway not much wider than the window continued a short distance into a larger room beyond. Still no sign of Menduarthis or Roakh, but she could hear frenzied movement inside.

"Hweilan!" Menduarthis called. "Do come in. It's rude to linger outside windows. Someone watching might think we were up to something."

She jumped inside. Keeping her back to the window, she walked forward, the knife held in front of her. She could feel her arms and legs trembling like plucked harp strings, and her breath seemed very loud in her ears.

The room beyond was a wreck. Round walls and a domed ceiling, it seemed—much like Menduarthis's dwelling had—to be more of a cave molded from the rock of the mountain. Shelves lined the wall to her left, each crammed full with bits of clothing, old boots, weapons, jewelry, brass lamps, scrolls, books and pieces of books, and many things Hweilan couldn't identify. Piles of similar items lay around the room, on tabletops, on the floor, and more bundles of sackcloth or net hung from the ceiling, every one packed full.

Menduarthis, a thin trickle of blood dripping down his chin, stood in front of the far door. Roakh, his mouth a mess of blood and broken teeth, one side of his face already swelling, stood pressed against the far wall, his breath coming in ragged gasps.

"Treachery!" Roakh screamed, and it came out more of a croak than a cry. "You know what happens to traitors here. Kunin Gatar will flay you for this."

"Perhaps," said Menduarthis. "But not today. Today, you will give us what we want."

"I'll tell you where he is," said Roakh. "Just . . . don't hurt me anymore."

"Where who is?" said Menduarthis.

"Lendri. Please! He's . . . he's still alive. The queen ordered him taken to the Thorns. She wants him to die where Miel Edellon died."

Menduarthis pursed his lips and nodded, taking this in. "Very nice," he said. "But that's not why we're here, old crow."

Roakh's eyes widened. "What . . . do you want?"

"Hweilan here has come for her things," said Menduarthis. "Her father's bow."

Hweilan nodded. "I want it."

Menduarthis smiled down on Roakh, and a shiver went down Hweilan's spine. It was the first time she had seen such an expression from him: pure, undisguised, joyful malice. "I think you know what *I* have come for, old crow."

Roakh pushed himself away from the wall and into a crouch, his limbs trembling with fury and pain. He glared at Menduarthis a long moment, then said, "Why?"

Menduarthis shrugged. "Why not?"

Roakh leaped at Hweilan. His form blurred and twisted to wings, feathers, and long, sharp claws, aiming for Hweilan's face.

Menduarthis flicked his wrist and thrust an open palm at Roakh. Wind roared through chamber, blowing scrolls off shelves, ripping pages from books, and setting the dangling nets and bundles to swaying. But one directed current of air struck Roakh full force and smashed him into an upper shelf. Hweilan winced at the sound of cracking wood and bone, then Roakh, shocked back into his elflike form again, hit a table below, smashing it beneath him and scattering jewels and coins all over the floor.

"Best not try that again," said Menduarthis. "Hollow bird bones break so easily."

Roakh lay writhing atop the smashed table, clutching at his right side and moaning.

"You broke my arm, you—" The rest of Roakh's rant faded into a long string of words in another language that Hweilan was quite sure were curses.

"Give the lady her bow," said Menduarthis as he walked over to stand over Roakh. He bent down and began to stuff his pockets with jewels and coins. "Be good, and I'll leave you tied and gagged in one of your nets. Continue being . . . *difficult,* and—well, have you ever seen an old wineskin filled with too much wine? Imagine what would happen if the air in your wretched frame did the same thing."

Menduarthis stood and twirled his fingers in an intricate pattern, and Hweilan felt a breeze waft through the room. Roakh gasped—

No, not a gasp. Air was rushing into his lungs, very much against his will. He clamped his jaws shut, then pressed his unbroken hand across his nose. His eyes widened with fear, and tears leaked down the sides of his face.

"I can shove it in through your ears," said Menduarthis, "though we won't be able to continue our conversation once all the little bones in there get shoved down your throat. So give"—he kicked Roakh in the ribs once, a rib cracking under the blow—"the girl"—another kick, and Roakh dropped the hold on his nose—"what"—another kick, this one aimed at Roakh's knee—"she wants!"

"Ah!" Roakh screamed. "Stop! Stop, please! I'll do it."

Menduarthis stopped his assault and dropped his hands to his sides.

"Just . . . just help me up," said Roakh. "I'll, ah!" He winced in pain. "I'll get them."

"No," said Menduarthis. "You point, and we'll get them."

Roakh glared at him. Menduarthis raised one hand again, his fingers already twirling again.

"No!" Roakh screamed. He pointed in Hweilan's direction. "Under the pile! There!"

She turned. Shoved up against the wall not far from the hallway was a jumble of cloaks, clothes, and what looked like an old tapestry.

"Careful, Hweilan," said Menduarthis. "This one's a trickster."

She peeled back and tossed aside the thick fabrics with the tip of her knife. At first there were just more of the same, then she came across a long tassel, a bit of rope that looked fit only for burning, then under an old leather jerkin was a familiar bundle. One of Lendri's belt pouches. The larger one. She grabbed it and opened it. Inside was a whetstone, bowstrings, arrowheads, a few wooden phials stopped with tightly rolled felt, and a ring. Not gold. Darker and redder. More like copper, with darker etchings all around it. The ring he had used to summon the fire for Scith's pyre. She closed the pouch and tucked it under her belt.

Digging through more clothes and another bit of tapestry, she found her old knife and her father's bow. She gasped with relief, tears welling in her eyes. She slipped the knife into her boot, sheathed the new blade Menduarthis had given her, and cradled the bow to her chest.

Standing and turning to face Menduarthis, she wiped the tears from her eyes. "It's here. Everything I need."

"Good." Menduarthis looked down on Roakh. "Now, back to business."

He raised his hand, his fingers twirling, and Roakh's eyes went wide. "No! You promised!"

"And I'm a liar," said Menduarthis, a stiff breeze already wafting through the room. "Even if I could trust you not to go cawing off to the queen the moment we leave—and I can't do that, can I?—the truth is I never liked you, you conniving, greedy, gluttonous little bastard. You've had this coming for a long time, and I am going to enjoy myself."

Roakh clamped his jaw shut again and grabbed his nose. Tears streamed out of his eyes. The air in the room moved, eddying currents twisting every which way and then coalescing around the two men.

But then another sound broke through the howling of the wind in the chamber. Horns. From outside. Dozens of them at least. Not the brass sound of the horns of Highwatch Hweilan knew so well. These had a lower, howling sound.

"What is that?" Hweilan asked.

"Ujaiyen clarions," said Menduarthis, and he dropped his hand. The air stopped dead in the room, though bits of it still seemed to be playing in Menduarthis's hair. Even the howling of the storm outside seemed to have hushed.

The horns continued, and amid them Hweilan could hear the cries of voices in the distance.

"We're under attack," said Menduarthis.

Guric spent the evening in prayer. The longest time he had ever done so since his knighthood—and the first time since Valia's death. The small shrine devoted to Torm was set in a bit of the mountain near the gardens where most of the High Warden's family had once had their apartments.

In the sacking of Highwatch, the shrine had been robbed of its gold, the jewels pried from the statues, and the silver chalice of the altar itself was long gone. Probably in some Creel chief's tent. But Guric had not allowed the altar to be desecrated. At the time, he wasn't sure why. But now, he was glad.

He did not feel at peace. Only death would bring him peace now. But at least he felt determined.

Where it had all gone wrong, he still didn't know, and if Torm knew, the god was silent. Guric knew his own center had never been right since Valia's death. But he often wondered if her death was Torm's judgment for Guric's defiance of his father, his family, and their house. In his heart of hearts, he did not believe that. Torm demanded justice, but there was no malice in his judgments. No, Guric believed his life had come to ruin at one critical juncture: Argalath.

Had Argalath used Guric from the beginning? Deceived him? Or did the man honestly see good in the horrors he had wrought? In the end, it didn't really matter. The man had to be stopped.

Guric's guards fell into step behind him as he left the shrine and crossed the winter-bare garden. Guric stopped in the middle of the garden and looked around. The ivy climbing the walls was brown, the branches on the bushes black and leafless. How fitting, Guric thought. He turned his attention to Boran and said, "Gather ten more guards. Men you trust. Hemnur and Isidor." He hesitated. "And Sagar."

"Sagar?" Boran whispered and looked at the other guards, standing a respectful distance away. "You're certain, my lord? His loyalty——"

"I have no faith in Sagar's loyalty to me," said Guric. "But I am quite certain of his . . . antipathy for others."

Boran's eyebrows rose, and he looked around. Not gathering his thoughts. He seemed to be searching for spies. "You mean——"

"You know who I mean. No need to speak it."

"If I may . . ." Boran swallowed, and Guric saw that a fine sheen of sweat had broken out on his brow. "For what am I gathering these men?"

"Nothing more than a walk, I hope," he said. "But they should come armed. Just in case."

• • ⊚ • •

Guric, fourteen guards at his back, stood before the arched doorway that led to the southern tower where Valia had been housed. Every guard had a sword at his belt, two carried axes in their hands, and every one wore mail and helm.

Two Nar guards had been here before. Now, nothing. The archway stood empty. Unguarded. Guric did not know whether to feel relief or dread. It delayed a possible confrontation with Argalath's men. But that Valia's chamber was unguarded . . .

A thin curtain of dread draped itself over Guric's mind,

and for the first time since leaving his prayers, he felt his determination cracking.

He turned to Boran. "I want you, Isidor, and two others with me. Everyone else, guard this entrance. No one comes in or out without my leave. And I mean *no one*. Understood?"

The men bowed.

Boran said, "Yes, my lord," and chose two men to accompany them. The axemen.

Guric's unease grew as they mounted the stairs. Something was not right. No lamps or torches burned in the sconces. It was cold enough in the tower that their breath steamed before them, and the sounds of their footfalls echoed against profound emptiness.

Long before they reached the top, Guric began to suspect. But before they rounded the final bend in the stairs to the top platform and the door, he knew.

No guards stood vigil on the platform. The door to her cell stood open. The chamber beyond still held a foul reek, but nothing stirred within. Even the rats had forsaken the chamber.

Valia was gone.

· · ⑥ · ·

Guric rejoined the rest of the guards at the bottom of the stairway. Seeing the fury on his face, they stepped back. Two bowed their heads and did not look up.

"Did anyone try to come this way?" Guric asked.

"No one, my lord."

Guric turned to Boran. He opened his mouth, then shut it again, reconsidering. He'd been about to say, *We must find Argalath. Now.*

But no. He would not go to Argalath, making demands and begging like a cur under his master's table.

No.

Argalath would come to him.

"My lord?" said Boran. "What are your orders?"

"I am going to my chambers. I want a flagon of wine

waiting for me when I get there. Before I am finished draining the dregs, I want Argalath in front of me."

Sagar smiled. "I'll fetch him, my lord."

CHAPTER TWENTY-SIX

"UNDER ATTACK?" SAID HWEILAN.

"Those clarions," said Menduarthis. "That is the call to arms. Something has come into the realm of Kunin Gatar."

Hweilan felt it then. The pulsing at the back of her skull. Not strong yet, but steady as a drumbeat. She had not felt it since . . .

And she knew who it was.

"Soran," she said. "That . . . that thing that looks like my uncle. It's him. I know it."

Roakh tried to laugh, but it came out more of a cough, and black blood dribbled out on his cheek. "Haak! They'll be coming for you, Menduarthis. Your Ujaiyen. And for me. You to lead your scouts. Me to . . . do what I do. They'll be coming. They'll . . . find you. See what y—"

Menduarthis kicked him again. Then he looked to Hweilan. "He's right. If we're under attack, the queen's hound and her favorite snoop will soon be summoned."

Roakh coughed up more blood, then began to roll away from Menduarthis, closer to the shelves.

"Where are you going, old bird?" Menduarthis asked. He bent down to turn the man over.

But Roakh rolled back on his own, and as he did so he used his unbroken arm to punch at Menduarthis.

Menduarthis jumped back, laughing, and said, "What do you th——?"

And then something struck him in the face. It hadn't been a punch from Roakh after all. A throw.

The small brown bag bounced off Menduarthis's forehead, surprising him more than anything, but as it did so, its contents spilled out in a cloud of white powder.

"Wha——?" said Menduarthis, then he screamed and slapped at his face. He lurched backward, stumbling as his knees gave way, then fell face first on the floor. Only the bundle of junk saved him from cracking his head on the stone.

Hweilan screamed, "Menduarthis!"

"Don't worry," said Roakh, as he pushed himself to his feet. "He's not . . . dead." He coughed, and a fine spittle of blood flew out of his mouth. "Not after what he's done. Death's"—he took in a deep breath, and Hweilan could hear the broken, wet rattle in his chest—"too quick . . . for him. Now, what shall we do with you?"

One twisted arm hung limp and useless by Roakh's side. He tried to move it, winced in pain, then gave up. He took a big step to Hweilan, almost slipped on all the detritus littering the floor, then leaned against the near shelf.

"Keep away from me!" said Hweilan, and she thrust the bow in front of her, holding it crossways like a staff. She glanced over her shoulder to the still open window. Beyond was the ledge, and after that a drop of a good forty feet or more. Too high.

"Half a . . . moment!" Roakh coughed up more blood. He turned and used his good hand to rummage through the shelf behind him. An old plate fell to the floor and shattered. He turned back to Hweilan. Still leaning on the shelf for support, he now held a small phial in his trembling fist. Wincing at the pain, he used his teeth to pull the cork, spat it out, then drank the contents of the phial.

Roakh screamed—an agonized shriek that caused

Hweilan to take an involuntary step back. He fell back onto the remains of the table where he had received his beating. His back arched. He hammered the floor with one fist, his scream growing into a ravenlike cry. Then, like the tension leaving a cut string, he collapsed.

For an instant, Hweilan thought—hoped—Roakh was dead.

But then he took a deep draught of air and sat up. He moved his right arm. It was no longer broken. He made a tight fist then wiggled his fingers.

"Ahh." Roakh chuckled and looked at Hweilan. "Much better. Still not quite hale as ever." His smile widened. The sharp teeth had mended, though blood from his previous wounds still smeared his face and mouth. In the fading light, it looked black against his gray skin. "A good meal will mend that, I think," he said, and pushed himself to his feet.

"Stay away!" Hweilan said, and raised her bow in both hands, like a club.

Roakh's smile melted, his face losing all semblance of emotion, and he cocked his head to one side. Like a raven. A raven scavenging the quiet battlefield, disturbed only by the endless drone of flies and the caws of his fellows. He charged her.

Hweilan screamed and swung the bow.

He laughed and caught the bow in one hand, the wood striking his palm with a loud slap. He tightened his grip, twisted, and yanked the bow from her hands. Hweilan tried to hang on to it, but he was too strong—unbelievably strong, considering his small stature and almost frail frame—and he almost pulled her off her feet.

Roakh caught her. She pushed at him, and again he used her own strength against her, throwing her across the room. Her back struck the wall under the window, knocking every last bit of breath from her body, then she hit the floor, and bright lights danced before her eyes.

Her vision cleared. Roakh advanced on her. She screamed

and scrambled to her feet. A forty-foot drop suddenly seemed a lot more inviting than it had a few moments ago.

She was halfway out the window when Roakh grabbed her, threw her to the ground, and put his full weight on top of her. He didn't weigh more than a child, but his strength was incredible. She aimed a backhanded punch at his face, but he caught her wrist and pinned it to the ground beside her head. She tried to bring her left arm around, but it was pinned beneath his leg.

Roakh opened his mouth, dark spittle fell down onto her cheek, and his teeth lunged down. Hweilan screamed, still unable to move her hands, and twisted beneath him. Strong as Roakh was, he was still much lighter than Hweilan, and she managed to get him halfway off her. His jaws snapped shut, barely missing her face and instead closing around a mouthful of hair. He growled and spat it out.

Hweilan's right arm was still pinned under his grip, but she'd wormed her left free. Rather than aiming another useless punch, she raised her knee and thrust her hand inside her boot. With the glove on, it took her a moment to find the knife. She managed to wrap three fingers around the hilt and pull, the knife coming halfway out.

Roakh used his free hand to grab a handful of Hweilan's hair. He gripped and yanked, turning her head to expose her throat.

Hweilan grabbed the hilt.

His lips wet with blood and drool, Roakh lunged.

Hweilan drew the knife. Her leg and arm were twisted at such an angle that the blade sliced through her trousers and nicked the skin beneath as it came free.

Sharp teeth and warm, wriggling flesh, like grave worms, hit her throat.

Hweilan screamed and stabbed upward.

Roakh shrieked, the sound deafening so close to her ear, and his teeth scraped away skin and flesh as he flung himself away.

Hweilan rolled to her feet and looked down. Dark blood drenched the entire length of the knife and much of the glove holding it. Roakh leaned against the opposite wall, both hands clutching his side just below his ribs. Blood wasn't leaking out from between his fingers. It was *pouring*.

"You stabbed me, you——!" Roakh pulled his hands away, twisting them into claws, and lunged.

Hweilan dodged sideways and swept the knife in front of her. She was too frightened to aim, to think of anything more than keeping the monster away from her. But the knife sliced one arm, opening another deep gash.

Roakh twisted and came after her.

She brought the blade around again, stabbing this time instead. She felt the shock up her entire arm as the point slid between two ribs, the blade catching there a moment before the force of Roakh's charge twisted the blade, forcing it in deeper.

They fell. One of Roakh's clawed hands went for Hweilan's throat while the other batted at her knife hand. She screamed through clenched teeth, desperate to keep hold of the knife, and pushed him with her free hand as they hit the floor. It forced Roakh away, the blade coming out with another gush of hot blood.

"You——!" Roakh screamed, and there was desperation as well as fear and anger in his eyes now.

But Hweilan gave him no time to finish. All the rage and fear of the past days——her family massacred; chased by Nar and some monster wearing her uncle's face; captured, having her mind violated by a capricious queen; and this foul creature putting his wet, slavering mouth on her——all the railing against her powerlessness and the injustice of the world . . . all of Hweilan's terror and rage twisted and tightened into a tight cord, humming and vibrating under the tension.

And then snapped.

She fell on Roakh, the knife rising and falling again and again, sometimes hitting bone and scraping away, tearing more skin and cloth than flesh. But others sinking deep. First into the soft flesh where his neck met his shoulder. The blade sank all the way in, and Roakh's black eyes went wide with shock and his mouth opened in a silent scream. She yanked it out, blood spraying over her, and then brought it down again and again and again, ravaging his neck and face.

She was still stabbing and pulling, stabbing and pulling, stabbing and pulling, long after Roakh stopped moving.

"Hweilan!"

A strong hand caught her wrist.

She shrieked and twisted, lunging after her new attacker.

"Hweilan, enough!" Menduarthis said as Hweilan came down on top of him.

She lay there, panting. The scarf on her head had been ripped off in the fight, blood soaked her hair, and it hung in matted lanks in front of her face. The knife, raised over her head and ready to plunge into Menduarthis's face, was trembling, and a steady drip-drip-drip of blood fell off the blade and pattered onto the floor.

Menduarthis still had bits of the powder on his face, and his lovely blue eyes were shot through with ugly red veins. Still, he gave her a weak smile and said, "I see my knife proved useful."

Hweilan slid off him and onto her knees. She clutched the knife to her chest in both hands, not caring in the least about the gore covering it.

"Lendri's," she said. She held the knife up. "Lendri's knife."

Now that her breath was coming easier and the hammering in her heart was slowing, she heard the horns again. She opened her mouth to ask, *What are we going to do?* But then her gaze caught the mangled mess that had once been Roakh.

She dropped the knife, fell forward on her hands, and vomited all over the floor.

Menduarthis let her finish, then pulled her gently to her

feet and held her against his chest.

"I killed him." He throat and mouth ached from the burning bile.

Menduarthis brushed the bloody hair out of her face and said, "The world is a better place without the little bastard. He can plague the Nine Hells with his chatter now."

She pushed Menduarthis away and retrieved her knife. Considering the bloody wreck of her clothes, it seemed pointless to clean the knife, but she did, kneeling down and wiping away the blood on an old curtain. The sounds of horns still wafted through the air.

"Hweilan, you're bleeding," said Menduarthis. He knelt beside her and gently turned her face aside. "I didn't notice it at first because of the *halbdol*."

She had completely forgotten about Roakh's bite, but now that Menduarthis had mentioned it, she could feel a throbbing sting along the left side of her throat, just below her jaw line.

"How bad is it?" She gave a sharp intake of breath at his touch.

"Nasty, but it looks like more torn skin than anything. We'll need to clean it. Come. But triple-quick. We *must* hurry."

He helped her to her feet and through the door. Beyond was an even larger room, a round door on the opposite wall, littered with even more piles of Roakh's possessions. Windowless, the room would have been black as starless midnight if not for one iron lamp hung from the ceiling. What sort of fire or magic lit it, Hweilan had no idea, but it cast sickly blue light throughout the room, casting all the piles and tables as little islands in pools of shadow.

One other object in the room cast its own light—a wide basin, crafted from some precious metal and encrusted with hundreds of jewels. The rim glowed vibrant green, the light rippling off the fluid filling the basin.

"What is that?" said Hweilan.

"Just a washbasin," said Menduarthis, "which you sorely need."

Together, they washed the worst of the gore out of Hweilan's hair. No matter how much blood stained the water, a swirl from Menduarthis's finger, and the water cleared again. Whether this was some trick of the basin itself or one of Menduarthis's spells, Hweilan couldn't bring herself to care. She'd just hacked a person to death. When she closed her eyes, she could still feel the shock traveling up her arm as each blow of the blade landed—the instant of resistance as the steel passed through flesh, or the harder strike of glancing off bone. His screams . . . Hweilan shuddered. No, it was when the screams had stopped and she'd kept hacking away. That had been the worst.

Hweilan's knees trembled, and then her legs gave out, depositing her on the floor. Lendri's knife, which she had completely forgotten she was still holding, clattered to the floor beside her. She would have retched again if anything remained in her stomach.

"Are you hurt?" Menduarthis asked, as he knelt beside her.

"I . . . I killed him, Menduarthis. I killed Roakh."

"That you did. He is most certainly dead."

Her body was shaking. She hugged herself tight but couldn't make it stop.

"Hey." Menduarthis grabbed both her shoulders and shook her. Not hard, but enough to get her attention. "Now, listen to me. It was him or you. Believe that. True, you did get a bit . . . carried away. One sloppy mess you made of the old bird. But it was your first time. A little more practice, and you'll be a cold killer."

She looked up at him. He was smiling. Not with his usual sardonic amusement. Something almost like genuine good will.

Her body was still shaking, but she managed to give him a faint grin in return. "It . . . it wasn't my first time."

His eyebrows shot up. "Really? Well, that sounds like a tale. But at the moment, Hweilan, we've got to survive today. Now let's get out of here. We've lingered too long already."

Menduarthis stood and extended a hand to help her up.

She grabbed his arm and stood. "Where are we going?"

"Those horns are coming from across the river, which means that whoever is attacking either came through the main portal or from that direction, which means that the Ujaiyen, the uldra, the eladrin, the elves, the everyone, they'll be scrambling to hunt down the invaders. That whole area will be thick with fey out for blood. But there are other ways out of here. We avoid being noticed and slip through in the confusion. Everyone will be looking for trouble coming in. Not trouble getting out."

She looked down at her clothes. Despite Menduarthis's efforts, the once-fine cloth was spattered in blood, and she was a solid black mess from her left elbow down. "Avoid being noticed? Look at me."

"Hm. I see your point. Wait here."

Menduarthis returned to the first room and soon returned carrying her father's bow and the red silk scarf he had given her. It was still clean.

"Cover your hair with this. You huddle under that cloak and cowl, nice and snug, and I'll give you a good coating of snow. Carrying the bow, you'll pass a quick look for one of us."

"And a longer look?"

"It's the best we can do under the circumstances."

She pulled her hair back and covered it with the scarf, knotting it in a sort of cap that would both keep her hair out of her eyes and hide the tops of her ears. Looking down to do so, she saw the knife she'd dropped on the floor. Lendri's knife. She picked it up.

She removed all the blood she could from Lendri's blade, but much of it had soaked into the leather wrapped around the hilt. Looking at the knife, looking at *Lendri's* knife, it came to her then. Even if they could make it out of Kunin Gatar's realm, she had nowhere to go. The most she could hope for among the Damarans was a life in hiding and the security of wedding some minor lord. A hunted woman with no lands, no riches, no dowry, she'd be lucky to bed some minor duke's man-at-arms. A friendly tribe of Nar? She'd do little better there. If Lendri was to be believed, the Vil Adanrath were gone . . .

Lendri.

She couldn't leave him. She knew it now. Not after everything he had done for her. The knife he'd given her had saved her life, and he himself had done so at least twice, risking his own life for hers. Was he using her as Menduarthis said? Perhaps. But if so, she needed to hear it from his own lips. Look into his eyes as he admitted it. And then—

A life on the run with Menduarthis? To what end? Where? And how soon before he expected to share her blankets in return for helping her?

"No," she said.

"No what?" said Menduarthis, his voice equal parts exasperation and fear.

"We can't leave yet. Not without Lendri."

Menduarthis's jaw dropped, shut again, and he laughed. "You're serious?"

"I'm not leaving without him."

"He's *using* you, Hweilan!"

"I won't forsake him unless I hear that from his own lips."

Menduarthis turned and kicked a pile of junk on the floor. Jewelry, utensils, an old shoe, and a few books went flying. He kicked another pile for good measure, toppled a small table, and screamed, "Are you serious?"

Hweilan opened her mouth to answer, but the sound of pounding cut her off. she could hear voices yelling outside, though they were too faint, the door too thick, for her to understand. But then she heard one, raised above all the others. "Roakh!"

"Gods buck my bottom, they've come for him," said Menduarthis. His eyes were round and shiny as new-minted coins.

"What do we do?" Hweilan whispered.

Menduarthis paced the room, muttering to himself the whole time, kicking aside piles of clothes as he went. Mice scuttled squeaking from a few of them. He ran out of piles to kick at the wall, then came back toward Hweilan, shoving Roakh's belongings aside as he went.

"What are you doing?" she said.

"Looking. Help me!"

"Looking for what?"

He kicked a large pile of robes, clothes, and old tassels aside, and said, "This!"

Hweilan stepped over, and Menduarthis pulled at an old iron ring set in the floor. A hidden door swung upward, revealing a ladder leading down into darkness.

"Roakh?" said a voice from the other room. Someone had come in through the window, the same as Menduarthis had.

"Where was it Roakh said Lendri is?" Menduarthis whispered.

"The Thorns?"

"The Thorns it is then. In you go." Menduarthis motioned to the ladder.

From the other room came a loud cry. *"Roakh! Aivilulta! Aivilulta! Roakh aiviluldulaik!*

In she went.

"WAIT HERE A MOMENT," SAID MENDUARTHIS, HIS voice scarcely above a whisper. "Don't make a sound."

He turned away and shuffled off around a bend in the tunnel. Hweilan was still trying to catch her breath, and she could hear little beyond the hammering of her own heart.

After their frantic flight down the ladder from Roakh's dwelling, Menduarthis had led Hweilan through a series of tunnels. For a while, they had been followed by the sounds of pursuit—light footsteps and the occasional shout. And once their pursuers had come close enough for Hweilan to catch the faint green glow of the lights they held. But then a strong breeze had shot through the tunnel—Menduarthis working his magic—and they scuttled quick as they dared down a series of steps and through a series of several quick turns. It had worked, and there had been no sounds of pursuit since.

They kept on for a long while after that, no longer running but keeping a quick pace. Hweilan's eyes strained, hungry for light, but there was only the dark, intense cold, and the sounds of their own footsteps. In places, Hweilan could feel fresh air against her skin as they passed fissures in the rock. But full night must have fallen outside, for no light leaked through. They walked in utter darkness, Menduarthis keeping a first grip on her cloak.

But then Hweilan realized she could see again. At first she thought it was only a trick of her eyes—the swirling lights and shadows that dance before everyone's sight at times. But no. It was not clear or distinct, but there was no mistaking the shape of Menduarthis before her—a solid blackness in front of only a slightly-less-than-black background. The farther they went, the stronger the light became. It was only moon and starlight, but so hungry were her eyes for even the tiniest fragment of light that by the time they neared the end of the tunnel, Hweilan could see quite well.

She heard furtive movement, and Menduarthis stepped back around the bend. He saw her and said, "All clear, as near as I can tell. Come."

Hweilan followed him out of a cave mouth only slightly larger than the door in Roakh's floor. She had to crouch to get through, and the back of her cloak scraped on icicles. She stood and was struck at the cold brilliance of the night. The storm clouds had broken, and only a few tattered remnants remained—black ribbons tinged almost white by the brilliance of the moon rising over distant mountains. Only a thin crescent, but it was huge, far larger than any moon Hweilan had ever seen, and its silver light was almost painful to her eyes. A million stars rode the sky. Under their combined light, the snow and ice of the world around her shone a brilliant blue, broken only by the black of winter bare trees and jagged rocks.

The cave from which they emerged wormed out of a broad riverbank, but the river itself was a jumble of ice rolling down a gentle slope. Presumably a smaller offshoot of the great river whose fall formed the main gates of Ellestharn. But rather than the sharp cliff of the palace, this bit of the river had taken more of a boulder-riding journey than a fall, before freezing, seemingly in an instant.

Nothing moved for as far as Hweilan could see. Even the wind had died.

"Where are we?" she whispered, and her breath fell as snow before her.

"Downriver from Ellestharn," said Menduarthis. He stood beside her, his gaze roaming over the wide valley before them, his face creased with concern.

"What's wrong?"

"The horns," said Menduarthis. "They've stopped."

"Is that bad?"

"Perhaps. It could mean that they've caught whoever was causing the trouble. Or it could mean all the watches are set, and the entire force of the Ujaiyen is waiting in ambush."

She followed his gaze, imagining the woods lining each side of the valley and every boulder hiding watching eyes. And there was something else. Something she had first felt in the Giantspires with Lendri. That pounding in the base of her skull, mingled with a growing dread. The way she imagined some animals could sense bad weather on the way. A heaviness. An itch. And it was growing stronger by the moment.

"I think we need to go now," she said.

Menduarthis still didn't move. Didn't even look at her. There was an edge to his voice when he said, "You're sure about this? About going after Lendri?"

"He saved my life. Twice."

"For his own reasons. He's *using* you."

She looked down at her hands, at the bow she held, already gathering a coat of frost from her breath. Were it not for Lendri, she would be some Creel bandit's slave right now, and her father's bow long gone.

"If that's true," she said, "I have to hear it from him."

"*If?*" Menduarthis's jaw clenched and his eyes went narrow as slits, though he still didn't look at her. "That's it, then? You don't believe me?"

She considered a moment, then said, "Much of what you

say rings true. Most, in fact. But damn it, Menduarthis, the man saved me from death and worse. If he is using me, perhaps there is more to it than you know. And even if there isn't, I have to hear it from his lips before I forsake him. I owe him that."

Menduarthis muttered something in his own language that sounded less than flattering.

"You can find him?" she asked. "You know where these . . . thorns are?"

"*The* Thorns," said Menduarthis, "and yes, I do."

"So we can find Lendri?"

"We?"

"You promised to help me."

"Escape. I promised to help you *escape,* not kill one of Kunin Gatar's chief servants, then deliver you to her with silk in your hair."

"*You* were going to kill him!" she said.

Menduarthis hissed and waved his hands at her. "Quiet, quiet. Sound travels far out here." He dropped his own voice to just above a whisper and finally looked at her. "True enough, though. I was. And then I was going to run fast and far away. Not run off rescuing the one person Kunin Gatar has dreamed of killing for years!"

"So you won't help me?"

"Why should I?"

"He's kin to me."

Menduarthis snorted. "No. He's blood brother to some distant forebear of yours. Hardly a favorite uncle."

"And blood oaths mean nothing to you?"

"Don't know. I've never been damned fool enough to make one."

"Very well," she said. "I'll do it on my own."

Menduarthis grabbed her shoulder. "Hold a moment! At least answer my question before trotting off to your untimely death."

Her hands stopped halfway to her hood. "What question?"

He smiled. The mischievous boy smile again. "Why should I help you?"

She tucked the ends of her hair into the hood and raised it. "Get to the point. What do you want?"

"For helping you steal from the queen and rescue an honor-obsessed elf?"

"Yes."

"A kiss."

Hweilan felt her cheeks and ears flushing and was very glad for the deep hood and the dark *halbdol* masking her skin. "That's it? Just a kiss?"

"Well, it's a start. But that's all I'll obligate to you."

"Very well," she said. "Get me to Lendri, then help us to get out again, and *afterward,* I will . . . kiss you."

"Us? Get us out? You mean you, me, and Lendri?"

"That's going to depend very much on what Lendri has to tell me."

• • ◎ • •

They took their time getting down the slope of the hill and into the valley proper. Menduarthis kept them to the shadows of the wood, going from shadow to shadow until they reached the wide expanse of the frozen river.

He stopped and gave Hweilan a chance to catch her breath. "This is where things get tricky," he said.

"How do you mean?"

He pointed across the river. It was hard to be certain by moon- and starlight, but it looked to be close to a mile across. A mile of flat snow and ice, with no cover. "We have to cross that," he said.

"Why is that bad?" Hweilan asked. "Is this ice thin?"

"Thin? Ha. No. Solid ice straight to the bottom, I'd wager. But we'll have no cover. Anyone watching for as far as eyes can see will see us—and many have eyes out there that are much sharper than mine." Menduarthis sighed. "We go. Quick, but not too quick. We want to look urgent, but not hurried. And if we do come across someone—or they come across us—you let me do the talking. *All* the talking, mind you."

Hweilan nodded.

"And one more thing. Where we're going . . . , the Thorns. Not a nice place. Not nice at all. I'll do my best for you, Hweilan, but no promises. We may not be able to get through there, much less get Lendri out. Not if the guards have been warned against me."

"You think they are? Looking for you I mean?"

He shrugged. "We know they've found Roakh. And since they don't know where I am or where you are . . . add to that the little trick I played back in the tunnels, and it won't take long for our people to start wanting to ask me a lot of questions. Much depends on how far word has spread and how fast."

The heaviness in her mind was almost pounding now. Hweilan could feel it, right behind her eyes.

"We need to go," she said. "Now."

They left the trees, hopped down the final bit of the embankment, and set off across a mile of frozen river.

They tried to run, but with no snow shoes and almost a foot of new snow covering the ice, the best they could manage was a quick shuffle, pushing their way through and sending waves of powdery white pluming in front of their knees.

Hweilan kept her eyes fixed on the dark line of woods ahead, fearing at any moment to see signs of movement. Once, she thought she saw a shape pass in front of the moon, but if so, it was either very small or very far away, and she could not find it against the night sky.

They were about halfway across when a great noise broke the silence. Not just horns this time, but horns, howls, and cries, wafting out of the distance to their right.

Menduarthis stopped in his tracks, listening.

"What is that?" said Hweilan.

"Kunin Gatar has returned to Ellestharn."

"Is that good or bad?"

"If we get out of here soon, it doesn't matter. Move."

They kept on, Menduarthis pushing them faster now. Hweilan's legs and back were beginning to ache, but she knew they couldn't stop. Not until they were well away from Kunin Gatar's realm.

The snow began to get shallower as they neared the far side. Most of the storm's fury seemed to have struck the palace side of the river. The bank and nearest trees were only a stone's throw away, and still there were no signs of pursuit. Hweilan believed they might actually make it. Still . . . that nagging weight in her mind seemed to grow with every step.

Looking at the dark line of the trees before her, the dream from days ago hit her again, not simply as a memory, but as an assault on her senses.

The smell—foul, putrid, rotting.

The black wolf, its yellow eyes suddenly brighter than the moon in her mind's eye, its voice—Run!

Laughter, devoid of all goodwill. The giggle of a girl ripping the wings of a butterfly. The eager smile of a boy, tearing the legs off a grasshopper and heading for the anthill.

Singing. Sweet voices. True melody. All set to blasphemies.

The motherly voice—

Death comes . . . be sure of it.

It hit her with such force that she stumbled, for a moment her mind separate from her body. She fell in the snow, her father's bow striking her painfully in the ribs.

"Hweilan?" Menduarthis's voice. "Are you—?"

She heard them before she saw them. Something large—or more likely many large somethings—breaking through the brush, and the sounds of many heavy hooves churning through snow. When the herd broke out of the woods just upriver from them, Hweilan actually felt the ice vibrating under their feet. Running against the dark backdrop of the forest, Hweilan could not make out what they were at first, but as they came out onto the snow-covered ice, she saw huge antlers crowning the herd. Swiftstags?

If so, they were the largest she had ever seen.

"Stay calm," said Menduarthis as he helped her to feet. "Act like we're going about our business. And remember, *I* do all the talking."

Hweilan opened her mouth to ask how he planned on talking to giant deer, but then she saw them. The creatures were almost upon them now, the sound of their hooves on the ice like slow thunder. She thought she saw nine, though it was hard to tell through the great cloud of snow and frost churned up by their legs. Every one of them bore a rider, and every rider carried weapons.

The herd split into a V formation to surround Menduarthis and Hweilan. As they rode past, spraying her and Menduarthis with snow, she saw the riders' pale faces turn to watch her. Beautiful, lean faces, but solemn. Starlight played off the frost in their dark hair—elves. She saw two carrying bows, but most bore long, black spears.

Menduarthis stood unmoving as the ring of creatures closed around them. Not swiftstags after all, but something like them. Draped in shaggy fur, the smallest of the beasts was easily seven feet tall at the shoulder, and their antlers, which ended in curved points, spread more than ten feet across, so that as their masters turned them to face Hweilan and Menduarthis, the beasts had to stand well apart. Their breath froze as they panted, painting Menduarthis and Hweilan in fine frost.

Hweilan looked wistfully past them. They'd been so close. The embankment and nearest trees were only a few dozen feet beyond the riders.

"Menduarthis?" said one of the riders, as he slid off the back of his mount and approached them. He held a spear in one hand, and he didn't even have to duck to make it under the antlers. He was nearly the same height as Menduarthis, but leaner, his features sharper, and his ears ended in an upward curve. Definitely an elf. He stopped a few paces away and said something to Menduarthis in his own tongue.

Menduarthis answered in kind, then said, "I am taking this one to the Thorns."

The elf glanced at Hweilan and scowled. "Why do you speak the vulgar tongue?"

"She goes to the Thorns." Menduarthis gave Hweilan a sly smile over his shoulder. "I wish to remind her of it."

"Why?"

"Pain tastes sweeter if it is seasoned with fear."

The elf's scowl deepened as his eyes lit on her bow, and his fist tightened around the haft of his spear. "You are taking her to the Thorns, but she goes armed?"

"It is my bow," said Menduarthis. "She bears it because I command her to carry it."

"You have no bow like this."

Menduarthis shrugged. "Recent spoils."

"Indeed?" The elf lowered his spear and used its point to peel the heavy fur cloak back from Hweilan. Several of the other elves, still on their mounts, tensed. One of the bowmen reached for an arrow. "Word flies on the wings that Roakh lies murdered in his roost. And here is this one, covered with blood. Recent spoils, you say. Spoils from where? Where *exactly*, Menduarthis?"

"You accuse me?"

The elf pulled his spear back and planted its butt in the snow. "Accuse? No. But . . . you never liked Roakh. That much is known. He lies dead, with you nowhere to be found. Until now. And I find you with a captive covered with blood. You can explain this?"

"I can," said Menduarthis. "But not to you . . . Tirron, is it? I don't answer to you."

"You may not answer to me, Hound. But I answer to Kunin Gatar, and she orders any who find you to bring you to her at once. So you will come with us. Both of you. Nicely"—five spears lowered in their direction, Hweilan heard creaking wood as the bowmen drew feathers to cheeks, and Tirron smiled—"or otherwise."

Menduarthis bristled, his back straightening, and he gave Tirron his best withering stare. "Your orders are old. Kunin Gatar herself ordered me to take this one away. I am taking her to the Thorns. I would demand your aid, but I tire of your insolence. Send us on our way, and I might forget to tell the queen that this happened."

A few of the riders exchanged nervous glances, and Hweilan thought she caught a hint of doubt in Tirron's gaze.

But then the elf looked at her again. She had neglected to close her cloak, and her blood-spattered clothes were still on display for all to see.

"I think not," said Tirron. "Something is amiss here. We will take the matter to the queen."

The heaviness in Hweilan's mind seemed to drop and shatter, shards stabbing her awareness. Not blinding her, but making her incredibly *aware*.

Death comes!

Every shade of light and shadow suddenly seemed clear and sharp as new steel. Every sound—the heavy breathing of the elves' mounts, the crunch of the snow under their hooves, and something . . . something else. Something coming closer. Its footsteps pounding her skull like a hammer.

Scent filled her head. Sweat from her body. The reek of Roakh's blood in her clothes. The musky scent of the huge elklike creatures, and the stink of their breath wafting over her. The wind-through-frosty-pines smell of the elves. And a slow rot, stirred to an agonizing mockery of life by the fire within. Closer . . . closer . . .

She felt every fiber of her clothes against her skin. The greasy coat of *halbdol* on her face. The bite of the cold night air in her throat. The shaking of the ice beneath her feet as some foul dread approached.

And so it was that Hweilan was the first to see it.

A tall, broad figure walked out of the shadow of the wood. Not rushing, but not hesitating either. Hweilan cried out and pointed.

At the same time, the elves' mounts began to snort, toss their heads, and fight the reins of their riders.

One of the riders shouted. *"Tir ened! Tir ened!"*

The figure stepped off the bank, landed on the snow-covered ice below, and continued its advance.

The elves' mounts scattered, forsaking Hweilan and Menduarthis for the moment to assess the newcomer. Tirron, lithe as a deer himself, leaped back onto his mount and turned it to face the newcomer, spear lowered. The huge elklike creatures snorted and fought their reins, and even in the dark Hweilan could see the whites of their eyes, wide and frightened.

"Rí ened!" Tirron shouted. *"Deth! Deth!"* Tirron's mount pranced sideways, spraying snow in every direction as it fought its master's control. *"Liikut! Liikut! Stop!"*

If the figure understood him, it gave no sign, neither slowing nor speeding up, just coming at that same implacable pace.

Tirron's mount had gone well to one side now, and as the snow settled, Hweilan saw the figure's face.

Soran. Or at least the cold mockery of his face. The same grim, square-jawed countenance that looked as if a smile might break it. The deep set eyes. The close-cropped hair. But it was an image only. A likeness. Devoid of all life.

Tirron shouted, *"Hled et!"*

Two arrows hissed through the air. One struck Soran in the chest and bounced away. The other buried itself up to the fletching in his stomach.

He didn't even flinch.

His eyes were fixed on Hweilan. She could feel the gaze burning her, like noonday summer sun. Pace unfaltering, he reached over one shoulder and drew a massive sword from its scabbard.

Two of the elves kicked their mounts into a charge, the great antlers lowered as they closed on Soran. He spared them a glance but did not slow his pace.

The first of the creatures veered at the last moment, and the elf threw his spear. Soran stopped long enough to smash the spear out of the air with his sword, then managed another two steps before the second creature was on him, raking with its sharp antlers.

Soran stopped. One hand brought the sword down on the creature's neck, while the other grabbed the antler. Hweilan heard a crack of breaking bone, a short scream cut off, the smash of bodies colliding, then all was lost in a cloud of snow.

Soran emerged from the settling snow, the broken body of the huge elk lying beside the motionless body of its rider. She could smell the fresh blood wafting off him.

He was less than twenty feet away now, and Hweilan could see his face clearly, even behind the mask of blood and snow. Another arrow struck him, then two more. He didn't even flinch.

"Hweilan?" Menduarthis said, and Hweilan heard fear in his voice.

"Run!" she said.

A spear struck the Soran-thing, hurled with enough force that it threw him off his stride as it pierced him, tearing flesh and shattering ribs.

Menduarthis and Hweilan ran downstream, away from the horror. Her senses were still sharp as a razor, and she heard every hoof breaking through snow, every cry of the elf warriors behind them. She heard a snap and risked a glance over her shoulder.

The Soran-thing still had the broken haft of a spear protruding from his side, but he had either hacked or broken off the spear's length. Seeing his quarry fleeing, he broke into a run. Even wielding the massive sword and bearing wounds that would have killed any man, he came at them incredibly fast. Another of the elves' mounts plowed into him.

"Hweilan, move!" Menduarthis shouted.

She turned and ran, fast as she could.

Menduarthis waved his hand, and a gust of wind struck the snow before them, clearing a wide path. Another wave, and the great cloud of snow swept over and behind them, hiding the battle. She could hear elves and their mounts screaming.

Two more riders were between them and the woods. The nearest seemed content to let them pass, concentrating on the graver foe at hand. But the second reined in his mount just under the boughs.

A pale man, dressed all in skins and furs, white hair flowing behind him, leaped from the tree shadows. A long blade, slightly curved near the end, caught the moonlight and flashed in his hand. The elf didn't see him.

"You two!" the elf called. "Stop or—!"

The pale man passed over the rump of the elklike creature, his sword swinging out beside him, and sliced the elf's head from his body. Elf, swordsman, and a great gout of blood hit the snow at the same time. The elf's mount screamed, almost humanlike in its fright, and bounded away.

The pale man stood and faced them, a smile playing over his lips. He was more than pale. His skin was as white as the snow.

"Kadrigul," Hweilan said.

Menduarthis kept his eyes fixed on the newcomer as he said, "Not another uncle, I hope?"

Kadrigul swiped his sword, cutting the air. "Been awhile since I killed one of your kind."

"Really?" Menduarthis smirked, and his fingers began their intricate motions.

Wind shot past Hweilan. Not a gale. Just a good breeze, but she could feel it narrowing and gathering force as it passed.

"Been awhile since I did this trick," said Menduarthis, "and the lady here ruined my last try."

Kadrigul's chest swelled, and his eyes went wide. He dropped his sword, fell to his knees, and clamped his mouth shut.

"Hmph," said Menduarthis, and twirled his fingers faster.

Kadrigul's nostrils flared, the air whistling as it forced its way in.

"You might want to look away, Hweilan. This can sometimes be a bit m—"

Something dark passed over Hweilan's right shoulder, spraying her with warmth and wetness, there was a *thunk,* and Menduarthis screamed and fell forward—

—the pale man fell on his hands and expelled a great gout of air—

—and Hweilan saw what had hit Menduarthis. An arm. By its size, she knew it had to have come from one of the elf riders.

Hweilan turned and saw Soran coming, black sword in one hand. She drew the knife Menduarthis had given her and stepped in front of Menduarthis. She dropped into a defensive crouch, just like Scith had taught her, and brandished the blade.

A gale swept down the hillside, spraying snow and branches and a million pine needles. It swept over Soran in a flood.

Hweilan felt a tug on her arm. "Don't be a fool, girl!" said Menduarthis. "Run!"

They turned and ran.

Kadrigul was back on his feet, sword in hand, fury in his gaze.

A great ram of air—the strength of a winter gale off mountain heights, but concentrated into the force of a giant's fist—tore through the snow beside Hweilan and struck him. He flew through the air in a cloud of snow and broken ice.

The sounds of a savage fight still raging behind them, Hweilan and Menduarthis ran up the embankment and into the woods.

CHAPTER TWENTY-EIGHT

THE WOODS TANGLED AROUND THEM. HWEILAN HAD never seen such trees, had never imagined such trees. Most grew no more than a few dozen feet, but hardly any grew up. Trunks twisted, turned, bent sideways, and smaller ones even wrapped around their larger neighbors. Deep winter as it was, still dark green leaves grew in abundance, so thick that they had blocked out nearly all the snow—and every trace of star- and moonlight.

Hweilan kept a firm grip on Menduarthis's arm and trusted that her feet would find their own way in the dark. She made it no more than twenty steps into the wood before striking a root or low branch and falling, almost pulling Menduarthis on top of her.

Menduarthis let her go, said, "A moment," and Hweilan could hear him searching his pockets.

Light bloomed, blue and cold, no brighter than a small candle, but in the nearly impenetrable gloom of the wood it seemed very bright to Hweilan's eyes. It shone forth from a round crystal, no larger than an owl's egg, that Menduarthis held in one hand.

In the near distance, an elf's voice cried out in a defiant battle cry, then rose into an agonized shriek.

"*Move,* girl!" Menduarthis pulled her to her feet and they plunged onward.

The land began to climb almost at once. The trees grew larger and even more tangled the farther they went, but Menduarthis always seemed to find a path—ducking under the great arch of a branch, pushing their way through the leaves; finding narrow paths that snaked among the branches; sometimes even running along broad trunks that grew along the ground, like slightly curved roads.

"Careful," said Menduarthis, and Hweilan soon saw why.

They were walking along the wide bole of a tree, but the ground fell away beneath them, the tree forming a natural bridge across a ravine. The sky opened above them, giving enough light for Hweilan to see that the cut in the ground was not that wide, and no more than thirty or forty feet deep. But the trees down there had been choked by vines covered with wicked thorns.

When they reached the other side and stepped off the tree, Menduarthis stopped and turned. Over the sounds of their heavy breathing, they listened for pursuit. Nothing.

Still, that nagging weight, that sense of dread pulsed in Hweilan's mind. It had lessened somewhat in their flight from the frozen river, but now that they'd stopped again . . .

"We need to keep going," said Hweilan.

"Half a moment," said Menduarthis. He pulled her behind him. "And hang on to something."

He stood away from the tree and threw back his cloak. He began waving his arms and hands in an intricate motion, faster and faster. Wind rushed past them, snapping branches and toppling smaller trees in its path.

It struck the tree-bridge. Roots broke and came up with such force that dirt exploded dozens of feet into the air, and the tree itself shattered in the middle. The wind died, and the broken tree fell into the ravine with a crash that shook the ground.

"That should throw off the pursuit," said Menduarthis.

Hweilan wasn't so sure.

More and more vines—their thorns ranging from small, almost furlike protrusions along the creepers to long thorns thick as nails on the stalks—crawled through the trees as Hweilan and Menduarthis climbed the final slope. But the trees themselves didn't seem to suffer. The foliage, rather than lessening, grew even thicker, and in some places Hweilan felt that their path was walled in by leaves and thorns. Menduarthis's light began to catch bits of white in the air. At first, Hweilan thought that it was snowing again, and some few flakes had managed to find their way through the canopy. But no. They were tiny moths, their wings white as new frost. How they managed to survive the cold, Hweilan had no idea. The close air of the woods was warmer than it had been out on the frozen river, but it was still cold enough for Hweilan's breath to steam before her.

Menduarthis stopped, their path seemingly ending in a great tangle of thorns. One hand grasping the little light stone, he turned and looked at Hweilan.

"This gets tricky here," he said. "Once again, you must trust me."

"Trust you how?" she said.

With the hand holding the light, he pointed at the wall of thorns before them. "This is our way."

The vines looked tough as wire, their thorns sharp as wasps' stingers. Even the leaves looked sharp. "You can't be serious," she said.

"Trust me. You'll be safe as a babe in her cradle *as long as you keep moving forward*. Don't stop. Don't slow. And whatever you do, do *not* move backward. As long as you move forward, these creepers are all bark, no bite. Soft as feathers. Stop or try to move backward . . . well, the only thing that'll get you out then is fire, and I don't think you'd like that much."

"Wh-what if I fall?"

"Don't."

She looked back. There was no other way.

"I'll go first," said Menduarthis. "But Hweilan, once I'm in, I can't come back for you. You understand?"

She swallowed hard and nodded.

Menduarthis pushed forward into the vines. They parted before him like smooth waters before a ship, then rustled shut behind him, thick as iron bars. He'd taken the light. Darkness engulfed Hweilan.

"Come along," he called, and she could hear the rustling of his movement.

Hweilan held her father's bow close, pulled her hood down as far as it would go, huddled in the cloak, and pressed forward. Even through all her layers of clothing, she could feel the vines. Not like wire at all. More like . . . snakes. They slithered and undulated around her as she moved forward, the thorns bending, pliable and harmless as feathers, just as Menduarthis had said. Unable to see anything, Hweilan squeezed her eyes shut and pushed onward, step by careful step.

She could still hear Menduarthis ahead.

"How much farther?" she called.

"Not long," he said. "Keep moving!"

She kept moving. Once, the bow caught on a particularly thick branch, and for one terrified moment, caught. Stifling a scream, Hweilan pushed hard. The bow broke through, and the branch snapped back, striking her in the face. Her hood caught most of the blow, but she still felt the branch brush across her nose and cheek. The thick autumnal scent hit her, but the thorns didn't even scratch, and she pressed onward.

Her eyes squeezed shut, her mind concentrating solely on forward, forward, forward, a slow panic began to rise in Hweilan. To fight it, she began counting her steps.

At forty-seven, another vine struck her face, harder this time. Still, the thorns brushed off her skin, but it startled her so that for an instant her step faltered. The vine's thorns stiffened, catching in her hood. A low moan escaped her throat and she surged forward. The thorns caught in her hood, pulling it off her head. She kept going. She heard fabric tearing, then she was through. The feel of the vines and leaves against her face sent her stomach churning, but she pressed on, even faster this time.

"Hweilan?" Menduarthis called, and she could hear the concern in his voice.

"Right behind you. How much farther?"

"Not long."

"You said that. Quite long ago, I'm certain."

"Keep moving."

She took a breath to scream at him, but a sound cut her off. Laughter. Light and gleeful. Almost childish. And very close.

Hweilan opened her eyes. Still she walked in darkness, vines and leaves and thorns thick about her, but she saw eyes watching her. Not the pale blue of the uldra. These eyes glowed verdant green. Two pairs of eyes off to her right, and one very close on her left. Just out of reach, in fact. Seeing her watching them, the watchers laughed, and the eyes were gone.

"Menduarthis!" Hweilan called, panic rising in her voice.

"Keep moving."

"There's something in here with us!"

"Many somethings," said Menduarthis. "Keep moving. We're almost through."

"Curse you, Menduarthis, how much far—?"

She shrieked as she fell forward into open air.

Menduarthis sat on a boulder a few paces away. The vine-wrapped trees still twisted all around them, but the light from Menduarthis's stone showed a small grove with paths branching off in several directions. He gave her a sheepish smile. "Not long," he said.

Then the thorns around them moved, and Hweilan saw that many of them were not thorns at all. At least a dozen figures closed in on them. Some stood on the ground, while others crouched on the thicker branches of the surrounding trees. They stood no taller than uldra, but their skin was green as moss, their meager clothing made up entirely of leaves. They had very narrow chins, almost pointed, tiny noses, and their sharp ears swept back, framed by thick brown or reddish hair that stood off their heads in lanky points. Theirs were the eyes she'd seen. Most held bows, arrows nocked and ready, but one held a sword of sorts in both hands. At least Hweilan thought it was a sword. There was no steel or metal. The entire thing—blade, hilt, handle— seemed made entirely of stiff vines, hundreds of sharp thorns sprouting off the blade.

"No sudden moves," said Menduarthis in Damaran. "Most of them know at least a little Common, so guard your words. Let me speak to them."

"Speak so I can understand you, Menduarthis," the creature with the sword said in Common.

"Forgive me, Grilga. This one"—he pointed to Hweilan— "knows little Common, and none of our speech."

"And who is this one?"

"A captive taken in my last hunt."

"The one who traveled with the Vil Adanrath?"

"That one, yes."

Grilga looked at Hweilan, his eyes narrowing in what she thought was a scowl. "And why is she here now?"

"Kunin Gatar ordered me to let her go."

Grilga's eyes widened, and he looked at Menduarthis. "Let her go?"

"I believe 'Get that creature out of my sight' were her exact words."

"Gods' truth?"

"Gods' truth," said Menduarthis.

"Then why not kill her?"

"Had Kunin Gatar wanted her dead, I'm sure she would have said so—or done it herself. You know as well as I that our beloved queen is seldom unclear on such matters."

The other creatures giggled at this.

"I see blood all over her," said Grilga. "And I smell it on you, Menduarthis. Elf blood. Explain."

"You heard the horns?" said Menduarthis.

"We did. You have news?"

"On the way here, the girl and I met Tirron's riders on the ice. While we were . . . having words"—at this, a few of the creatures laughed softly—"we were attacked. By two. One was a Frost Folk warrior. The other . . . some vile thing I have never seen before. Whether they were the entire invading force or only part, I don't know. But Tirron's riders"—Menduarthis shuddered—"they couldn't stop the thing."

A collective gasp rustled through the group. Even Grilga seemed caught up in the tale.

"I took the girl and ran," said Menduarthis. "I can't be sure, but I think these invaders, whoever they may be, are after her."

All eyes turned to her, and several pulled their bowstrings to a half draw.

Hweilan looked back into the wall of thorns. The weight in her mind was growing heavier again, the pulsing alarm faster.

"Then I ask you again," said Grilga, "why not kill her?"

"Marauders invade our realm," Menduarthis said, anger in his voice, "kill our people, defy our queen, and you suggest we give them what they want? Besides, Kunin Gatar ordered her gone. Until Kunin Gatar orders otherwise, I hear and obey."

Hweilan watched the creatures. They glanced at one another, and every one pointedly avoided looking at Grilga, whose scowl deepened. It struck her how magnificent a liar Menduarthis really was. Everything he'd just told them was the truth. Every word. But the many words he'd left out made all the difference. It made her very glad that she'd insisted on seeing Lendri for herself. Menduarthis had been wounded defending her, and was even now committing treachery against his queen. She had no reason to doubt he was helping her. But why? *I'm bored,* he'd told her, *starting to feel dead.* True? Perhaps. But what truths was he keeping from her?

"If Tirron's people couldn't stop this thing," said Grilga, "and if it is hunting her, then where is it? And what of the Frost warrior?"

"I dealt with that one," said Menduarthis. "The other . . ." He shuddered. "I don't know. I destroyed the Byway Bridge. I'm sorry. I had to. But for all I know, that thing is on its way here right now."

The creatures all went very quiet. They cast furtive glances over their shoulders into the surrounding woods.

"What is this thing?" said Grilga.

Menduarthis glanced at Hweilan, then said, "I don't know. I've never seen its like. He seemed like a man—taller than me, but much stronger. A very formidable-looking fellow. Human by the looks. But I saw him take an arrow and a spear in his body—wounds that would have killed any creature with sense enough to die—and it barely slowed him. He ripped off an elf's arm with his bare hands."

The creatures all looked to their leader. Grilga stood straight, puffing up all of his three-foot height, and said, "Nothing comes through the thornway without our knowing."

The pounding in her head felt like iron hammers now. It was closing in.

She opened her mouth to tell Menduarthis, when hundreds—hundreds of thousands—of the tiny white moths poured out of the thorns, like a fluttering geyser.

Grilga shouted orders. The creatures—all but one—split into groups and shot back into the thorns, quick as squirrels. Hweilan had no idea how they navigated the deadly tangle, but the branches closed around them, the leaves rustled a moment, and they were gone.

Grilga looked at Hweilan, seemed to weigh her in his mind, then said, "My folk will do what we can, but I won't spend their lives on this one. Get her out of here."

"Nothing would give me greater pleasure," said Menduarthis.

Grilga took what looked like a long, thin bone from his belt, set it to his lips, and blew. Hweilan heard nothing, but a shudder seemed to pass through the branches.

"The way is open to you, Menduarthis," he said. "Move fast."

CHAPTER TWENTY-NINE

Guric slumped in his chair. He'd turned it to face the door of his personal chamber, but Argalath still had not come. The flagon dangling from Guric's right hand had been empty a long time. The wine had thickened his head, making him feel warm and the world around him soft, but it had not dampened his ire.

He heard voices. Someone knocked on his door.

"Enter," Guric said. He did not get up, did not even straighten in his chair.

The door opened, and Sagar stepped inside. "He's here, my lord."

"Send him in. Alone. And shut the door behind you."

Sagar turned and left the room. Guric could see more guards, and beyond them, Argalath, head buried deep in his hood against the light. Vazhad and Jatara lurked beyond their master. Argalath entered the room, and Sagar slammed the door behind him.

Argalath bowed. "I come as bidden, my lord."

"Drop your cowl, counselor. I would look at you when you speak."

"The light, my lord . . ."

Guric had ordered the hearth packed full of wood and blazing, every lamp in the room lit, and more candles brought in. One might have thought it was High Festival by the look of things.

"Then close your eyes. I like to look at a man when he lies to me."

Argalath laid the palm of one hand against his chest and bowed even deeper. "You wound me, my lord."

"Drop that cowl, damn you!"

Slowly, Argalath straightened and lowered the hood. He squeezed his eyes shut and placed one hand over them. "How have I lied to you, my lord?"

Guric stood. He towered over the spellscarred man by more than a head, but he still found himself hesitant to approach. "I have two questions for you, Argalath, and I want the raw truth. No evasions."

"Might you dampen some of the lamps, my lord?"

"No," said Guric. "Where is my wife?"

Argalath licked his lips. "We have been over this, my lord. I assure you, your beloved's body is being well cared for until we can return her to you."

"*Where* is her body being well cared for?"

"Someplace safe."

"She's down beneath the fortress, isn't she? In those caves. Down there with your other monsters. Isn't she?"

Argalath stepped toward Guric and laid one hand on his shoulder to push him toward the bed. "You sound so tired, my lord. You aren't thinking clearly. Please, take your rest. I will see to everything. If you so wish it, I will have her brought back to the tower at once."

Guric took one step back, his legs crashing into the chair behind him, then smashed the empty wine flagon against Argalath's skull. The baked clay was thick, but it shattered. The man grunted and went down in a tangle of his own robes.

The door slammed open, and Sagar and Isidor rushed in, swords drawn. Jatara stood just outside the door, struggling with two guards, who were keeping her out of the room and preventing her from drawing her sword.

"Do you need assistance, my lord?" said Isidor.

Guric looked down at Argalath, who was rubbing the side of his head and brushing shards of pottery off his shoulder.

"No. Everyone out. If *anyone*"—Guric caught Jatara's gaze—"enters without my word, Sagar, you have my leave to run them through."

Sagar smiled and gave the fallen Argalath a rather disbelieving—and very relieved—glance before following the other guard out. Guric walked past Argalath and shut the door behind them.

Argalath pushed himself unsteadily to his feet.

"What was the other thing you wished to know of me?" Argalath said. His voice lacked his usual deference, and he seemed more angry than hurt.

The first pang of doubt hit Guric, like a little shock at the bottom of his skull. "What?"

"You asked where Valia is," said Argalath. He stood before Guric, eyes still closed, but he stood straight now, not cowering against the light. "But you said you had two questions. What is the other?"

"I trusted you," said Guric. "I trusted you with everything. My life. My future. Everything I had. Even after you turned Valia into that . . . that thing, still I clung to your word. But I was wrong, wasn't I? This was your game all along, wasn't it? Those Nar I saved you from all those years ago, they were right, weren't they? You are a . . . a monster."

"Am I a monster? What is a monster but a trial for the hero in bards' tales? I gave you all you asked for, never asking anything in return. And you are no hero, Guric."

A low growl built in Guric's throat. *No one* had ever spoken to him in such a fashion. Had he been sober, he might have given Argalath a cold laugh and summoned the guards. But the wine had opened his eyes, had showed him that when the really important things of life are at stake—and nothing was more important than his beloved Valia—all the trappings of society, of court, of civilization, all the bows and "by your leaves" were only so much pretty ribbon on an unbroken horse. Pretty it up all you like, the horse still would suffer no master—unless the master broke it.

He had a dagger at his belt. No. Too swift. Guric wanted to beat this monster with his bare hands. He balled both fists and charged.

The patches of pale skin mottling Argalath's skin suddenly flared with cold, blue light, and pain—agony like he had never known, like he had never imagined any one person *could* know—struck Guric in the chest, then radiated outward. He couldn't cry out. Couldn't even draw breath. His entire chest seemed to constrict, and he fell at Argalath's feet. Darkness was closing in around the edges of his vision.

"Guric," said Argalath, "because you have been such a useful tool in my hand, I will answer your last question. And it will be your last. Those men you *rescued* me from all those years ago were doing exactly what I told them to do. They played their roles perfectly."

The pain evaporated, and Guric spent every ounce of his strength drawing breath into his body. He opened his eyes. His vision was clearing, though the room seemed to dance and swirl. All the lamps had gone out. All the candles. Only the fire in the hearth remained, bathing Argalath's robes in a hellish light.

On the other side of the door, he could hear men screaming. The clash of steel on steel.

He looked up at Argalath. The man was smiling.

Guric tried to push himself up, but a new pain struck him, right in the middle of his head.

"That is a vein in your brain bursting," said Argalath. "That warmth, that . . . fuzziness you're feeling is your own blood flooding the inside of your skull. Your own heartbeat is killing you. So, Guric, I will answer your question: Yes. This was my game all along. Thank you for playing."

THIRTY

CHAPTER

Hweilan and Menduarthis crouched in the trees on the top of a small hollow. Menduarthis had put his light away. After leaving Grilga and his band, they had gone swiftly downhill, and the foliage was not as thick down here. Parts of the path were even open to the sky, and there was enough moon and starlight that even Hweilan could see fairly well. A wall of trees and vines ringed the hollow, but farther down, the brush seemed to thin out, and Hweilan could see bits of snow here and there.

"Damn," said Menduarthis. "There are guards."

"Where?"

"In the hollow. I'd hoped Grilga might summon all his forces to go after . . . that thing."

"I don't see any guards."

"Of course you don't."

The pounding in her mind had dampened somewhat, but it had not gone away. "We don't really have time for this, Menduarthis."

"If the guards had gone off with Grilga and his band, this place would be alive with birds. Owls mostly. But it's dead quiet. That means sentries."

"We need to hurry," she said. The feeling of approaching doom was getting stronger again. Making her bones itch. "You have a plan for getting past the sentries?"

"Bluffing. Seemed to work on Grilga, eh?"

"And Tirron?"

Menduarthis sighed. "You have a better idea?"

"No."

He stood and offered his hand. "Then let's do this."

They walked down a winding path toward a thick wall of trees and vines. As they drew near, Menduarthis said, "Now, remember——"

"I know. You do the talking."

Several steps later, leaves rustled over them and two of the green creatures, much like the ones from Grilga's band, dropped onto the path, one before them, one behind. Both had bows, with arrows pulled to their cheeks.

Menduarthis stopped and spread his hands. Hweilan followed his example.

The one in front of them relaxed his blow slightly and said, "Menduarthis? Why are you here?"

The one behind Hweilan lowered his bow.

"We need to see the prisoner," said Menduarthis.

The first creature narrowed his eyes to glowing slits and said, "Why?"

Hweilan could barely keep herself from bouncing on her toes. Her entire head was thrumming. "Menduarthis," she said in Damaran. "Hurry. Please."

"What's this?" said the first guard, his words harsh and angry. "Who is this one?"

Menduarthis turned to Hweilan and spoke in Common. "It is most rude to speak of our hosts in front of their backs."

"What is the meaning of all this?" said the guard.

Horns broke the surrounding silence of the wood. The same warning clarions as before, but these were *much* closer. Definitely this side of the river. Perhaps even just over the crest of the hill, Hweilan thought.

"Invaders are in the woods," said Menduarthis.

"We heard. Drurtha and I guard the prisoner. Why are *you* here?"

"Just you two?" said Menduarthis.

"We two. Now why—?"

"That simplifies things," said Menduarthis. He thrust his hands outward, one toward each of the guards. Currents of air, focused like battering rams, shot through the trees and hit the guards, snapping both arrows and knocking the bows from their hands. He flicked his wrists again, and the currents came back around, striking each of them from behind and pummeling them to the ground. Bits of leaves went flying from their clothing.

"Get that one!" Menduarthis shouted, and leaped for the first guard.

Hweilan threw down her bow and jumped for the second guard. His quiver had spilled its arrows all over the ground, and he was still stunned from the pummeling, but as soon as Hweilan grabbed his arm, he screamed, kicked at her, and tried to twist around to bite. Only her thick glove and coat sleeve saved her. He was no larger than a six-year-old child, and very thin, but he twisted and thrashed like a sack full of cats. Hweilan yanked him up by the arm, spun him around, and grabbed him in a fierce hug. Still he kicked and thrashed.

"I thought you were going to talk our way past!" she screamed.

Menduarthis had the other guard in a similar hold. "Changed my mind."

"Now what?"

The little creature was still thrashing and wailing in her arms.

Menduarthis walked over, his own prisoner putting up quite a fight. "Listen, you two!" he said.

It did no good.

Menduarthis threw his charge to the ground, belly first, and straddled his back, pinning the creature's arms underneath his own knees. His hands now free, Menduarthis twirled his fingers, and the guards' screams suddenly stopped.

"That's right," said Menduarthis. "I can rip the breath right out of you. Or"——he twirled a different pattern, and Hweilan heard a great gasp forced into each of the creatures——"or I can pop you like pustules. So you will both calm yourselves. Now."

Air exploded out of both guards. The one in Hweilan's arms went limp, as did the one beneath Menduarthis.

"Much better," said Menduarthis. "Now, the girl and I are going to see your prisoner. Then we'll be leaving. You can tell Grilga whatever you want. Never saw us. Ate us. I don't care. But you *will* cease to bother me. Understood?"

Hweilan retrieved her bow while Menduarthis kept a tight grip on the guards' arms. But it seemed unnecessary. After Menduarthis's threat, all the fight had gone out of them. There was still anger and hurt in their eyes, but a great deal of fear as well.

The horns had stopped, but the wind had picked up again, setting the entire wood to rustling. Knowing Menduarthis as they did—at least by reputation—this only served to make their captives even more nervous. Wisps of cloud were racing past the moon and gathering overhead.

"Oh, damn," said Menduarthis.

"What?"

Menduarthis spoke as he led Hweilan along the wall of vines and trees. "Kunin Gatar. I think she might be headed this way. And I don't think she's happy. Let's make this doubly damned quick, shall we?"

Prisoners in tow, they ran.

"How far is the way out of here?" Hweilan asked.

"Skip, hop, and a stone's throw," said Menduarthis, and they came to an opening in the wall. "Let's see to your pup," he said, and rushed inside.

They ran through a tunnel formed of foliage, leaving the soft ligh of the night behind. Holding the prisoners, Menduarthis could not retrieve his light. Hweilan followed the sound of his movement, his boots kicking their way through eons' worth of dead leaves.

They emerged from the tunnel and into a large area devoid of trees. Clouds hid the moon entirely now, and the last of the stars were fading behind their haze. But faerie light lit the area before them. A fall of glowing frost, much like the ones Hweilan had seen in Ellestharn, only much larger, fell over a low cliff to their right and gathered in a narrow pool. Small orbs of light, none larger than her fist, floated soundlessly throughout the area, reflecting off the fresh snow in every color of the rainbow.

A huge tree, shaped like an ancient oak but utterly black and leafless, grew out of the glowing pool at the bottom of the glowing fall. It towered at least fifty feet in the air, but its lower branches, thick as battering rams, bent low to the ground. Vines draped the tree, and thorns covered the vines. Tangled among the vines, like a fly in a spider's web, was Lendri. Naked, his pale skin bled from dozens of places where the thorns had raked away great gouges of skin or cut deep into the flesh beneath.

"Quickly, Hweilan," said Menduarthis. He was watching the sky nervously. "Every moment counts now."

He needn't have said so. The pounding in her brain told her all she needed to know.

She ran to Lendri, Menduarthis following with their prisoners.

Mindful of the vines and thorns, Hweilan knelt in front of Lendri. He raised his head to try to look at her. She reached in among the thorns, slow and careful, and brushed the hair from his face.

"Hweilan?" he said. "Are you—?"

"I'm well enough. But we need to get you out of here and be gone." The words from her dream came to her suddenly—
Death comes . . . empty dens, dead hearts.

"Leave me," said Lendri.

Much to Hweilan's surprise, Lendri looked even better

than he had when she had last seen him in the queen's palace. Not good. But not just half a shade from death either. He bled from dozens of cuts, but few of them looked very deep. Hweilan suspected the worst of his injuries were more to his spirit than his flesh.

"How badly are you hurt?" she asked.

Hweilan heard Menduarthis walk up behind her, and Lendri's eyes focused on him. "What's *he* doing here?"

"Helping us escape."

Lendri barked something that was part laugh and part sob, then let his head fall again. "Get out of here while you still can, Hweilan. But don't trust that one."

"Weak words, coming from you," said Menduarthis. "But we can play Menduarthis-was-right-all-along-and-oh-how-I-should-have-listened later. After we are well away from here."

Hweilan looked up at Menduarthis. "What's the matter with him? He looks better than when we saw him at the palace."

"The queen's had him tortured," said Menduarthis. "Several times. But before he can die and be out of misery, she has him healed again, then starts over."

"Help me free him," she said.

Menduarthis looked down at his two captives. "You heard the lady. Double quick!"

The sentries stared spears up at Menduarthis. They'd heard that Menduarthis suspected that Kunin Gatar was headed their way, and a great deal of defiance had returned to their gazes.

"Don't make me twirl my fingers." The one Menduarthis held with his left hand tried to thrash out of his grip, but Menduarthis held on and shook him. "Just for that, I'll burst your chest first. Go on! Free my hand!"

Wind gusted, rattling the branches of the old tree and spraying them with snow. By the slight widening of Menduarthis's eyes, Hweilan knew he hadn't done it. But that was apparently lost on the guards, and they jabbered something to him in their own tongue. Menduarthis answered in kind, then let them go. They stepped away, each of them rubbing their arms where Menduarthis had held them.

"Stand back, Hweilan. Let them work."

She did. The two guards stood in front of Lendri. They began a sing-song chant, more mutter than song, and passed their open palms over the thorns, beginning low down where thick tangles of vines held him around the waist. As they did so, the vines peeled away, unwrapping themselves.

"Why didn't they bind his legs?" Hweilan asked Menduarthis.

"He can struggle more that way. The more he struggles, the deeper he cuts himself."

The nagging beat in her mind was screaming at her now. "Hurry!" she told the guards.

Lendri seemed to sense something as well. He raised his head and sniffed at the air. "Hweilan, run!"

The guards had removed most of the vines from his torso and shoulders, and as Hweilan watched, the last coils sloughed off his neck. But many still encased his arms, holding him upright but limp, like a puppet hung from a peg on the wall.

"We're not leaving without you," she told Lendri.

"Don't be foolish," Lendri and Menduarthis said at the same time, then glared at each other.

Seeing the vines sloughing off him, more and more skin revealed, Hweilan realized a flaw in their plan. They'd brought no clothes for Lendri. After they left the Feywild, it might not be as cold, but winter was still holding on in the mountains.

She turned to Menduarthis. "Why didn't you tell me he'd be naked?"

"How would I know?" he said. "But this one can take care of himself."

"He'll freeze!" Hweilan took Lendri's pouch that she'd

rescued from Roakh out from her belt and laid it on the ground before her. She knew there were no clothes in there, but there might be something to give him a little modesty at the least.

"He won't," said Menduarthis. "Trust me. He can—"

Lendri screamed and lunged for Menduarthis. Most of the vines had been taken away by the guards, and the few that still clung to his arms ripped away, taking more skin with them.

But Menduarthis sidestepped, and Lendri sailed past. He hit the ground and turned, already preparing another lunge. Menduarthis stood ready, one hand held before him, another raised over his head, the eldritch glow of a spell pulsing in both fists.

"Stop it!" Hweilan screamed, and jumped between them.

Lendri crouched before her, hands like claws before him, lips pulled back over his teeth like some rabid beast.

"Stop this! Lendri, stop! Menduarthis saved my life and risked his own to free you. We're leaving here with him."

Lendri recoiled as if slapped. The fury melted from his face, but he didn't relax. "You can't trust him, Hweilan."

"More so than you," said Menduarthis.

The two guards, seeing their captors distracted, fled. One headed for the tunnel, the other ran over the lip of the hollow and disappeared into the woods.

"Let them go," said Menduarthis. "Doesn't matter now." Still holding his magic and standing guard against Lendri, Menduarthis spared a glance at the darkening sky and the wind rattling through the branches of the great tree. "Come with us or don't, Lendri, but we *are* leaving. Now."

Hweilan winced. The pounding in her head was so intense now that it had gone beyond annoyance or anxiety to actual pain. She took Lendri's pouch that she'd found in Roakh's roost and handed it to him. "Please," she said. "Let's just go."

Resigned, Lendri stood, took the pouch, and reached inside. He pointedly avoided looking at either Menduarthis or Hweilan.

Menduarthis straightened, the magic in his hands dissipating.

"You have something for the cuts?" said Hweilan.

"I'll be fine," said Lendri. He took out the copper ring she had seen in the pouch and slid it on one finger. Hweilan could see his hands trembling.

Menduarthis shouted, "Hweilan!"

She turned. A figure stepped from the tunnel. Or shambled more like, as if it were hurt or carrying a great weight. Shadows seemed reluctant to leave it. Darkness clung to the thing like a cloak. But as the figure stepped onto the snow, the fey light illuminated his features.

Soran.

But he had been . . . not hurt. Savaged. The flesh and skin along one side of his face hung in bloody tatters, and the eye in the midst of it was only a dark, wet socket. The lips and cheek were gone, showing his teeth in a lopsided, savage grin. His few remaining clothes hung off him in tatters, and great gouges of flesh along his torso had been ripped away. He dragged his right leg as he walked. In his left hand, he held a sword, broken about halfway above the crosspiece and ending in a jagged shard. Bits of vine hung off him, and in his right hand he held what Hweilan first took for a tree branch. But as he walked, the thing in his hand flopped, and she saw that it was an arm, still dripping blood and steaming in the cold air. Hweilan feared she knew what had happened to the guard who had fled into the tunnel.

The thing fixed its one good eye on Hweilan, its bloody half-grin widened, and it increased its pace.

"Run!" Menduarthis spread his arms in a flourish worthy of a tavern bard, and his fingers began to twist in their intricate pattern.

Lendri grabbed Hweilan by the forearm and pulled her after him, heading downslope toward the woods.

She looked back.

Menduarthis brought both hands around in a sweeping motion. Wind crashed down like a wave, driving snow and ice and compressing it into a wall that rolled toward the Soran-thing. It struck him full force, stopping him in his tracks. Snow and ice continued rolling over him, encasing him.

"Ha!" Menduarthis cried.

But then the spell was spent. Thick ice encased Soran up to his waist. He thrashed like a live fish thrown onto a hot pan, striking at the ice again and again with his sword and fist. His strength was far beyond anything human, and the ice was not glacier solid.

"He's breaking free!" Hweilan shouted.

"Duly noted," said Menduarthis. He stood his ground.

Soran broke through the last of the ice and charged.

Menduarthis's hands were forming another spell.

Soran plowed into him. But Hweilan was his target, his one blazing eye fixed on her, and he simply crashed through Menduarthis like a stallion breaking through a half-open gate. Menduarthis hit the ground several feet away.

"Keep going!" Lendri said, and shoved Hweilan in front of him.

She went all of five steps before turning and drawing the knife sheathed at her back. She held the knife in one hand and brandished her father's bow in the other. Her body trembled, and the warning inside her seemed to be trying to claw its way out of her skull, but she would not run while her only remaining friends fought.

Lendri kept himself in a low crouch between Hweilan and Soran. Covered in blood, his long hair in a wild tangle, muscles trembling, the elf was a fearsome sight. He threw back his head and screamed. It struck Hweilan like a physical blow, and she realized there was nothing remotely elven in the cry.

But it didn't affect Soran in the least. He brought the broken sword around in a savage arc, aiming to cut Lendri in half. But Lendri ducked under the blow and lunged. He latched onto Soran and buried his teeth in the man's throat.

Soran didn't scream, didn't cry out in pain. With his sword arm pinned, he could not bring the blade to bear. But his strength far outmatched Lendri's. He grabbed Lendri's forearm and threw the elf off, sending him sailing through the air. Lendri landed not far from Hweilan, hitting the snow and skidding a ways before coming to his feet. When he rose, the wind blew his hair out of his face, and Hweilan screamed at the sight.

The bones in Lendri's face had thickened, his jaw elongated, and when his lips peeled back in a snarl, he revealed sharp teeth.

Soran swung his sword, but not in a strike. Lendri was too far away. He threw the broken blade, and it cut through the air, twirling end over end. Just before it was about to strike Lendri, a shard of ice, thick as a lance but moving swift as an arrow, slammed into the steel, shattering it into several pieces and sending the frost-covered shards into the snow.

Hweilan followed the path from which the shard had come and saw Menduarthis standing again, frost still leaking from one fist, like heavy smoke.

Weaponless, still the Soran-thing kept coming. But he was not coming for Lendri. Hweilan had half-turned to flee before she realized she had no idea where to go.

The wall of vines and trees at the edge of the hollow exploded in a gust of snow and wind. The blast shattered all but the thickest branches of the great tree and struck Hweilan like an avalanche. She flew through the air and hit the ground hard. She tried to breathe, failed, then tried again, forcing frigid air into her lungs.

She rolled over and sat up. A section of the wall wider than Highwatch's main gates had been completely blasted away. Leaves and shards of shattered wood and vines still rained from the sky. In the gap in the wall, framed by a storm of wind and snow, draped in feylight frost, stood Kunin Gatar.

How Hweilan had ever seen the queen as a young woman her own age, she could not imagine now. The being that stood at the rim of the hollow was ancient of days, queen of winter and wielder of all its power. She held storm in her hands, and in her eyes swirled the darkest moonless midnights. All the fey lights now shone cold and white, and they swirled around her in dozens of tiny cyclones.

Kunin Gatar spoke, her voice shook the ground, but the words were in a language that meant only storm and ice.

Lendri and Menduarthis were both on their hands and knees, looking up at her—Lendri in defiant fury, Menduarthis in a sort of resigned despair.

From a pile of forest debris and snow, Soran rose to his feet. More of his skin had been stripped away by the blast. But he did not even glance in the queen's direction. His eyes, one all dead flesh, the other a blazing red, fixed on Hweilan.

Lendri stood between them.

Kunin Gatar rose, lifted into the air by currents of air at her command, and entered the hollow.

The queen turned her gaze on Lendri. *"You* brought this on us? On *me?"*

The winds calmed around her, and when her feet touched the snow, she was already storming toward Lendri. He looked up at her, then spared Hweilan a glance. In his eyes, Hweilan could see that he knew he was about to die. He looked more relieved than frightened.

Soran, thinking perhaps that the queen was coming for Hweilan, lurched toward her. His muscles trembled and convulsed so strongly that his entire body seemed to be shaking itself apart, and tiny tongues of orange flames began to dance up his arms and crown his head with fire. He spared Hweilan only a glance before charging the greater threat.

Seeing Soran advancing on her, Kunin Gatar shrieked, "You *dare?"*

She thrust her hand, one finger pointing at him, like an angry teacher disciplining a rebellious pupil.

Hail and ice shot out of Kunin Gatar's body and struck Soran like a storm of nails, stripping away what remained of his skin and taking large chunks of flesh. His remaining eye exploded, and both empty sockets blazed like tiny forge fires. The flames dancing along his arms and head fell flat, but they grew in power, and although his gait slowed, he did not stop.

Soran struck the queen like the tide striking the shore. His fists ripped through her. She wailed, the sound of wind breaking rocks. Her physical form melted into the storm, wrapping round Soran, and pounding him again and again. The thinner bits of flesh round his skull, hands, and shoulders flew away, and the flames on him grew brighter still, burning away the frost in a hissing steam.

"We should go now!" said a voice beside her, shouting to be heard over the storm. Hweilan tore her gaze away from the battle. Menduarthis, wide-eyed and trembling, crouched next to her.

Lendri was just beyond him. He looked down at her and said, "Go!"

"What about you?" she said.

"I'll follow. I know the way. Now go!"

Menduarthis pulled her to her feet, she snatched her bow from where it had fallen in the snow, and together they ran for the woods.

Just before they reached the shelter of the trees, Hweilan risked a look over her shoulder. Kunin Gatar and Soran had separated, and both now seemed more elemental than physical—one of malicious winter, the other consuming fire. Lendri huddled in the snow not far away, watching them. The two combatants struck each other in a clash of howling wind and hissing steam. Hweilan felt the ground shake.

Lendri shouted something and pointed one fist—the one on which he had put the ring, Hweilan remembered—and fire spewed out from his fist, enveloping the queen and her adversary.

As Hweilan and Menduarthis plunged into the wood, a terrible shriek filled the world. Fury, fire, agony, ice . . . all combined into one great scream that rattled the trees around them.

The incessant pounding in Hweilan's mind exploded.

CHAPTER THIRTY-ONE

ARGALATH'S EYES ROLLED BACK INTO PLACE. THE final shudder shook him so hard that he fell to his knees, and his free hand came down right in the middle of the corpse. He could feel the hot blood and viscera between his fingers. The reek wafted upward so strong that he could taste it in the back of his throat, coppery and searing.

But he could see again. The eviscerated corpse of the Damaran. Sagar . . . ? Had that been his name? It no longer mattered.

The other corpse—the one kept so carefully whole, tended so well after death, and laid so carefully beside the sacrifice—was sitting up. The corpse that had once been Guric turned its head and smiled down on Argalath.

Half of Argalath's vision was still in the other world, and he could see the furnace of black fire blazing behind those eyes.

"Well come, brother," he said.

"Come at last," said the thing inside Guric.

They stood together and turned to face the Ring of Ten—Vazhad, Jatara, and eight of Argalath's acolytes. The last of his acolytes. The strongest. The others had not been found worthy and had been put to other uses. They stood round the basin on the great rock shelf where once the

Knights of Ondrahar had held their holy rites, where the final stages of Argalath's plan had begun with Valia. How fitting that Guric should now join her. Sooner than expected, to be sure. The man had surprised Argalath, had come to his senses and seen through the lies far sooner than Argalath had thought he would. No matter. The hardest part of the plan was done. Planting season was over. From here, it would be a matter of tending the healthy crop of his designs.

Guric's corpse lurched and would have fallen had Argalath not caught him.

"So . . . hungry," he said.

Argalath waved to his men. "Bring him. Quickly!"

Vazhad took two of the acolytes back into the tunnel. They returned, dragging a bound and gagged Damaran soldier. His eyes were wide, and the blood and tears had frozen on his face, but still he thrashed and screamed behind the gag.

The thing in Guric hissed in delight and fell on his meal before the three men had even brought it to the basin. Argalath and the others left him to it. It was over in moments.

Guric stood, his eyes and teeth shining bright in the starlight amid their mask of blood. The ravaged body of the soldier steamed in the cold at his feet.

Argalath opened his mouth to speak—

The world spun around him, light lancing through his brain, shattering the darkness there. In the roar of the world's passing, he heard—far, far away—his brother screaming.

With every beat of his heart, the world came back into focus, and the roar in his mind fell away. When Argalath could finally see again, Vazhad and Jatara were leaning over him, concern written on their faces. He realized he'd fallen and was lying in the blood-spattered snow.

"Are you hurt, master?" said Jatara.

"Ukhnar Kurhan has fallen." The words had passed Argalath's lips before he realized them, but he knew they were true.

"What does this mean?" asked Vazhad.

At the same time Jatara, face filled with worry and shock, said, "Kadrigul . . . ?"

"Help me up," said Argalath.

They did. The other acolytes were looking on, impassive. Unmoving. Not even a hint of worry—or worse, ambition—in their eyes. He had trained them well.

"Master," said Jatara. She was trembling, her grip on his arms too tight. "Master, my brother . . . ? Please."

"I do not know," said Argalath. "All I know is that Soran's body has been destroyed. Ukhnar Kurhan will seek another or return here, weakened, bewildered, and hungry."

"Seek another?" said Jatara, and Argalath knew her meaning.

"The only way he could possess a living being is if the person were to invite him."

"And if the person was . . . not living?"

Argalath turned away from her. "I need rest. This has been . . . most trying. Have the acolytes see to our new guest. You should help them, Jatara. Vazhad, take me back to my rooms."

"Master?" Jatara called after him.

Leaning on Vazhad's shoulder for support, Argalath headed for the passageway that would take him through the tunnels and back to Highwatch. Back to his bed. Vazhad cast an apologetic glance over his shoulder, but he did not slow.

"Master!" Jatara said. "Master! My brother?"

● ● ⓖ ● ●

Carnage. Absolute carnage.

On the frozen river where Tirron and his hunters had been slaughtered, a band of uldra worked in the bloody snow, gathering the corpses of the dead. They dragged the broken and torn elves onto litters. Their dead mounts they left where they lay.

Near the steep bank where the trees drew in close, one of the uldra found another corpse, neither elf nor one of their mounts. A human, dressed mostly in skins and leathers. His skin and long hair were as pale as the snow in which he lay. His limbs were twisted and back broken as if he had been pummeled by a giant.

One of the Frost Folk. The uldra who found him had fought his kind before. On hunting trips to the far north of the outside lands, where the cold almost matched that of the queen's domain.

The horizon beyond the shore suddenly lit up, as if by a great fire, and the ground shook. In the distance, the uldra heard a scream. It hit beyond the ears, striking their very bones with its fury and pain.

The sound died away. The rumble in the ground stilled to a tremble, then stopped.

The uldra felt a stray breeze waft past his face. It almost felt . . . hot. But not in a pleasant way. Scalding.

He looked back down on the pale corpse. Something was different. Something—

The corpse's hand shot out and gripped the uldra's ankle in a crushing grip. The eyes opened. Red fire burned in their depths.

CHAPTER THIRTY-TWO

THE LITTLE STONE PRESSING BACK THE DARK WITH IT pale light, Menduarthis led Hweilan out of the hollow and down a steep path to a clearing in the wood. A mound sat in the very center. Something about it set Hweilan's teeth on edge.

Menduarthis dragged her to it. "Quickly!"

He fell to his knees at the foot of the mound and pressed both hands into the snow. He closed his eyes, and for a moment Hweilan thought he was praying.

"What are you doing?"

He stopped his chant and glared at her. "Trying to make sure no one follows us out of here."

"What about Lendri?"

"If he isn't here by the time I finish, he won't be coming." Menduarthis closed his eyes and resumed his chant.

Hweilan looked back the way they had just come. Wind still tore through the wood, its howl masking all other sounds. No sight of Lendri.

"Time to go."

Menduarthis stood and tossed his light stone in the snow. It was no longer glowing with a pale blue light. It pulsed yellow, and with each pulse it quickened and darkened, becoming an angry red.

"What is that going to do?" she said.

He grabbed her wrist and pulled her behind him. "Blow this mound to the bottom of the Nine Hells, I hope."

"But Lendri!"

Menduarthis ignored her and pulled her behind him. They circled the mound, and on the first full circuit, Menduarthis began an incantation. Hweilan looked back up the rise. It was hard to be certain through all the snow stirred by the wind, but she thought she saw a pale shape bounding toward them.

"Menduarthis, I think I see him!"

"Too late," he said, and in the next swirl of shadow and light, Hweilan looked up at a clear sky, set with a million stars. Stars she recognized. And Selûne was the moon Hweilan knew. Just the right size. Her court of stars in the old familiar patterns.

Menduarthis pulled her behind him. "Not safe yet!"

Stumbling behind him down a frost-covered slope, Hweilan looked back. The mound was a mirror image of the one they had just left in the Feywild, but the shadows seemed thinner here. Less vital. Starlight glimmered on the rime-covered rocks, almost sparkling.

She tripped, righted herself, and when she looked back again, Lendri was running toward them.

Hweilan opened her mouth to call—

And the mound exploded.

She saw Lendri lifted through the air, then Menduarthis fell on top of her, taking her to the ground. A tide of rock, ice, and grit washed over them in a roar of sound. When it passed, smaller stones and a storm of soil began to rain down around them.

Menduarthis rolled off her, and she sat up on one elbow. Back where the mound had been was only a smoking crater. Eldritch lights sparked and fumed, and tiny lightnings struck the ground. They were growing with each strike.

And then Lendri was beside them, bleeding from dozens of scrapes and cuts, still naked as the day he was born.

"Whatever you did . . ." He looked back at the magic fury eating away at the crater. "We should go."

Hweilan looked back at the conflagration. "That thing and the queen . . . ?"

"The thing is dead," said Lendri. "Kunin Gatar? I very much doubt it."

In the crater, several bolts of lightning crackled around one another, each increasing in fury as they struck the ground.

"We need to leave!" said Lendri.

"Damned if I don't agree with him for once," said Menduarthis.

● ● Ⓢ ● ●

They were deep in the Giantspires, in the high mountains, and the stars seemed very close. Cold as it was, it was a cold Hweilan knew, and after the realm of Kunin Gatar, it almost seemed warm.

Menduarthis led them into a high valley flanked by three peaks. In the bottom of a gully choked with boulders and bushes of iron-hard branches, he took them to a small cave. No more than a large hole in the ground, it looked like the entrance to an oversized warren.

"What is this place?" said Hweilan.

"The Ujaiyen used to camp here when they hunted this region."

"Used to?"

"They don't come here anymore."

"Why?"

Menduarthis looked to Lendri. "Yes, why would that be?"

Lendri scowled, then looked to Hweilan. "Inside. Then I'll tell you everything."

It was a simple shelter. A cave with a dirt floor. Its low ceiling was stained black by old fires, and a fissure where one wall met the ceiling let out most of the smoke. A small basin, dusty dry, hugged the back wall, but when Menduarthis chanted and waved one hand over it, it filled with clear, cold water. There was even an old cache of supplies—firewood, kindling, blankets, and food that had long spoiled or been eaten by mice. No clothes for Lendri, but he covered himself in one of the blankets while he set about fashioning a sort of loincloth and sleeveless shirt.

After they had slaked their thirst and got a small fire going, Hweilan looked to Menduarthis. "Are you certain we're safe here?"

Menduarthis snorted. "We're a damned long sight from safe. But with the mound gone, the Ujaiyen will have to come at us from another. That will take them most of a day at least. Still . . . I don't think they'll come here. We're very close to a part of these mountains where I doubt even Kunin Gatar would come." He looked to Lendri, who stared in the fire. Lendri would not meet Hweilan's gaze.

"Lendri," she said, "who is Nendawen?"

He flinched and looked up. "Where did you hear that name?"

"Menduarthis said I called it out in my sleep. But . . . but I don't remember."

Lendri's eyes widened at that, and he mumbled something in his own tongue.

"Time to bare your soul, cub," said Menduarthis. "What's your game?"

Lendri swallowed hard and looked at Hweilan with haunted eyes. "I didn't know it was you," he said. "I swear it. I didn't know. I never *imagined* it was you."

His words, the desperation in his eyes . . . it seemed to stir a deep pool in Hweilan's mind. She remembered parts of her dream that night she'd slept in the frozen branches of the fallen tree.

The howl of wolves . . .

Time to grow up, Hweilan inle Merah. Time to hunt.

You do not need understanding. You need to choose. Understanding will come later . . . if you survive.

And the image of the antlered man that haunted the shadows at the edge of her vision.

Then Lendri began his tale.

● ● ● ●

"Our people were not born to this world, but in a place we name the Hunting Lands. Long ago, a fell being of great strength made war on the gods of our people and the primal spirits who served them. Jagun Ghen we named him. Burning Hunger. The Destroyer. For generations we fought him, but he grew stronger, destroying our homeland. We fled in exile to this world, where we have lived for many long years. But some twenty years ago, the great god Dedunan——"

"Who?" said Hweilan.

But it was Menduarthis who answered her. "Silvanus."

Lendri and Hweilan both looked at him in surprise.

He shrugged. "I know things."

Lendri scowled. "Yes. Silvanus. He intervened on our behalf, and for once the winds turned in our favor. Jagun Ghen was cast from the Hunting Lands, and after generations in exile, the Vil Adanrath returned home. Except for me."

"Because of your oaths to my forefather," said Hweilan. "Because of me."

"In part," said Lendri. "After my people left, I wandered for a while. I even visited Highwatch once, but Merah had no interest in renewing her ties to her heritage. I left, lost in my heart." He looked up at Menduarthis. "It was at this time I came to live in the realm of your queen."

Menduarthis snorted. "Hardly *my* queen anymore."

"I escaped," said Lendri.

"After betraying them and murdering their king," said Menduarthis. He looked to Hweilan. "He's leaving out quite a lot."

"And so are you," said Lendri. "I——"

"Enough!" said Hweilan. "Menduarthis, be quiet. Lendri, what does any of this have to do with me?"

"After I escaped Kunin Gatar," said Lendri, "I fled, but

the Ujaiyen pursued me. I fled to the one place I knew the Ujaiyen would not dare go. To a region of these mountains sacred to Nendawen. We are close to them now."

Menduarthis shuddered and looked at the exit of the cave. "*Very* close."

"Truth be told," said Lendri, "I went there with little real hope. Nendawen is sacred to the Vil Adanrath. Not one of the great gods like Dedunan, but Nendawen serves him in his own way, as we serve our gods. Nendawen is a hunter. *The* Hunter. But to come to him without sacrifice, without blood . . . it is death. Nendawen loves our people in his own way, but he is not a kind master. Not forgiving. I'd hoped he might take the Ujaiyen on my trail as sacrifice, but if not . . . well, I thought it better to die at the hands of one of my own than *his* ilk." He looked at Menduarthis.

"*This* ilk just saved your life, I'll remind you," said Menduarthis.

"He killed them?" said Hweilan. "Nendawen killed the Ujaiyen?"

"Oh, yes," said Lendri. "But he did not count it as sacrifice. He . . ." His brows creased as he searched for the word. "Put off payment, you might say."

"You mean *her?*" said Menduarthis. He raised one fist and glared at Lendri, and Hweilan knew he was considering which spell to use on the elf. "You're delivering Hweilan to this monster as some sort of blood sacrifice? That . . . that's—"

"No!" said Lendri. His lips pulled back in a snarl, and in the firelight Hweilan thought his teeth seemed sharper. "I would never do such a thing." His countenance softened and he looked to Hweilan. "I would die first. I swear it."

She believed him, but something in his gaze sent a shiver of fear through her.

"It's . . . more complicated," said Lendri. "Nendawen told me that Jagun Ghen—the Destroyer who made a wasteland of our home—had not been killed. Only vanquished. He fled the Hunting Lands. Fled here, to this world. Though his power was much reduced, it will grow again. He will bring his brothers and servants—fell spirits like him—to this world to kill and destroy. His hunger is never satisfied. He does not care to conquer. Only consume."

Lendri looked into the fire, and Hweilan saw its warm light glistening in his eyes. They were filling with tears.

"I thought he meant me," said Lendri. "I swear it. Nendawen said that Jagun Ghen must be stopped. But this world . . . it is not ours, nor our gods. Even Nendawen, his power is very limited here. Only on certain nights may he roam. Other times, he is confined to his holy places. To stop Jagun Ghen, the Hunter requires someone to go in his stead. The Hunter needs a Hand."

Both men were staring at Hweilan, Lendri with tears in his eyes and Menduarthis with his mouth hanging open.

"You mean me?" she asked.

"I did not know," said Lendri. "Nendawen would not tell me who. He told me only that his chosen would hold 'death in her right hand.' "

Hweilan's mind reeled. She looked down at her hand.

"Wait," said Menduarthis. "Death in her right hand? You mean . . . ?"

Lendri nodded. "Show him," said Lendri.

Hweilan pulled off her glove, spread her palm, and turned it so that the firelight caught it full force.

"I've seen it already," said Menduarthis.

"Death," said Lendri. "Hweilan holds 'death' in her right hand."

Hweilan stood.

"Where are you going?" said Menduarthis.

"I need to be alone."

"It isn't safe out there."

"The sun will be up soon," said Lendri. "She'll be fine." He looked at her. "Don't stray far. If you need me, use your *kishkoman*."

Behind her, she heard Menduarthis ranting. "Are you mad? One of your bloodthirsty beast-gods wants her and you tell her to blow a damned whistle?"

Hweilan ran, leaving them behind.

• • ◉ • •

She wandered out of the gully and sought the heights. As the stars began to fade in the lightening sky, a sudden hungry longing to see the sun woke in Hweilan. How long had it been since she'd watched the sun rise? She couldn't remember. Since well before the fall of Highwatch.

She found a way up a low offshoot of the nearest peak, her boots often slipping on the slick rocks or ice-covered grass beneath. But she made it up and found a nice perch, where she had a clear view of the eastern sky between the mountains. The Giantspires towered around her.

Nendawen . . .

Jagun Ghen . . .

She shivered. Not so much at the horror of Lendri's tale, nor that it had a sharp ring of truth. No.

She'd heard those names before. She knew that now. Never in her waking memory, not until Menduarthis and Lendri had spoken them. But those names had haunted her dreams.

Nendawen. The Hunter. The antlered man she kept seeing from the corner of her eye. *Time to grow up. Time to choose. Understanding will come later. If you survive . . .*

Jagun Ghen. Destroyer. That voice out of the darkness. The stench of death, of rot, of carnage unimaginable.

And familiar. It hit her then. Her dream had met the waking world. When that . . . that thing, that monster wearing her uncle's face had come after her. It wasn't even a scent so much as a complete miasma. A reek that sank into the spirit.

This Nendawen had sent Lendri to claim her: Had Jagun Ghen sent something as well? That thing, that mockery of Soran? And would he keep sending them?

With a jolt, she realized something else. That thing had not come alone. The first time he'd found her, Creel had been with him. Creel had taken Highwatch. Had killed her family.

And Kadrigul had been beside Soran too. Kadrigul who served Argalath.

Hweilan had heard the whispered tales that Guric's chief counselor was more than spellscarred. Though the man himself had always denied it, more than a few had said the man was a demonbinder, that he sacrificed to the ancient devil-gods of the Nar.

Jagun Ghen.

"Damn," said Hweilan. It all made sense.

Highwatch had fallen and her family had been murdered. And all because of some conflict that went back thousands of years.

Sitting there surrounded by mountains, weighed down by her thoughts, Hweilan felt very small.

And terrified. She'd lived a sheltered life at Highwatch. The world was much bigger, harder, and *meaner* than she had ever imagined. Every person she'd ever loved was dead. Murdered.

That didn't make the terror go away. A little pit of it still churned in her stomach. But it shrank as something else grew inside her. Something stronger.

Anger. Fury.

It cleared her thoughts.

She was alive. Through all the horror, the fear, and the uncertainty of the past days, one fact remained, pure and cold in the growing predawn light: she was alive. Her breath came cold and plumed before her. The *halbdol* was beginning to lose its potency, and she could feel the first pangs of chill against her skin, but it was a *good* feeling. She was hungry, tired . . . but those feelings seemed to strip her to her purest essence. She was alive. She still had her breath, her blood, and her freedom. If anyone or anything wanted those things, they would have to take them. Hweilan was tired, yes. Tired of running. Tired of being hunted.

She remembered a lesson Scith had given her in her eighth year. Her first time in the wild without her family. Only her, Scith, and a few guards. But she and Scith had roamed away from the others for much of the day, Scith teaching her the ways of the wild. His first lesson, the one on which all others had built, came to her now.

"There are two types of beings in the world, Hweilan, neither better than the other, and both depending on one another, blood and breath, for survival: the hunter and the hunted."

Hweilan was tired of being the hunted. Whatever the days ahead brought, she would be hunted no more. Time to stop running. Time to stop being hunted. Time to hunt.

CHAPTER THIRTY-THREE

THE SUN WAS CLIMBING INTO THE SKY WHEN HWEILAN
returned to their shelter. Menduarthis was pacing
outside, and Lendri crouched just outside the entrance.
When Menduarthis saw her approaching, the tension
left his shoulders.

"We were getting worried," he said.

Hweilan took a deep breath, then said, "I'll go."

Menduarthis looked at her, looked at Lendri, then
back at her. "Go? Go where? What are you—?"

"To Nendawen," she said.

"You can't be serious."

"I want to find the people who killed my family. I want to
kill them. If this Nendawen can help me do that . . ."

Menduarthis opened his mouth to reply, but Lendri
spoke first.

"Hweilan, it isn't . . ." He stood and gazed off northward to
the pass between two of the peaks. "Not like that. Nendawen
isn't one to be bargained with. He wants Jagun Ghen, and
that is that. Your family—"

"Was killed by Jagun Ghen," said Hweilan. "Or by those
who serve him, at least."

Lendri scowled and Menduarthis rolled his eyes as
Hweilan laid out her reasoning to them. Lendri's eyes
sharpened, but she could see his attention focused inward.

Menduarthis's eyes widened in dawning horror.

"Am I the only one here who hasn't lost all sense?" said Menduarthis. He pointed at Lendri. "Just because *he* made some deal with a barbarian demigod doesn't obligate *you* to help him. He wants to honor his people's ways by jumping face first into the fire? Let him. But don't jump in with him."

"They're my people too," said Hweilan.

"Oh, for—"

"They killed my family! Do you remember what you told me? 'The world isn't a nice place,' you said. 'Fools say it's unforgiving, but that's why they're fools. The world doesn't forgive because it doesn't blame. And the world doesn't blame because *it doesn't care*.' You were right, you bastard. The world doesn't care. But there are people in the world who do. I loved my family. They loved me. And they're dead now. Murdered. And those who did it are sitting in my home. My home! And if Jagun Ghen is responsible, I swear to my family's gods that I'm going to make him regret the day he—"

An arrow hit Menduarthis in the chest. He still wore his armor, and the shaft bounced off, but it struck with enough force that it knocked him to the ground.

They looked up. An archer stood on the southern rise that they had come down earlier. He was already reaching for another arrow. Below him, two tundra tigers were descending the slope, each carrying a rider. Other figures—some small, their odd hats giving them away as uldra, others taller, their long hair blowing in the morning breeze—crested the rise and fanned around the archer.

"Ujaiyen," said Menduarthis. "How . . . ?"

Lendri grabbed Hweilan and pulled her behind him. "Run!"

• • ⊛ • •

They had no real chance. Their weapons were down to Hweilan's two knives and a bow she could not use. The Ujaiyen had the element of surprise, superior numbers, and Hweilan, Menduarthis, and Lendri were still hungry and haggard from their escape. Still, desperation lent them strength and speed, and they were halfway up the northern slope when the tigers' roars washed over them.

Hweilain's knees buckled, and she hit the ground. Lendri grabbed her elbow and yanked her to her feet.

"Move," he said. His eyes shone with a cold fury, and his teeth had lengthened to points.

The tigers flanked them, passed them, then stopped on the rise above them as the Ujaiyen on foot closed from below. The tigers' riders lowered long spears.

Menduarthis flicked an intricate pattern with the fingers of his right hand, then thrust both fists forward. A wind swept across the slope, driving frost and grit across the riders, blinding them. He finished with a flourish of arms and hands, and snow and sharp bits of hail wove into the wind, striking their pursuers below.

"Keep going!" he shouted to Hweilan.

They made it over the rise and kept going. The next valley was choked with evergreens and winter-bare underbrush. Behind her, she heard the roar of a tiger, a shout from Menduarthis, and the roar of more wind.

Lendri fell back to put himself between Hweilan and their pursuers. She spared a glance back and saw Menduarthis coming over the rise. An arrow shot through his cloak, and another bounced off his armor.

"Keep moving!" he shouted. "Don't wait for me!"

Lendri looked at Hweilan, said, "Get to the trees," then charged back over the hill.

"Where are you going?" she called, but he ignored her.

Menduarthis grabbed her and pulled her after him. "He can take care of himself. Move!"

A tundra tiger roared, and mixed with it Hweilan heard the angry growl and bark of a wolf.

"Lendri!" she screamed.

But Menduarthis held her tight. "He's buying us time. He'll be along. Now *move!*"

She turned and ran, Menduarthis a few steps ahead of her. The slope was steep and covered with ice and snow. She could hear footsteps behind her, gaining, but she didn't dare look back. Near the bottom, a rock under the snow turned beneath her boot, and she fell, hitting the ground hard.

It saved her. She felt something pass over her, and when she looked up, she saw that one of the riders had tossed a net. It had just missed her, and instead caught Menduarthis around the legs.

The rider snarled and reined the tiger back, tightening the noose threaded around the net. It pulled Menduarthis down in a tangle of his own cloak.

Hweilan let go of her father's bow, grabbed the nearest rock, and lobbed it at the rider as hard as she could. Her thick gloves affected her aim, and the rock hit the tiger instead. It stopped and turned its yellow eyes on her. As did its rider. He let go of the rope holding the net, lowered his spear, and with his knees turned his tiger toward her. The tiger's ears flattened, and it lowered its head as it charged.

A spear struck it in the soft flesh between its jaw and shoulder. The tiger screamed and thrashed, throwing its rider.

Hweilan grabbed her bow and looked up. Lendri was coming down the slope, a small knife in one hand. Blood covered his face and chest, and as near as she could tell, none of it was his own. He must have killed one of the Ujaiyen and taken his weapons.

"Go!" he shouted.

More Ujaiyen—uldra and elves, all on foot—were streaming down the hill behind him. Except for the archer, who stood on the crest, bow bent, arrow to cheek, the point of his arrow aimed at Hweilan. He loosed. His aim was flawless, but the distance was enough that Hweilan had time to dive out of the way, scramble to her feet, and run. She heard the arrow strike the rocks a few paces away.

Menduarthis had disentangled himself from the net and

was on his feet again. Together they made it into the trees.

Hweilan slowed. "Where is Lendri?"

Menduarthis pushed her onward. "If he's alive, he'll find us. If not, there's nothing you can do for—"

Menduarthis screamed and shot into the air. A thick tendril of vine, covered in wicked-looking thorns, had snaked around his torso and yanked him into the air. Hweilan looked up and saw two uldra, their faces split by wicked grins, crouched in the thick green boughs of a pine.

And then the net fell over her.

• • ⊙ • •

Three uldra and an elf reached through the net, taking Hweilan's weapons, then hung her from the next tree. More vines encased Menduarthis, pinning his arms to his sides. Even his fingers, bloody and ripped by the thorns, were bound in smaller tendrils.

Hweilan dared hope that Lendri might come to their aid, but when the rest of the hunting party arrived, they were dragging Lendri in another net.

An eladrin who wore his black hair in dozens of tight braids, all pulled back and bound with a green cord, stood in their midst and looked up at Menduarthis.

"Nikle's plan worked," he said, and bowed to one of the uldra. It was the first one Hweilan had met her first night in the feywild. The little creature's eyes sparkled at the praise. "Just like deer. Spook them and they run right into the trap. I said you were far too smart to fall for that. I am most pleased to see how wrong I was. Most pleased."

Menduarthis cursed him in his own language, and Hweilan could tell by his voice that the thorns were cutting through more than his clothes.

"Most impolite, considering your current predicament," said the eladrin.

"How in the unholy hells did you get through the mound?" said Menduarthis.

The eladrin chuckled. "The one you destroyed? Oh, we

didn't. We had to come through the crystals. But really, Menduarthis, are you so smitten with this little wench that you've forgotten how to think? We came through the crystals, yes, but how hard is it to teleport once we are here? Quite a mess you made of the place, I will say. Still, it wasn't hard to pick up your trail."

"I really didn't think you'd come here," said Menduarthis, and he managed an insolent grin through his mask of pain. "I thought you too much a coward."

The eladrin went very still and paled. Finally, he said, "Whatever devil you let into our realm, Menduarthis, it failed. Kunin Gatar was hurt, yes, but your little ruse only fueled her anger. She has plans for you three. For you, Lendri . . . she's going to cut off a new appendage every day, then grow it back. That will be your food for the next year. Eating yourself." He shuddered. "Still, bloody monster like you might enjoy that. You, Menduarthis? She's still contemplating your fate, though I dare say it is going to make you pray to take Lendri's place. And you."

He walked over to Hweilan, looked down on her, and poked at her with the toe of his boot.

"I confess I've forgotten your name."

She glared up at him. "Hweilan."

He grimaced. "Not worth remembering. You girl . . . well, perhaps our queen still has a warm place in her heart for young girls. I have orders to find a low-hanging branch, nail you to it, palms and wrists, and leave you to the mercy of whatever foul power haunts these lands."

Lendri snarled and thrashed in his net, but two of the uldra laid into him with whips fashioned from the thorn-covered vines. Blood splattered, freezing on the ground as it hit, and he quieted.

"Well," said the eladrin, "let us do our duty. Sooner done, sooner we are gone."

One of the uldra said something in his own language. A single syllable, but Hweilan heard the fear tinging it. He pointed, and the eladrin looked up. Hweilan followed his gaze.

Ravens filled the nearest trees. They had not been there before, Hweilan was sure of it. Dozens of ravens looked down on the hunters and their catch. Thick wings flapped, and even as Hweilan watched, more landed. And more. Dozens at first. But then they grew to a hundred or more. In the bits of sky she could see between the branches, she saw more circling overhead, some close enough to be seen for the huge ravens they were, but others only distant specks. There were hundreds of them. Perhaps thousands.

The eladrin opened his mouth to speak, but even as he did so, a howl broke the silence. Then another and another and another. From every direction.

The Ujaiyen called out in alarm. Dusky shapes were making their way through the surrounding wood, and here and there, yellow eyes watched from the shadows.

Menduarthis laughed. "I'd watch the 'foul power' insults if I were you, Losir. And if you have any sense at all, you'll let us go. Someone much more powerful and much meaner than Kunin Gatar has a claim on that girl. And you're pissing on his threshold."

CHAPTER THIRTY-FOUR

"MENDUARTHIS SPEAKS THE TRUTH—FOR ONCE," said Lendri. "Hweilan is Chosen of Nendawen. Harm her, and by dawn all that will be left of you and all your hunters are your bones."

Losir looked around at his men. They did not look away, but Hweilan could see the fear in their eyes.

"If we go back without you," said Losir, "Kunin Gatar will put your fate on us."

"Then run," said Menduarthis. "Get as far away as you can from the queen. You'll be surprised how good it feels."

The two uldra holding him snarled at his insult and pulled the vines tighter, shoving the thorns deeper into his arms.

Menduarthis cried out, then said, "Though not so much right now, I will admit."

"I am not like you," said Losir. "Faithless. The lord of this place claims the girl? Fine. I will leave her here unharmed and hope that the queen is in a forgiving mood. But you two are returning to face her judgment."

"No!" Hweilan screamed. But Losir ignored her.

Hweilan thrashed and kicked in her bindings. One of the uldra stepped forward and brought his thorned whip across her. Her thick clothing protected her from the worst of it, but a long tendril raked down her cheek, barely missing her eye.

Every raven in the trees cried out, their caws loud as thunder, and the wolves' howls changed to low growls that shook the ground.

They quieted.

"I wouldn't do that again," said Menduarthis.

Losir nodded and spoke to the uldra in his own language. The little creature coiled his whip and stepped away.

"Let us go!" Hweilan screamed.

Losir glanced at the ravens, then looked down at Hweilan. "Calm yourself, and I will free you before we leave."

Hweilan screamed and kicked at him, but he bounced away, light as a dancer.

"As you wish," said Losir. He called out to his troop, and they began to file away, every eye turned warily up to the trees or watching the thick brush. The two uldra let Menduarthis down from the tree and fitted his bindings to drag him behind them.

"Losir!" Lendri called. "Leave the girl her weapons. The knives and bow. They are hers, and she is Nendawen's. Steal from her, and you steal from him."

Losir stopped, considered, then waved to an elf and issued an order.

The elf stepped forward and dropped both knives and the bow on the ground several paces away.

Losir looked back at her, "This Nendawen claims you? Let him untie you."

And with that, he walked away, his troop following, dragging Lendri and Menduarthis between them.

In moments, Hweilan was alone under the eyes of the hungry ravens.

She screamed.

"Hweilan!" Menduarthis called from the woods. "Stop. This doesn't help us. I got away from Kunin Gatar once. I can do it again." Hweilan heard the lie in his voice. "You take care of yourself now, little flower."

● ● ◉ ● ●

Hweilan let out a final scream, then stopped. She had no idea how long she'd been at it, but her throat was raw. Taking deep breaths, she realized how absolutely silent it was.

She looked up. The ravens were gone. The skies were clear again, and there was no sign of a wolf in the brush.

Have to think, she told herself.

She was still bound in the net, but the net's leash was not tied to anything. Scooting like a caterpillar, she worked her way over to her weapons. She worked three fingers out of the net, managed to grab the knife Lendri had given her, and set to work.

It was a painstaking process, and more than once she dropped the knife or sliced into her jacket. But bit by bit she managed to slice through the net, and before too long she had freed one arm. After that, it was easy, and she freed herself in moments.

She stood and sloughed off the remains of the net.

Looking around, the Ujaiyen and her friends gone, she realized she had absolutely no idea what to do.

She could not forsake Lendri and Menduarthis. Not after all they'd done for her. She knew if she did so, the disappointed faces of Scith and her family would haunt her dreams forever. But what could she do with only two knives and a bow she could not bend?

"Nendawen," she said.

And then a new realization hit her. She knew she was near his sacred lands. But near which way? Lendri had said north. But how far? And how could she find him?

Standing there, wrestling with indecision, hungry, tired, and very, very frightened, she felt her head begin to hurt.

No. Not just a headache. It was pounding. A steady pulse in the base of her skull. And a cold dread was building. A familiar dread.

Her eyes widened and she gasped. It was the same feeling that had dogged her whenever that Soran-thing drew close. The closer he got, the harder the pounding in her brain.

Lendri had been wrong. That monster had somehow survived, and it was hunting her again.

It gave her an idea.

• • ◎ • •

The sun was disappearing behind the wall of the western peak when Menduarthis saw Lendri again. The Ujaiyen had dragged them through the rocky country, and if Menduarthis had a square inch that hadn't been bruised, scraped, or raked by those damnable thorns, he swore he would never tell another lie. Never. For at least a tenday.

But as they began to climb a large offshoot of one of the peaks, a treeless expanse, the hunting party had gathered in again, and Lendri's captors came in close to Menduarthis.

The pale elf was covered with blood, dirt, and snow, but none of the fury had left his eyes. His gaze locked on Menduarthis.

"You think the girl will be all right?" Menduarthis asked.

Lendri opened his mouth to reply, but the uldra laid into them with the whips again.

"No talking!" one of them said in his own language. Menduarthis had squeezed his eyes shut against the thorned whips, but he thought he recognized Nikle's voice. Unappreciative little whelp. Since being captured, Menduarthis had begun to compile a list of names on whom he would rain his vengeance as soon as he escaped. Nikle had just moved up five spots on the list.

Menduarthis heard a chuckle and opened his eyes. Losir was walking behind him, a smug look on his smug face.

"Feeling more contrite?" said Losir.

Menduarthis ignored the barb. "May I ask you something?"

He looked askance to make sure the uldra weren't coming in with the whips again. They weren't.

"What?" said Losir.

"If you could teleport from the crystals to the mound,

why can't you just teleport back to the crystals from here? Are you really enjoying bruising us that much?"

Losir frowned. "We tried. Something about these cursed lands . . . it interferes with our magic. We need to get well away first. We intend to try again at the top of the next height."

"Oh, good," said Menduarthis. "Then home to bed and supper."

Losir laughed. "Eager are you? Which part do you hope to taste first? A hand perhaps? Don't get your hopes up. I think the queen intends to start with other appendages first. She'll save the bony parts for later when you've developed a taste for it."

"I thought you said that was Lendri's fate."

Losir shrugged and smiled.

A ways later the hunters cried out, and the party stopped. Menduarthis wiggled and craned his neck around to see what they were pointing at.

"Oh, no," he said. "That little fool."

At the crest of the height, profiled against the sky, no more than a long bowshot away, stood Hweilan.

Losir laughed. "Looks like we get to take all three back after all."

He issued an order and several of the hunters ran forward. Lendri had killed both tigers, so Menduarthis half-hoped Hweilan might run. If her luck held, she might get away.

But no. She simply stood there, watching them come.

Menduarthis watched, sick at heart, as the two elves and four uldra escorted her down. They didn't net or bind her, or even take her weapons. Just kept their spears at her back or naked swords in hand.

Hweilan stepped among the hunters, and Menduarthis saw that she was not well. She was trembling and squinted as if the light hurt. Her jaw clenched and she did not even look at Menduarthis or Lendri as her captors brought her before Losir.

The eladrin chuckled. "I must admit, you do surprise, girl. You were free. Why come back?"

Hweilan did not meet his gaze. "Let them go. Both of them. Let me go. Do it quick and run. Fast as you can. Heed me, and I think you might have time to get away."

Losir threw his head back and laughed. "Get away? From you?"

She did look up then, and Menduarthis saw the gleeful fury in her eyes. "No."

Several of the Ujaiyen cried out and pointed.

"Now what?" said Losir.

Menduarthis looked up.

A figure was coming over the rise. Not running, but approaching in a steady unwavering gait. Pale skin. Long hair tossed by the wind. For a moment, Menduarthis thought it might be some of Lendri's kin come to rescue him. But no. They were all gone, weren't they?

And then he drew close enough for Menduarthis to make out the details. He felt his blood frost at the sight.

It was that pale warrior. The Frost Folk. The one Menduarthis had most assuredly killed back in the Feywild.

"This is your plan?" said Losir, and he looked on Hweilan with disdain. "We hunt Frost Folk for fun. Whole clans of them. This one will be no more than a distraction."

He said something to his hunters in his own language, then drew his sword and stepped forward to meet the newcomer.

The pale warrior only glanced at him. His eyes were fixed on Hweilan. Now that he saw her, he increased his pace, coming swiftly down the slope.

Losir stepped in front of him and brandished his blade. He said something that Menduarthis did not catch, then attacked.

Losir was a fine swordsman, Menduarthis knew. One of the best among the Ujaiyen. But perhaps he was in no mood to play. Or perhaps at the last moment he sensed something amiss and chose a simple attack—one quick thrust between the ribs, aimed to skewer the heart.

The pale warrior turned his gaze on Losir, locked one fist around the eladrin's sword arm, and twisted. They were at least a hundred feet away, but still Menduarthis heard the bone snap like a dry branch. Losir shrieked and went down. The pale warrior drew the sword out of his own chest, bent down, and lopped off Losir's other arm. He picked it up in his other hand and stepped over Losir, who kicked and screamed on the ground as his lifeblood poured out.

The Ujaiyen charged.

All but two. One elf who stood guard over Lendri and one uldra over Menduarthis.

Their attention was focused on the fight. The elf never saw Hweilan step up behind him and bring the hilt of her dagger down on the top of his head. He flopped to the ground like wet dough.

The other uldra cried out and flicked his arm, uncoiling his whip. He charged her, swinging the weapon in swipe after swipe. Hweilan danced out of the way—the girl was good on her feet—but each strike was coming closer.

Menduarthis squirmed and struggled, but he only succeeded in tightening his bonds and losing more skin.

Snarling, Lendri thrashed and threw off his bindings.

Little bastard chewed through the ropes, Menduarthis said to himself.

He had. His teeth had gone long and sharp, his fingers curled into claws, and his hair was thickening around his face and shoulders.

One look, and the uldra fled.

Hweilan ran to Menduarthis. Lendri was right behind her, and by the time they knelt beside him, he was fully an elf again. She handed Lendri her other knife, and the two set about cutting away the vines.

Menduarthis hissed through his teeth. "Careful! Some of those thorns are caught in more than cloth."

Lendri looked up to the battle. Menduarthis saw his eyes widen, and he gave Hweilan back the knife.

"Back the way we came," said Lendri. "Over that northern rise and down in to the next valley. Once you cross the river—frozen most likely—you should be safe. Get him free and go!"

"Where are you going?" Hweilan and Menduarthis said at the same time.

"To buy you some time," he said, and bounded off.

Menduarthis looked the way he had gone. The pale warrior brought his sword down, killing the elf who held the shaft of the spear piercing the warrior's gut. The eladrin went down and did not move. The rest of the Ujaiyen—the few survivors whose corpses were not littering the slope— were disappearing over the hill.

"Forget the thorns," said Menduarthis. "Just cut, girl. Cut!"

CHAPTER THIRTY-FIVE

DOZENS OF TENDRILS OF VINE AND THORNS STILL CLUNG to Menduarthis, but once he could move again, they were on their feet and running. He picked at the tighter creepers and smaller thorns around his hands as they ran.

Hweilan looked back.

A huge wolf snapped at the pale warrior, raking at his legs then bounding away. Each time the warrior would pursue, the wolf bounded off. The warrior would break off the chase and continue after Hweilan, and the wolf would charge in again.

"Go! Toward the river!" said Menduarthis. "Once we're away, he'll follow."

Knowing Menduarthis was right, Hweilan turned and ran. She was utterly exhausted. When had she last slept? In the Feywild, and that hadn't been a rest so much as a mental pummeling by the queen. But her fear and desperation lent strength to her limbs. She knew in her heart that the thing didn't care for Lendri in the least. The wolf was only an obstacle in his way. The best thing she could do to help Lendri right now was to get away.

But just before they crossed a bend in the hill, she heard the wolf let out a yelp of pain. She turned. Less than a quarter mile away, the pale warrior was headed straight for her. The wolf lay motionless on the frost-covered rocks behind him.

"Lendri!" she screamed. "No!"

"Run!" Menduarthis pulled her along.

They did, rounding the bend in the trail and losing sight of the pale warrior. They kept going, and when the thing next came in sight, he was much closer. Despite the broken spear shaft still protruding from his midsection and the gaping sword wound in his ribs, he was running.

"Up here!" said Menduarthis, and he tried to pull Hweilan up a narrow trail. She saw that it wound up the arm of the mountain to a cliff overlooking their present trail.

"No!" she pulled back. "That isn't the way."

He grabbed her again and shoved her before him. "I know. I have an idea."

Their path ended at the cliff. Before them an old rockslide had collapsed the rest of the trail into the valley, which was a dizzying distance below them.

"A wonderful idea you had," said Hweilan.

She looked back. The pale warrior was still coming. He'd be on them in moments. She gripped her bow tight and pulled Lendri's knife.

"None of that," said Menduarthis, and he pulled her to him in a tight embrace.

She struggled and pounded his chest with the handle of her knife. "What are you——?"

"No one likes a coward. Trust me."

And then she knew what he had in mind.

"Oh, gods," she said.

The air hit them, swirling tighter and tighter, taking them in an embrace of storm that drowned out all other sound. Hweilan squeezed her eyes shut.

"Mind the blade!" said Menduarthis, and an instant later they lifted in the air, shot away from the cliff, and down.

Near the end, it was more fall than flight. They landed

in a thick bank of snow crusted by ice. It was soft enough, but Menduarthis ended up on top of her.

She shook her head and spat snow. "You need to work on your landings."

He grinned. "Seems fine from my vantage point."

She pushed him off. They stood and looked up to the cliff where they had just been. The pale warrior was standing there, sword in hand, looking down on them. Hweilan saw the glimmer of red in his empty eyes. What had become of the Soran-thing, why it was now Kadrigul, she didn't know. But she knew that gaze.

Kadrigul jumped.

She heard Menduarthis gasp, then the pale warrior hit the ground in a racket of tumbling stones and cracking bones.

Kadrigul pushed himself to his feet. Broken bone protruded above and below his left shoulder and above his left knee. Part of his skull had caved in, and Hweilan could see shattered ribs poking under his clothes. He raised his right fist. The sword had broken just above the hilt, and he tossed it aside.

"Hm," said Menduarthis. He winced at the pain from his torn fingers as he began twirling them.

Hweilan heard air rushing, and she saw Kadrigul's cheeks puff and flutter. She remembered how Menduarthis had threatened to kill Roakh. *Have you ever seen an old wineskin filled with too much wine? Imagine what would happen if the air in your wretched frame did the same thing.*

Kadrigul stopped and looked down at his expanding chest. It only took a moment, then Hweilan heard a distinctive *pop!* of tearing tissue as his chest deflated in a rush. She even saw a fine blast of fluid shoot out of both Kadrigul's ears. Then he looked up and kept coming.

"Well, I'm out of ideas," said Menduarthis, and she heard real fear in his voice. "Back to running now."

They turned to do just that. Menduarthis made it three steps. Hweilan heard *clonk,* and then he dropped like a torn pennant. She screamed and looked down in time to see the rock fall away. Blood gushed from his scalp. He was still breathing, but she knew she'd never revive him before Kadrigul was on top of them.

"Alone," said Kadrigul, his voice a broken rasp. She looked to him. The red in his eyes blazed. "Just you . . . and me. Come. I will . . . end it quick. Join . . . your family."

For a brief instant, two beats of her heart at most, Hweilan was tempted. Exhaustion pulled at her. She knew it wouldn't be long before she gave out entirely. It would be easy to stop running. To stop the pain and struggle. See her family again. See Scith.

That decided her.

She knew that even if she did stand before Scith in the next life, if she stood before him a victim, come before him in defeat, she would see the disappointment in his eyes.

Hweilan raised her knife. "You first."

The thing in Kadrigul smiled, a horrid pulling back of dead lips over broken teeth. "Good," he said, and lurched toward her.

She side-stepped quickly, testing whether he would follow her. She had to know he'd leave Menduarthis alone. He did.

"You're going to kill me?" she said, walking backward.

"I'm going . . . to eat . . . your heart."

"Catch me first," she said, then turned and ran.

The Kadrigul-thing shrieked. Remembering how he had felled Menduarthis, she ducked and swerved as she ran. Stones skipped off the ground around her, and one bounced off her back. Only her thick clothes saved her a broken bone. The pain was incredible. Her vision darkened for a moment.

But she kept going.

She remembered Lendri's words.

"North," she panted as she ran. "Over the rise. Next valley. Frozen river."

When she came to areas of open ground, she'd look back.

She had managed to put a good deal of distance between her and Kadrigul, but he was still coming, lurching along on his shattered leg. As the late afternoon sky darkened toward the deep blue of evening, his eyes seemed all the brighter, two points of red fire gazing at her from that dead white face.

The pounding in her head was so strong that she could barely think. Still she ran.

She came to the woods where the Ujaiyen had captured them. Shadows lay thick in the dusk light. She half hoped and half feared to see the ravens and wolves again, but the wood was empty, silent save for the sounds of her own ragged breathing and footfalls.

The land climbed again, the trees gave out, and she crossed into the next valley.

There, below her, she could see the river. Only slightly wider than the path through Highwatch's main gate and frozen solid. It looked no different from hundreds of other streams she'd seen in her life, but something about it made her bones itch. Something beyond that river watched.

She stumbled down into the valley, her muscles burning with exhaustion. Every step was an effort. Her knees trembled, and she had to focus all her attention on forcing one foot in front of the other.

She came to the bottom, wove through the ice-slick rocks that lined the bank, then fell, her hands striking the frozen river. A pulse seemed to radiate outward, just beyond her hearing.

Hweilan pushed herself up, crossed the river, then collapsed on the other side. Dark pines, ages old, leaned over, covering her in their shadow.

"Safe," she said. Lendri had said so. *Once you cross the river you should be safe.*

She rolled over on the bank and looked back. Evening was giving way to night. The brightest stars were out, but shadows clung thick among the rocks of the far side. Amid those dark shadows, something pale moved.

Kadrigul.

Hweilan watched, her ragged breathing calming, but her heart beating faster than ever.

The pale warrior stopped on the opposite bank and looked down. She heard him snarl.

Safe, she thought. I'm safe.

A small laugh—no more than a cough of air—escaped her, and the Kadrigul-thing looked up, its red eyes blazing in the growing dark.

He stepped onto the river. His snarl choked off, as if he were in pain, and his gait slowed, as if he were wading through onrushing water. But he kept coming, step by lurching step, dragging his broken leg behind him.

"No," said Hweilan, and it came out half a whimper.

She didn't have the strength to get to her feet, but she crawled backward as best as she could. She made it perhaps a dozen feet before the bank became too steep, and she slid back down a ways until her foot caught on the exposed root of one of the old pines.

Kadrigul stepped onto the bank.

Her heart was beating so hard that it drowned out all other sounds. She couldn't even hear his footfall as he came toward her, his hands reaching out.

A snarling shadow bowled into him, and they both hit the ground.

Wide-eyed, Hweilan watched. It was Lendri, back in elf form, though the growls coming from him were all wolf.

The Kadrigul-thing screamed—more in fury than pain, Hweilan knew—and stood, Lendri's jaws locked around his throat. Kadrigul grabbed his hair with one hand and lower jaw with the other, then wrenched the elf off. With one hand around Lendri's throat, he held the elf at arm's length. Lendri screamed, clawing at Kadrigul's torso with his feet, his fingers—now tipped with claws—raking at his face and eyes.

Kadrigul smiled, even as Lendri tore his eyes away, leaving only the red fire behind.

"I know your stink," said Kadrigul. He breathed in deep through his nose. "I remember now. I killed your mother. Ate her heart."

Lendri managed one last shriek of defiance, then Kadrigul struck with his other hand, punching through Lendri's gut, up and into his chest cavity, breaking through muscle and bone. He yanked and pulled out the dark, dripping mass of Lendri's heart. Lendri's arms and legs went limp, a final shudder passed through him, and then Kadrigul dropped his lifeless body.

Tears froze on Hweilan's cheeks.

Kadrigul dropped the heart into the snow. Those red eyes turned to her. "Now, to the main course."

A curtain of light, pale and cold, washed over them, and a ripple of *something* passed through the ground and air.

When Hweilan was a little girl, she had once sneaked into her parents' bedchamber very early one morning, coming forward on tiptoes over the thick rug. Her father lay nearest, eyes closed, breathing deep and steady. She had said, "Father?" His eyes remained closed, but something had changed. Between one breath and the next, some indefinable something told Hweilan that her father was awake.

That same feeling filled her now. Something had woken.

She turned to see where the light was coming from and saw the first pale rim of the moon climbing over the black horizon. Full and fat. With so much snow on the ground, once the moon rose high, it would be almost bright as day even at midnight. The Hunter's Moon.

Howling filled the air. But like no howling Hweilan had ever heard. This was a call of thunders.

The red light in the Kadrigul-thing's eyes flickered and dimmed.

"No." He gasped and lurched backward. But then his gaze fixed on Hweilan, and the fire blazed again. *"No!"*

He came at her, arms outstretched, and a storm of ravens struck him, wings flapping as they pecked and tore at him. He stumbled, righted himself, then fell as a black wolf ran in and sank its jaws into his good leg.

A shriek cut through the night air, and Hweilan knew it did not come from the animated corpse before her, but from the dark will inside it.

The Kadrigul-thing fought its way to its feet. Orange flames had broken out along the surface of the pale skin. It caught in the feathers of the ravens, setting them alight. The wolf shrieked in pain and fled.

Dead ravens, still smoldering, fell to the snow. Hweilan could not look away. Torn flesh hung off bones. The remaining clothes had burned away, and still the flames grew. He took one step toward Hweilan.

And something landed between them. A huge figure, taller than any man Hweilan had ever seen. Moonlight glinted off pale scars that ribboned his muscled frame. His left hand dripped blood. In his right he gripped a long spear, its black head barbed and cruel. Antlers sprouted from his skull.

It was the shape that had haunted her dreams.

Nendawen had come.

A green eldritch light sparked around the barbed point of Nendawen's spear.

The thing of flame shrieked. Defiance, agony, and futility. The spirit fled the remains of Kadrigul's body and shot across the river, like flames borne by storm winds. Nendawen took one step forward and threw his spear. The light crackled around the shaft as it flew. It struck the heart of the flames, and in the resulting maelstrom of darkness and light, Hweilan knew—knew in the deepest well of her heart—that something wild and hungry ate the fiery spirit. Swallowed it whole.

The fire went out.

Nendawen turned. A mask of bone hid his face, but

behind the empty sockets glowed the same green light that bathed his spear.

Why have you come? It was a growl in her mind, but she understood the meaning.

She looked into those eyes and saw that what Menduarthis had told her was true. There was no malice there. Nothing so petty. But something far stronger. Far older. Primal. There was no word for it, for it had been born long before there were such things as words in the tongues of men.

"I come to hunt," she said.

Good. And who are you?

"Uh . . ." She searched for the words. Could Lendri have been wrong? Worse, could Menduarthis have been right in telling her not to trust him? "I was told——"

Who are you?

He took a step toward her, and the green light began to glow around his hands. They curled into sharp claws.

"H-Hweilan," she said. "My name is Hweilan."

Do you know the covenant, Hweilan?

"Uh . . . I . . ."

To come without sacrifice means death.

Lendri had told her much the same thing, had he not? Just earlier that day. *To come without sacrifice, without blood . . . it is death.* Lendri . . .

She looked down at his lifeless, ravaged body. Her gorge rose. But looking down on him, it stoked her anger again.

"There." She pointed. "There is my sacrifice."

Ukhnar Kurhan slew that one.

"He was *my* friend. He died protecting me."

Nendawen looked down. He stared at her a long time, as if considering. Finally he said, *Then the sacrifice was his. Not yours. To come without sacrifice means death.*

Hweilan's breath caught. She felt her chest constrict. After all she'd lost . . . to have come so far . . .

Death.

A small part of her wondered, Why fight it? After all she'd lost, after all she'd ever wanted had been taken from her . . . why fight? Would death really be that bad? But that was the little girl in her talking. Wanting the simple way out. Wanting her way or nothing. And the little girl was almost gone.

The larger part of her, louder, was just plain angry. Furious in fact. She might die, yes, but not without a fight.

"My family," she said. "My father. My mother. Their fathers and mothers. All dead! Everyone I loved. Everyone who loved me. They died that I might come here. To you. If that isn't enough . . . then to the hells with you! I have nothing more to give."

Nendawen's eyes blazed, and a thousand howls filled the night. A storm of raucous cries rained down from the boughs overhead.

Hweilan looked up.

Hundreds of ravens looked down on her, their black eyes reflecting the moonlight. Yellow wolves' eyes watched her from the shadows under the trees.

Nothing more to give? said Nendawen. *You are wrong. There is you. You are mine, Hweilan. You were always mine.*

He took off his mask.

Hweilan screamed.

FORGOTTEN REALMS

Award-winning Game Designer

BRUCE R. CORDELL

Abolethic Sovereignty

There are things that we were not meant to know.

Book I
Plague of Spells

Book II
City of Torment

Book III
Key of Stars
September 2010

". . . he weaves a tale that adds depth and
breadth to the FORGOTTEN REALMS history."
—Grasping for the Wind, on *Stardeep*

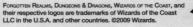

FORGOTTEN REALMS

Ed Greenwood
Presents
Waterdeep

Explore the City of Splendors through the eyes of authors
hand-picked by FORGOTTEN REALMS® world creator Ed Greenwood.

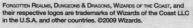

FORGOTTEN REALMS

The New York Times BEST-SELLING AUTHOR

RICHARD BAKER

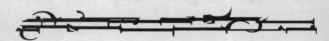

BLADES OF THE MOONSEA

". . . it was so good that the bar has been raised.
Few other fantasy novels will hold up to it, I fear."
—Kevin Mathis, d20zines.com on *Forsaken House*

Book I	Book II	Book III
Swordmage	**Corsair**	**Avenger**
		March 2010

Enter the Year of the Ageless One!